She had been caught
by the talk of moon and lovers

"I've wanted you, Red, ever since I saw you again at the hotel," Chance murmured against her mouth.

The use of her nickname set off alarm bells. This was not an innocently romantic kiss in the moonlight, not with Chance Barkley as a participant. She twisted out of his arms.

"You are still making the same mistake about me," she accused with a painful catch in her voice.

His head drew back, a hint of arrogance in his look. "Am I?"

JANET DAILEY AMERICANA

Every novel in this collection is your passport to a romantic tour of the United States through time-honored favorites by America's First Lady of romance fiction. Each of the fifty novels is set in a different state, researched by Janet and her husband, Bill. For the Daileys it was an odyssey of discovery. For you, it's the journey of a lifetime.

The state flower depicted on the cover of this book is magnolia.

Janet Dailey Americana

Don't miss any of our special offers. Write to us at the following address for information on our newest releases.

Harlequin Reader Service
901 Fuhrmann Blvd., P.O. Box 1397, Buffalo, NY 14240
Canadian address: P.O. Box 603,
Fort Erie, Ont. L2A 5X3

Janet Dailey
Americana

THE BRIDE OF THE DELTA QUEEN

Harlequin Books

TORONTO • NEW YORK • LONDON
AMSTERDAM • PARIS • SYDNEY • HAMBURG
STOCKHOLM • ATHENS • TOKYO • MILAN

Janet Dailey Americana edition published February 1987
ISBN 373-89818-5

Harlequin Presents edition published May 1979
Second printing May 1982

Original hardcover edition published in 1978
by Mills & Boon Limited

CHAPTER ONE

HER FINGERS CURLED around the post supporting the balcony overhead. Green flecks sparkled in her hazel eyes as she surveyed the narrow, bricked street. This was it—Vieux Carré, the French Quarter of New Orleans with its brick buildings decorated with ornate Spanish grillwork making balconies of iron lace.

After almost two full days of sight-seeing, Selena Merrick still hadn't become accustomed to the wonder of it. She had planned this vacation for years, it seemed. Not that everything had gone according to her plan. Her best friend, Robin Michels, was to have come along but had to cancel her reservations at the last minute owing to a family crisis.

It had never crossed Selena's mind to cancel the trip or postpone it because of Robin. As she looked down the picturesque streets, a faint smile curved her lips. Selfishly she was glad she had come alone. She could tour the Quarter at her own pace, see as much or as little as she wanted without consulting the wishes of anyone else. And there were times when Robin, good friend or not, could be a soppingly wet blanket.

On the opposite side of the street, a white lace balcony caught the rays of the setting sun, the white ironwork reflecting the gold tint. This silent reminder of passing time prodded Selena into movement. Threading her way through the stream of fellow tourists, she crossed the street and directed her footsteps toward her hotel.

The sunlight warmed her shoulders, bared by the halter sundress in a springlike apricot print. The closeness of the air, heavy with humidity, made Selena think of summer instead of the last week of April. It tightened the natural wave of her light auburn hair and made her skin feel sticky with moisture. She would definitely need to shower before changing for dinner.

A sidewalk café bar added to the congestion of pedestrian traffic on the narrow sidewalk. A passerby accidentally jostled Selena, knocking her sideways into one of the wrought-iron chairs and its occupant.

"Sorry," Selena said, offering a quick, smiling apology to the man she had bumped.

A glancing look caught the movement of crisp black hair as the man nodded his head in acceptance of her apology. The incident forced Selena to change her path, skirting the edge of the tables that intruded out onto the sidewalk.

Selena paid no attention to the men grouped around the next table. Their loud talk and raucous laughter blended in with the street sounds. But she had not escaped their notice, with her gleaming bare shoulders and copper hair.

As she drew level with their table, one of the men rose and staggered into her path, checking her steps. Selena smiled briefly in apology, unaware that he had deliberately blocked her way, and paused to wait for a break in the steady stream of tourists to walk around the man.

"Why don't you join us for a drink, Red?" The man's voice was slurred, indicating the he had already indulged in more than he could hold.

Startled only momentarily, Selena cast a sweeping look over the group of men, noting the conventioneers' badges on the pockets of their jackets. Amusement flickered in her eyes. They were undoubtedly respectable businessmen who, in their own home towns, would not be caught dead inviting a strange girl to drink with them in a place as public as this café bar.

"Thanks, but no," she refused, unable to take offense at their invitation.

An empty chair was being offered to her. "Come on, honey, sit down with us," another voice spoke up.

"Thank you, boys. It's really nice of you to offer, but—" Selena refused again with an eloquent shrug, the sparkle of laughter remaining in her eyes.

"Aw, come on, Red," the first man cajoled. "Have a drink with us and later I'll buy you dinner," he promised with an expansive sweep of his hand.

Still smiling, Selena shook her head. She

found no threat in the situation. It was broad daylight and the streets and sidewalks were crowded with people. She had opened her mouth to refuse again when the first man bent his head toward her in an attitude that suggested secrecy. But he didn't lower the volume of his voice.

"You can call a couple of your friends for the guys and we'll really do up the town."

At first, Selena was astonished. "My friends?" she echoed, before suddenly realizing that they thought she was a native of New Orleans instead of a tourist like themselves.

"You know," a third voice chimed in to prompt her, his sotto voice ringing loudly for all to hear. "Your cohorts, other ladies of the evening like yourself. I like blondes," he proclaimed.

Selena nearly choked on a bubble of laughter. Try as she would, she found the situation much too funny to feel insulted or degraded. Simultaneously she also realized that they wouldn't believe her if she denied her alleged profession. To assert her valid claim that she was a minister's daughter would only add to their romantic image of what a fallen woman should be.

Assessing the group of men eagerly awaiting her reply, she couldn't help thinking that they were overgrown little boys. They were all dressed in the best suits and ties, good material and well tailored, but none of the suits was expensive—a fact she could attest to, thanks to her eye for clothes and four years of experience as inventory clerk and part-time buyer for an exclusive department store in Des Moines. She had often railed at the job since the only reason she had ever been promoted was because other employees had left, but now she was glad of her experience.

"Sorry, boys." Laughter riddled her voice despite her attempts to restrain it. There seemed to be one safe way out, and Selena intended to take it, seeing only harmless fun in choosing pretense. "No offense intended, but I don't think you could afford me."

Her response set them back in their chairs, except for the one who was standing beside her. His expression was wreathed in curious awe.

"How much?" he whispered, holding his breath.

Selena named the first sum that came to her mind in an answering whisper. The man's mouth opened and closed several times, and Selena's lips twitched in an effort to control her laughter at the whole ludicrous situation.

"Goodbye, boys," she beamed.

As she half turned to slip into the throng of tourists, her attention was caught by a pair of dark eyes assessing her with sweeping coolness. They belonged to the man seated alone at the next table, the one she had accidently bumped into. Selena recognized the ebony black hair growing so crisply, and there was something speculative in the arch of his eyebrow. It seemed to be mocking and interested, in an amused sort of way.

Unfortunately, as far as Selena was concerned, her dumbstruck friend chose that moment to recover his voice and answering the whispered question of, "How much?" from his friends, he breathed, "Five hundred!"

And the dark eyebrow lifted a fraction of an inch higher. Selena's stomach muscles constricted. A slowly spreading warmth started to fire her skin as she escaped into the concealing stream of pedestrians. It had seemed harmless fun to pretend to be the shady lady of the evening the elderly gentlemen had been seeking, but Selena discovered that she didn't care to have the dark-haired man see her in that light.

Within a couple of blocks, she arrived at her hotel. In the interim, she had managed to shake the disturbing sensation as she stored up the incident in her memory, a tale to tell her friends when she returned from the vacation. It smacked of naughty adventure while being amusing at the same time.

But it also caused her to pause in front of the vanity mirror in her hotel room as she tried to discover what there was about her that would have led those respectable and elderly gentlemen to believe that she was a member of that old profession.

Was it the shimmering copper color of her hair, she wondered curiously. Red, the color for a scarlet woman? Between the humidity—which increased her hair's tendency to wave—and the occasional breeze that had sneaked down the narrow streets, her shoulder-length style was in charming disarray.

Sighing, Selena dismissed the color of her hair as the cause. Perhaps it was the bold gleam in her green-flecked eyes, but it had always been there, shining through long, sun-kissed lashes.

Her father, the Reverend Andrew James Merrick, had often accused her of embracing life too passionately. Of course, he never meant it in the lustful sense of the word. He was referring to her lack of fear; Selena's inclination to rush in where angels would fear to tread.

Strangely enough, this inclination had never been true when it came to relationships with the opposite sex. With projects and friends, yes— Selena would tackle anything and anyone if it was for the benefit of someone else—but when it came to her own emotions and feelings, she was very cautious.

There was nothing outstanding about the rest of her features, just the usual forehead, nose, cheeks, jaw and chin that are required to make a face complete. Maybe it was her lips, she considered. A friend had once described them as full and sensuous, but she hadn't paid too much attention to the remark. Looking at them now, shining with gloss, Selena admitted without conceit that her mouth was nicely shaped and possibly inviting.

But she was no nearer to discovering what it

had been that had prompted the gentlemen to make such a mistake. Shaking her head in bewilderment, she took a step away from the mirror. That was when she saw it—the composite picture of herself.

Wholesome beauty met with the boldness of her eyes, the sensuous lines of her lips and the attracting brightness of her hair. It was nothing blatant, Selena realized. Probably it could be discovered in any attractive woman if that was what a man was looking for. It was a case of seeing what a person wanted to see.

It was almost a relief to discover there was nothing abandoned or wanton about her looks. Striking, yes—attractive, yes—and a well-rounded figure, too, but nothing licentious.

Laughing at herself, Selena turned away from the mirror and began untying the halter straps of her sundress. Robin would have been appalled at the reason Selena had so minutely dissected her appearance. As far as that went, Selena smiled to herself, her girl friend would have been appalled at the incident.

No, she corrected, Robin would have been indignantly outraged by the mistake and would never have dreamed of perpetuating the impression, even in good fun. Selena decided maybe it was just as well that Robin hadn't been able to come along on the trip. She was probably going to have more fun without her.

Later, as she finished dressing for dinner, she retracted the last thought. It would have been more fun if Robin was along. No matter how liberated the times were supposed to be, it still raised eyebrows when a woman went to a bar or a nightclub alone. As it was, Selena knew she would draw a lot of curious glances sitting alone in the restaurant.

New Orleans was a city renowned for its nighttime entertainment. Judging by some of the posters and advertisements Selena had seen on the famed Bourbon Street, there were some clubs that she wasn't interested in but there were other, reputable night spots that she would have liked to experience.

With her hair secured in a sophisticated pleat, Selena smoothed the sides absently with her fingertips and reached for the tricorner shawl that matched the flame-orange dress she wore. It was an unusual shade and one that oddly accented and complemented the fiery lights in her hair. She draped the shawl around her shoulders and tied the ends in a loose knot.

Stepping out her door into the carpeted hotel hallway, she paused to make certain the room key was in her evening purse, then closed the door. She had barely taken two steps from her door when a door farther down the hallway opened and a man stepped out.

It took Selena about as long to recognize where she had seen him before as it took him to remember her. It was the man she had bumped into before encountering the older group of men.

Her first sinking thought was—why had she chosen such a brilliantly colored dress to wear? Why hadn't she picked something from her wardrobe that was more demure and unobtrusive? Fighting the urge to scurry back into her room, Selena continued down the hallway. Her steps had slowed as she crossed her fingers, hoping he would ignore her and continue on his way.

Of course, he didn't. He stood waiting expectantly for her, those glinting dark eyes sweeping her from head to toe. The look branded her with the iron Selena herself had put in the fire.

"Hello, Red." His voice was huskily pitched, carrying that note of amused interest.

It seemed pointless to ignore him or pretend that she didn't recognize him. Selena was positive that she had already made him aware of her recognition. *What a fine mess I've got myself into this time,* she thought.

"Hello," she returned the greeting accompanied by what she hoped was a detached and disinterested smile.

Slipping his room key in his suit pocket, he stepped forward to meet her. Selena couldn't make up her mind whether she should walk past him or stop.

Her fleeting glimpse of him at the café had not prepared her for his bulk. Several inches taller than her five-foot-six frame, the man was huskily built. He was wearing a light tan suit, the jacket unbuttoned to reveal a matching vest.

Selena didn't need to see the lining to know it had been hand-tailored to fit his muscular frame. The richly textured fabric cried "money," as did the assurance in his craggy male features.

"Are you coming or going?" he inquired, meeting her boldly inspecting stare and returning it with a mirthless quirk to his mouth.

In the glinting blackness of his eyes, Selena saw what he had left unsaid in his question. The very fact that they had met a second time in the hallway of the hotel indicated that she must have come from one of the rooms. And in that silently suggestive look of his, he was considering what had gone on in that room.

Her anger boiled near the surface, but Selena determinedly cooled it. She had no one to blame but herself for what he was thinking.

At some point in his approach, she had stopped. It was a mistake, she realized, and one not so easily rectified, since the breadth of his shoulders blocked her way.

"Going," she answered his question and made an attempt to pass him, hoping he would move out of her path.

He didn't budge an inch. "Where?"

Her father had often told her that the truth could never hurt. Selena hoped he was right as she answered frankly, "To dinner."

Unknowingly she was clutching her purse, knuckles white with the tenseness of her grip. His gaze slid to her hand, drawing her attention to her death hold on her evening bag. She guessed what construction he placed on that—that she was protecting her monetary payment for services rendered. She seethed with frustration.

"Did you work up an appetite?" The question was almost a taunt.

This time Selena didn't attempt to contain her anger, letting it blaze in her eyes. "I find that remark crude, sir. Excuse me." And started to push her way past him, all stiff and proud.

His large hand rested on the bareness of her arm to stop her. "That was crude," he acknowledged smoothly. "I had no business saying it to a lady of your caliber. I'm sorry."

"Of your caliber." The words taunted her. If he had just left it with the word "lady," Selena might have been more willing to accept his apology.

Instead all she could manage was a freezing, "That's quite all right," that made a lie of her acceptance.

His dark gaze scanned her features, his own expression inscrutable. "Will you be dining alone?"

He was making no attempt to hold her, but Selena found she couldn't move or pull her arm from the light touch of his sun-browned hand. Yet her muscles were rigidly resisting his nearness.

"Perhaps," she answered noncommittally.

He interpreted her reply to mean she was dining alone. "As luck would have it, I'm without a dinner companion myself tonight." His right hand was thrust in his trouser pocket, holding his jacket open with studied casualness. "Would you join me?"

Moments before leaving her room Selena had wished for a table companion to share her meal, but she knew instinctively that the company this man would supply would be dangerously stimulating. It was there in his shuttered dark eyes that glinted with mockery yet never revealed what he was thinking.

"No, thank you." Her rejection was coolly abrupt.

It piqued his interest even as it deepened the dimpling grooves next to his mouth. "Why not?"

"Because I choose who I dine with," Selena retorted, wishing she could bring an end to this ridiculous meeting. Why wouldn't he let her pass?

"Just as you choose who you go to bed with?" he countered in a low mocking taunt.

"Exactly!" The word burst from her in an explosion of temper.

In the back of her mind, she had been wondering how she could convince him that she had gone along with the elderly group for a harmless joke. But a red flash of anger made her feel that she owed him no explanation at all.

Something cynical flickered across his expressio as one corner of his mouth slanted without humor. "I'm well aware there's a price for your time, Red. I'm prepared to pay it."

His right hand was withdrawn from his trouser pocket. A freezing burn seemed to hold Selena motionless as he reached out to tuck folded bills into her cleavage. At the brush of his fingers against her bare skin as his hand withdrew, the spell of immobility was broken.

Bending her head, she looked down at the green bills, aware of a distant sensation of degradation. Slowly she removed the money and lifted her gaze to his. Still no words of denunciation left her lips.

"I'm surprised," she heard herself say evenly. "You didn't strike me as the type who would have to pay for his pleasure."

He cocked his head slightly, his dark gaze sweeping over her. "Maybe I'm curious what 'pleasure' you have to offer that would be worth so much," he countered.

Something in his tone or his look, or maybe it was the sheer magnetism of his presence, warned Selena of the dangerous game she was playing. Her pulse accelerated in alarm.

"I don't happen to be selling right now," she rushed, and tried to force the money into his hand while pushing her way by him.

His hand closed around the fingers holding his money at the same moment that he took hold of her elbow. "This isn't the place for a discussion."

He was propelling her stilted legs forward.

Selena's initial reaction was that he was going to force his company on her at the dinner table by directing her down the hallway to the lobby and restaurant. Her mouth was open to protest, her widened and slightly angry gaze on his strong face when he paused to reach in front of her. Her gaze swung forward as he opened a hotel room door, obviously his.

"This will be more private," he announced with a lazy, mocking glint in his eye.

Panic screamed through her nerve ends. "No, listen, please!" But she was already through the door and it had closed behind her.

She pivoted, ready to bolt out the door, but he was there, blocking her escape and regarding her pale complexion with curious bemusement. She could feel her heart thumping against her ribs.

"I think we can make a satisfactory arrangement, don't you?" he questioned, his voice smooth and husky, his expression experienced.

"Look," Selena took a shaky breath and swallowed, "this is all a mistake—"

The folded bills were still in her hand. He took them from her clenched fingers, then removed her evening bag from her other hand. Fear strangled the protest in her throat as she watched him unsnap the purse and slip the money inside.

"My purse!" she squeaked when he gave it a toss to some point behind her.

She started to turn but managed only a glance

over her shoulder, enough to see her evening bag slide to a stop on top of a low dresser. The strong hands closing around the bare flesh of her upper arms kept her from turning around completely to retrieve it.

"It will be perfectly safe there," he assured her.

But she wasn't perfectly safe. The fact was driven sharply home to her as she felt his hands slide to the shawl, freeing the ends from the loose knot with the simplest of tugs. She clutched at the trailing ends, but they escaped her grasp as he let the shawl fall to the floor.

Selena would have stooped to pick it up, but his hands were on her arms, drawing her to his chest. Hunching her shoulders, she used her forearms to wedge a small space between them. His chest was like a solid wall, immovable.

"Don't!" she struggled.

His cheek and jaw were near her temple, the clean, spice-scented fragrance of his after-shave lotion assailing her nose. His fingers were spread across the bareness of her spine, pressing her ever closer.

"Stop acting." His breath stirred the hair near her ear as he spoke.

"I'm not acting!" Selena flared, breathing in sharply when he began nuzzling the sensitive area of her neck below her earlobe. "Did it ever occur to you that the lady might not be willing?" she gasped, twisting her head toward her shoulder to stop his exploring mouth.

He merely laughed. "It's your profession to be willing."

"Well, I'm—" Her indignant protest was lost as she made the mistake of lifting her head to deliver the protest to his face. Immediately his mouth muffled the rest of her words.

Startled, for several seconds Selena was passive under the mobile pressure of his male lips. There was a quality of arrogant mastery to his kiss, commanding rather than bruising. It was this assertion of rights that she rebelled against rather than feeling repulsed by his kiss. That, coupled with fear. She wrenched her head away from his mouth, drawing back, the storm of anger flashing green in her eyes.

A dark brow was raised in cynical mockery of her action. She was conscious of the large hand at the base of her spine, pressing her hips and legs to his taut-muscled and long-bodied frame. Fiery lights glittered behind the thick screen of his lashes, amused and passionate and confident.

"Will you let me go?" she blazed in a temper born of desperation.

She pressed her hands against his shoulder bones and strained with all her might to break out of the steel trap of his embrace. All she succeeded in accomplishing was to arch the lower half of her body more fully against his.

Impatience hardened the firm set of his mouth. "Look, this game of hard-to-get might work with your older clients, but it doesn't impress me," he stated.

Her chin and jaw were captured by long fingers to hold her mouth still for his possession. Selena was helpless to prevent it, unable to move her head, and her hand and arms were pinned between the crush of their bodies.

Soon the long, drugging kiss began to make its effects known to Selena. Like a narcotic, it weakened and relaxed her rigid muscles, and for a moment she allowed his roaming hands to mold her pliant flesh to his male form. The sensation of the kiss was threatening to become addictive.

When the fingers on her chin relaxed their hold, it took all of her willpower to slide her lips free of his kiss. He permitted it, tipping her head back in order to explore the smooth column of her neck and the hollow of her throat.

The nibbling caresses aided the drugging, and molten warmth spread through her limbs. But Selena's senses were not totally numbed. She heard the zipper of her dress being released and felt the coolness of air against her skin. At the tug on the fragile straps of her dress, she knew she was lost unless she did something quickly.

She had tested his strength and knew she was no match for it. As long as he remained the aggressor she had no hope. Her only chance was to turn the tables.

Taking a deep breath for courage, she was filled with a strange combination of fear and exhilaration. His hand was on her shoulder now, pushing away one of the offending straps, her dress hanging loosely about her.

"If you tear the dress, it will be extra," she warned on a bold and breathless note.

For a split second, he didn't move, his mouth pressed against the curve of her neck. Selena was so scared she was afraid to breathe. Thick jet-black hair brushed her jaw as he lifted his head, a complacent curve to his mouth.

There was space between them now, but his hands were still resting on her shoulders. Selena attempted an alluring, if tremulous, smile and raised sweeping eyelashes to look at him. Gently and carefully, he slipped the spaghetti straps from her shoulder and the flame-orange dress fell around her ankles.

Her lashes fluttered once, but it was the only outward sign she gave of embarrassment. Inwardly she knew her knees were threatening to buckle, and it took all her nerve not to cover the scanty lace of her strapless bra with her hands. Luckily a matching half-slip of lace kept the rest of her well covered.

Keeping the smile painted on her lips, she reached out for his hand. The smallness of her hand was soon lost in the largeness of his.

She stepped out of the dress, which lay around her ankles and unfortunately stepped out of one of her shoes, too.

She kicked the other one off as she led him farther into the room and away from the door. She stopped short of the bed, a fact the fathomless black eyes made note of while continuing to watch her with burning brightness.

Releasing his hand, she reached for his jacket, sliding a hand along the lapel. "Shall I help you off with your clothes?" The huskiness of her voice was due mainly to the fear of the moment.

A dark brow briefly flickered upward. "I think I can manage," he assured her.

Shrugging, she turned away, relief washing through her with the force of a tidal wave. But he was still watching her as he peeled off his jacket and began unbuttoning his vest. Selena wandered to the mirror, patting the escaping tendrils of copper hair back into place and keeping him in view via the mirror.

After the vest came the white shirt. Selena quivered at the sight of all that naked muscle. Without an ounce of spare flesh on his torso, sunbrowned to a teak shade. All that male virility oozing from him was not a sensation to settle her already taut nerves.

When he unfastened his trousers and stepped out of one leg, she bolted. There wasn't time to worry about shoes or her red dress lying on the floor. She made a sweeping grab to retrieve her purse and darted to the door, ignoring his muffled curse.

For the first time in this misadventure, Selena felt luck was on her side. There was no one in the hallway, no one to see her racing to her hotel room in her lacy underwear. She wasted a precious second fumbling for the room key in her purse, inserted it quickly in the lock and turned it.

Opening the door and slipping into her room, she darted one last glance down the hall just as he appeared, bare chested and fastening his trousers. He looked toward the lobby instead of in Selena's direction and she quickly and silently closed the door.

Her knees buckled and she leaned weakly against the door, taking deep, quaking breaths. Sounds that were somewhere between laughter and sobs came from her throat. She sobered quickly into silence when she heard footsteps in the hall, but they gradually receded.

Gathering strength, she walked into the room to take the cotton robe from the foot of the bed and wrapped it around her. The red orange dress had been one of her favorites. It was gone for good now. Selena doubted that she would have worn it again even if she could have managed to bring it with her out of the room.

Her stomach growled, reminding her that she still hadn't had dinner. She shook her head, knowing there was no way she was going to risk bumping into that man again. Selena walked to the telephone and dialed room service.

CHAPTER TWO

DETERMINED NOT TO BE a prisoner in her room, Selena slipped out of the hotel early the next morning. She took precautions to keep from being readily recognized, by donning dark, owl-shaped sunglasses and wearing a floppy-brimmed straw sunhat to cover her auburn hair piled beneath it.

Her fear of meeting the man a third time vanished when she stepped outside the hotel into the sunlight of a spring Sunday. Indeed, she felt like both—spring and Sunday—in her pristine white skirt and silk blouse of lime green with large white polka dots, a matching scarf and the same material tied around the hatband.

There was no hesitation in her footsteps as she left the hotel entrance. She knew exactly where she was going—to the French market to breakfast on *beignets* and chickory coffee. The route she chose was not the most direct, but Selena decided it would be picturesque, although she doubted that there was any place in the French Quarter that was not picturesque.

The French Quarter—wandering down a narrow street, Selena wondered again at the misnomer because all the architecture was decidedly Spanish. But of course, she conceded that the name was really derived because of the French who lived in this section of New Orleans, especially when the Americans took over and attempted to anglicize the city. Selena doubted if they had ever succeeded completely.

Emerging from the shaded coolness of Pirates' Alley, she paused near the entrance of St. Louis Cathedral and marveled again at the fairy-tale turrets and steeples of its building, the oldest cathedral in the United States.

As she crossed the street, she noticed the artists setting up their wares outside the iron fences surrounding Jackson Square and promised herself she would browse through them after she had breakfast.

She took the shortcut through the square to the French market and quickly discovered that she wasn't the only one who had decided to breakfast early. The café was filled with the aroma of fresh doughnuts and *beignets*, and hungry customers, and Selena felt her appetite increasing as she sought and found an empty table and chair.

The square-shaped doughnuts, minus the hole and covered in powdered sugar, were still warm when they were served. She took a wake-up sip of the black coffee and immediately added a liberal amount of cream to weaken its potency. Chickory coffee was an acquired taste, she decided.

Later, wiping the floury sugar from her lips and hands, she hoped she had rid herself of all the powdery sweet. The coffee, she had discovered after finishing the cup, was really more palatable than she had first believed, and she accepted the refill the waiter offered.

A young boy at a nearby table grabbed his mother's arm and exclaimed excitely, "I just heard a man say the *Delta Queen* is in! Can we go look at her?"

The mother's reply was too low for Selena to understand, but the nod of her head and the boy's hoot of joy convinced her that it had been in the affirmative. As she watched the family leave the café, the name *Delta Queen* kept running through her mind, but she couldn't remember why it should be so familiar.

The question nagged her until she finally stopped the waiter to ask him, "I heard someone say the *Delta Queen* was in. Is that a ship?"

"It's a riverboat, ma'am," he answered. "An old-time paddle wheeler, one of the last on the river that carries overnight passengers."

The pieces began to fall into place. "It's the boat that was almost forced out of service a few years ago because it was made of wood, isn't it?"

"Her superstructure is made of wood, but she has a steel hull," he corrected. "Congress has granted her a temporary exemption to keep her on the river." One corner of his mouth lifted in a half smile. "A stay of execution, you might call it."

Selena remembered the publicity that had surrounded it and her lips echoed his faint smile. "Where is she docked?"

The waiter hestitated, then answered, "At the Poydras Street wharf, I imagine. Do you know where that is?" Selena shook her head in regretful acknowledgment that she didn't. "It's on the other side of Canal Street, near where the International Trade Mart is."

"I know where that is," Selena nodded. "Thank you."

She knew generally where the boat was docked. With the towering trade center building in sight, it was easy to walk to it. Once there, she had to ask for more specific directions to the wharf. Reaching the wharf buildings, she stopped at the parking garage to ask again.

"The *Delta Queen*? She'll be tied up by the excursion boats," a security guard informed her. "You can walk through the garage, if you like, then turn right."

A sudden breeze tugged at her floppy hat brim as she walked on to the concrete walkway running the length of wharf buildings on the riverside. Holding onto the brim, Selena turned right, moving past the silver-painted monolith called The Admiral.

Farther down the dock, she could see a stirring of activity and walked toward it. Her view of the *Delta Queen* was blocked by other boats until she was almost upon it. At the first glimpse of the name painted on the black hull, she slowed her steps, letting her gaze run up the four-storied lady of the river.

Deckhands were moving around the forward deck, while uniformed porters carried luggage off the boat, followed by strolling, unhurried passengers. A few other spectators had gathered along the dock, some to meet disembarking passengers while others, like the family Selena had seen in the café, were simply there to see the *Delta Queen*.

At the head of a gangplank, a sign was posted that read Sorry, No Visitors At This Time, and Selena experienced a feeling of regret as she walked toward the stern. The polished teak handrails circling the top three decks and the black smokestack with its gold crown perched behind the pilothouse made her wish she could explore the interior. At the stern the red paddle wheel rested, not required to churn muddy water until the boat again left port.

One of the crew—judging by the curved figure Selena realized it was a female—was repainting the *Delta Queen*'s name on the large signboard above the paddle wheel. The gold whistles of the calliope gleamed in the morning sunlight.

Here and there, Selena caught glimpses of the boat's age, most of them artfully concealed with a fresh coat of paint, reminders that the legendary *Delta Queen* was the grand old lady of the riverboats.

"Like something out of the past, isn't it?" a voice said.

Startled, Selena turned, becoming aware only at that moment of the older woman standing near her. "Yes, it is," she agreed, recovering quickly to smile. "Somehow I never realized it was such a large ship."

"Boat," the woman corrected gently. "Any vessel that plies the river is a boat, no matter what her size."

"A large boat, then," Selena conceded, her smile widening.

"Yes," the woman nodded. "She'll accommodate one hundred and ninety-odd passengers and a crew of seventy-five," she added in a knowledgeable tone.

"You know a lot about the *Delta Queen*, don't you?" Selena commented running a considering eye over the woman.

Almost as tall as Selena, the woman had dark hair except for a pair of silvered wings at the temples that gave her a distinguished air. There was a suggestion of crow's feet at the corners of her brown eyes, but otherwise her facial skin was relatively unlined. Selena guessed that the youthfulness of the woman's features was due to the strong bone structure of her face, because she was certain the woman was in her late fifties or very early sixties.

Although the woman was large boned, she was trim and neat in her blue summer suit. The simple lines of the tailored outfit bespoke class and the woman wore it with the ease of one accustomed to wearing good clothes. Selena suspected that the woman had never been a beauty, even in her youth, but she decided that she had probably been attractive in the same strong sort of way that she was now.

"I am very familiar with the boat and her history," the woman answered.

"You're from New Orleans?" Selena was positive that there was something in the picture the woman was presenting that she wasn't seeing.

"Yes," was the brief reply and then the woman's brown gaze was riveted on the steamboat.

Selena let her attention slide back to the boat, trying to disguise her sudden intense curiosity about the woman beside her. She couldn't stop herself from probing further.

"Have you ever taken a trip on the *Delta Queen*?" she asked, certain the woman didn't work for the company.

"Yes, I have...many times." There was the slightest pause in her words, the length of a heartbeat, leaving Selena with the impression that the woman had a catch in her voice.

With a sideways glance, she studied the woman again. Initially she saw the same image as before—an older woman, calm and composed and completely in control. Then Selena noticed the flaws.

A white linen handkerchief edged with lace

was being twisted by agitated fingers. And the luminous quality of the woman's brown eyes was produced by a fine mist of tears. Too many times, members of her father's congregation had come to the parsonage, ostensibly for a friendly visit, only to have something in their behavior betray an inner turmoil, as this older woman was doing now.

Selena was not her father's daughter for nothing. "Excuse me, but—is something wrong?" Unconsciously she adopted the gentle, consoling tone she had so often heard her father use. She removed her sunglasses so the dark lenses would not shade the woman's reaction.

"I—" Instant denial formed on the woman's lips. As she caught sight of the compassion gleaming quietly in Selena's eyes, she checked the denouncement and turned away. "It's—nothing."

"I don't mean to be personal, but I can tell something is troubling you. Sometimes it helps to talk about it—to a stranger." Selena noticed the faint quivering in the woman's chin.

"You're a very astute young woman." The reply was accompanied by a stiff smile. "Not many people your age would be concerned enough to inquire," she sighed.

"It's probably a case of environment and upbringing." Selena dismissed the idea that she was in any way special, only different. "My father is a minister."

"That no doubt accounts for it." The woman

glanced at her lace handkerchief and nervously tried to smooth out the wrinkles she had twisted into it.

"My name is Selena Merrick." Selena offered her hand to the woman.

"Julia Barkley," the woman returned, clasping Selena's hand warmly but briefly. "Are you here on vacation?"

"Yes. I'm your typical tourist, sight-seeing and all." Selena understood the woman's reluctance to confide in her and let the conversation take its own direction. "That's what brought me to the wharf. I heard the *Delta Queen* had docked and wanted to see her."

"Where is your home?"

"In Iowa," Selena acknowledged.

"Coming from the farmlands of the prairie, you probably don't mind the flatness of our delta land, do you?" the woman who had identified herself as Julia Barkley asked, smiling.

"No," Selena agreed with a wry twist of her curved lips, "although we do have more hills than you do. Do you live in New Orleans?"

"Actually my family's home is outside of New Orleans, but I keep a small apartment here so I can get away every once in a while to be on my own." Unconsciously the older woman stressed the words "get away."

Selena immediately guessed there were family problems at home, possibly a daughter-in-law that Julia Barkley wasn't able to get along with. That thought became sidetracked as she caught

the woman staring again at the massive paddle
wheeler in an attitude that could only be
described as wistfully reminiscent.

"You have a special attachment to the *Delta
Queen*, don't you?" Selena observed softly.
"Because of something that happened to you."

The woman's tears were in definite evidence,
welling diamond bright in her eyes, but there
was a radiant happiness, too, about her expression. Her reddened lips curved into a faint
smile.

"I met Leslie on that boat," she whispered
absently.

"Your husband?" Selena guessed.

"No." Julia Barkley blinked away her tears
before glancing at Selena. "I'm not married.
I'm the old maid of my family, literally," she
tried to joke about her advanced years as Selena
reacted with surprise. "That's why they think
I'm being overly romantic and silly now. Wom-
en of my age aren't supposed to act the way I
do."

"What do you mean?" Selena was thoroughly confused. Her guesses about the elderly
woman and her family problems had obviously
not been accurate.

"Do you believe in love at first sight,
Selena?" she responded to the question with an-
other question, then added, "may I call you
Selena?"

"Of course you may, but as for your first
question—" Selena laughed "—I'm not exactly

an expert. I've never been in love before—a few near brushes here and there, but never the real thing. I have no idea if it can happen the first time you meet.''

"Believe me, my dear, it can. It did for me—with Leslie.'' Her brown gaze swung again to the boat, distant and vaguely dreamy.

"What happened?" Selena dared the question.

"He asked me to marry him.'' A mixture of pain and confusion seemed to flicker across the woman's smooth forehead. It was quickly masked with a polite smile as Julia Barkley turned to Selena. "I was on my way to church. Would you like to join me? Afterward, if you have no other plans, perhaps you'll have Sunday dinner with me at my apartment? Don't hesitate to say no if you'd rather not come. I'll quite understand.''

"I would like to come," Selena accepted without hesitation.

Despite the wealth and status implied by her clothes and manner, Julia Barkley was a lonely woman plagued at this moment by memories of a lost love. Selena sensed it as surely as if it had been put into words.

And Selena enjoyed people too much to even consider that a few hours in the older woman's company would prove boring. Besides, she had twelve full days of her vacation left, so what did a few hours on a Sunday matter?

Just for a moment, she imagined she could

hear her mother laughing and exclaiming, "Stray dogs and orphans couldn't find a better home than with you, Selena." Even at twenty-three, Selena had to admit she was sometimes too trusting of strangers.

Look what had happened yesterday with the dark-haired man in the hotel passage. She smiled to herself. Obviously she hadn't learned a thing about strangers, because here she was going to dinner and church with another. She pushed the thought of the tall, muscular man to the background of her mind.

It returned to haunt her at an inopportune moment. It had happened during the church service while the collection was being taken. Her handbag slipped from her lap, nearly spilling all its contents onto the floor before she could catch it. But the large denomination of bills the man had tucked in her purse did slide silently to the floor. Selena had forgotten all about the money until that embarrassing moment.

A frown of concern creased Julia Barkley's forehead as she whispered to Selena, "You shouldn't carry so much cash with you. It really isn't wise."

"It's n-not mine," Selena explained nervously and self-consciously. "I'm just keeping it for someone. I'll be returning it. . .later."

Just how, she wasn't sure, but she would think of some way to return the money to the man, short of knocking on his hotel room door, of course.

Fortunately Julia Barkley accepted her explanation. Or at least, she was too polite to question Selena about it any further.

At the conclusion of the church service, a car was waiting outside for them, a previous arrangement made by Julia Barkley before she had left her apartment.

But Selena was a bit confused when the car stopped at the canopied entrance of a building complete with a doorman. It had all the earmarks of a hotel. When she stepped out of the car, her suspicions were confirmed by the name, Hotel Ponchartrain.

"The hotel has suites they let on a permanent basis," Julia explained as they entered the marbled lobby.

It was a beautiful suite of rooms that Julia guided her to, a luxurious apartment filled with lovely old furniture. Some of the pieces, Selena was positive, were valuable antiques. Yet it was a very comfortable place.

Selena was quick to attribute the atmosphere of the rooms to her hostess, who was both charming and friendly, if at times a bit preoccupied. Their dinner, an oven meal prepared in advance by Julia and served on genuine china, was simple and excellent.

As Selena helped clear the dishes from the table, she noticed a bedroom door ajar in the hallway. Selena happened to glance inside and her eyebrows lifted curiously at the suitcases and clothes covering the bed.

"Are you going on a trip, Julia?" she questioned, not wanting to stay if her hostess had more urgent plans to attend to.

Julia's hands trembled slightly as she set the china plates on the counter. "Do you know, I can't make up my mind?" The hiccupping sound that came from her throat was half laughter and half sob. "Isn't that silly?" She looked at Selena, tears gathering in her eyes again.

Not since they had left the wharf had Selena noticed any crack in the older woman's composure. Now it was there and widening.

"There are some decisions that are difficult to make at any age," Selena offered. She hesitated to probe, but she felt Julia wanted her to ask. "Were you planning to return home to your family?"

"No." Julia turned away to discreetly wipe the tears from her eyes and smooth the silvered wing of hair into the dark. "I have a passage booked on the *Delta Queen* tomorrow—to meet Leslie."

"Leslie?" Selena echoed, grateful the woman couldn't see her startled expression. For some reason she had thought Leslie was dead.

"Yes," she answered with a hesitant nod. "He's to meet me in Natchez—where we're to be married."

"Really?" This time Selena couldn't mask her incredulity. Then she saw the woman's tightly clutched fingers and the frown of pain wrinkling her brow. "You are going, aren't you?"

"I don't know," Julia murmured uncertainly, shaking her head.

"But you said you loved him." It was Selena's turn to frown.

"I do," the older woman hastened, then sighed in frustration. "I don't know what's the matter with me. I'm as nervous and unsure of myself as a schoolgirl."

In a gesture of bewilderment, Selena ran her fingers through the auburn hair near her ear. "I think there's some point in all of this that I'm missing. You love Leslie and he wants to marry you, but there seems to be something that's holding you back. What is it, Julia?"

"My family," the woman admitted. "My brother thinks I'm crazy. He insists that Leslie is only interested in the family money and the doors the Barkley name can open for him. My sister, everyone, agrees with him."

"Have they met him?"

"Oh, yes, they've met him," Julia assured her, and Selena realized it had been a foolish question to ask a woman of Julia's maturity and status. Of course, she would have introduced him to her family. "Leslie and I met on the *Delta Queen* during its autumn cruise last year. We corresponded for a time. In one of the letters, he proposed to me." Selena could well imagine that his letters were tied up in a pretty blue ribbon and secreted away in some safe place to

be read over and over again. "I was so delirious-
ly happy. I invited him to New Orleans after the
winter holidays to meet my relatives. It was—"
Julia stopped, unable to finish the sentence.

"Disastrous?" Selena completed it for her.

"Totally," Julia sighed the admission. "My
brother, Hamilton, insisted there was too large
a difference in our ages."

Selena gave an involuntary start of surprise.
Was Leslie younger than Julia? It seemed unlikely at Julia's age—whether it was fifty-five or
sixty—that her brother should protest about her
marrying a man fifteen or twenty years older.

If he was that age, what would Julia's status
and money mean to Leslie? If a man in his
seventies proposed to a woman in her sixties,
Selena felt he should be applauded instead of
condemned.

"And the rest of my family," Julia continued, "believes that I'm foolish to take this
romantic fling, as they call it, seriously. They
absolutely forbid me to have anything more to
do with him."

"They forbid you?" Selena repeated. Surely
the woman was old enough to behave or misbe-
have as she wanted. "You obviously didn't
listen to them."

"No, though perhaps I should have," the
woman murmured with a rueful twist of her
mouth. "But I had to write him to explain why I
couldn't marry him. Initially I did refuse him,"
she added in quick explanation. "Then Leslie

wrote me back and I answered it. Before I knew it we were exchanging letters again. In one of his letters, he told me how much he loved me." There was a definite throb in Julia's voice as she added, "And how much he wanted me to be his wife, a-and suggested that we elope...."

"Now you can't decide whether you want to marry him or not," Selena concluded.

"Oh, I want to marry him. But my family—" Her voice trailed off, the tug-of-war still going on inside. She looked beseechingly at Selena. "What would you do?"

"Don't put me on a spot like that, Julia," she declared. It seemed impossible that a woman old enough to be her grandmother would be asking her, Selena, for advice about love and marriage.

"There isn't anyone else I can ask," the woman replied with a despairing shrug. "My family is so prejudiced against Leslie. You, at least, are impartial."

"You have to live your own life, Julia." Selena fell back on the advice her father had always given to her when she had sought him out. "Whatever decision you make will be the one you'll have to live with and not your family."

Julia murmured absently, "It's the things in life you don't do that you regret." She glanced at Selena and smiled. "That's what my nephew always says when my brother begins to lecture him about his questionable escapades."

"There's a great deal of truth in that," Selena

agreed, thinking to herself that there was a member of the Barkley family who evidently didn't always obey the family's edict.

"Yes, and I would always regret it if I never saw Leslie again," Julia declared in a wistful sigh.

"I think you've just come up with your own solution," Selena smiled gently.

"I have?" she returned with a startled look.

"Take the trip and see Leslie again," Selena explained. "Maybe what you once felt for him won't be there anymore. You would still have time to back out before the marriage takes place."

"You're right. That's exactly what I will do!" The shadows left her brown eyes at last, leaving them clear and sparkling. "What would I have done without you, Selena?" Julia declared. "If I hadn't met you today—"

"You still would have made a decision," Selena interrupted, unwilling to take any credit for prompting Julia to a decision.

"But would it have been the right one? And I know in my heart that this one is right."

"I'm glad," Selena said, and meant it.

"I wish you were coming with me. I would so like to have you meet Leslie." The words were no sooner out of her mouth than Julia's expression brightened as an idea flashed through her mind. "Would you come, Selena?"

The request caught Selena completely by surprise. "I—" She couldn't seem to get any answer out.

"As crazy as it sounds, I've never traveled anywhere alone," Julia admitted with a self-deprecating laugh.

"Never?" echoed Selena, although she didn't know why she was astounded. Julia had obviously led an unusually sheltered life.

"Never. Sophie, my cousin, usually goes with me. She accompanied me on the cruise where I met Leslie."

"Well then, maybe she—" Selena began.

"Could come along this time?" Julia finished the phrase and laughed, a throaty, amused sound. "I think not. She despised Leslie. I think she was jealous. Sophie is a few years younger than I am and much more attractive, but Leslie didn't look at her once on the cruise."

It was unnecessary for Julia to explain that her cousin would violently oppose the elopement.

"I suppose it wouldn't be a good idea to have her go with you," Selena conceded.

"But I would enjoy it very much if you could come along, Selena. And I know you'd enjoy the cruise. It's eleven days up the Mississippi River into the Ohio to Cincinnati. There's entertainment and dancing aboard as well as other activities. And the *Delta Queen* stops at various river ports along the way, interesting and historical cities that I know you would like to see."

It did sound tempting, Selena admitted silently. She would certainly see more of the country than just New Orleans and more than the mile-high jet flight home would permit.

"I'm sure it would be very interesting," she admitted as she tried to find a gentle way to refuse the request. "But—"

"You did say you were on vacation," Julia reminded her, not appearing to understand Selena's hesitation.

"I am."

"How silly of me!" Julia exclaimed suddenly. "Of course, you're hesitant because of the cost. You mustn't worry about that, dear. I'll gladly pay your fare."

"It isn't a question of money. I can pay my own way," Selena asserted quickly.

"Gracious! Here I am making all these plans and I don't even know if there's a room available. Sometimes you have to make reservations for these cruises months in advance," Julia explained, as she walked toward the telephone in the small sitting room. "I'll call to see."

"But it's Sunday," was the only protest Selena could offer in her astonishment. She felt as if she was caught in a whirlwind.

Julia tossed her a twinkling glance that made her look very young. "This is one time when it's an advantage to have Barkley for a surname." And she picked up the telephone receiver.

Later that afternoon in her hotel room, Selena wondered how in the world Julia had succeeded in persuading her to go on the cruise.

Somehow she had been gently bulldozed into agreeing. Not that she minded, since the cruise on the old steamboat sounded as if it would be interesting and unusual.

Selena had convinced Julia that she would pay her own way before she had left the apartment, assuring the older woman that she didn't require or expect financial assistance from her. Besides, the fare wasn't that much more than Selena had expected to pay for her hotel and meals during her stay in New Orleans.

She was to meet Julia at four o'clock the next afternoon at the riverboat terminal on the wharf. Glancing at her luggage, Selena was glad she had unpacked less than half of her clothes. It wouldn't take her long to pack, which meant she would have time to see more of New Orleans before she left. Flexibility had always been one of her key traits, she reminded herself.

However, there was one thing she had to take care of before she left. Opening her purse, she took out the folded bills and removed a hotel envelope from the drawer of the nightstand. The simplest and least risky way of returning the money to the man would be to slip it in an envelope under his door.

Sealing the money in the envelope, she reached for the telephone and dialed his room number. When it rang the fourth time with no answer, Selena was convinced the coast was clear and started to hang up.

The receiver was halfway to its cradle when

an impatient male voice crackled into the room, "Yes?" Her hand froze guiltily. At her continued silence, the commanding male voice came came over the phone again. "Who is this? What room were you calling?"

There was no question in her mind that the voice belonged to the man whose money she held in her hand. Very quietly, she hung up the telephone. She would have to wait until later to return it to him when there wasn't a chance of her being caught slipping the envelope under his door.

At midmorning on Monday, there was no answer when she dialed his room. With the envelope in hand, Selena left her room and started down the hallway to his. She nearly turned around and darted for the safety of her own room when she saw his door standing open. Then she heard the hum of a vacuum cleaner and walked closer. The maid was in the room cleaning.

Sighing in exasperation, Selena decided there had to be another way of getting the envelope to him. That was when it dawned on her that she could leave it at the desk for him. Immediately she took the elevator to the lobby.

"May I help you, miss?" One of the younger male clerks inquired when Selena approached the front desk. The sweeping look of admiration he gave her was thinly disguised behind a polite smile.

"Would it be possible to leave a message for

one of your other guests?" Selena fingered the envelope nervously.

"Of course. What room number, please?" he requested with an intensely curious gleam in his eyes.

Selena gave it to him. He frowned and glanced at his records. "I'm sorry, miss, but that room is vacant."

"Vacant? But there was a gentleman—" she began.

"He checked out this morning," the clerk explained.

Selena nibbled at the inside of her lower lip for a thoughtful second, then asked, "Would you give me his name and address, please, so I could mail it to him?"

"I'm sorry, miss," he said smiling apologetically, "but the hotel isn't permitted to give out that information."

"I see," she murmured dejectedly, and managed a smile. "Thank you."

As she walked slowly away from the desk, she wondered what she was going to do with the money. She couldn't keep it, that was certain. But now it was impossible to return it to him. That only left one choice—to give it away to a charitable institution where it would do some good.

She walked to the nearest phone booth and copied the name and address of a local branch of a national organization onto the envelope. With a postage stamp from her purse, she stuck it in the corner and dropped the envelope in the hotel's mailbox.

A wry smile tugged at the edges of her mouth. At least the incident had ended on a redeeming note, she thought.

CHAPTER THREE

FOLLOWING JULIA BARKLEY over the gangplank onto the boat, Selena felt a rush of excitement and nostalgia fill her. If it wasn't for the orange Volkswagen with the black letters *Steamer Delta Queen* painted on its doors that was parked on the bow of the boat, she could have been stepping into another era.

Polished wood gleamed darkly in the wide stairwell leading to the second deck of the boat where fellow passengers were milling around the large and gracious sitting room. Julia didn't pause to let Selena take in the furnishings but continued straight to the purser's office at the end of the room.

A tall, uniformed man was talking to one of the porters, but when his ever-roving gaze touched on Julia Barkley, a smile wreathed his face. With a quick word to the white-coated porter, he stepped forward to meet her, extending his hand.

"Miss Julia, it's good to have you aboard with us again," he declared with beaming sincerity. "I understand congratulations are in order," he winked, and squeezed Julia's hand.

Selena smiled at the blush that colored the older woman's cheeks. It made her look very youthful and vulnerable and also very happy. "Yes, they are, Douglas. Thank you," Julia said. "And it's good to be aboard the *Delta Queen* again. How is your father?"

"He's fine, Miss Julia, just fine." His blue eyes flicked their attention to Selena, then beyond her. "Where's your cousin, Miss Sophie? Isn't she with you?"

"No, not this time. She wasn't able to come. But Selena—Miss Merrick—is traveling with me." Julia turned to draw Selena forward. "Selena, this is the chief purser, Douglas Spender."

"We're pleased to have you aboard with us, Miss Merrick," he said as he shook her hand.

Selena had the distinct impression that he meant it and was not simply issuing polite words of welcome. Neither, on the other hand, was he making a pass. In his midforties, he was a tall and slender man with brown hair and blue eyes. There was a pleasant drawl to his voice and a decidedly charming way to his manner. Selena decided that she liked him.

"I know I'm going to enjoy it." Her smile widened into dimples.

"This is your first cruise?" he inquired.

"Yes," Selena nodded.

"Then I and my crew will do everything we can to insure that it will be enjoyable for you," he smiled. He clasped his hands in front of him in a gesture of decision. "I'm sure you'll want to see your cabins. Kevin—" he motioned to one of the porters, a young fair-haired man "—would you show Miss Julia and Miss Merrick to their cabins?"

"Yes, sir." He smiled at both of them, his gaze lingering a fraction of a second longer on Selena's youthful face. "This way, please, ladies." He led them through an opened door into the wide, interior passageway leading to cabins on the same deck. "You have your customary stateroom, Miss Julia," he said, pausing in front of a door numbered 109 to open it with a key before handing it to the older woman. "Your luggage is already inside. Is there anything else you'd like right now?"

"No, I don't believe so, Kevin." Julia smiled and glanced at Selena. "I'll meet you in the forward cabin in about twenty minutes."

"Fine," Selena agreed, then frowned in bewilderment after Julia had closed the door.

"Are you wondering where the forward cabin is?" the porter asked grinning.

"Yes," she laughed with a trace of self-consciousness.

"You just left it," he explained. "It's the sitting room where you met Doug Spender, the chief purser."

"Thank you." She glanced over her shoulder, hoping to keep her bearings.

"Your cabin is 237, up on the texas deck, Miss Merrick. I'll take you there now." The porter reclaimed her attention.

She followed him as he led her down the passageway, smiling to herself. "Where is the texas deck?" she asked.

"One floor up."

"I'm never going to get these terms straight," Selena demurred.

"It's easy. You're on the cabin deck," he explained. "Front and back are forward and aft or bow and stern. After a few days on board, they'll come naturally to you."

"I hope so," Selena murmured with a skeptical smile. He was dealing with a landlocked girl from Iowa!

He turned right down the short hall toward an exit door leading to the outer passageway. There was also a door on the opposite side of the boat, Selena noticed.

As he turned to make certain she was behind him, the porter saw her glance at the other door. "We'll use this one," he said, pushing the door open. "Watch your step." He indicated the raised threshold over which Selena carefully stepped. "The odd-numbered cabins are on the port side of the boat," he said, explaining his reason for using this exit.

"Oh, dear!" Selena laughed softly.

Walking only a half a step ahead of her, he turned his blond head to give her an understanding grin. "As you face the bow of the boat—the front—the port side is left and the starboard is right."

"Of course," she nodded, but the sparkling

gleam in her eyes said she would never remember and the porter laughed, his gaze openly admiring. As they ascended the covered stairwell to the next deck, Selena said, "I know I'm being foolish because I'll probably forget your answer, but why is it called the texas deck?"

"It's texas deck with a small 't'. It's customary on a riverboat for the largest deck to be called the texas deck after the largest state, Texas. At least at the time of the riverboats, it was the largest state," he explained. "And staterooms derived their names from the fact that they were named after states—the Kentucky Room, the Vermont Room, and so on."

"Fascinating," murmured Selena.

At the top of the stairs he stopped, producing a key from his pocket. "Your room, Miss Merrick," he announced and opened the door.

"Thank you." She nodded, and added with a smile, "And thank you for the lessons, too."

"Definitely my pleasure," he declared, and handed her the key.

With a bobbing nod to her, he turned to retrace his steps. Selena hesitated, then stepped over the raised threshold into her cabin.

A single chest of drawers stood against the wall just inside the door. Two single berths flanked the room. Her luggage was sitting on the floor at the foot of the bed, her garment bag hanging on a clothes rod in the corner. A full-length mirror covered the door leading to the bathroom. The room was compact and efficient and very comfortably adequate.

Unpacking only the clothes that had a tendency to wrinkle, Selena left the rest of it till later. She freshened her lipstick and ran a brush over her copper hair. Slipping her room key into her bag, she left the cabin a few minutes ahead of the agreed time to find her way to the forward cabin lounge. She retraced the exact route the porter had taken and met Julia just as she was stepping out of her stateroom.

"Selena, come see what was waiting for me in my room," Julia exclaimed with delight.

Following Julia into her cabin, Selena stopped just inside the room. A dozen long-stemmed roses glowed velvet red from their crystal vase atop the dresser.

"They're beautiful, Julia," Selena smiled, knowing instinctively that the bouquet was what the older woman had wanted her to see.

"They're from Leslie, of course." There was extra warmth in her voice as she said his name. "Here's the card that came with them."

She handed Selena a small envelope, opened to reveal the card inside. Selena read the personal message written on it somewhat self-consciously. The words were simple but eloquently touching. "I love you, Julia. May I always and forever be—your Leslie." Silently she handed it back to Julia. All the comments that came to her mind seemed inadequate and trite.

Julia read it again before slipping it back in its envelope. "It's moments like this that make me wonder why I have any doubts," she sighed. Again Selena couldn't think of a suitable response and remained silent. As if pulling herself out of her reverie, Julia turned to Selena, fixing a bright smile on her face. "Have you done a bit of exploring yet?"

"No, not yet," Selena admitted. "With all the coming and going of passengers and crew, it's a bit crowded and confusing."

"That's true. And there'll be plenty of time for you to discover every nook and corner of the boat before the cruise is over," Julia stated with a knowing gleam in her brown eyes. "Since the weather is so nice, shall we go up to the texas lounge? Perhaps there'll be a table free. We can relax and have a glass of sherry."

"Sounds fine," Selena agreed.

In the interior passageway, Julia stopped to obtain their table assignment in the dining room from the head waiter before continuing, with Selena at her side, to the forward cabin lounge. Stopping abruptly just inside the lounge, Selena breathed in sharply at the sight of the grand staircase leading to the texas lounge.

"It takes your breath away, doesn't it?" Julia commented.

"Indeed it does," Selena declared, staring at the gleaming wood columns that stood regally at the fanning base of the stairs.

Brass kickboards shimmered gold on the steps. The sweeping curve of the banister railings was inset with lacy scrolled wrought iron. An arched opening had been carved into the ceiling and a chandelier suspended in the aperture.

"I expect to see Rhett Butler appear any minute and carry me up the stairs," Selena confided to Julia in a somewhat awestruck tone.

"Yes, it does remind one of the 'grand old manor' and the days of gracious living," Julia agreed, moving forward to ascend the stairs. "In her day, the *Delta Queen* was the epitome of luxury living and modern conveniences. Her woodwork and paneling is all oak or mahogany. Of course, most of it's covered now with fire retardant paint—Coast Guard regulations."

"It's a pity." Selena observed all the wood moldings and paneling that were painted a cream white.

"It's a compromise with modern times and the need for passenger safety, but it doesn't diminish her charm."

"It certainly doesn't." Selena could already feel the gentle atmosphere warmly enveloping her.

The sensation was intensified as she reached the top of the grand staircase and entered the horseshoe-shaped texas lounge, windowed all around. The rich luster of the wood was free of paint, its casual elegance enhanced by the plaid carpet underfoot.

Furnished with small square tables and captain's chairs, the room had a bar with tall stools in the center of its horseshoe. Double doors on either side of the room opened onto the outer deck where white wrought-iron tables and chairs were waiting.

As Selena and Julia walked toward one set of double doors, a bartender leaned over the bar. "Hi, Miss Julie. I heard you were aboard."

After an initial blank look, surprised recognition flashed across the woman's strong features. "Greg! I didn't expect you to be here. I thought you were quitting to go to college."

"I was." He ducked under the narrow opening cut into the side of the bar and walked over to meet them. "But I decided it would be financially wiser to work through the summer and sign up for the fall term."

"Be sure that you do," Julia insisted in a matronly tone. "You need to complete your education."

Light brown eyes swung to Selena to regard her with studied intentness. Despite his full brown mustache, Selena decided he wasn't any older than she was, possibly a year or two younger. He was good-looking, and there was something in his expression that said he knew it. His charm was evident in his engaging smile and his slow, drawling way of talking.

"Is this your niece, Miss Julie?" he asked, his gaze remaining fixed on Selena.

"No, Miss Merrick is a friend. This is Greg Simpson, an incorrigible but likable young man," Julia introduced them. "And the only one who uses the diminutive of my name, irrespective of my wishes."

"Miss Julie, you know you like it," he chided teasingly, and Selena guessed he was right, judging by the twinkle in Julia's otherwise sternly composed face.

"If I didn't know how hard you work in this job, I would say you rely too heavily on sweet talking," Julia stated.

The bartender laughed off her words of reproof and smiled at Selena. "How do you do, Miss Merrick. And welcome aboard the *Delta Queen*."

"Thank you," she nodded.

"The chief purser, Doug Spender, gave orders that your first sherry of the cruise was to be on him, Miss Julie," he announced, swinging his attention back to the older woman. "Would you like it on the outer deck?"

"Please," Julia agreed.

He turned to Selena. "And what would you like to drink, courtesy of the chief purser?"

Hesitating for a fraction of a second, she said, "I'll have the same."

"My name is Greg," he offered in invitation of its use. "We'll be living together aboard this boat for the next ten days, so we might as well start right out with first names."

"Very well, Greg," Selena agreed, her naturally outgoing nature accepting his friendly advance.

"I'm sorry, but I'm afraid I've forgotten your first name," Greg smiled.

"That's because I didn't give it to you," Julia inserted dryly.

Selena supplied it with a laugh, "It's Selena."

"I like it," he winked before moving off toward the bar. "Two sherries coming right up."

"Incorrigible!" Julia clicked reprovingly under her breath, but Selena noticed the indulgent gleam in the older woman's eye.

On the outer deck, the air was humid and still with only an occasional breath of breeze to stir it. Seated in the wrought-iron deck chair, Selena enjoyed the warmth of the late-afternoon sun on her face.

Her back was to the doors of the texas lounge as she faced the Mississippi River. She missed Greg's approach until he was at their table setting their sherry glasses on cocktail napkins.

His gaze touched the fiery crown of Selena's hair, flaming brighter in the sunlight. "If there's anything else, just call me," he said as he withdrew.

More passengers were migrating toward the lounge, some of them spilling onto the deck where Selena and Julia sat. Their happy, laughing voices were in keeping with the bustling activity Selena was witnessing on the river.

A large oil tanker was moving slowly up the river while other ships, freighters mostly, were docked along the wharves. There seemed to be an almost constant stream of towboats pushing barges up or down the river. In the middle of all this activity, the ferryboat to Algiers was darting back and forth across the Mississippi.

Selena was absorbed by the river scene until she heard a sharply indrawn gasp from Julia.

She glanced at the older woman curiously and frowned at the dismay in the woman's expression. Her concern was immediate.

"Julia, what's wrong?"

"It's my nephew. He's here." She bit at her lower lip, her gaze focused on an object beyond Selena. "I should have known my brother would send him to try to stop me!"

Selena didn't want to be caught in the middle of a family dispute. "I'll leave so you can speak to him alone." She started to rise, but Julia lifted a hand to stop her.

"Please stay," she requested with a hint of panic in her low voice. "I'm afraid I'll need your moral support."

There didn't seem to be any way to refuse without appearing heartless. After the way Julia had befriended her, Selena knew she couldn't treat the older woman that way. But she promised herself she wouldn't become any further involved as she sat back in her chair, aware of the firm, steady strides approaching the table.

"Hello, Julia." At the sound of the male voice, cold fingers ran down Selena's spine.

It couldn't possibly be the same man who had propositioned her in the hallway of the hotel, her mind cried in disbelief. Her fingers closed around the stem of her sherry glass, shock waves vibrating through her body.

"What a surprise to see you here, Chance." Julia's voice wavered as she greeted the man.

Selena dared an upward glance at the man

who had stopped at their table. Her look was returned, coal black eyes hard with recognition, slicing her to the bone before directing their attention to the older woman seated opposite Selena. With an alacrity that surprised her, he assumed an expression of gentleness and patience.

"Is it a surprise, Julia?" There was affection in his mocking tone.

"How did you know where to find me?" the older woman sighed heavily.

Part of Selena wanted to bolt for safety, but she remained rooted to the chair. Staring blindly at her glass, she was uncomfortably aware of the thoughts and opinions that were probably going through the man's mind. She tried to comfort herself with the knowledge that she had been the innocent victim of an unfortunate set of circumstances, but it didn't lessen the disturbance trembling through her.

"I stopped by your apartment," he answered his aunt's question. "The girl at the desk told me you'd left on a trip. After that, it was simple deduction that brought me here."

"I suppose Hamilton sent you," Julia declared with a trace of resentment.

"Yes, he was hoping I would be able to persuade you not to do this," he admitted.

"He should mind his own business." Agitation quivered in Julia's reply, drawing Selena's gaze to the moisture glistening in the liquid-brown eyes.

"Hamilton is your brother. It's natural for him to be concerned about you and what you're doing with your life," was the calmly reasoning response. Selena sensed that he was choosing his words with care, not wanting too much of the family linen to be aired in front of her.

"But it is my life. And I want to do this, it's my right," Julia insisted with a traitorous lack of conviction in the strong words.

"He doesn't want you to be hurt—none of us does. What you're doing is foolish and it's only going to bring unnecessary anguish. Come home with me now, before it goes any further." His tone was cajolingly persuasive. Even Selena could feel its pull. "I—"

"Chance," Julia interrupted to protest, "you know how I feel about Leslie."

"Julia—" Impatience flashed in his voice, making Selena's gaze lift to see the grimness in his features.

"No," Julia stopped the rest of his sentence. "I know what you're going to say. I've heard it all before and it isn't going to change the way I feel. Please, I'm going to do this," she appealed to him to understand. "Don't try to talk me out of it."

Covertly, Selena watched his reaction to the plea. At first there was a stubborn set to the sharply etched line of his jaw, his narrowed black gaze unrelenting.

Then suddenly his eyes smiled. There was no other way to describe the change in his expression. There was no movement of his mouth, nothing except his eyes crinkling at the corners.

"All right, I've tried. My duty to the family is done," he stated. "All that's left is to have a bon-voyage drink with you and the young lady."

There was no smile in his eyes as his gaze swung to Selena. Only a faint challenge glittered through the black shutter he had pulled over them. It was his first formal acknowledgement of her existence and Selena felt trapped. Every nerve end tautened into alertness.

"Where are my manners?" Julia exclaimed in embarrassed agitation, and she hastened to correct her omission of an introduction, one that Selena would rather have avoided. "Selena, this is my nephew, Chance Barkley. Chance, this is a new friend, Selena Merrick."

"How do you do, Mr. Barkley." The words sounded stilted and cold even to her own ears.

"Miss Merrick." He made a mocking half bow to acknowledge her greeting, his gaze hard and glittering as it rested on her upturned face. Drawing an empty chair to the table, he directed his next remark to his aunt. "She must be a very new friend of yours, since I don't recall ever seeing her with you."

There was the faintest emphasis on the last two words, but Selena heard it, as Chance Barkley had guessed she would.

"Oh, yes, as a matter of fact we just met this weekend," Julia admitted.

The upward flick of his dark brow seemed to

say, "You, too." Selena felt like squirming in her seat. It didn't help that he was aware of her discomfiture and was enjoying it.

"You must have a facility for making new friends easily." If it was possible for a man's voice to purr like a smug cat, his did.

His double-edged meaning was not lost on her. "I try, Mr. Barkley," she retorted in a voice riddled with fine tension.

"Call me Chance. You see—" again the taunting smile returned to laugh at her predicament "—already I feel as if I've met you before."

Troubled, green-flecked eyes lowered their attention to the quirking line of his mouth, which was subtly drawn, very masculine and provoked the memory of his potent, drugging kisses. Unnerved, Selena curled her fingers around the glass, ordering her hand not to tremble as she lifted it to her lips. A gulp of the amber-brown wine didn't dull her senses, which leaped in alarm.

His glittering regard was distracted by the appearance of the bartender, Greg, at the table. "Would you like something to drink, sir?"

"Scotch. Chivas Regal on the rocks." Chance Barkley leaned back in his chair, relaxed and insolent, but Selena knew it was only a pose. Despite those lazily drooping eyelids, he was just as alert as she was.

"Very good, sir," Greg nodded. "And how about you, Miss Julie? Would you care for another sherry?"

"One is my limit, Greg," she replied in an apparent reminder.

"Yes, ma'am," he smiled and turned to Selena, his light brown eyes flirting with her—a fact Chance Barkley was quick to note, sardonic mockery flicking across his chiseled male features. "And you, Selena?"

She stared at the glass her fingers circled and the sherry that barely covered the bottom. "Nothing, Greg, thanks," she answered stiffly.

When Greg left, Chance said, "I'm curious. How did the two of you meet?"

"Here," Julia answered. At his sharply questioning look, she laughed and explained, "We met on the dock. We'd both come to see the *Delta Queen* when she docked. We started talking, then one thing led to another, and I invited Selena to church and Sunday dinner."

"To church?"

If he had laughed aloud, his ridiculing amusement couldn't have been more evident as his derisive gaze swung to Selena. Her chin lifted in defensive challenge.

Julia seemed ignorant of the byplay. "Yes, Selena is a minister's daughter."

"Really? I would never have guessed." His voice was bland, but the jeering light in his eyes raked her with contempt. Selena burned slowly in helpless anger, unable to find convincing words to offer in her own defense.

"We had a very enjoyable time together yesterday," Julia went on blithely. "And when

I decided I was going to take this trip, I—"

"It was only yesterday that you decided to go on this trip?" Chance questioned sharply, looking at his aunt with thoughtful contemplation.

"I d-did have a few doubts before then," Julia hesitated, glancing anxiously at Selena. "But it was entirely my own decision."

Selena winced inwardly. Julia wasn't a very good liar, even though her statement was half true. Selena knew she had influenced the decision, however inadvertently, and Julia's assertion to the contrary held a false note. Selena saw the slight flaring of his nostrils as Chance Barkley heard it, otherwise he masked his reaction completely.

"In fact," Julia went on, as if to cover her previous words, "once I decided to go, I convinced Selena that she should come, too." At the harmless and completely true statement, Chance Barkley's gaze narrowed into black diamond chips, slicing over Selena. "You know how I hate to travel alone, Chance." She smiled at Selena. "And Selena is such good company."

"How fortunate that your work permits you to take off at a moment's notice." His smiling comment was double-edged, its sharp side gibing at Selena to remind her of his knowledge of her alleged profession.

"I came here on vacation," she retorted.

"Everyone needs one now and again," Chance stated with an expressive shrug, the hard glint not leaving his eyes, "regardless of his or her line of work."

It was on the tip of Selena's tongue to inform him of her true occupation, but Greg's arrival with Chance's drink checked the words. When he left, Selena decided it would be useless to tell him. Chance Barkley would simply assume that it was a story she had concocted to make herself appear respectable in Julia's eyes, and would make her the recipient of more of his mocking scorn.

"Aren't you concerned that you might find this cruise boring, Selena?" Chance sipped at his drink, making his query with apparent nonchalance.

"I think it will be interesting," Selena countered. "Why should it be boring?"

"Haven't you noticed?" He swirled the ice cubes in his glass, glancing at her over its top and making her aware of his powerfully handsome features. "The majority of your fellow passengers belong to my aunt's generation."

"That won't be a deterrent to my enjoyment of the cruise, Mr. Barkley—"

"Chance," he corrected.

"Chance." Her teeth grated as she uttered his name, pinning a cool smile on her mouth.

There was something coldly calculating in the look he returned that made her want to panic. She sensed a determination in the makeup of his character that could border on ruthlessness if the situation warranted it.

But she couldn't gauge just how vengeful he felt over that incident in his hotel room and the money she hadn't been able to return to him. If only she hadn't been so quick to mail that money to a charity, she could have handed it over to him and vindicated herself to some degree.

The hoarse whistle of the steamboat blew a long and two shorts, hesitated and repeated the sequence. At its cessation a monotone voice issued an announcement over the public-address system.

"All ashore that's going ashore. All aboard that's coming aboard."

"Oh, dear," Julia murmured ruefully. "That means you have to leave, Chance."

"So it does," he agreed with a certain grimness. He downed most of his drink, setting the glass on the table as he pushed himself to his feet. He towered beside Julia's chair. "There isn't anything I can say to persuade you to come home with me?"

"No." She shook her head in negative answer to his half statement, half question. "Don't be angry with me, Chance," she pleaded softly.

A warm and gentle smile softened the hard contours of his face, crinkling his eyes. "I'm not angry, Julia, never with you. You should know that."

"Perhaps," she conceded, with a wealth of affection gleaming in her brown eyes as she gazed up at him. "But it makes me feel better to hear you say it."

Bending down, he kissed her rouged cheek. Selena glimpsed the springing thickness of black hair curling around his white collar. As Chance straightened, his gaze sought Selena. Briefly he inclined his head in her direction and walked away, disappearing into the interior of the texas lounge.

What had it been—a concession? Selena wondered. She was fully aware that she had been spared because she was with Julia. The boat would be leaving in a few minutes or he might have separated her from Julia. And that might have been very humiliating and difficult.

"Chance is almost like a son to me," Julia remarked, pride and sadness mixing in her expression. "He used to call me his 'other mother.' He was always so protective when he was young. He still is, in his own way. It wasn't fair of Hamilton to send Chance to stop me."

"He did seem very fond of you." Selena knew her remark was inadequate, but none other came to mind.

"Yes, he's often said that his mother and I are the only women he needs in his life on a permanent basis." Julia sipped at her sherry, thoughtful and vaguely reminiscent. "Not that he has much time for a private life now that Hamilton has turned everything over to him except the stud farm. And Chance hasn't been content to just manage. He's had to build and expand, take risks and experiment. Never foolishly, you understand."

Selena nodded. She suddenly felt weak and nerveless. She finished the last of her sherry, hoping it would somehow fortify her. It didn't. She hadn't realized how much of a strain she had been under until this minute. It had been like waiting for a bomb to go off and discovering it was a dud. It left her shaky and limp inside.

Assured by the nod that Selena was listening, Julia continued her dissertation. "Chance always holds on with one hand and reaches out to take what he wants with the other. Of course, he's always willing to pay the price. He doesn't expect to get it for free." Selena paled at that— the words were coming too close to her own experience. "I've often wondered if his name had anything to do with the type of man he is. I suppose not, because his grandfather was very much like Chance, too—willing to take risks."

"I hope he's a good loser," Selena commented.

"Oh, he is," Julia insisted. "Before he makes a move, he weighs the odds. No matter how much he loses, Chance doesn't blink an eye because he's already considered that possibility from the first. Unless he's been cheated, then it's an entirely different matter."

And he believed she had cheated him. Her stomach fluttered queasily. A series of wheezing discordant notes sounded from the stern of the riverboat, distracting Julia from her subject.

"Listen! They're going to start the calliope concert. Would you like to walk to the sun deck? There's also a welcome-aboard party in the aft cabin lounge if you'd rather attend it," Julia suggested as if suddenly aware her younger companion might prefer something more in the way of entertainment than listening to an old woman's ramblings.

"Actually, Julia, I think I would prefer to go to my room. I'd like to shower and do some unpacking before dinner," Selena said with an unsteady smile.

"You go right ahead, my dear. Dinner is at seven in the Orleans Room. We're seated at table 40."

The band had finished playing in the texas lounge, although the banjo player was plunking out a few notes as Selena made her way around the bow of the boat to the side of the texas deck where her cabin was located. For a time, the banjo vied with the calliope notes—festive sounds. Soon the texas lounge was behind Selena, and all she heard was the calliope.

Pausing at the railing outside her cabin, she didn't feel very festive. In the windows of the river terminal building where they were docked, she could see the reflection of the passengers gathered on the top deck listening to the musical steam whistles of the calliope. Her gaze strayed to the spectators scattered along the dock below her.

A little girl waved to her and Selena smiled and waved back, the smile soon fading to a faint curve. Her gaze wandered the length of the dock forward to the gangplank. There it was arrested by the tall, muscular figure of Chance Barkley, standing with his hand thrust negligently in his pants pocket, talking with the security guard on duty at the gangway.

As if he possessed an inner radar attuned to her, Chance turned his head, seeming to look directly at her. Shaken, Selena stared back, a fiery heat licking through her veins.

A gambler of sorts, Julia had called him. Selena conceded that he had some of the necessary qualities: the facile charm to trip the innocent; the unrelenting confidence to bluff his opponent; and the black shutters that could keep any of his thoughts from being revealed in his eyes.

Perhaps most of all Chance Barkley had a certain aura of danger about him gained from taking risks, a calculating recklessness that attracted. Combine that with his vital maleness and hard good looks and the end result was potent.

The dark head turned back to the guard, releasing Selena from his ensnarling gaze. She pivoted abruptly, searching through her purse for the cabin key. Her hand shook as she inserted it in the lock and opened the door.

CHAPTER FOUR

THE SHOWER HAD THE NECESSARY reviving effect on Selena, leaving her flesh alive and tingling. Slipping into clean undergarments and her lemon yellow housecoat, she stepped into the main area of the cabin. With the louvered wood insets raised, she couldn't see out of the window.

Walking over, she slid the shutter halfway down. Instead of looking out through the glass at the windowed terminal building, she saw a strip of brown river water and a large freighter docked in front of one of the warehouses that lined the river.

How strange, she thought. There was no sensation of movement at all. Then she listened and heard the rhythmic thump of the engines, distantly, almost a vibration instead of a sound.

She turned from the window after raising the louver and walked to the chest of drawers. The hands of her traveling alarm clock said twenty minutes to seven, ample time to dress before dinner. Picking up her hairbrush, she began stroking the bristles through her hair until it was crackling and glistening like burnished copper.

A sharp rap at her cabin door brought a puzzled frown to her forehead. She hesitated, still holding the hairbrush in her hand.

"Who is it?" she called, certain Julia wouldn't be there.

"The steward," came the response, partially muffled by the door between them.

The wing of a brow lifted in confusion. Setting her brush on the dresser, Selena glanced over her shoulder to see if any of her luggage was missing. It was all there. With a little shrug of bewilderment, she reached for the door, unlocking the deadbolt and holding onto the knob to open the door a crack.

With the first sliver of outside light running the length of the door, it was yanked from her hand. In the next second, she was pushed backward. Her startled cry ended the instant she recognized the towering bulk. The door was shut.

"You!" she choked, her hazel eyes blazing with green flecks as they met the glittering black lights shining from Chance Barkley's eyes.

"I think we have some unfinished business, you and I." His voice was threateningly low.

Her hands were doubled into fists. She was too surprised and angry at the way he constantly kept popping up to be afraid. She stamped her bare foot in rage.

"Get out of here! Get out of my cabin this minute!" she ordered in a hissing rush.

"I don't think I will," he said, defying her complacently and taking a step toward her.

Instinctively she backed up. An ashtray sat on

the small, narrow shelf beside the bed. She grabbed for it, desperate fingers clutching the smooth glass.

"Keep away from me!" She hurled it at his head.

He ducked and the ashtray careened loudly off the door frame, bouncing intact onto the carpeted floor. Her blood was thundering like an express train through her veins, her breath coming in quick, short gasps. She reached for the ashtray on the shelf on the opposite wall.

Long, talon-strong fingers caught her wrist, jerking her away and capturing her other wrist. Her straining and twisting struggles were wasted as Chance hauled her effortlessly against his chest.

"Didn't your mother ever teach you not to throw things, Red?" The low, taunting voice was smooth and complacent. "You could have hurt me with that ashtray."

"I wish it had bashed your head in!" Selena declared, and gasped in pained surprise as he twisted her arms behind her back and crushed her soft shape to his length.

"You're a bloodthirsty little thief," he reproved mockingly.

"Let me go or I'll scream," she threatened, tilting her head back to glare at him. "I mean it!"

He shifted the position of her arms behind her back, the long fingers of one hand easily gripping both wrists. "We can't have that," he murmured.

And Selena realized he was ignoring her warning. Taking a quick breath, she opened her mouth to scream, but his free hand was at the back of her head, holding it still while he smothered her cry in a punishing kiss. Valiantly Selena resisted, muted cries and words of damnation coming from her throat, to be swallowed by his mouth.

Powerless against his superior strength, she kicked at his shins with her bare feet, nearly breaking her toe. He forced her backward, somehow lifting her feet off the floor. She writhed against him and realized with sickening panic that the buttons that had always been too small for the buttonholes of her robe were beginning to slip free from the material in her struggle.

That discovery was quickly replaced by another, one as alarming as the first. With a balancing knee on the mattress, Chance was lowering her to the bed. Waves of panic swamped her, almost paralyzing her lungs and her heart. She glimpsed a ray of hope. As the solidness of the bed formed beneath her, he released her wrists.

Selena didn't question his reason, but took advantage of it to bring her arms around, spreading her hands against his chest before his weight crushed her. He seemed content to let her stop him stretching his length beside her, even slackening his hold on her neck to permit her to twist away from his bruising mouth.

With her lips throbbing from the grinding kiss, Selena tried to roll away from the tautly muscled man lying beside her, but his large hand covered her hipbone to force her back. She realized with a start that that wasn't all his hand was doing. It was dispensing with the last remaining buttons of her robe.

"No, don't!" she gasped in panic.

"Such modesty, Red?" His throaty voice laughed at her attempt to stave off his hands as they pushed aside the covering robe. "You act as though I haven't seen you before similarly unclad."

Her mind whirled desperately, wildly seeking an answer, thoughts jumbling one on top of the other, making no sense. The only coherent thought that pierced her confusion was that Chance wasn't even supposed to be here.

"Why aren't you in New Orleans where you belong?" Selena accused breathlessly. "Don't you know the boat has left port?"

"Yes, I know." He was nibbling at her collarbone.

Her face was turned against the pillow as she struggled to stop his roving hands. Her nerve ends were tingling where his firm mouth explored, his warm breath caressing her sensitive skin.

"You were off the boat. I saw you," she declared on a frantic note. His attention had shifted to the pulsing vein in her neck with disturbing effect. "How did you get back on?"

"I slipped aboard when no one was looking," Chance murmured against her skin.

"What?" Selena was certain she hadn't understood him, the clamoring of her other senses possibly dulling her hearing.

She stopped trying to ward off his wayward hands. The priority had shifted to ending the devastation those male lips were wreaking. Her hands cupped his smoothly shaven jaws to push his face away as she twisted her head to bury her chin in her neck.

Selena partially succeeded in lifting his head, her fingers slipping into the midnight black of his hair. The silky crispness of the thick strands curled around her fingers and against her palms, the feel of it virtually sensual.

"I stowed away," drawled Chance, and began an intimate exploration of her face, the wing of her brow and the curving sweep of her lashes. "You'll have to hide me."

Her fluttering lashes sprang open at the last low statement, while her hands slipped to his shoulder, splayed and resisting. "I'll do no such thing!" she denied hotly. "I'll turn you over to the captain and he'll put you ashore immediately."

Lifting his head a few inches, he studied her lazily, mockery glinting in his jet dark eyes at indignant flames flashing in hers. His hand raised to cup the underside of her jaw, his thumb rubbing the point of her chin.

There was something threatening in his action, as if at any provocation, his thumb would slide down to throttle her throat. Like a wild animal, Selena sensed the danger, saw it in the straight, ruthless line of his mouth, and remained warily motionless under his stroking thumb.

"If you turned me over to the captain, Red, I'd simply have to tell him about you." His thumb slid upward to move across her trembling lips as he added, "and the money you stole from me."

Swallowing, Selena tightly insisted, "I didn't steal your money." Her lips moved against his thumb as she spoke. It was not an altogether unpleasant sensation.

His veiled look focused on her mouth, sending her pulse rocketing, while his thumb directed itself to a more thorough exploration of her lower lip. His expression was completely masked as his gaze flicked to the round alertness of her eyes.

"Am I supposed to regard the red dress and shoes you left as equal to the value of the money you took?" he inquired in soft challenge. "Neither of them happen to be in my size or my color."

"That isn't what I meant," Selena protested.

"Then what did you mean?" His voice was as smooth as polished steel. "I gave you the money—you took it. And I didn't get what I paid for. I don't like being conned, Red. Nobody cheats me and gets away with it."

Selena could feel the silent menace of his words. "I didn't mean to take your money." With an effort, she kept her voice calm and firm.

"Didn't you?" A black eyebrow arched in mocking skepticism as his thumb moved away from her mouth.

"Honestly, I didn't," she insisted with a trace of taut anger. "When I grabbed my purse, I'd forgotten you'd put the money in it. All I was interested in was my room key that was in it."

"Your room key? You had a room at the hotel?"

"Yes, I was staying there."

"How convenient for your clients," Chance drawled.

"I don't have any clients," Selena retorted in exasperation. "It was all a joke."

"Then why am I not laughing?" he countered.

"Because you took everything seriously," she explained earnestly, her brows drawing together in a slight frown.

"When money is involved, I'm always serious." Flat black eyes regarded her steadily and her own faltered under the look.

"Look, it was all a mistake," she began nervously. "I'm—"

But Chance interrupted to derisively mock, "A minister's daughter?"

"From Iowa," Selena tacked on unconsciously.

Laughter rolled from his throat, rich and deep, as he threw his head back in amusement. Dying to a low chuckle, it glinted brightly in his eyes, teasing and taunting her assertion.

"A minister's daughter from Iowa," he repeated. "Is that supposed to make your claim legitimate? Because you're from Iowa?"

He laughed softly again, infuriating Selena to

the point where she almost choked on her own anger. "It happens to be the truth! And I don't give a damn whether you believe me or not!"

His eyes widened in pretended shock. "What would your father say if he heard such language?" he murmured reprovingly.

A frustrated moan was wrenched from her throat. "Why won't you listen to me? I tried to return the money to you."

"I'm sure you did." There was a single trace of disbelief in his voice.

"I did," Selena snapped. "When I discovered it in my purse, I sealed it in an envelope. I was going to slip it under your door when you were out. Don't you remember those phone calls you got where there was nobody on the other end? It was me, calling to see if you were in your room."

"How can you prove that when there was no one on the other end?" Chance continued to bait her, seeming to derive amusement from her anger.

"Surely the fact that I know about the phone calls proves something," she retorted.

"It might prove that you were trying to figure out a way to get back into my room to retrieve your dress and shoes," he pointed out.

"I wasn't," Selena denied his claim in an impatient burst. "As a matter of fact, I even tried to leave the money for you at the desk this morning, but you'd already checked out."

"Why didn't you just return it in person instead of supposedly trying all these covert attempts?'' His look was bland, unrevealing and unconvinced.

"Are you crazy?" she expelled in a laughing, scornful breath. "And risk ending up like this—in bed with you?" Suddenly aware of their prone position she tried to push away and sit up, but his hand pressed her shoulders to the bed. "I ran out of your hotel room to avoid this!" she hissed.

His gaze narrowed thoughtfully as he weighed her words. "All right," he conceded. "Return my money and I'll forget the whole thing."

Selena paled, the anger flowing out of her with a rush. "I don't have it anymore," she said in a small voice.

She hadn't been aware of any softening in his expression until it hardened. "You don't have it anymore," he repeated her statement. "You had it this morning, but you don't have it now. I suppose I'm wasting my time by asking you what happened to it?"

"The desk clerk wouldn't give me your name or address so I couldn't mail it to you," Selena tried desperately to explain the dilemma she had been in. "And it wasn't mine, so I couldn't keep it."

"Oh, no, a minister's daughter couldn't keep money that didn't rightfully belong to her," he agreed wryly. "So what did you do with it?"

"I gave it away." She couldn't tell whether he was believing any part of what she said. "To a charity."

A smile seemed to play with his mouth, the corners twitching. "Do you expect me to believe that?"

"It's the truth, I swear," Selena vowed.

"It seems to me," he said, pausing to watch his finger as it traced the sensitive cord on the side of her neck, "that we're back to where we started—with the money paid and the goods still to be delivered."

"Will you stop?" Panic bubbled in her throat and she swallowed it down. His mouth descended towards her and she turned her head to elude it. "Don't!"

Winding a bunch of auburn hair around his fingers, Chance tugged her back, capturing her lips with practiced ease. His other hand slid over the bareness of her stomach, arousing a tumult of emotion that she was powerless to control. His seductive mastery was completely beyond her experience.

When he felt her trembling and unwilling response, he lowered his head, seeking the hollow of her throat. Selena's resistance stiffened as she felt the bra strap slipping from her shoulder and the trailing tips of his fingers making their way to the exposed swell of her breast. She clawed at his hand, only to have it closed firmly over the lacy cup of her brassiere.

"Don't do this, please," she repeated an earlier plea. "I'm not that kind of girl."

He followed the curve of her neck to her ear, nuzzling it, his warm breath arousing and stimulating. "Are you trying to convince me that you don't sell your favors despite what I overheard at the café?"

"I don't, no," Selena protested, fighting the breathlessness that had attacked her voice. "Those men thought that was what I did and I just went along with it. It was. . . . It was just a little harmless fun, a joke. When I saw you later at the hotel, I didn't know what to do. One lie just led to another."

He moved, his mouth playing over her lips, teasing and tantalizing them into wanting his kiss. "Isn't that a strange kind of joke for a minister's daughter to be playing?"

"I don't think you've known many minister's children," she breathed tightly. "We tend to be more mischievous than other kids."

A swift, hard kiss effectively silenced her before Chance unexpectedly levered himself from her. Propped up by an elbow, he studied her flushed and shaken expression.

"Suppose I believe that you aren't that kind, what then?" he challenged.

"Do you believe me?" She searched his dark, unreadable features.

"I believe at least part of your story, although I find your tale about what happened to my money is a little hard to swallow," he returned.

"It's true," Selena rushed. "You can look through my bag and see that, apart from some traveler's checks, I only have a little cash."

"That doesn't prove anything. You could

have spent it to pay for this cruise." His gaze narrowed. "Unless my aunt paid your passage."

"I paid my own fare," she flashed, resenting his accusation, "with my own money."

"Or was it mine?" Chance taunted softly.

"It wasn't. I told you what I did with your money!"

"I know what you told me." Skepticism was etched in his words. "But there's still the very real possibility that you used it to finance this cruise, investing it in the hope of a larger return."

"What are you talking about?" Selena frowned angrily.

"I'm sure there are several wealthy widowers on board."

"I'm not looking for a husband," she interrupted coldly.

"And my aunt is a trusting, vulnerable woman," he concluded. "She's completely taken in by you. You know that, don't you?"

"I don't think I like what you're implying." Wary, irridescent fires smoldered in her eyes and her auburn hair fanned over the pillow like a flaming crown.

"Not any more than I do," Chance stated. "But if you were planning to con any money out of her, on whatever pretext that red head of yours has dreamed up, you'd better forget it. Because, honey, I'm going to see to it that you don't get a penny."

Selena was indignant. "It was never my intention!"

"As if you would admit that it was," he jeered.

"You disgust me!" Her voice trembled with the violence of her emotions. With a surge of strength, she pushed him away. "Get out of my cabin!"

As she sat up, Chance rolled over onto his back, folding his hands beneath his head. "But, there is still the matter of where I'm going to spend the night, isn't there?" he asked, looking very much at home.

"Well, you certainly aren't going to stay here!" she snapped.

His gaze slid over the single bed and Selena already cramped against the wall. "No, it would be too crowded with both of us, but luckily you have a spare bed that's empty."

"I'd sooner have a snake in my room than you!" Selena hissed, discovering she was treacherously close to tears. "So you can just get out and see if the Barkley name can work any wonders with the captain."

Laughter again rolled from his throat as he swung himself to his feet with an ease unexpected in a man of his size. His hand was in front of him, holding a key.

"What's that?" Selena eyed it warily, almost afraid that he had somehow managed to obtain her cabin key from her purse.

"The key to my cabin," he informed her.

"You see—" he was confident now; it was written in every line of his stance "—when I found you sitting with Julia, I arranged for a passage on this cruise so I could keep an eye on you."

"Does Julia know?"

"Not yet. I wanted to find out what your game was first," he answered.

Resentment seethed in Selena. "Julia told me what an important and busy man you are. I suppose I should feel flattered that you canceled everything and came on this cruise because of me." She stiffened as another thought occurred to her. "Or is it entirely because of me?" At his silence, she pursued it. "You want to stop this thing with Leslie, don't you?"

"That's a personal, family matter and none of your business," Chance stated coldly.

"Then I'm right," Selena concluded. "How can you be so heartless? Julia is old enough to make her own decisions. Your family has no right to stand in the way of something that will bring her happiness."

"I have no intention of discussing it with you. And I suggest that you stay out of it." There was a deadly calm about him.

"Is that right?" Although intimidated, Selena still defied him.

"Yes." His gaze glittered over her, implying amusement at her challenge. "Put some clothes on. Unless you intend to go to dinner like that?"

"I'll get dressed—" she paused pointedly, her lips tightening "—when you leave."

"You're only going to be putting clothes over what I've already seen." His eyes were crinkled, laughing at her again. "Is this what you're planning to wear?" Turning, he nodded to the pink-flowered dress laid out on the other bed.

"It is," Selena acknowledged stiffly.

"Very pretty." Chance picked it up, fingering the synthetic material. "Although it isn't nearly as sexy as the red one." He tossed it to her. "Put it on."

Glaring at him, Selena had the distinct impression that if she refused, he was quite capable of taking a hand in it himself. This was one time, she decided, when discretion was the better part of valor. Clutching her robe tightly shut and holding the dress in front of her for added protection, she slid from the bed and retreated behind the closed door of the bathroom.

When she emerged from the bathroom several minutes later, fully clothed and with fresh makeup, Chance was standing at the window. He turned, running a practiced eye over her.

"It took you long enough," he observed, but without complaining.

"I had trouble with the zipper," Selena admitted, smoothing the obi sash at the waistline.

The dress was superbly and simply styled, from its slender band neck with its demure front slash to the artful seaming curving the material over her torso and sweeping to a full skirt. The delicately flowered print was in the softest pinks imaginable, flattering the copper tint of her hair.

"I could have given you a hand with the zipper," Chance stated, watching as she slipped her sheer stockinged feet into her shoes.

"It occurred to me, and I rejected the thought just as quickly," she retorted.

"Shall we go?" Her purse was in the hand he extended to her.

Holding her tongue was an effort since the urge was strong to tell him where she thought he should go, but wisdom and temperance prevailed. Taking her purse, she walked to the door. As she reached to unlock it, his hand was there to turn the key and push the door open, his arm brushing her shoulder.

Selena stepped quickly over the raised threshold onto the outer deck. Anxious to escape the confining intimacy of the cabin, she nearly walked into the path of two other couples heading for the stairs. Chance's hands were there, curving into the short sleeves covering her upper arms and pulling her back, and she tensed under his hold.

One of the men glanced from her to Chance to the cabin door swinging closed. He couldn't possibly know that she and Chance weren't married, but she felt the growing pink of embarrassment warming her cheeks. The boat was not so large that at some point the man would discover they weren't.

As the two couples descended the stairs,

Chance released her to move from behind Selena to her side. She averted her head, but not quickly enough to escape his observant gaze. She tried to hurry to the stairs, but his hand gripped her elbow to forestall her rush.

"Are you blushing?" he questioned, tipping his head down for a closer inspection.

"Yes," she muttered the admission under her breath.

"Why?" Chance sounded amused.

"Because I don't like the idea of those people seeing you come out of my cabin," she retorted. "They might get the wrong idea."

"Just as long as they believe that you're with me, I don't particularly care what other ideas they get," Chance stated.

"Well, I'm not with you!" Selena flashed.

"For the duration of this cruise, everyone is going to think you are," he informed her. "Because I'm going to keep you in my sight every waking minute."

"Is that right?" Her chin lifted in the beginnings of defiance.

His mouth curved into a smile, one that didn't reach his eyes as she knew it could if it was genuine. "I suggest that you be glad I said every *waking* minute."

"If that's supposed to be a threat, I'm not frightened," she countered.

"Suit yourself," Chance shrugged, and released her elbow. "But you'd do well to remember all that I've said."

Selena turned up her nose at his advice and walked to the stairs, well aware that he was following her. And she was also aware that there was very little she could do about it, short of pushing him overboard, and she didn't have the strength for that.

Not until she had reached the cabin deck did Selena realized that she had no idea where the meals were served. She glanced around, hoping to see fellow passengers on their way to dinner so that she might follow them. There wasn't a soul in sight.

It grated to have to turn to Chance. "Do you know where the Orleans Room is located?" she requested stiffly.

Slashing grooves were etched from nose to mouth on each side of his tanned face. They deepened now as his mouth tightened to conceal a smile. He knew how it irritated Selena to ask his assistance and was complacently amused.

"I believe I do, yes," he drawled, and guided her to the area where the forward cabin lounge was located.

As Selena entered the lounge ahead of Chance, Julia saw her. "I was wondering where you were, Selena," she exclaimed. "I was about to go down without you." Then she saw the man following Selena. "Chance! What are you doing here?" Julia greeted him with surprise and delight, with none of the trepidation she had voiced at his appearance before the boat left the dock.

"I decided to come on the cruise with you," was his brief reply. He nodded to Selena adding, "I found...Selena." He paused deliberately before using her given name while his gaze flicked to her red hair, reminding Selena of his nickname for her. "She was wandering about lost and I volunteered to show her where the dining room was."

"Oh, dear," Julia exclaimed in dismay. "I didn't tell you where it was located, did I?"

"It's all right," Selena assured her.

"Thank you, Chance, for directing her here," Julia smiled at her nephew, then sighed happily. "I'm so glad you've come, Chance." She clasped one of his hands warmly between her own. "I so wanted a member of my family at the wedding and now you're here."

"Yes, I'm here," Chance agreed blandly.

But Selena noticed the way his jaw had hardened when Julia had referred to her marriage to Leslie. She knew intuitively that if Chance had his way, the marriage would never take place. Obviously he was going to do everything in his power to stop it. Selena resented, on Julia's behalf, this desire to dominate.

CHAPTER FIVE

"SHALL WE GO DOWN to dinner?" Chance suggested, distracting the conversation from Julia's elopement.

Behind the grand staircase was a stairwell leading below. The identifying words Orleans Room were in open view. At the base of the stairs, double doors of cream white stood open in welcome, the head waiter standing just inside, resplendent and distinguished in an excellently cut black suit, and smiling a greeting as the trio descended the stairs.

"You and your companion have table 40 as usual, Miss Julia," the man announced with grave courtesy, before turning to Chance. "And your table, sir?"

From his suit pocket, Chance withdrew a round, numbered disc indicating table 83. He handed it to the maître d'.

Selena darted Chance a look through sweeping lashes. He caught and read the message written in her eyes, triumphant relief that she wouldn't have to suffer his presence at the dinner table.

"Your table is on the starboard side sir," the head waiter explained. "Your waiter will show you."

"This is my nephew, André," Julia spoke up. "Chance Barkley."

"Mr. Barkley," the man bowed slightly as he shook Chance's hand. "It's a pleasure to have you aboard." Then, to all three of them, he said, "Enjoy the buffet."

The tables of food ran the length of the room down its center, splitting the dining area in half. Most of the passengers had already helped themselves and were seated at their assigned tables. Filing behind Julia, Selena noted the spaciousness of the room. There was no suggestion of crowding, and the leisurely atmosphere invited her to take her time over the varied selection of salads, vegetables and entrées.

Their waiter was at the end of the buffet to carry their plates to the table for four. An elderly couple were already occupying two of the chairs, and there was a friendly round of introductions as Selena and Julia joined them.

Selena couldn't remember the last time she had enjoyed such an unhurried meal. Against the middle of the far wall was a bandstand, complete with a grand piano. A man sat at the keyboard, softly playing a medley of show tunes. Her gaze wandered to the opposite side of the room and glimpsed the satin blackness of the back of Chance's head, but he was too far away to disturb her serenity.

Their waiter, another college-aged boy, appeared unobtrusively at the table, refilling Selena's coffee cup and whisking away her dessert plate. Selena relaxed in her chair to listen to the dreamily soothing piano music.

The arrival of night had darkened the windows. Water shimmered occasionally beyond the panes where the lights from the steamboat touched the river's surface.

Yet the sun-yellow walls of the dining room kept the mood mellow, enhanced by the glow of Tiffany lamps located on the walls between each of the green shuttered windows. The individual lights resembled a trio of palm fronds, their stalks secured with a gold bow, while crystal pendants were suspended from the tip of each golden spiked leaflet.

The hoarse whistle of the steamboat blasted a single, long wail. In the distance came a long, answering toot, low and deep, reverberating into the interior of the boat. Curious, Selena waited expectantly for something to happen. Julia noticed her expression and smiled.

"Our captain just signaled to another vessel coming down river that we would pass on the port side," she explained. "The other vessel, probably a towboat with barges, returned the signal. Two whistles would mean the starboard side."

"I see," Selena said, nodding her understanding.

"It's written on the walls by the door," Julia pointed.

Selena turned slightly in her chair. On the wall to the left of the double doors was written

"One whistle port." On the right it read, "Two whistles starb'rd." The sign also signified which side was which.

"The vessel will be going by shortly," Julia added. "Would you like to go up for a better view?"

"If you're ready?" Selena agreed with qualification. The other couple at their table had already left.

"I am," the older woman acknowledged, folding her linen napkin and placing it on the table near her coffee cup.

It was cool outside and Selena chose to watch the massed barges and pushing towboat go past from the shelter of the forward cabin lounge. She had seen similar barges and towboats from the New Orleans dock, but it was a much more impressive sight from the interior of the moving steamboat as the two vessels met and glided slowly and silently past one another.

When the towboat was gone, there was only shadowing darkness outside the window. Selena turned away and found Chance standing behind her, smoke curling from the slender cigar between his fingers.

"You'll get used to it." His perceptive eyes had noticed the bemused look that hadn't completely left her face and recognized its cause. "In a few days, you won't even glance out the window when the pilot blows the whistle."

Selena didn't respond to his cynical observation, but she hoped he was wrong. Instead she remarked, "I hope you enjoyed your meal."

"I did. Did you?"

Selena managed only a nod before Julia broke in to ask, "Chance, do you recall what time the show in the Orleans Room is this evening?"

"Nine-fifteen, I believe," he answered.

"You are going, aren't you?" Julia directed the question to her nephew.

"I thought I would, yes."

"It should be very good," Julia remarked idly. "They have some excellent entertainers aboard. I know you'll enjoy it, Selena."

"Oh, but I'm not going." She had made up her mind the instant that she heard that Chance Barkley was.

"But it's your first night," Julia protested, while Chance smiled knowingly.

"Yes, I know, but it's been a full day and I want to write to my parents. I haven't let them know yet about my change of plans." Selena felt her excuse was excellent, even if Chance did guess why she was making it. "There'll be other nights and other shows."

"I suppose so," Julia conceded gracefully.

"Excuse me. I noticed the gift shop was opened and I'd like to pick up a few postcards." She was already moving away, making her escape while she could. "I'll see you in the morning, Julia. Good night."

There was an interesting assortment of souvenirs displayed on the gift-shop counter, but

Selena didn't take the time to look at them. She purchased a few cards to send to friends at home and left.

An hour later, the letter to her parents was written—to fulfill the excuse she had made—as well as one to her girl friend Robin. Selena glanced at the turned-down covers of the bed, courtesy of a dinner-time visit by the maid, and knew she wasn't ready yet to sleep.

She hesitated, then took a white crocheted shawl from the chest of drawers and the cabin key from her handbag. Wrapping the shawl around her shoulders, she stepped out of the door onto the outer deck. At first, she was struck by the silence of the night, broken only by the rush of water cascading from the paddle wheel and the muffled throb of the engines.

Moving to the railings, she leaned against the teakwood handrail and stared at the glow of light from New Orleans. Rising above it was a big, full moon, looking like a fat Georgia peach. Selena corrected the thought, deciding it was more salmon-colored, but breathtaking just the same.

"It's beautiful," she murmured aloud.

"Yes, it is."

Selena turned with a start as Chance separated himself from the shadows and moved to the railing. "Why don't you quit spying on me?" she demanded and pivoted back to stare at the river.

Chance ignored her question, seeming to indicate that he didn't believe it warranted an answer, and remarked, "You didn't mention that you were going to take a romantic stroll around the deck."

"I just wanted some fresh air before I turned in," she replied, and immediately wished she hadn't offered an explanation. It was none of his business. "What are you doing out here? I thought you were going to the show." Her sideways glance found him negligently leaning a hip against the railing to face her profile.

"I wanted some fresh air." He used her excuse deliberately, Selena thought, to mock her somehow.

"Go and find it somewhere else," she retorted, her nerves stretching thin like a piano wire.

"Have any suggestions?" Chance sounded amused.

Selena felt an unreasoning irritation, a desire to lash out, to claw. "Why don't you try the bottom of the river?"

Silence followed. In the stillness she had an inexplicable urge to retract her words, to make peace whatever the cost.

When Chance did speak, it was in a voice that reminded her of velvet. "Do you really want to be on deck alone—under that moon?" Her gaze slid to the full moon, bathing her with the serenity of its light and catching her in its romantic spell. "It seems to say, 'for lovers only,' doesn't it?" His voice sounded dangerously close.

When Selena turned, she turned into him. Her hands, clutching the crossed ends of the shawl, brushed against his jacket. The moonlight was masking his compelling features in glistening bronze, but his eyes, black midnight pools, fathomless and shimmering, were focused on her lips. Everything seemed to come to a standstill, her heart, her breath, her thoughts.

His hands settled lightly on her shoulders as his head bent lower. She knew what he was going to do, but Chance had kissed her so many times before, it seemed natural. At the warm touch of his mouth she responded, hesitantly at first, then with increasing ease. She let his shaping hands mold her to him, his oak-strong solidness something she could lean on.

The pressure of his kiss relaxed, although his firm, male lips continued sensually playing with hers, their warm breath mingling. "I've wanted you, Red, ever since I saw you again at the hotel," Chance murmured against her mouth.

The use of her nickname set off the alarm bell, making her aware of the danger in his embrace. This was not an innocently romantic kiss in the moonlight, not with Chance Barkley as a participant. Why had she let herself be caught up in all the talk about the moon and lovers?

She twisted out of his arms. "You're still making the same mistake about me," she accused with a painful catch in her voice.

His head was drawn back, a hint of arrogance in his look. "Am I?"

"Yes, you are." Chance made no effort to stop her as she stepped away, aware that in her weakness and foolishness she had given him cause to think that way. "I'm going to my cabin," she announced, adding a definite "alone" when he started to follow her.

His mouth quirked. "A gentleman always sees a lady to her door."

"You aren't a gentleman," Selena retorted.

His eyes said, "You aren't a lady," but they had already crossed the few feet to her cabin. Selena tried to ignore him as she inserted the key into the lock. When she started to pull the door open, his hand was there to stop it.

"Don't you think I should check to make sure there aren't any unwanted visitors in your room?" he queried mockingly.

"Such as?" she asked in caustic challenge.

"Spiders, mice, the odd creatures that might have slipped aboard."

"Like rats," Selena suggested with a cloyingly sweet smile, and ducked under his arm to slip inside the door.

She heard his soft chuckles as she closed it behind her. She waited just inside until she heard his footsteps moving away from her cabin.

After changing into her nightclothes, she switched off the light and crawled between the covers of her bed. A couple walked by her door, passengers murmuring a greeting to someone. There was a tightness in her chest as she heard Chance's familiar voice respond.

He was still outside her cabin, somewhere close. She rolled onto her side, punching her pillow with the unladylike wish that it was his face. But that wasn't really what she wished and she knew it.

Morning brought renewed zest and a firm resolve that she wasn't going to let Chance Barkley get under her skin—or anywhere else!

Her clothing was casual for the day of cruising up the river. The loose-fitting sweater top was a natural shade with toast and black stripes ringing the bodice, the hips and the hem, the short sleeves cuffed at the elbow with more stripes. Natural linen pants matched the top, and a black and tan plaid scarf secured her hair at the back of her neck, the silk material brushing the skin left bare by the boat neckline of the sweater.

Breakfast was being served in the Orleans Room, and Selena skipped lightly down the stairs, the brilliant sunlight shining outside reflected in her bright, carefree spirits.

Inside the dining-room entrance, she stopped dead. Chance was sitting at her table, sipping a cup of coffee. When he saw her poised inside the doorway, he rose and pulled out a chair for her with mock courtesy.

Numbly Selena moved to the table, her resolve vanishing in a rush of irritation. "What are you doing here?" she demanded.

He continued to stand beside the chair, waiting for her to be seated. "I arranged to have my table changed," he explained with a wicked glint in his eyes. "The head waiter quite understood that I would prefer to sit with my aunt."

She wanted to turn and stalk from the room, but that would give him too much satisfaction. She ignored the chair he held out for her and chose one that seated her opposite him.

The long, narrow menu card was leaning against the crystal vase of carnations in the center of the table. Selena picked it up and forced herself to concentrate on the selections, ignoring Chance as he took his chair.

"Are you ready to order?" Dick, their waiter, asked as he appeared at the table.

"Selena?" Chance directed the inquiry to her.

"I haven't quite decided. You go ahead."

He hesitated, then ordered a full breakfast. The waiter turned to Selena. "Have you made up your mind, miss?"

"I think I'll just have orange juice and a sweet roll," she stated, replacing the menu. "And coffee."

When the waiter left for the kitchen, Selena felt Chance's gaze center on her. "I expected an Iowa girl like you would eat a hearty breakfast," he commented.

"Did you?" Coolly, Selena lifted her gaze to meet his. "But then you've consistently misjudged me, haven't you?"

Chance made no reply, his gaze narrowing briefly. Silence reigned through the morning meal with Selena naturally finishing first and excusing herself from the table to leave him there alone.

Later she saw him on deck, but he made no attempt to approach her, although she noticed, with irritation, that he kept her in sight. Soon his presence lost the ability to chafe as she became caught up in the spell of the Mississippi River.

The *Delta Queen* steamed up the river with majestic slowness, a stately, old-fashioned lady taking a leisurely paddle up the Mississippi. Levees, emerald green with thick grasses, paralleled the river's winding course as it sometimes seemed to attempt to twist back into itself.

Trees forested the banks. Cottonwoods, cypress, sycamores—an almost endless variety—grew there to baffle and break up the raging current when the river went out of its banks at flood stage. Through breaks in the trees, there were glimpses over the levees of sprawling flatlands, cotton and sugar plantations.

A trio of egrets was perched on a fallen tree near the river's edge, and a deer grazing in a grassy glade flicked his white tail before bounding into the trees. The river itself was a dirty brown, rushing full between its banks, creating eddies and then destroying them. Logs and tree branches were swept helplessly in its current, along with a million spring seeds. The river was showing a face that had changed little since the days when steamboats ruled its waters and Mark Twain described its lure.

But there were other faces; buoys marked the channel and industry spilled onto its banks. Vast chemical plants and refineries with their complex network .of intertwining pipes and towering stacks rose above the levees. Water towers and church steeples marked towns that were hidden from view.

Except for the Crescent City of New Orleans, nowhere did the modern face become more evident than at Baton Rouge. The highrise buildings of the city proper marked its center. On either side of the river loading terminals lined the banks with oceangoing ships of every description. Some were being unloaded and giant cranes were loading others. Selena left her comfortable deck chair to walk to the railing for a better look.

"Baton Rouge is the farthest inland, major port in the States," said Chance, appearing at her side.

Selena found the scene all too fascinating to object to his presence. "It's an impressive array of ships, but why are they all flying the American flag? Surely they can't all be American ships?"

"It's a courtesy to fly the flag of the port nation. The flag of the ship's country is on the stern," he explained.

"I see," she nodded. "There's one from Holland," she pointed.

"The next one is from Glasgow, Scotland, where the *Delta Queen* was made."

Selena faced him in surprise. "The *Delta Queen* was made in Scotland?" she repeated. "I didn't know that."

"Yes, the steelwork for her and the *Delta King* was fabricated in Glasgow and temporarily assembled on the River Clyde. The parts were all marked, then torn down and shipped to California where she was reassembled and finished. But it was the same shipbuilding center in Scotland where the *Queen Mary* was fitted out that this riverboat had her start," he concluded.

"Amazing!" she breathed, and looked back at the freighter from Scotland.

Several crew members had gathered on the bridge of the freighter to watch the *Delta Queen* steam by, her paddle wheel churning tan foam. One of the crew was taking pictures of the riverboat and Selena wondered if he knew of the *Delta Queen*'s beginnings in his homeland. Or did she just seem an anachronism gliding slowly past the sleek, ultramodern tankers and freighters?

"When was she built?" Selena questioned absently.

"In the mid-1920s I think. She carried passengers on the Sacramento River back and forth from San Francisco to Sacramento, California."

"Yes, I remember the couple at our dinner table last night mentioned that one of their older relations had been on the *Delta Queen* when she was in California many years ago," she nodded.

The breeze had picked up, whipping around the stern. It tugged a strand of hair free of Selena's scarf and laid it across her cheek. Before she could push it aside, Chance's hand was there, smoothing it behind her ear and making her conscious of him.

He was tall and vital, his dark eyes glinting with an inner light. With the breeze ruffling the thick crispness of his black hair, he looked rugged and manly, totally in command. His silk print shirt was plastered to his torso by the wind, the material alternately clinging and billowing to enhance his muscular physique.

The cuffs of his shirt sleeves were rolled up twice to reveal a portion of the rippling muscles in his forearms. The top two buttons of the shirt were unfastened, exposing his throat and the tanned column of his neck. Chance Barkley was a handsome brute, a black-haired devil, and the heady sight of him shook her senses.

She tore her gaze away from him, suddenly finding it very essential to speak and break the silence. "The *Delta Queen* has a very interesting history, doesn't she?" Her voice was much steadier than she had expected and she could feel her pulse settling into a more even rhythm.

"Yes, it has," Chance agreed.

Another couple moved to the railing near them, an older man and his wife. After several minutes, the man struck up a conversation with Chance and Selena drifted away to reclaim her deck chair and watch the outskirts of Baton Rouge slip by.

She hadn't been there long when Julia stopped, saying, "Good morning, Selena. Are you going to take your 'eleven at eleven'?"

"I beg your pardon?" Selena blinked.

Julia laughed softly, "Eleven laps around the sundeck—which is a mile—at eleven o'clock, with the calliope providing the marching music."

"I don't think so," she said, smiling wryly at her own lassitude. "I feel too lazy." Overhearing their conversation, Chance caught her eye, a mocking reminder in his that an Iowa girl should be more industrious. Selena ignored the look with an effort.

"Are you going, Julia?"

"Oh, yes. I have so much energy I must channel it somewhere," she declared, and moved toward the stairs. "See you at lunch."

Watching her leave, Selena knew that the bright sparkle in Julia's eyes came from more than just energy. She was sure it was born of excitement because the next day they would be arriving in Natchez, where Leslie was waiting for her.

Selena felt a pang of envy, hoping that some day she might have that special glow the older woman possessed. Almost of its own volition, her gaze swung to Chance, leaning backward against the railing, his arms crossed in front of him.

Something jolted through her as she found him watching her, but the emotion was fleeting and indefinable, and Chance's attention was soon claimed by the man standing beside him.

The sensation didn't return. In the afternoon Selena attended a lecture on the *Delta Queen*'s history. Julia didn't go because she had heard it all before. Neither did Chance, and Selena guessed that he was equally well informed on the subject.

His sketchy outline had whetted her appetite to hear more and she was not disappointed by the lecture. Mike, the cruise director, spoke of her construction and the almost one million dollars that had been spent to build the *Delta Queen*, a phenomenal sum to pay for a riverboat in the 1920s. He told of her life on the Sacramento River in California and the years that she had been laid up when the Depression hit.

During World War II the U.S. Navy took over the *Delta Queen,* using her as a troop carrier in San Francisco Bay, ferrying soldiers to and from ocean vessels. With the navy's predilection for battleship gray, every inch of her was painted—including the stained glass panels set with copper, which were set in the top of the windows in the lounges on both the cabin deck and the texas deck.

After the war the *Delta Queen* was auctioned off, sold to the Green Line that was already operating overnight passenger trips on the Mississippi River. It was then that she was shored and crated like a huge piano in a box, and towed down the Pacific Coastline, through the Panama Canal into the Gulf of Mexico to the Mississippi River. This riverboat was not designed for the ocean or its fury, yet the *Delta Queen* had made it intact, to the stunned amazement of many an ocean man who had predicted her doom on the high seas.

The story of the Congressional battle to keep her from being banned forever from traveling the western rivers was recounted, along with the tale of the ultimate, though possibly temporary success. Finally, the cruise director told of the recent construction of her sister ship, the *Mississippi Queen,* a sleek modern paddle-wheel steamboat with a personality all her own.

Selena came away from the lecture with a new appreciation for the riverboat and the feeling that she had only heard the highlights, that there was much of the *Delta Queen*'s rich history she didn't know.

At dinner that evening it was their scheduled arrival at Natchez the following day that indirectly dominated the conversation—at least between Julia and Selena. The older woman talked about her anticipation of being with Leslie and reminisced about their previous times together.

Chance was almost grimly silent. As far as Selena was concerned, his dislike of Leslie and his disapproval of the coming marriage was practically a tangible thing. She considered his attitude autocratic and insensitive.

"I've decided to buy a new dress in Natchez for my wedding," Julia announced. "But I can't make up my mind what color. I think it would be in bad taste for a woman my age to wear white, even though I've never been married before. I was considering something in cream or beige or perhaps yellow. Leslie always said yellow was my color."

Selena was about to comment when Chance broke in curtly, "Julia, you're boring Selena with all this nonsense about your wedding."

"That's absurb!" Selena flared, her spoon poised above the peach melba. "What woman would find wedding plans boring? And personally I find it reassuring that a woman of Julia's age can love as deeply and as romantically as a younger person."

She observed the hardening of his features at her quick and vigorous defense of Julia and turned away, fixing a determinedly interested look on her face as she glanced at the older woman.

"With your hair, I think something in silver gray might be very complimentary," she suggested, noting the silver wings at the temples of Julia's otherwise dark hair.

Julia hesitated for a second, glancing apprehensively at her nephew before picking up the conversation where Selena had left off, and Chance's disapproving silence was ignored. But a strained atmosphere remained.

It wasn't relieved until the three returned to the New Orleans Room after dinner for the banjo concert. The room had been tránsformed into a nightclub with tables—minus their linen and silverware—chairs, the lights dimmed, and drinks being served from the Mark Twain Saloon.

The banjo player sat on a stool in front of the band. Mustached, with brown, waving hair, he wore black pants, a white shirt and red vest with garters around his sleeves.

He introduced himself in a drawling voice and said, "You all have come here tonight to hear a banjo concert. That's good, 'cause that's what we got planned." He plunked a few strings and looked out at the audience. "Banjos and riverboats almost seem synonymous. You think of one, then the other." A shyly mischievous smile curved his mouth. "Course, you all know that the banjo is the only musical instrument invented in America and you are about to find out why we're the only country that had the nerve." With that, he immediately broke into a rousing version of "Waiting for the Robert E. Lee."

Before the song was over, everyone in the room was clapping along, and Selena felt the tension leave her, extinguished by the gay, infectious spirit of the music.

After the concert Julia left, insisting it was time for her to retire with all the things happening the next day. Selena lingered to sample the late-night snacks, as did Chance. Somewhere along the way, they were separated as Selena paused to chat with some of her fellow passengers.

When the band began playing some dance music, she saw Chance at the crew's table in the far corner of the room, talking to the chief purser. He seemed to have forgotten about her, and Selena was positive she was glad about it.

Sipping at her hot chocolate, she watched the older couples on the dance floor, marveling at their grace and ability. When the chocolate was gone, and with it her reason for staying, Selena walked to the stairs.

Before she reached the first step, Chance was at her side.

"I'll walk you to your cabin," he stated.

"There's no need," she balked.

With typical arrogance, he ignored her protest and pressed a hand against the small of her back to guide her up the stairs. She submitted to his lead, however ungraciously, and they walked in silence up the stairs through the forward cabin lounge to the outer deck.

Ripples of moonlight danced over the river and the cobweb silhouettes of trees along the banks. A corner of the full moon was lopped off, making it look like a chipped silver dollar in a velvet sky. The stars were big and bright, so close Selena felt she could reach out and touch them. It was a warm and languid southern night with a moist breeze stirring the air.

"Don't you think this charade has gone far

enough?" Chance issued the demanding question in a cold, hard voice that shattered the evening's mood.

Selena's eyes widened, partly in anger and partly in fear that they were back to the question of her profession. "What are you talking about?"

"I'm referring to the way you keep humoring Julia, of course," he snapped, impatient with her obtuseness.

"Humoring her?" she repeated, her resentment at his attitude at dinner returning to fuel her anger. "I am not humoring her! I'm glad she's found someone to love. And you should be, too, instead of trying to spoil her happiness. She's a warm, wonderful person. She doesn't deserve to have a family like yours!"

She didn't flinch under his piercing regard, his eyes narrowing to black slits as he searched deep into her soul as if testing the sincerity of her words. Turning, he said nothing in defense but merely escorted her up the stairs to the texas deck and her cabin.

He left her at the door with a brusque goodnight, which, still simmering from their exchange, Selena didn't bother to return. As she closed her door she saw he had moved to the railing.

A lighter flamed in his hand. He cupped it to the slender cigar in his mouth, the lighter briefly illuminating his features and revealing an expression of grim thoughtfulness.

As Selena got ready for bed, the humid breeze carried the aromatic smoke from his cigar through her open cabin window. The scent lingered long after she had fallen asleep.

CHAPTER SIX

SELENA AWAKENED FAIRLY EARLY the next morning. The river was shrouded in fog when she stepped from her cabin. It seemed a white world with the sky paled to a pearl gray. Even the sun was a white glare in the east. The damp coolness seeped through her sweater to chill her skin, making her hurry down the stairs to the forward cabin lounge.

The first person she saw as she entered the lounge was Chance. He was standing at one of the windows and staring out, and as if sensing her presence, he shot her a glance. An impassive mask had been drawn over his compelling features, making his thoughts unreadable.

Then Selena noticed Julia, looking dejected sitting in one of the chairs. Selena's mouth tightened; she was certain that in some way Chance was to blame for his aunt's expression. She walked directly to the older woman to offer moral support and perhaps undo whatever damage Chance had done.

"Good morning, Julia," she greeted the woman quietly.

Looking up in surprise, Julia recovered to

respond, "Oh, good morning Selena." But it was an absent greeting, her thoughts were obviously far away.

"Is something wrong, Julia?" Selena probed gently.

"The chief purser just brought me this message," was the sigh.

Selena noticed the crumpled slip of paper between Julia's twisting fingers. "From Leslie?" she guessed.

"Yes, he won't be able to meet me in Natchez." Disappointment, intense and painful, clouded her expression.

"Oh, no!" Selena breathed out, an instant frown of compassion drawing her eyebrows together.

"He said he'd meet me in Vicksburg instead." Julia attempted to fix a reassuring smile on her face, but she couldn't conceal her regret for the postponement.

"What happened?"

"His car broke down," Julia explained. "Something major, I guess, since he says it's going to take a couple of days to fix."

"I'm so sorry," Selena offered, knowing it was poor comfort.

"It's all right. We'll be in Vicksburg tomorrow, and the day after that Leslie will be there, so I don't have long to wait. It's you I feel badly about," she murmured apologetically.

"Me? Whatever for?" Selena exclaimed.

"My dear, I know you didn't book for the

tour of Natchez because you expected to meet Leslie in the afternoon. Now it's too late and you're going to miss seeing it altogether," Julia sighed.

"I don't mind, really," she insisted.

"Of course you do," Julia dismissed Selena's protest. "You're on vacation. You should be going places and doing things instead of letting me interfere in your life, boring you with my troubles."

"You're not boring me and you aren't interfering," Selena stated flatly. "You've been listening to Chance too much." She flashed an angry glance in his direction, throwing invisible, flaming daggers at a point between his broad shoulders. "I enjoy your company and I'm excited about your wedding. Don't pay any attention to what he says."

"You're such a good girl." Julia patted her hand, adding, "And you're so good for my ego."

"I'm glad," Selena smiled, her affection for the older woman steadily growing.

"Before you came in the lounge, I was feeling so low. Now—" the other woman shrugged and smiled "—I even think I could eat some breakfast. Will you join me?"

Selena hesitated. "Not right away," There was something else she wanted to do first. "But I'll be down before you're through."

"Very well," Julia agreed, rising from her chair.

Selena waited until Julia had started down the steps to the Orleans Room before she walked to where Chance stood.

His glance and his voice were indifferent. "Good morning."

There were other passengers around the lounge helping themselves to coffee. Selena's mouth tightened into a hard line. She wasn't in the mood to exchange pleasantries.

"Would you come outside with me?" she requested stiffly. "I want to talk to you."

A brow lifted briefly at her request, his flat black gaze making an assessing sweep of her, noting the light of battle in her eyes, before he complied with her request.

The instant they were outside and out of earshot of their fellow passengers, Selena turned on him, her eyes flashing green sparks.

"Was this your doing?" she demanded.

Chance tipped his head slightly to the side. "I'm afraid I don't follow you."

One of the deckhands was polishing the brass kickboards of the stairs leading to the texas deck. Selena lowered her voice so she couldn't be overheard, but that didn't lessen the heat in her tone.

"You follow my meaning all right," she retorted. "I'm talking about the message Julia supposedly received from Leslie, the one saying he wouldn't be able to meet her in Natchez."

"That message," he nodded in understanding, his bland expression not changing.

"Yes, I know about it. What has it to do with me?"

"That's what I want to know," Selena challenged. "What was your part in it?"

"As I recall the message, Leslie had car trouble," Chance remarked with infuriating calm. "I've been on the boat with you ever since we left New Orleans, so I don't see how you could accuse me of possibly tampering with his car. That is what you're suggesting, isn't it?"

"That's presupposing, of course, that Leslie sent the message."

"Meaning, you think I did and signed his name to it?" His gaze sharpened.

"It's possible," she said grimly. "I saw you talking to the chief purser last night. You could have paid him to deliver the message to Julia this morning. I wouldn't put it past you—you're so determined not to let them get married."

"It could happen that way," he admitted. "But your theory has a flaw."

"What's that?" Selena didn't hide her skepticism.

"If I sent the message and not Leslie, then he'll be waiting at the landing when the boat docks in Natchez, won't he?" Chance reasoned smoothly, causing Selena's doubt in her suspicions to flicker across her face. "Unless you're going to accuse me next of sending a message to Leslie from Julia calling off the wedding?"

She hadn't thought of that. "You could have."

"Perhaps. But I didn't. The message Julia received this morning was not sent by me," he said firmly. "Nor did I arrange to have it sent. I guess you'll have to assume it came from Leslie."

He sounded as if he was telling the truth, but Selena wasn't sure if she could believe him. "Maybe," she submitted grudgingly. "But if I ever have proof that you're lying, I'll—" She compressed her lips tightly, unable to think of the words to complete the threat.

"Yes?" Chance drawled the word, his eyes taunting her.

Her anger was now an impotent thing. Pivoting, she stalked to the lounge door and jerked it open. She had her temper under control by the time she joined Julia for breakfast. Chance had already eaten, she learned, so she wasn't forced to endure his company for the morning meal.

Three whistle blasts signaled their arrival in Natchez shortly before noon. Along with many of the other passengers, Selena moved to the starboard railing to watch the tying-up process. There was no indication of a city, just a few scattered, old buildings, mostly wood and a few brick, with a sheer bluff rising behind them. A treed, parklike veldt stretched several hundred yards downstream.

The boom swung the landing platform to the ramp running down into the river. Deckhands jumped off to drag the heavy ropes to the tie pins. Selena glimpsed the historical plaque identifying the location as Natchez-under-the-Hill, once the most wicked hellhole on the river, peopled with thieves, murderers, gamblers, prostitutes and cutthroats. The river had carried away most of the old town, leaving a row of ramshackle buildings as a representative of the town's sordid past.

On top of the bluff was the city of Natchez where the respectable citizens had lived. Selena knew the glory of its history was duly represented by the more than one hundred antebellum houses that had been restored to their previous grandeur. The Natchez Pilgrimage tours were some of the most famous in the country, and she regretted that she wasn't going.

A few curious townspeople had driven to the waterfront to watch the *Delta Queen*'s arrival. Some sat in their cars, while others, especially those with children, stood on the banks. The arrival of a steamboat was still an event in this river town.

But there was no middle-aged man alone on the landing, searching the faces of the passengers along the railing for a familiar one. Leslie was not there. Even though Selena didn't know what he looked like, she was certain he wasn't there. She sighed with relief, then wondered why. Because Chance hadn't lied to her? Selena shook her head. It couldn't be that.

When the boat was secured, she went ashore, strolling along the worn path in the parklike area. As the trail curved over a knoll, she stopped at the top to lean a shoulder against a tree and stare at the red paddle wheel of the *Delta Queen*, framed by two trees.

The flags circling the top deck ruffled in the breeze against an intense blue sky and a warm, golden sun. Two deckhands were in a rowboat at the bow, applying a fresh coat of paint to the hull.

The leaf of a twig tickled her cheek. Unconsciously she pulled it off and fingered the green leaf. She was in an oddly silent and thoughtful mood, and her mind seemed to be blank. Then she saw Chance coming toward her with slow, purposeful strides. She hesitated and finally stayed where she was.

"They're serving lunch. Aren't you coming?" he asked, stopping beside her.

"I'm not hungry." Her voice was low and flat.

"Watching your diet?" he returned with a teasing inflection.

"I'm just not hungry," Selena said, shrugging and looking away. She became aware of the leaf in her hand and released it, watching it spiral to the ground.

"What's bothering you, Red?" His voice changed to a serious tone.

"Nothing." She slipped the tips of her fingers into her pants pocket, indifferent to his searching gaze.

"Something is," Chance insisted.

Irritation flashed at his persistence. "If there was something, would you really care?" she challenged.

He continued his quiet study of her without offering a reply. Finally her gaze fell from his, her annoyance burning itself out.

When Chance did speak, he asked, "Were you considering going into town?"

"I thought I would," admitted Selena.

"It's a long walk up that hill." She shrugged her indifference to his comment. "I've hired a cab. You could come along with me, if you'd like, and we'll have lunch and drive around to some of the plantations," he invited in a calm, unemotional tone.

She was surprised and wary of his offer, certain he had some reason for asking her that he wasn't saying. A thought occurred to her.

"Is this your idea or Julia's?" she wanted to know.

"Do you really care?" Chance countered with mocking coolness.

With a painful jolt, Selena realized that she did. She didn't want Chance to be making this invitation out of a sense of duty prompted by his aunt.

"You haven't said whether you'd like to go," he reminded her.

Selena hesitated, then decided it didn't make any difference why he had asked her. This was her chance to see Natchez and she would be a fool to turn it down.

"I have to get my handbag," she said in the way of an answer.

"The cab is at the landing. I'll wait for you there."

"I won't be long," Selena promised, and started back to the boat.

After lunching at Stanton Hall, Chance arranged with the cab driver to take them by many of the antebellum homes. They stopped at three that were open to the general public and not restricted to private tours, giving Selena an opportunity to see the interior of these gracious homes.

They returned to the boat half an hour before it was scheduled to leave. As they walked onto the gangplank, Chance asked, "How did you like Natchez?"

"I enjoyed it," Selena answered with genuine enthusiasm. "Thank you for taking me."

"Are you going to your cabin now?"

She nodded. "I thought I'd freshen up and change for dinner."

"It isn't required, you know," he commented.

"Yes, I know, but I feel like it," she shrugged as they climbed the stairs to the cabin deck.

As they reached the top of the stairs, Selena turned toward the double doors leading to the outer deck, but Chance stopped. "Meet me in the texas lounge in a half hour for a drink," he suggested.

"All right." Selena was surprised at how quickly she agreed.

When she left her cabin to meet Chance, the boat was just getting under way. As its stern swung away from the river bank so the boat could back away from the landing, the calliope played a farewell concert on the sundeck.

Its music was interrupted by an announcement over the public address system requesting the passengers to move to the stern of the steamboat. The *Delta Queen*'s bow was temporarily stuck in the Mississippi mud, and the captain wanted as much weight as possible to the rear of the steamboat.

Obligingly, Selena waited by her cabin, smiling to herself at the simple remedy. Soon the bow was free and the steamboat was reversing into the channel, once again heading upstream.

Chance was waiting for her at a table in the lounge when she walked in, a drink already in front of him. Greg, the bartender she had met the first day aboard, was at the table almost before she sat down.

"What will you have, Selena?" he asked with familiar ease.

Selena felt the speculative look Chance gave her. "I'll have a margarita," she decided.

"Good choice," Greg winked. "I make the best margarita aboard this boat." And he moved away.

"Do you know him?" questioned Chance, in a bland and impersonal tone that was at odds with the look in his eyes.

"I met him the first day," Selena explained

somewhat defensively. "It's a very friendly crew."

"Especially around passengers like you," he added dryly.

Her chin lifted as she had the impression of something derogatory in his remark. "What is that supposed to mean?"

"That you're an attractive young woman, as if you didn't already know," he answered.

As much as she tried, Selena couldn't interpret that as a compliment. Chance had been stating what he saw as a fact, not making a personal comment.

Greg returned with her drink. "The word is out that we'll be meeting the *Mississippi Queen* on her way downstream," he said, referring to the *Delta Queen*'s new, modern sister ship.

"When?" Selena's interest was immediate.

"Sometime tonight. It will depend how fast we go upstream and how fast she comes downstream," he smiled. "The captain will be in contact with her by radio before we ever see her. He'll make an announcement ahead of time, letting you know when she'll pass. It'll be a sight to see," Greg declared.

"Where is she coming from?" Selena asked.

"Vicksburg, I think."

"That reminds me. What time will we get into Vicksburg tomorrow?"

"Haven't you heard?" Greg looked at her curiously. "We aren't going to stop at Vicksburg this trip."

"What?" She frowned and glanced at Chance who was studying his drink. But Julia was to meet Leslie in Vicksburg, she thought. "Why not?" she demanded of Greg.

"The river is high from all the spring rains and runoffs, which means the current is swifter, and it's going to take us longer to go up," he explained. "And no one wants to risk getting into Louisville late and missing the steamboat race."

"The steamboat race?" Selena repeated, thinking to herself, *but what about Julia and Leslie*?

"Yeah," he nodded, finding her blankness curious. "The one between us and the *Belle of Louisville*. We won it last year, and nobody wants to give up the golden antlers, especially by default." A passenger at another table called to him for a round of drinks. Greg excused himself and returned to the bar.

Selena darted an accusing look at Chance. "Did you know we weren't stopping at Vicksburg?"

Impassively he met her gaze. "I heard about it the other day."

"And you didn't say anything to Julia? You know as well as I do that she's planning to meet Leslie in Vicksburg!" She was angered by his indifference.

"She'll find out about it soon enough, if she hasn't already."

"And you didn't see fit to warn her this

morning when she was suppressing her disappointment with the knowledge she'd be meeting him in Vicksburg?''

"No, I didn't,'' Chance admitted without a flicker of remorse.

"I don't know whether you don't have a heart or if you're just naturally cruel,'' Selena declared, almost choking with the effort to keep her temper in check.

He seemed unmoved by her caustic description of him. Lifting his glass to his mouth, he said, "Memphis is our next scheduled stop. I imagine Julia will plan to meet him there.''

"Unless you can find a way to prevent it,'' she added bitterly, and rose from her chair. "You can keep your drink. I'm not interested.''

Chance made no attempt to stop her as she walked swiftly from the room. As she neared the grand staircase, she overheard a low comment from one of the passengers, "A lovers' quarrel.'' It only made her more anxious to leave the room.

At dinner that evening Selena pointedly ignored Chance, her dislike of his heartless ways feeding on itself. It made the meal miserable, turning delicious food into tasteless mush. Julia gave no indication that she was aware they wouldn't be stopping at Vicksburg. She didn't mention either Vicksburg or Leslie at the table. Her conversation was centered on Natchez and the sights that Selena had seen.

The gift shop in the forward cabin lounge was

open when Selena left the dining room. She spent some time looking over its items, then wandered up the grand staircase and out through the double doors of the texas Lounge to the outer deck.

It was a warm, languid night with a three-quarter moon slipping out from behind a cloud. Selena leaned against the railing and gazed out at the shapeless black shadows darkening the banks, trying to convince herself that she was content with her own company.

At eight-thirty the announcement came that the *Mississippi Queen* would be passing them in fifteen minutes on the port side. Selena walked to the left side of the boat to sit in one of the wrought-iron chairs near the fan-shaped air duct. She was soon joined on deck by other passengers, invisible excitement building as the time approached.

Someone said, "There she is, dead ahead."

And a crew member groaned, "Don't put it that way!"

Selena leaned forward to look over the railing and saw the big steamboat coming around the river's bend. She caught her breath at the sight of it. All the decks were ablaze with light, like a tiered birthday cake with all the candles lit in a darkened room.

In the clear night air came the vociferous music from the *Mississippi Queen*'s calliope. A murmur ran through the passengers as they recognize the tune, "Cruising down the River."

A spotlight was shining—from the *Delta Queen*, playing over the water ahead of her. The rasping whistle was blown once to officially signal to the *Mississippi Queen* that they would pass on the port side and her whistle blasted once in agreement.

As the large paddle wheel steamboat drew steadily closer, one of the bartenders crowded into the railing beside Selena, a flashlight in his hand. He smiled a quick apology, then began flashing the light at the approaching vessel. She caught the answering flash from the forward deck of the *Mississippi Queen*.

The bartender let out a short whoop of delight and began flashing in earnest. "That's my brother," he said, offering Selena a quick explanation. "He works on the *Mississippi Queen*. This is about the only time we see each other."

The bows of the two boats were nearly even now, spotlights roaming over each other's decks. The passengers of the *Mississippi Queen* were all gathered on the outer decks, too, and they shouted in unison, "Hello!" Automatically, Selena heard herself and the others respond with the same greeting. Everyone was waving. It seemed the thing to do.

Slowly the two sister ships glided by each other, the *Mississippi Queen* floating along in the current, her red paddle wheel motionless to prolong the moment of meeting. Then she was past, and her paddle wheel reluctantly began churning the river water again.

Selena leaned back in her chair as the other passengers began leaving the railing. The night was once again ink black, the moon and stars unable to match the brilliant lights of the *Mississippi Queen*.

"Here." A white cloth was offered to her.

Selena glanced up at the donor in surprise. It was Chance, smiling gently as he looked down at her. She was about to protest that she had no need for a handkerchief when she realized that her throat was tight, gripped by the craziest mixture of nostalgia and happiness and the magical beauty of the event. What was more surprising were the welling tears in her eyes.

"Thank you," she muttered, and took the handkerchief to dab her eyes. Laughing, with an emotional catch in the sound, she declared, "I don't know what's the matter with me!"

"I'd say you're turning into a steamboater."

"What's that?" Selena asked, too unnerved by her reaction to remember that she was supposed to dislike Chance actively.

"That's a person who loves steamboats," he answered, taking the handkerchief she returned to him and stuffing it back in his jacket pocket. "Do you feel like a stroll around deck?"

"Yes, I think so." The lump in her throat was beginning to ease as she rose to walk with Chance.

A companionable silence lay between them, his arm curved lightly and impersonally along the back of her waist. Their circuitous route eventually brought them to the stern of the boat near Selena's cabin. In silent unison, they paused at the rear railing to gaze at the waterfall created by the spotlighted paddle wheel.

Other passengers, too, were strolling the decks, exchanging quiet greetings as they passed Selena and Chance. However, one man stopped when he saw them, smiling broadly.

"I see the two of you finally made up after your little tiff this afternoon," he commented, and walked on just as Selena recognized him as being the man she had overheard remarking about their "lovers' quarrel."

Stiffening under the light pressure of Chance's hand, she gave him an odd look. "Why didn't you correct him?"

"What was the point?" he shrugged.

"He thinks we're...."

"Lovers?" supplied Chance, his mouth quirking in mockery at her hesitation over the word.

"Yes," Selena clipped out the answer.

"It's only natural. What do you expect the other passengers to think when they see us together almost constantly?"

"Maybe if you quit following me around all the time, they wouldn't get the wrong impression," she retorted. "And stop hanging around outside my cabin at night!"

"Outside your cabin?" he repeated, a dark brow arching.

"Yes, my cabin," she repeated.

"It just so happens, Red, that I'm hanging around outside my own cabin."

"Your cabin? Where's your cabin?" she demanded in disbelief.

"Number 239, the one right beside yours," he said with a complacent light in his eyes.

"You're lying," Selena accused.

Chance reached into his pocket. "Would you like to see my key?"

She believed him. "No, I wouldn't."

"Which bed do you sleep in?" he asked. "The one on the right as you walk into your cabin?"

"I don't see that it's any of your business, but yes, that's the one," she retorted, still trying to recover from the shock that he had the cabin next to hers.

"We're sleeping side by side with only a wall between us. It's a pity the wall isn't removable," Chance commented in a low voice. "Then I could start collecting on that promise you made in my hotel room."

"I didn't make any promise." She twisted away from the hand on her back. "I keep telling you that, but you refuse to listen. So, from now on, you can just stay away from me."

As she turned away, he caught at her hand. "Where are you going?"

"To my cabin." She slipped out of his grasp. "Good night."

"Selena, one word of caution," he followed her to the door. "Don't start sleeping in the other bed or the maid will get suspicious and think someone else is sleeping in your room. And you know how fast rumors spread on this boat!"

Inserting the key in the lock, she jerked her cabin door open and slammed it in his face. But it didn't shut out his remark. When she crawled into bed that night, it was the one she had always slept in.

CHAPTER SEVEN

SHORTLY AFTER SUNRISE Selena stepped out of her cabin, unable to sleep, and tiptoed by Chance's. The chill of the night was still in the strong breeze whipping around the stern. She buttoned the last two buttons of her jacket and tucked her hands in its pockets.

Streamers of scarlet pink trailed across the eastern horizon and the sun was a heavy orange ball. Bluffs rose high along the river banks, the water's course a twisting nest of oxbows.

She wandered around the empty deck and descended the stairs near the bow to the cabin deck. A coffee urn was in the forward cabin lounge for early risers, and Selena helped herself, warming her hands around the steaming cup.

A figure was standing on the outer deck at the bow, wearing a suede jacket and a scarf tied around her head. It took Selena a few minutes to recognize it was Julia. With her cup in her hand, she walked back on deck to join the woman.

"Good morning, Julia."

The woman turned, smiling automatically yet

with a touch of absentness. "Good morning, Selena. You're up early."

"I couldn't sleep."

There was silence as Julia gazed intently ahead. The *Delta Queen* glided under a railroad bridge. Around the bend, a highway bridge stretched high across the river. There was a suggestion of activity concentrated behind the river's treed banks. It was this that held Julia's attention.

As if sensing Selena's curious eyes on her, Julia explained, "That's Vicksburg ahead."

Selena hesitated an instant before saying, "You do know we aren't stopping, don't you?"

"Yes." It was a quiet word, but it spoke volumes about Julia's disappointment.

Again there was silence as the boat moved steadily nearer. The wind gusted, tearing through Selena's uncovered hair. The sun was yellow, the streaks of dawn gone from the sky.

"I sent Leslie a wire telling him we wouldn't be stopping here," Julia said softly, "I hope he received it."

"I'm sure he did," Selena consoled.

Selena waited with Julia while she maintained her silent vigil on the bow until the *Delta Queen* followed the channel markers past the mouth of the Yazoo River. Only then did the older woman suggest that they go inside. Vicksburg was behind them and Memphis was ahead.

Later that afternoon, Selena came up from the Orleans Room after watching a navigation film. Afternoon tea was being served in the aft cabin lounge. Wanting some fresh air, she decided to walk along the outer cabin deck to get to the aft section instead of using the wide passageway through the center of the deck.

At a leisurely pace, she began walking beside the railing to the stern. A cabin window was open, releasing familiar voices from within. Selena realized she was approaching Julia's stateroom. When she heard her name on Chance's lips, she stopped.

She didn't hear what Chance had said about her, but she heard Julia reply. "How can you say that? Selena is such a wonderful girl. You should know that by now from spending time with her on this cruise."

Since her insistence last night that Chance leave her alone, he had been remarkably absent all day. Selena didn't know how long it would last, but she realized that even Julia had noticed how much time he had been spending in her company.

There was a moment of pregnant silence from the cabin. Selena was afraid that Chance was going to tell Julia the sordid circumstances of their first meeting.

Instead he offered an impatient, "You're entirely too trusting, Julia. Sooner of later—"

"You think she's going to hurt me, don't you?" came Julia's gentle response.

"In one way or another, I can practically guarantee it," he retorted.

A fellow passenger was walking toward Selena and she realized she didn't dare tarry any longer outside Julia's window or she would risk being discovered eavesdropping. She moved on, knowing Chance was still wrong about her. And she certainly would never do anything that would hurt Julia.

Two mornings later the *Delta Queen* steamed into Memphis. The sky was slate gray with a steady drizzle of rain coming from its clouds.

Selena stood beside Julia on the outer cabin deck beneath the overhang of the deck above them as the boat maneuvered to tie up. Despite the miserable weather, spectators were on the river front to watch the boat's arrival.

It was these faces that Julia searched so anxiously. When the lines were tied and the gangplank secure on the cobblestoned ramp, she turned to Selena.

"Leslie isn't there," she announced, pain obvious in her expression.

"It's a little before nine and we weren't scheduled to arrive until nine, so maybe he doesn't know the boat is in yet," Selena suggested. "He still might come."

"I'll bet he didn't get the message to come to Memphis," Julia sighed.

As the minutes stretched into half an hour, Selena had to admit it was possible that Leslie had not received Julia's message. Silently she berated Chance for not being here to comfort his aunt.

"Listen," Selena said, refusing to give up, "why don't I go ashore and telephone the different hotels to see if I can find out where he's staying? Maybe he overslept."

"Oh, thank you, but I can't ask you to do that."

"You aren't asking me. I'm volunteering." She opened her purse and took out a piece of paper and pencil. "What's Leslie's full name?"

"Leslie Reid." Julia spelled it for her.

Selena slid the paper into her purse. "Is there any chance he might be staying with family or friends here in Memphis?"

"I don't think so," Julia replied, shaking her head uncertainly. "When Leslie and I were on the autumn cruise, we stopped in Memphis. He didn't mention knowing anyone here and I'm sure he would have."

"That just leaves the hotels and motels," Selena smiled, trying not to think about what a daunting list that would prove to be in a city the size of Memphis. "I'll be back as soon as I can. Wish me luck."

She was off, entering the forward cabin lounge and descending the stairs to the main deck and the gangplank. The light rain made the cobblestones slippery. It was tricky going until Selena reached the sidewalk.

The downtown shopping mall was only a few blocks from the dock. Every other building along the waterfront seemed to be occupied by cotton brokers or cotton warehouses. As she crossed the street, the clouds opened up, nearly drowning Selena in a downpour. No umbrella, bareheaded, wearing a cotton jacket that wasn't waterproofed, she was soon soaked to the skin before she could reach any kind of shelter.

Two hours later, with a pocketful of change consumed by the telephone booth in her fruitless search for Leslie's hotel, she made her way back through the driving rain, now being whipped by a cold north wind. Her feet slithered and slipped down the slanting cobblestones to the boat.

She was drenched by the rain, nearly frozen into an ice cube by the cold wind and disheartened by the long list of calls she had made in vain. At the back of her mind, she kept hoping that Leslie would be aboard the boat when she got there.

Someone was walking up the cobblestones directly toward her. At the moment her footing was fairly solid. She didn't care who it was, she wasn't going to give ground. He could just go around her.

The person kept coming directly toward her, not altering his path an inch. She didn't dare take her eyes off the uneven ground for fear of slipping and landing ignominiously on her backside.

"I thought country girls like you were supposed to have enough sense to come in out of the rain," Chance declared in an exasperated and mocking tone.

Selena stopped at the sound of his voice, glaring at him through the strands of the hair plastered across her eyes. "That's what I'm trying to do, if you'd get out of my way." Her teeth chattered uncontrollably when she spoke.

His arm circled her waist, providing solid support as he half lifted and half carried her to the more secure footing of the gangplank. He didn't slow the pace until they were under the shelter of the main deck.

"Where were you during the first half of that descent?" Selena muttered between shivers.

"You look like a drowned rat," Chance observed.

"Thanks a lot!" She was shaking all over, frozen to the bone.

The arm around her waist pushed her to the staircase. "What was so urgent that you had to go out in the middle of a downpour?" he demanded.

"I had to make some telephone calls," she answered, gritting her teeth to keep them from clattering together. "To see if I could find where Leslie was staying. Did he show up here at the boat?"

"Of all the harebrained, wild-goose chases—" Abruptly he cut off his exclamation and snapped, "No, he didn't."

"Poor Julia," Selena sighed. "She'll be heartbroken. You should be with her."

"I'm going to talk to her, all right." There was an ominous note in his voice. "But first you're going up to your cabin and get out of these wet clothes."

"That is where I was going," she retorted

with as much strength as her shivering voice could muster. "Or did you think I was going to wear them until they dried?"

"I wouldn't put it past you," Chance muttered, forcibly ushering her through the forward cabin lounge, unmindful of the gawking passengers. "Any fool that would go out in a downpour without a raincoat or an umbrella—" he pushed open the door to the outer deck and shoved Selena through "—might not have enough brains to change into dry clothes."

"It was only drizzling when I left," she defended. "And I'm not made of sugar. I don't melt."

He gave her a cutting look and demanded, "Where's your room key?"

"In my bag."

Before Selena could open it, he was taking the bag from her shaking hands and pushing her up the stairs to the texas deck. Her reactions weren't as quick as they normally were.

Before she could stop her impetus forward and protest at his taking of her purse, Chance had found the key and was handing back her purse. He hustled her the rest of the way up the stairs to her cabin door, opening it and pushing her inside.

Now that she was out of the wind and the rain, she was shivering even worse. She stopped short when she realized that Chance had followed her into the cabin.

"Get out of here," she shuddered impatiently. "I want to change my clothes."

He gave her a raking glance that told her what a sorry sight she was. It didn't do much for her self-confidence. "I brought you here to change your clothes, so get undressed."

Her mouth opened to order him out, but he was already brushing past her into the bathroom. He emerged a second later with a bath towel in his hand.

"Are you going to undress yourself or am I going to do it for you?" he challenged.

The hard set of his jaw warned her that there was no use arguing. She would simply be wasting her time and expending energy in a useless effort. Shuddering from the bone-chilling wetness of her clothes, she gritted her teeth and lifted her numbed fingers to her blouse buttons. If they had been all thumbs, they couldn't have been more awkward.

"You could at least turn around," she snapped, blaming his intent gaze for her fumbling efforts.

Chance ignored her request. "The clothes will be dry before you ever get them off." He pushed her hands away and began unbuttoning the blouse.

"I can do it myself," Selena protested almost tearfully, angered and miserable to the point where she wanted to cry.

"There is a time for modesty, Red—" he stripped the blouse from her shoulders and gave it a toss into the bathroom "—and this isn't it."

He shoved her down to sit on the bed while he knelt to remove the saturated leather shoes from her feet. They followed her blouse into the bathroom, along with her socks. Impersonally, Chance reached up and unsnapped her pants. Grabbing the sodden material of the pants legs, he pulled those off, too. Then he rose and pivoted to pull down the covers of the other single bed.

"Wrap the towel around your head and get into bed, little miss prim and proper," he ordered. "While you're hiding under the covers, you can take your underclothes off."

He waited until Selena had done as she was told. When the underclothes were lying in a wet heap beside the floor, he turned and left the cabin. Continuing to shiver, Selena closed her eyes and snuggled deeper under the covers, certain she would never be warm again. But at least Chance was gone.

After fifteen minutes, she began to warm through and feel like a human being again. There was a warning rattle of metal, then the door opened and Chance walked through, carrying a tray.

"The door was locked!" she protested angrily.

"I took the key with me," he explained offhandedly, and slipped it into his pocket.

"Why don't you go away and leave me alone? You've had your laugh at my expense. Now go away!'' Selena cried in frustration, in no position to enforce her demand. "I—"

"I've brought you some soup from the kitchen," Chance interrupted as if he hadn't heard a word she'd said.

"Leave it on the chest of drawers."

He sat down on the edge of the bed beside her, balancing the tray on his knees. As he removed the cover from the bowl, the mouth-watering smell of chicken soup filled the room. Picking up the soup spoon, he dipped out some broth and carried the spoon to her lips. Selena couldn't believe it. He was actually going to feed her.

"Come on, eat up," Chance ordered calmly, forcing the metal spoon between her lips.

She swallowed it, the liquid warming her throat as it went down. When he put the spoon in the bowl again, Selena couldn't help smiling.

"You look ridiculous," she said. He flicked an impassive glance in her direction and started to bring the spoon to her mouth. "Any minute I expect to hear you say, open the hangar, here comes the airplane, just as if you were feeding a child."

"Are you going to eat or talk?" he questioned.

"I'm going to eat." Selena pushed herself into more of a sitting position, taking her arms from beneath the covers while keeping the blankets tucked securely across her front. "But I'm going to feed myself."

With a shrug of acceptance, Chance shifted the tray so that it was on her lap and slid another pillow behind her head to prop her up.

"Have you seen Julia to tell her I couldn't find Leslie registered at any of the hotels?" Selena asked between spoonfuls.

"Not yet," he answered with a grim look.

"I feel so sorry for her," she sighed.

"My aunt doesn't need your pity."

"Well, she certainly doesn't get any from you!" she retorted, stung by his roughness. "You couldn't care less if Leslie ever shows up and you know it."

Chance eyed her narrowly. "There's a great deal that you don't know about my aunt and me and my family. I suggest that you aren't in any position to condemn my behavior since you aren't in possession of all the facts."

"Then tell me the facts," she challenged.

"I don't discuss personal family matters with strangers. And you, Red...despite all the intimate moments we've shared or almost shared—" there was a mocking glint in his steady look "—you're a stranger."

Selena's hunger for the soup ended with his words. She set the spoon on the tray and handed it to him. "I don't want any more," she said stiffly. Grudgingly she added, "Thank you for bringing it."

"It was the least I could do," he said, accepting thanks indifferently, "since it was at my aunt's instigation that you ended up half-drowned."

After Chance had left with the tray, Selena pulled the covers around her neck and slid down into a horizontal position. All his concern had been prompted by a sense of duty and responsibility. Nothing more.

She felt let down somehow, cheated out of a feeling that could have been exceedingly pleasant. She closed her eyes, trying to shut out the sensation. It wasn't long before she was asleep.

A hand touched her shoulder and she rolled over in alarm. She had difficulty focusing her vision, which was fuzzy from sleep. Chance was sitting on the bed, watching her with those intent black eyes.

"How do you feel?" He pressed his palm across her forehead, then turned it to let the back of his hand rest against her cheek.

"I'm fine." Her insistent voice was thick and husky from the sleep. He took his hand away in apparent satisfaction, assured that she wasn't running a fever.

"What are you doing here again?"

"I wanted to see how you were and whether you were going down to dinner tonight," he explained with a faintly amused twist of his mouth. "It's six o'clock."

"It can't be!" she frowned in protest.

"I'm sorry. Maybe it can't be, but it is," Chance shrugged. "So what's the decision? Are you coming down or do you want something sent up?"

"I'm coming down," Selena answered.

"Good. I'll wait for you outside." He straightened from the bed.

As he walked to the door, she said, "And leave my key on the chest of drawers."

There was a jangle of metal as the key was deposited on the wooden top before Chance walked out of the door. She heard the click of the lock and slipped out of bed to dress hurriedly.

Most of the passengers were already in the dining room when Selena and Chance arrived at the staircase leading to the Orleans Room. Another couple approached the stairs at the same time. Both men gave way to permit the women to go first.

"How are you feeling?" the woman inquired of Selena.

"Fine," she blinked in surprise.

"That was quite a drenching you got today. It's a miracle you didn't catch your death of cold."

"I never get sick," Selena replied.

"A person can never be too careful at this time of year. I've had more colds in spring than any other time of year," the woman remarked. "It was probably a good thing that you stayed in your cabin and rested and kept warm this afternoon."

"Yes." *Good heavens,* Selena thought, *how much more does this woman know about me?*

At the bottom of the stairs, the woman paused and smiled. "It must have made you feel good the way Chance looked after you, bringing you hot soup and all. I couldn't think of anyone nicer to take care of me than him—unless of course it was my husband," she laughed.

Selena echoed it weakly before the couple separated from them to go to their own table. If every person in the dining room had turned to look at her with Chance, she couldn't have felt more self-conscious.

As Chance escorted her to their table where Julia waited, Selena asked in a low, accusing tone, "Does everyone on board know about my rain-soaked morning?"

"Probably," he conceded, amusement glinting in his downward glance at her rigidly set expression of composure.

"Did you have to tell them?" she muttered in an aside before greeting the woman at the table. "Hello, Julia."

"How are you feeling, Selena?" came the question of concern.

"Fine," she said, and wondered how many times she was going to have to repeat the answer before the evening was over.

She sat down in the chair Chance held out for her. As he helped her slide it closer to the table, he bent low to murmur a taunt near her ear. "Would you have preferred that I didn't explain what I was doing in your cabin in the middle of the day?" Her color rose briefly, giving him the answer that didn't need to be put into words.

Straightening, he took the chair opposite Selena while she attempted to concentrate her attention on Julia. "I'm sorry I—" She was about to apologize and offer her sympathy for not being able to find any trace of Leslie.

Julia broke in with a radiant smile, "Did Chance tell you the news? I've heard from Leslie!"

"No, he didn't." She flashed him a reproving glance, not understanding why he had omitted that when he knew how concerned she was for Julia. "That's wonderful!"

"Yes, it is." The older woman was brimming with happiness.

"Did you explain why he wasn't in Memphis to meet you?" Selena asked.

"Yes. There was some mix-up and he didn't receive my message in time to get to Memphis before the boat left. He's driving to Louisville now," Julia told her.

Again Selena couldn't help noticing the profound silence surrounding Chance, just as it had other times when the subject of discussion was Leslie. She also noticed the way he deftly changed the subject at the first opportunity, drawing Selena's attention to the menu choices so that the waiter might take their order.

When the main course was served, Julia asked, "Are you wearing a costume to the Mardi Gras party tomorrow night, Selena?"

"Is it tomorrow night? I hadn't realized," she replied. "I had thought about dressing up in costume when I heard about it, but. . . ." She let the sentence trail off. Tomorrow night didn't give her much time to come up with anything. She cast a curious look at Chance. "Are you going to wear a costume?"

"I might. I hadn't thought about it."

"You could always come as a riverboat gambler," Selena suggested, half seriously, "with a string tie and brocade vest."

"That's an idea," Chance agreed smoothly. "And you could be a saloon girl."

"Except that I don't have the costume for that," she corrected, not liking his needling innuendo.

"Of course, you don't have to be in the costume to attend the party," Julia inserted. "The majority of the passengers probably won't, but it does make it so much more fun when you participate in the spirit of the event."

Selena started to make a comment, but Chance's low voice came first. "Your orange dress would work well as a costume."

She was about to remind him that she didn't have it anymore when she realized that he undoubtedly did. "Perhaps," she agreed curtly, expecting any second for Julia to ask how Chance knew about a dress that Selena hadn't worn while on the boat. "But there are other parts to the costume than just the dress."

"You'd need to wear your hair up, glue a

black beauty spot on your cheek and wear a black ribbon around your neck,'' Chance listed. "I'm sure one of the boys in the band would lend you his garter."

"And I have a black boa you could borrow," Julia offered. "One of those silly feathery things. There's crêpe paper you could use to make an ornament for your hair. I think it's a terrific idea."

Selena had little room left for argument. "Okay, I'll go as a saloon girl—as long as you go as a riverboat gambler, Chance," she qualified.

"You have a deal, Red." His mouth twitched in amusement, his expression otherwise bland.

She had once said she wouldn't wear that dress again if she did get it back. And here she was, blackmailing herself into wearing it to a party—with Chance. She didn't understand how she had talked herself into it. But it had been easy. The words had come out before she had the sense to say she wasn't going to wear a costume.

Suppressing a sigh, she sliced a bite of stuffed pork chop. With her mouth full of food, surely she wouldn't have room for her foot.

CHAPTER EIGHT

SELENA KNEW she wouldn't have missed the party the following night for anything. An extraordinary number of passengers came in costumes, parading down the stairwell to the Orleans Room. There was a highly imaginative assortment from sheeted ghosts to a Roman warrior, courtesy of the pots and pans from the kitchen. The range went from the ridiculous to the sublime.

After the parade of costumes and entertainment by the crew and passengers alike came the late-night snacks followed by dance music from the band. Selena was too caught up in the party spirit to leave when the music began, nor did Chance suggest they should.

Instead he turned to her and asked, rather mockingly, "Is it permitted for a minister's daughter to dance?"

Selena was simply in too good a mood to take offense. "It is for this minister's daughter," she smiled, and let him lead her onto the floor.

As he turned her into his arms, she felt again his manly strength, the power contained, the firm arm around her waist. She remembered the other times Chance had held her in his arms to kiss her, make love to her, and immediately shied away from those memories.

Chance bent his head slightly to better see her face. "I never thought I'd see you again in that red dress," he smiled wryly.

"I never thought I'd wear it again," Selena returned in a matching tone.

He was dangerously charming tonight, flirting with her in his mocking way. The admiring light in those lazy black eyes made her feel very special. She would have been neither human nor female if she had tried to deny that she liked it.

With each dance, it became easier to match his steps, to let her body sway with his in tempo with the music. Her senses came alive in his embrace. Whatever resistance she might have had melted under the warmth of his body heat and the intimate pressure of his thighs brushing against hers. With each breath, she caught the scent of the lotion on his smooth cheeks, a heady mixture of spice and musk. And the steady rhythm of his heartbeat was hypnotic.

It was with regret that Selena left his arms when the last song ended. She shifted the feathery boa higher up around her shoulders as the hand at the small of her back guided her from the floor to the stairs.

"Shall we take the long way to our cabins?" Chance suggested.

Selena nodded an affirmative answer, trying to steady the leap of her heart at his suggestion.

At an unhurried pace, they wandered onto the outer cabin deck to slowly make their way around the bow to the texas stairs. A half moon was beaming a silvery light from the midnight sky. The air was briskly cool, invigorating to senses already sharply aware of everything around them.

Climbing the stairs, they made a circuitous route around the texas deck. Neither spoke, not wanting to break the spell that was somehow making the evening seem so special.

As they rounded the stern where the paddle wheel splashed rhythmically in its circle, a sudden breeze whipped the trailing end of the black boa, sending it across Selena's face before the gust of wind faded. The fluff tickled her nose and she sneezed.

"Are you catching cold?" Chance stopped, studying her intently.

Selena shook her head. "No. It was just these feathers."

"It is chilly, though, and you should have something on your arms." He took his hand away from her to slip off his jacket, mocking himself as he said, "Therefore I will do the gentlemanly thing and offer you my coat."

"I'm all right, really," Selena protested.

But he was already swinging his jacket behind her to drape it over her shoulders. As he drew the lapels together in front of her, his enigmatic dark eyes focused on her lips. She held her breath, her heart beating a mile a minute. His fingers tightened on the material, pulling her toward him. And she realized it was what she had been waiting for all evening.

His head blacked out the half moon as he moved toward hers. His mouth was hungry in its possession, its appetite insatiable, taking, devouring and always demanding more. His hard length pushed her into the shadows of the overhang, pinning her against the wooden frame of the boat.

There was no pressure, no force to make her submit. No, the insidious seduction was taking place within her, making her hands weak and trembling as they spread across the solid muscles of his shoulders.

When he lifted his head, it was to bury his cheek in the flaming silk of her hair. "Selena." His demanding voice was rough, his breathing equally so. "If I ever find out you aren't a minister's daughter, I'll wring your neck!"

She laughed softly, but it hurt, as did the unsatisfied ache she felt inside. "I never felt less like a minister's daughter in my life," she answered.

Chance nipped at her earlobe. "I never felt more like saying to hell with propriety."

She shuddered against him, knowing how much she echoed his sentiments, and he gathered her close, pressing her face into his chest, his hands running caressingly over her spine.

"Cold?"

"I wish I were," Selena murmured, and felt him smile against her hair.

"Now you know at least a little of the way I feel," he said, and sighed heavily. "I'm not used to playing these games, of being satisfied with kisses. In the past, I've always taken what I wanted with few exceptions. Then you come along with your damned red hair and green eyes—and the menacing specter of your father, the reverend. And I get the awful feeling I'm being reformed."

Selena drew her head away from his chest to look up at him. "Chance, I—"

He kissed her hard to silence the response, leaving her breathless when he was through. "Let's get to your cabin before my better judgment gets pushed aside," he said roughly.

But it was a gentle arm that encircled her shoulders and guided Selena to her cabin. Chance took the key from her hand and unlocked the door, but she didn't immediately enter. Flirting with danger, she looked up at him, her eyes still luminous with the emotions he had aroused.

"Chance, I—" she tried again to speak.

His mouth tightened as he pressed his hand across her lips. "Just say good night, Red," he ordered.

"Good night," Selena complied, and returned his jacket before slipping quietly inside the door.

In the room, she listened to him walk to the railing. She partly understood his reluctance to talk about what was happening between them.

She was confused, too. At times, she disliked him intensely, distrusted him. She didn't know what her true feelings were. Possibly he didn't, either.

With a sigh, she began undressing. As she hung the red dress up on a hanger, she remembered that Chance still hadn't returned the matching shawl. She would have to ask him about it tomorrow.

Although he was outside, she knew he was right that the evening was at an end for them tonight. There were a few things they had to think about before they met each other in the morning.

The next morning Selena awakened to discover the boat was tied up at Paducah, Kentucky, to take on fresh water for the boilers. In the night the Mississippi River had been left and the *Delta Queen* had entered the Ohio River.

When she went down to breakfast, Julia was at their table, but not Chance. There were indications at his place setting that he'd been there and gone.

"Good morning, Selena. Did you and Chance dance all night?" Julia had retired the past evening when the dancing had started.

"We tried," she admitted, taking her chair. Her gaze slid to the empty chair opposite hers. "He must have been up early this morning."

"Yes. He was leaving as I came down," Julia told her. "He seemed restless, as if he had something on his mind. He said he was going to walk into town."

Regret swept through Selena. She would have gladly gone with him if he had asked. Subdued, she ordered her breakfast, discovering that she wasn't nearly as hungry as she had thought.

She was in the forward cabin lounge when Chance returned, within minutes of the boat's departure. A newspaper was tucked under his arm as he climbed the stairs from the main deck. He smiled and wished her good morning, then walked to the coffee urn to pour himself a cup before settling in one of the sofas to read the paper.

Expecting something more demonstrative, Selena managed to hide her disappointment and began chatting with some of the other passengers in the lounge. When the boat was well under way, she wandered outside.

After a week of viewing the levee-lined banks of the Mississippi and the flatlands stretching beyond them, the scenery along the Ohio River provided a startling contrast. Massive hills came right up to the water's edge on one side, their heavily treed slopes permitting occasional glimpses of rock faces.

The other side of the river was valley farmland with more hills in the distance. Selena noticed these features alternated. One time the hills would be on the right and the valley on the left. Around the bend, the positions would be reversed.

The buildings along the river ranged from farm homes to ramshackle huts to beautiful country homes. The wind turned brisk and blustery, forcing Selena to the lee side of the boat, where she watched the changing scenery alone.

Not until the afternoon did Chance seek her out. He was friendly and charming, but something was missing. She had the distinct impression that he had withdrawn behind that bronze mask his features could set to conceal his true feelings from the outside world.

The previous night with all its hinted-at changes might never have happened. Selena wondered if it had or whether she had only imagined the difference in Chance's attitude last night.

The next afternoon there was kite flying off the stern of the sun deck. Selena had assembled her kite in the aft cabin lounge and was carrying it up to the sun deck when she met Chance.

"Well, if it isn't Mrs. Benjamin Franklin!" he mocked, his eyes crinkling at the corners.

"Why don't you go fly a kite?" she suggested laughingly.

"I certainly hope you don't intend to fly that one," Chance commented, eyeing her kite skeptically.

"Why not?" She looked at it, finding nothing wrong.

"Because it won't fly. Didn't you follow the instructions when you put it together?"

"I couldn't understand the directions." Selena gave a helpless little shrug. "But I thought it looked like a kite when I was through."

"Here." He reached for the kite. "The string is tied wrong, I'll fix it for you."

Obligingly Selena handed him the kite and its ball of twine. With quick, sure movements, he cut away her work and rethreaded the string properly through the kite before he gave it back to her.

"Have you ever flown a kite before?" he asked.

"No," she admitted with a dimpling smile.

"Then may I come along to view the launching? It's bound to be something to see." The grooves around his mouth were deepening in an effort to hold back a smile. It didn't matter because his eyes were laughing at her.

"Very well," Selena agreed readily. "But don't make fun of me."

"Would I do something like that?" His voice was heavy with mock innocence.

"Yes."

There were quite a few fellow kite-flying passengers on the sun deck when they reached it, but only two kites were actually in the air. The rest were still trying.

After Selena made four unsuccessful attempts to get her kite airborn, Chance stepped forward to offer some advice. Under his direction she succeeded on the next attempt.

"Give it a little more string." Chance stood close behind her, and her shoulder brushed against his chest as she obeyed his instructions.

"More string."

"It's flying! It's actually flying!" she breathed, her eyes sparkling. The words were barely out when the kite began looping crazily like a wild thing trying to free itself from a tether. "What's wrong?" she asked, frantically feeding out more line.

"I think it's caught in the down drafts created by the paddle-wheel's rotation," Chance answered, watching the erratic behavior of the kite. At that moment it swooped, diving for the red paddle wheel. "Look out! You're going to lose it."

Jointly they attempted to reel the string in to rescue the kite from the churning paddles. For a few seconds, it looked as if they were going to save it. Then it was gone.

"That red monster ate my kite!" Selena declared with a mock sigh.

"We'll see how everybody else fares," Chance smiled.

No longer participating in the flying, they stood to one side and watched the others. The "red monster" had a voracious appetite. It gobbled up more of the kites until there were only six left, soaring high out of reach of the paddle wheel. It became a contest to see which kite could fly the highest, and more balls of string were added to each kite.

A practical joker in the spectators called out, "Bring them in. There's a bridge just around the bend!"

There was a moment of panic until the kite

flyers realized their legs were being pulled. There were numerous threats to throw the joker overboard, but all six kites remained on the boat.

Gradually the crowd of spectators thinned, and Chance and Selena wandered to an empty section of the port railing. Chance rested his elbows on the teak wood and leaned forward, clasping his hands in front of him. The sun was hot and the breeze was cool, a perfect combination. Selena laid her hands on the railing and lifted her face to the wind and sun.

With no advance warning of his topic, Chance said, "I had my secretary call the charity you said you sent the money to in New Orleans."

His announcement caught Selena completely off guard. Stunned, she could only look at him, unable to make any response. He glanced over his shoulder, noting her reaction.

"The charity admitted that they had received that amount of cash from an anonymous donor," he finished.

Finally she found her voice. "Are you convinced now that I've been telling you the truth?"

"Yes." He straightened from the railing and turned to her, his gaze steady as it met hers. "I owe you an apology, Selena, for my behavior in New Orleans and aboard this boat."

Her smile was a mixture of chagrin and ruefulness. "It wasn't entirely your fault that you got the wrong impression about me," she felt bound to admit.

"Do you forgive me?"

"Of course."

"You're very generous," Chance remarked dryly, turning away to study the valley farmland the boat was approaching. "If the situation was reversed, I don't know if I would be that ready to forgive." She was about to make a response when he distracted her attention. "Look!"

She followed the direction of his pointing finger and saw a small boy racing across a plowed field toward the river, running and stumbling over the clods of dirt. He wanted to reach the bank before the *Delta Queen* went by. Selena held her breath, afraid he wouldn't make it and knowing he was running his heart out.

"He's going to make it," Chance announced.

"Do you think so?" Selena doubted.

"This isn't exactly a speedboat," he chided.

Just as the bow of the steamboat glided past a grassy area on the bank, the boy reached the same spot. Winded, a sandy mop of hair tousled by his race, he began waving wildly, a broad grin slitting his freckled face. Selena waved back with equal enthusiasm along with Chance.

When they had glided past and the red paddle wheel was churning its goodbye, Selena continued to watch the figure on the bank growing steadily smaller.

"How exciting it must be for a small boy to see a boat like the *Delta Queen* steaming up the river," she commented. "How exciting for anyone. I guess children can just better express it."

"True," Chance agreed absently, and moved away from the railing, unexpectedly adding, "I'll see you at dinner."

After his apology, she had thought that his air of remoteness would leave. But there was a part of him that was still reserved and aloof. He was holding back and she didn't know why.

On Wednesday, the *Delta Queen* arrived in Louisville, Kentucky. For the third time, Selena stood on deck with Julia as the boat docked, unable to believe that Leslie would fail to appear again. Yet there was no one waiting on the waterfront except an obliging deckhand from the *Belle of Louisville* to help them tie up.

Cars and trucks whizzed by on the elevated interstate highway system passing above the wharf, some honking at the *Delta Queen* as she docked. The crew members not involved in the tying up were busy decking out the boat in all her finery. Pennants streamed from her landing boom and bunting was draped on her railings, all in festive preparation for the great steamboat race later in the day.

Neither woman felt festive as they turned away from the railing. Selena was confused and concerned. The same expression was mirrored in Julia's face along with aching disappointment.

"What do you suppose happened this time?" Selena asked.

"I don't know," Julia shook her head bewilderedly. "Leslie said he was driving straight here. He should have arrived at least by Monday. I can't think why he's not here."

"Would you like me to go ashore and make some telephone calls?"

"Oh, no, I can't let you do that—not after the last time," Julia refused hurriedly. "Chance would never forgive me."

"Chance doesn't have any say in what I do," Selena answered with a trace of irritation.

"Perhaps not." But Julia didn't exactly concede the point. "But I think I should make the calls. Would you stay on the boat in case Leslie comes while I'm gone?"

"Yes—"

"He's a tall, rather strongly built man, plain-looking, with a mustache, and he always wears a hat." A smile touched the older woman's mouth as she described him.

"I'll watch for him," Selena promised.

Twenty minutes after Julia had left, Chance came by, looking vitally masculine in a blue blazer and gray slacks. He gave Selena one of those disarming smiles that reached his eyes. She felt her heart flutter at the sight of him, so handsome and so male.

"Shall we do some sight-seeing in Louisville?" he suggested. "Go out to Churchill Downs and see if we can pick the Derby winner on Saturday?"

"I'm sorry." She hated to refuse, wanting

very much to accept his invitation. "I promised Julia I'd wait here in case Leslie arrived while she was gone."

His mouth immediately thinned, his features chilling into hard lines. "Leslie isn't—" he began impatiently, then abruptly cut off the rest of the sentence.

But Selena had heard enough to take a wild guess that it would have been, "Leslie isn't coming." Her look became wary and accusing.

"Leslie isn't coming?" She demanded that he finish it. "What do you know about this?"

The bland mask slipped into place. "I don't know anything about it," he returned smoothly. "I was simply going to say that Leslie isn't your affair."

"I don't see it that way." Her reply was stiff; she still did not quite believe his explanation.

He seemed to shrug although Selena detected no movement. Perhaps it was his attitude of indifference that gave her that impression.

He moved away, adding coolly, "I'll see you later," over his shoulder.

It was the middle of the afternoon before Julia returned, disheartened by her fruitless efforts to find or contact Leslie and upset by his unexplained absence. The state of her nerves wasn't improved by the influx of photographers and cameramen and various other members of the news media aboard to cover the race, or the hundred or so extra passengers who were coming on the *Delta Queen* just for the race.

"Why don't you lie down in your room for a while?" Selena suggested. "I'll tell the chief purser and the porters where you are. If a message comes from Leslie, then they'll know exactly where to find you.

"Yes, perhaps you're right," Julia agreed, her hands twisting in agitation. "I'll do that."

Selena spent some time in Julia's room, trying to calm her down and offer some words of reassurance, however meager. When she returned to the outer deck, the railing was crowded with passengers, the regular list and the new intruders.

The deep, rasping whistle of the *Delta Queen* blasted its long-and-two-shorts signal that it was leaving port. The *Belle of Louisville* was already in midstream along with the starter's boat. A crowd of spectators stood behind the barricades on the dock. The great steamboat race was about to get under way. Reversing into the channel, the *Delta Queen* moved upstream to draw level with the *Belle*.

"The railroad bridge overhead is the starting line." Chance was at her elbow, holding a mint julep in each hand.

"Thank you." As Selena took one of them, the paddle wheels on each boat stopped turning and they floated toward the bridge.

When the bows of the boats reached the imaginary line, the cannon on the starter's boat went off. Smoke billowed from the stacks and the paddle wheels began rotating again, churning up the water.

Yet nothing seemed to be happening. They were inching forward at a snail's pace, no explosive acceleration, no leap forward. The passengers on each boat were yelling. "Go! Go! Go!" Selena couldn't help laughing at the exceedingly slow start, so very different from the beginning of any other race.

"I told you before, this isn't a speedboat," Chance murmured dryly. "The *Belle* is shorter and lighter. She'll get up steam and power first and move into the lead. It takes the *Delta Queen* a little longer to get going. Then we'll catch up—I hope."

As he predicted, the *Belle of Louisville* took the early lead with the *Delta Queen* slowly closing the gap. Selena sipped at the sweet drink in her hand. The race was a very novel experience.

"How long is it?" she asked.

"Twelve miles. We go up to Six Mile Island and turn around," he explained. "The starting line is the finishing line, too. The race takes about two hours."

Both sides of the bank as far as Selena could see were lined with people, sometimes four and five rows deep, family groups picnicking while they watched the two old-time riverboats churning up the Ohio. The helicopters carrying more members of the news media followed the race's course, swooping low, sometimes hovering above the two boats.

A roar went through the passengers on the *Delta Queen* as they realized she was pulling ahead. The crowds on the bank saved their cheers to encourage the hometown favorite, the *Belle of Louisville*.

They had not reached the halfway point when Chance suggested, "They have a buffet set up in the Orleans Room. Shall we eat before the rest of the passengers decide to crowd down there?"

Selena agreed readily, knowing they would have plenty of time to eat and be back on deck for the finish of this unique race. Only a few other people had the same idea as Chance, so the room was fairly empty. They helped themselves to the buffet and sat down at their regular table. They were halfway through the meal when the *Delta Queen* was jolted.

"What was that?" Selena looked up in alarm.

"A towboat," Chance explained as they were jolted again. "We've reached Six Mile Island and are turning around. There are two towboats waiting, one for us and one for the *Belle*, to help us make a sharp, clean turnaround."

With the turn complete, the *Delta Queen* headed downstream, tooting her hoarse whistle twice. For a moment, Selena didn't understand the implication of the signal. Then it struck her. The pilot was signaling to the *Belle* that they would be passing on the starboard side.

The *Belle of Louisville* was still coming upstream, not having reached the turnaround point, and they were heading down, well in the lead. Suddenly the whistles carried the sweet ring of victory.

"We're going to win, aren't we?" she smiled at Chance.

"Barring a catastrophe," he agreed.

Her gaze slid to the empty chair Julia usually occupied, and some of the delight left her as she remembered that the older woman was in her room, heartsick and worried by Leslie's absence.

"I wonder why Leslie wasn't here to meet Julia," she mused aloud.

"I don't know," was the sharply clipped response from Chance.

Her temper flared at his curt words. "What you mean is that you don't care!"

"I don't know exactly what I mean." This time he spoke calmly and concisely. "But I don't want to get into a discussion about it now."

"You never want to discuss it." She was suddenly very close to tears.

"Selena—" His voice was husky, stroking her like thick, rough velvet.

"You can save your charm. It isn't going to make me forget how you're treating Julia, trying to deprive her of what future happiness she might find with Leslie."

There was more she wanted to say, but there was a painful lump in her throat. Jerkily she pushed away from the table and walked stiffly from the room, ignoring his low command to come back.

It was easy to lose herself in the crowd on

deck. If Chance searched for her in the milling throng, he didn't find her. As the *Delta Queen* crossed the finish line first, Selena cheered along with the rest, but hers rang hollow amidst the whistles of victory. She felt chilled and empty inside. Her heart was elsewhere.

CHAPTER NINE

THE NEXT DAY Selena stood on deck alone and watched the *Delta Queen* pulling away from Madison, Indiana, after their morning's stop, a town renowned for its classic examples of fine architecture. Everything and everyone on the riverboat seemed quieter, the excitement of yesterday's race over and the realization that tomorrow morning they would be in Cincinnati, journey's end.

With an sigh, she turned from the railing and walked into the forward lounge. Just as she entered, she saw Julia walking toward the passageway leading to her stateroom. There was no spring to her step and no happiness in her expression. A surge of compassion swept through Selena at the agony of uncertainty and confusion the older woman was going through.

"My, you look glum, Miss Merrick," a voice commented. "I hope your cruise with us has been more enjoyable than your expression indicates!"

Selena turned to find Doug Spender, the chief purser, standing beside her. She forced a smile, "I've enjoyed the cruise very much. I was thinking about Julia. . . Miss Barkley—'' she glanced in the direction the older woman had taken "—and wishing there was something I could do. I feel so sorry for her.''

"Yes, I know what you mean," he agreed. "All of us in the crew, especially the ones that have been with the *Delta Queen* for several years, are very fond of Miss Julia. It seems a shame that she keeps putting herself through this year after year."

Selena found his comment curious and looked at him with a frown. "I beg your pardon?"

"Don't you know?" An eyebrow arched in faint surprise.

"Know what?" she questioned.

"Leslie has been dead for fifteen years. He was killed in a car crash on his way to Louisville to meet Miss Julia," the chief purser explained.

"No!" Selena paled. "No, I didn't know that."

"It's true. Tragic but true," he concluded.

"Mr. Spender!" One of the other passengers approached to claim the chief purser's attention.

Shaken by the information, Selena left the room in a daze, unaware of where she was going until the briskness of fresh air touched her skin. She was on the outer deck. With a trembling hand, she groped for the support of the railing.

She couldn't take it all in. Leslie was dead. He had been for fifteen years. And Julia, dear sweet Julia, was going through the whole sequence of events again, probably just as it had happened fifteen years ago. A sob bubbled in her throat, and she swallowed it back. Poor Julia, she thought.

"Selena, are you all right?" Chance was beside her, studying her waxen complexion with concern.

She looked at him, a fine mist of tears blurring her vision. "I've just found out...about Leslie," she explained tightly. "He's dead."

"Ah, yes." His features were suddenly grim and there was a sardonic inflection in his voice. "Julia must have got the message about the accident now."

His response struck a raw nerve. "You're a cruel, heartless man. You don't have any compassion at all!" Selena flared bitterly. "The happiest day in my life is going to be the day I get off this boat and see you for the last time! You're disgusting! Totally disgusting!"

With the last spitting word, she swept away from him to reenter the lounge. Inside the door, she hesitated for only a second before making her way to Julia's stateroom. It didn't matter that Leslie had been dead for so long. Julia still needed some comforting, and it was certain that Chance wouldn't provide it. Besides, Selena wanted to understand why Julia was doing this.

She knocked twice on the door, lightly, and heard Julia's muffled voice bid her enter. As Selena walked in, she saw the older woman tucking the message card back in its small envelope, the one that had accompanied the bouquet of roses delivered the first day of the cruise, the one that read "I love you. May I always and forever be—your Leslie." Selena felt the grip of poignancy in her throat.

"Selena, my dear, come in and sit down," Julia welcomed her graciously. "I was just—" she fingered the small envelope in her hand and smiled wistfully "—rereading the note Leslie sent me with the roses."

Selena took a seat on the bed near Julia. "I don't know how to say this exactly," she began hesitantly. "But I just found out that Leslie is dead."

Julia frowned, "No, that isn't until tomorrow." Then she lifted a hand to her lips, discovery of Selena's meaning dawning in her eyes. "Oh, someone has told you that he's been dead for some time. You must think I'm crazy for pretending he's still alive."

"No." Selena shook her head and would have added more.

But Julia interrupted with a wry smile. "If not crazy, then just a little bit eccentric."

"I just don't understand why you put yourself through this."

"But don't you see? It was the happiest time of my life," she explained. "Oh, it did end tragically for me when Leslie died, but before that I felt warm and alive and wonderful, knowing I was going to marry him."

Selena still didn't understand. It was revealed

in the confusion of her green eyes. Julia took her hand gently, as one would take a child's, and patted it.

"I was an old maid threatening to turn into a starchy, stiff, older old maid, when I met Leslie sixteen years ago. My father always accused me of being too choosy. The truth was that I'd only received two proposals in my life, both from men I abhorred," she said with a mock shudder. "Then when Leslie came into my life, I began feeling like a real woman instead of an aging imitation. Maybe our marriage wouldn't have worked, as my family said, but I'll always be grateful to him for the way he changed me. When I lost him, I was afraid I'd turn into a bitter, starchy old maid, that I would shrivel up inside myself again. That's when I decided I had to keep taking this cruise."

"To renew the memories of how you felt." Selena was beginning to follow Julia's reasoning.

"It's a harmless game of make-believe I play in my mind. Until this trip, I've never involved anyone else in my pretending except a few members of the crew, whom I have know a long time."

"Yet this time you included me."

"Yes, I did," Julia admitted somewhat ruefully. "Perhaps I shouldn't have, but your reactions, your concern and interest made all the sensations so very real again. I hope you don't think badly of me. I truly meant no harm."

"I don't—I couldn't," Selena assured her, affection for the older woman gleaming in her eyes. "You've merely found an uncommon way to stay young at heart. It was just a shock to learn that Leslie was dead, has been dead for some time. I was worried that—" she hesitated, uncertain of how to phrase it.

"That I was trying to bring Leslie back from the grave?" Julie inserted in the blank.

"Something like that, yes," Selena nodded.

"No, I only want to keep the gift of life that he gave me," Julia explained. "I loved him and I'm sorry I lost him. But it doesn't accomplish anything to forever mourn the loss of a loved one. You must learn to rejoice in the good things they left with you. That's all I'm trying to do."

"I understand." And she did.

"I was sure you would," Julia smiled. "After all, you know how it feels to be in love, how warm and deliciously alive it makes you feel inside."

"Me?" Selena echoed with a blank look.

"You've fallen in love with Chance, haven't you?" Julia tipped her head to the side on a questioning angle.

"I—" Selena started to deny it, then was jolted by the discovery that it was true. "I . . . have, yes."

"It's a grand feeling, isn't it?"

"It is," she agreed weakly, but the realization was too new for her to know exactly what her reaction to it was. An announcement came over the public-address system, but she was deaf to the sound, listening only to turnings of her own mind.

"They're serving tea in the aft lounge. Shall we go have some?" Julia suggested.

"What?" For a moment the question didn't register, then Selena shook her head, copper-colored hair moving briefly against her shoulders. "I have some packing to finish yet and I want to shower and change before the Captain's Dinner tonight." She rose from the bed and Julia stood, too.

"I think I will have a cup," she decided, then smiled. "In a way, it's something of a relief that you know about Leslie. I knew I had to tell you the truth before the cruise was over. I do feel better now that you know and understand."

"So do I," Selena agreed, but her mind was elsewhere and she took her leave of Julia the instant she could.

The Captain's Dinner that evening was the only meal on the cruise where the passengers were required to wear formal dress. Selena dressed with elaborate care, her stomach feeling as if there was a convention of butterflies held within its walls.

Her gown was a special one, saved for this occasion, although at the time she hadn't known this last dinner of the cruise would be specially significant in another way. It was quite likely her last evening meal with Chance.

As she walked down the grand staircase, the busboy was going through the forward cabin lounge ringing the dinner chimes. Chance was near the base of the stairs with Julia. Selena hesitated for a split second when he glanced up, her heart pounding against her ribs. She felt the assessing sweep of his gaze and was reassured by the knowledge that her appearance was flawless.

Her dress was a filmy chiffon print of flowerets against a background of royal blue with bolder floral panels. It had a peasant neckline and billowy raglan sleeves with a long, shirred skirt. Its overall effect was totally feminine, a perfect foil for the gleaming copper of her hair.

Her heart leaped into her throat when he stepped forward to meet her. Tall and devastatingly handsome, he wore a rich black suit that emphasized his dark looks and that aura of something dangerous. There was an admiring glint in his eyes, but he offered no verbal compliment regarding her appearance.

"Shall we go down?" he addressed the question to both Selena and Julia.

"Yes," was all Selena managed. Her tongue was all tied up by her heartstrings.

It proved to be a difficulty that she couldn't overcome. She felt awkward and unsure of herself, unable to behave naturally in his presence. The champagne, courtesy of the captain, she barely sipped, afraid it would loosen the knots and let something slip.

Her silence went unnoticed, thanks to the

numerous toasts by the captain and crew before dinner and the entertainment afterward thus making conversation at their table almost unnecessary. At the close of the entertainment before the dancing started, Julia made a discreet withdrawal to leave the two of them alone.

But Selena knew the kindly attempt was wasted. She was too uncomfortable and self-conscious to be alone with Chance and much, much, too aware of the way she truly felt toward him to behave as she had on previous evenings.

"Excuse me, I think I'll call it a night," she declared with a stiff smile, and rose from the table.

"Aren't you going to stay for the dancing?" he questioned mildly.

"I still have some packing to do," Selena lied. "Good night."

"Good night," Chance returned.

At the stairs leading to the cabin deck, Selena paused to glance over her shoulder. Chance had lit one of his cigars and was absently watching the smoke spiraling from the burning tip. He seemed not the least interested in her departure. It looked like a case of "out of sight, out of mind." Selena turned and walked slowly up the steps, trying to keep her head held high and not reveal how much his attitude wounded.

She wakened early the next morning. She had barely slept all night. The most she had managed was fitful dozes. Rising, she dressed and did the last of her packing, setting her luggage outside the cabin door.

There was already a line at the purser's office in the forward cabin lounge when she entered the room. Moving to the end of the line, she waited with the other passengers to settle what charges she had to pay. She saw Chance walk in and tried to ignore him as well as the crazy leaping of her heart.

His searching gaze found her in the line and he made straight for her. The boat's whistle blew the signal that it was coming in to dock. They had arrived at Cincinnati. Selena supposed Chance was coming to say goodbye and she wished he wouldn't.

When he stopped beside her, she offered a tense, "Good morning, Chance."

He didn't bother with a greeting. "I want to talk to you, Selena." His dark gaze flickered to the other passengers covertly observing their exchange. "Privately if you don't mind."

Her nerves started jumping. She didn't want to speak to him alone. She was afraid she would blurt out something that she would regret and make a terrible fool of herself in the process.

"I'd lose my place in line," she protested lamely. "Can it wait until I'm through?" Maybe then she could slip away and cowardly avoid the meeting.

"No, it can't," he insisted, eyeing her steadily.

She couldn't hold his gaze and glanced at her

watch. "I don't have much time, Chance. I have a flight to catch back to Iowa."

"You can always catch a later flight." There was a hint of impatience in the line of his mouth.

"Maybe I can, but I'm not going to," she retorted.

Chance moved a step closer, his gaze narrowing in an intimidating fashion. "We are going to have this talk," he said, lowering his voice to a level of dangerous quiet. "I'll make a scene if I have to, Selena. Is that what you want?"

Compressing her lips tightly, Selena swept past him with a slightly angry toss of her head. His hand immediately clasped her elbow to guide her onto the outer deck, up the stairs to the texas deck and ultimately to his cabin.

"We can talk outside," Selena declared nervously as he inserted a key into his door lock.

"I said privately." He gently but firmly pushed her resisting figure into the cabin ahead of him, then closed the door.

Instantly she turned to face him, her pulse behaving erratically at the implied intimacy of his cabin. "All right, you've bullied me into agreeing to this conversation," she attempted to challenge him. "What is it that you have to say that can only be said in your room?"

"I simply chose a place where we couldn't be seen or overheard," he reasoned, that dark, enigmatic gaze of his studying her closely. "My cabin seemed the place that would provide that."

"What is it you want to say?" she demanded again, her breath not coming at all naturally.

"My aunt tells me that you've found out about Leslie and her little pretense," he stated.

"That's true," she admitted.

"And?" A dark brow lifted with a touch of arrogance.

"What do you mean—and?" Selena asked, frowning.

Chance took a minute to study the cabin key in his hand. "Don't you find her behavior a little strange?" When the question was out, he glanced at her, his eyes shuttered by a black wall.

"By strange, I suppose you mean weird or crazy." An angry hurt began fuilding, making her voice quiver slightly. "I expect you think I'm going to condemn her behavior the way you do. Well, the truth is, Mr. Chance Barkley, that I find her little pretense unusually touching. So if you think for one minute that you've found an ally in your attempts to end these trips—and I'm presuming that is what you've been doing, rather than trying to stop an imaginary elopement—then you're very sadly mistaken. I applaud what Julia is doing and I'm going to do everything I can to encourage her to keep right on doing it. If you had an ounce of feeling for her, you'd do the same. Instead you're just a self-centered, insensitive brute who tries to bully everyone into doing what you want—"

His arms were around Selena and his mouth

was crushing hers into silence before she knew what was happening. For an instant, she was rigid in his embrace, then she melted, unwilling to deny her heart what it wanted. She was breathless and shaken when he finally lifted his head.

"I only asked for an answer to my question." There was a peculiar glint in his eyes that puzzled her. "I didn't expect to receive a lecture."

His arms were still locked around her, holding her close. Finding his mouth too compellingly close for her peace of mind, Selena stared at his shirt buttons.

"Then you shouldn't treat your aunt the way you do and you wouldn't be getting any lectures," she replied defensively.

"And just how do I treat my aunt?" Chance bent his head, tipping it slightly in an effort to see her face.

"You know how you treat her," she insisted weakly. "Every time she mentioned Leslie's name on the boat, you'd go all cold and hard, totally unsympathetic to her feelings. And look at how you tried to stop her from even taking this cruise—you and your high and mighty family. You did your best to persuade her not to come. Don't forget, I was there," she finished more strongly.

His mouth twitched. "That was part of the act, Red."

Warily, she met his gaze, dark and sparkling with an inner light. "Do you mean you were only pretending that you didn't want Julia to take this cruise?"

"That's right," he nodded.

"And you came on the boat with her as—"

"No," Chance quickly corrected that delusion. "I came on the boat because of you and that little matter of the money you took from me."

"Oh!" Selena breathed.

"The second reason I came aboard," he continued, "was because I'd found you with Julia and the two of you were very cozy and friendly. At the time I had every reason to suspect your motives for befriending an elderly and wealthy woman."

"I suppose so," she conceded.

"As far as my reaction to Leslie's name was concerned, I didn't like the idea that Julia was involving you in her little game of make-believe. At first I thought you knew it was only a game and were going along with it. When I realized you didn't, I knew eventually you would find it out and I kept imagining what your reaction would be. Julia is very fond of you, and I didn't want to see you hurt her with any biting comments about her sanity," he explained. "Julia accuses me of being overly protective. Perhaps she's right. All I know is that I was irritated because I couldn't protect her from your ultimate discovery."

"But I don't think she's crazy for doing it," Selena protested.

"That's what she told me this morning. She said you understood her reasons, but being the cynical skeptic you've often described me as, I had to find out for myself."

"And that's why you brought me here," Selena concluded.

"That's it." His eyes smiled.

She struggled, trying to twist out of his arms. "Now that you have, you can let me go. I still have to go to the office and catch my flight." There was a catch in her voice, part of her desperate need to get away from him.

The steel band of his arms tightened the trap, keeping her in his embrace. "There's one more thing."

"What's that?" she breathed impatiently.

"Julia also told me that you're in love with me. Is that right?" he asked calmly.

Selena froze, a sickening sensation turning her stomach. "She had no right to tell you that," she choked.

"Is it true?" Chance persisted.

"Yes, it's true," she retorted, "but she had no business telling you."

"How else would I have found out?" His voice was complacent and infuriatingly calm.

"I have no idea!" Selena tried desperately to blink back the tears scalding her eyes.

"I suppose the next step is for me to fly home with you to ask your father's permission to marry you, wouldn't you say?" Chance suggested in the same composed tone.

"What?" Her head jerked up at his question, not believing she could have possibly heard correctly.

Those dark eyes were laughing silently into hers. "I hope he isn't one of those fathers who believes in long engagements. I don't think I could stand up under the strain."

Selena was still wary. "Chance, if this is your idea of a joke, I'm not going to find it very funny," she declared tightly.

"It's no joke." He stopped smiling, gazing at her so intently that she was certain he could see into her soul. "I love you and I want you to be my wife."

"Oh." The word slipped out as a bubble of happiness escaped.

"That had better be 'yes,'" he warned.

"It is!" Selena assured him, laughing and crying at the same time. "It most definitely is!"

Her arms wound around his neck as his mouth sought her lips. "Can you imagine," Chance murmured against the pliant curve of her lips, "how we're going to explain to our children the way we met? With you a minister's daughter?"

"It will be difficult," Selena laughed softly before he effectively silenced her, and not for the last time.

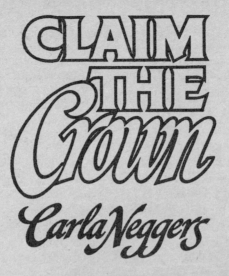

CLAIM THE Crown

Carla Neggers

**The complications only begin
when they mysteriously inherit
a family fortune.**

Ashley and David. The sister and brother are
satisfied that their anonymous gift is legitimate
until someone else becomes interested in it, and
they soon discover a past they didn't know existed.

THE
GIRL CRIED
MURDER

Orig. title: "Murder, My Dear!"

DOROTHY WOOLFOLK

Blairsville High School Library

SCHOLASTIC INC.
New York Toronto London Auckland Sydney Tokyo

For Donna and Donald, who know why

Cover Photograph by Owen Brown

ISBN 0-590-05810-X

12 11 10 9 8 7 6 5 4 3 2   4 5 6/8

THE
GIRL CRIED
MURDER

A Windswept Book

WINDSWEPT TITLES
FROM SCHOLASTIC

Don't Walk Alone by Mary Bringle
Someone Is Out There by Carole Standish
Girl in the Shadows by Miriam Lynch
The House of Three Sisters by Virginia Nielsen
Yesterday's Girl by Madeline Sunshine
The Snow's Secret by Carole Standish
The Red Room by Kaye Dobkin
The Silvery Past by Candice Ransom
Dreams and Memories by Lavinia Harris
A Forgotten Girl by Elisabeth Ogilvie
The Ghost of Graydon Place by Dorothy Francis
The Silent Witness by Meredith Hill
The Empty Attic by Jean Francis Webb
Murder by Moonlight by Dorothy Woolfolk
The Girl Cried Murder by Dorothy Woolfolk

CHAPTER ONE

EVEN as I woke up that morning, I had a premonition of disaster. From the kitchen downstairs came the aroma of coffee, the normally friendly clink of dishes, the smell of bacon frying in the pan — but the only effect it all had on me was to make me feel even more depressed. I knew they were waiting for me. My father was probably getting ready to call upstairs right this moment. I'd heard my brother Bob whistling his way downstairs long minutes ago, and Mother, of course, was the early bird who set everything in motion in our house.

With a heavy sigh, I had forced myself up out of bed. I had padded in bare feet to the bathroom and, holding my toothbrush midway between the basin and myself, I remember how shocked I was when I saw my face reflected in the medicine-chest mirror. There were dark circles under my eyes, my face had that yellowish sickly pallor I always got when I hadn't been able to sleep. My eyebrows seemed to peak, then descend, over my eyes with a kind of Pagliacci-the-Clown expression that was so ludicrous I could almost have laughed if I weren't so near to tears.

"Melissa!"

There it was, right on schedule. My father's voice scraping like a steel file against my nerves. I flung cold water into my face, grabbed a towel, dried with one hasty motion, and hurried back into the bedroom.

"Melissa! You get right down here this minute!"

I got into my clothes hastily, ran a brush through my hair, grimacing at my reflection as I so often did. I ran down the stairs and slid into my chair, hoping my father would let me be. Of course he didn't.

My brother Bob, my mother, and my kid brother Jody were all at the table. That made it just right for father. If anything, he was always worse in front of an audience.

"Why do I always have to call you down to the breakfast table?"

"Please, George! Let's not have arguments this early in the morning," my mother cut in.

"Yeah, Dad," my little brother said. "You're always picking on Melissa."

"I didn't ask for your opinion," my father said sharply to Jody. "Eat your breakfast."

Jody touched his foot to mine under the table. But it didn't help the sick feeling in the pit of my stomach. My father was really on the warpath.

"Just look at yourself! Your hair's a mess and you look like you fell out of bed. Sometimes I think you're not even a Prescott. Look at Bob."

6

My brother Bob, blond, handsome, beaming confidence with every one of his twenty-one years, grinned at me across the table.

"Pass the jelly, inferior one," he said. "I'm perfect and I'm starving."

I knew what my father wanted to talk about — my future. I didn't want him to, because right at this moment it seemed I wasn't having any. Only yesterday I had gotten the rejection notice from El Cameno College. "We deeply regret that at this time we are unable to accept anymore students for matriculation in the fall of 1974. . . ." It had been a terrible blow.

But that wasn't all. My dearest friend Paige had broken more bad news to me later that day in the ice-cream parlor.

"What'll we do, Melissa, without each other? If only they weren't moving my father so far away! Six hundred miles," she said mournfully.

Paige and I had been closer than sisters ever since the second grade. Her family life wasn't much better than mine. Her mother was a semi-invalid who needed constant care, and Paige waited on her hand and foot. Meeting each other and talking about the injustice of a life that gave a complaining, difficult mother to Paige and a demanding, never satisfied father to me, was a wonderful way of letting off steam and getting things into perspective. And now I was losing her.

"Melissa! I want an answer." I hadn't even heard my father. He eyed me sternly. "What I want to know is what you're planning to do. Now that El Cameno turned you down, and your friend Paige is moving away . . ." I felt as if he'd been reading my mind.

"I . . . I'm not sure," I answered slowly. "I

7.

thought I was going to work at Ridgefield Camp again this summer, but they've had to cut back. They don't have as many kids this year, so they don't need me."

"But why did they let *you* go?" my father asked imperiously. "Why not one of the others?"

"I don't know." There was a lump forming in my throat.

My father finished his coffee and wiped his mouth with a napkin. "You'd better have an answer soon, Melissa. I have no intention of letting you sleep away the days, moping around the house doing nothing. Bob is all set."

"Bob, Bob! He's perfect!" The words came out of my mouth differently from what I'd intended. They sounded mean, biting.

"It's not a question of being perfect. He plans his life. That's why he succeeds."

I pushed my chair back from the table. "I'm sorry I'm such a disappointment to you, Dad. . . ."

My father pointed an angry finger at me. His cold voice pushed me to the brink of tears. I swallowed hard.

"Just think about it, Melissa. The way I see it, you're going to fritter your life away!"

I'd heard it so often, but it hurt just as much every time. I wanted to fight back, to speak up in my defense, but I couldn't. The few times I'd stood up to my father I'd ended up in tears. I didn't want that to happen now. But just then Jody's voice, high, questioning, broke in, "Gee, Dad! You're always yelling at Melissa for something. You're always saying how Bob's great and she's awful. Don't you *like* her?"

"Don't, Jody," I said. I tried to control my tears,

8

but as I ran from the room I could no longer hold back. They could have heard my sobs in the house next door.

As I ran up the stairs, my father's voice was going on relentlessly, "I don't care if she's not as smart as Bob. That can't be helped. But Bob has *character*."

I flung myself on my bed. My mother was knocking at the door. "Let me in. Melissa, please. Your father doesn't mean anything. It's just his way." She came into the room and sat on my bed. "He loves you just as much as Bob."

I knew and she knew it wasn't so. To my father, Bob was everything he'd always wanted — a son, good-looking, good in school, good in athletics. I was a girl — two strikes against me there, and a not very good looking girl at that. I hadn't asked to be born a girl, or to grow up at age eighteen a little too tall, with not much bosom, and a kind of angular body that wasn't very "feminine." Right now as I sat up on the bed I could see my blurred image in the mirror of my dressing table. My hair was long and straight, an odd shade of brown that was neither chestnut nor real brown. My features were as unspectacular as the rest of me; my blue eyes turned to gray or green depending upon what I wore. At this moment, to myself, I was homely.

My mother tried to comfort me. I pretended to listen, but my mind was elsewhere.

"I've *got* to do something," I thought. "I can't stand anymore!"

Paige left on Monday as scheduled. I watched them load the huge van; then Paige and I waved to each other till the family car was out of sight.

With a heavy heart, I turned toward town. Eleven o'clock, and the day, hot and humid, stretched endlessly ahead of me. When I got to Ashton Place, I saw the low red brick building — the public library. I entered, and was instantly grateful for its cool comfort.

"Well, Melissa!" Miss Anderson, the librarian, smiled her welcome. "It's good to see you. I've missed you." Her eyebrows raised the question.

"Oh, I've been around." I tried to sound casual, but something in my voice must have reached her.

"Is something wrong, Melissa?" she asked gently.

I had to tell someone and soon the whole story came out. Paige's leaving, my turndown from college, and then losing the job at Ridgefield that would at least have kept me occupied and in pin money for the summer.

Miss Anderson listened intently. When I finished she looked at me for a few long moments before speaking.

"You're not going to change your father, Melissa," she said. "He loves you in his own way. Unfortunately, that way is a very old-fashioned one. From that viewpoint, boys are automatically superior to girls. It's a holdover from middle-European thinking. Working people, peasants — especially the very poor — all wanted boys because it meant they'd have help some day. Sons would earn money, work the farms, eventually take over the responsibility from the father. It's old hat, of course. Women are not just decorative. They can do almost any job a man can."

Until that moment I really hadn't thought about it very much. In my world, girls became secretaries and nurses and teachers, things like that. Boys were doctors, builders, truck drivers. Maybe not that simple, but not that different either.

"You mean my father thinks I'm inferior only because I'm a girl? But that isn't fair."

"No it isn't." Miss Anderson said.

"What does my father think I can do in Wellsville, anyway? Get a job in the five-and-dime? Or in some office? I can't type very well, and besides I don't think I'd be any good in business."

Miss Anderson nodded understandingly. She reached to the wide wooden rack behind her desk and pulled out several newspapers. On top was a copy of the *Boston Transcript*.

"Start thinking *ahead*, Melissa. The way to find a direction is to be able to make some choices."

"Choices? I have to make money. That means the five-and-dime, if they'll take me."

"I'm aware of that, but have a look at the Help Wanted section." Her thin, pale face was serious now. "Maybe you'll find something there to interest you."

I took the papers and sat down at one of the long oak tables. What was Miss Anderson thinking of? There wouldn't be any ads for local help in a big city paper like the *Transcript*. However, I began to turn the pages until I came to the Help Wanted. "Art Director, experienced . . . ," "Assistant Manager, dress shop . . . ," "Bookkeeper, double entry, manufacturing . . . ," "Clerk, must be able to file . . ."

This was getting me nowhere. I started to close the paper when the ad caught my eye:

"COMPANION: Well-bred young lady to help with bedridden older woman. Must be quick, intelligent, kind. Summer

11

job only. Prefer college student. Write
Box 117, Cranston, Mass., giving full details."

I read the ad over again; a sudden hope surged
through me. Here was an opportunity to get away
from Wellsville, even if just for the summer. But
could I do it? "Well-bred." What did that mean?
A debutante? That was silly. I didn't know where it
came from, but I had a feeling that this was exactly the kind of job I needed right now. A job
would ease the tension between my father and me.

My father! He'd never let me go away from
home.

A feeling of helplessness swept over me, but I
walked over to Miss Anderson and asked for a piece
of paper so I could copy down the information.

"Take the newspaper with you," she said. "It's
three days old."

My heart dropped. What good would it do to
apply now? Surely the job was already taken.

"Go ahead," she said. "Take it."

When I got home I sat down and composed a
letter, "To Whom It May Concern." I told everything about myself I thought they would be interested in. When I finished, I typed it up pains-
takingly and took it to the post office.

For the next few days, my father had to work
late and I must admit I was glad. He'd given
me until the end of the week to tell him my plans.
I had avoided him, since I couldn't tell him about
a job with an old woman that I didn't even have.

I spent the days in the public library, and at
night I either read or watched TV — endless shows
they were replaying for the summer months. I
missed Paige desperately.

When I got into bed one night, I was so unhappy I couldn't sleep. My head was splitting. "If only something would happen," I thought. "Anything."

The next morning the telephone rang and I answered it.

"Miss Prescott, please." The voice was very cultivated.

"This is she," I said. My heart was turning over violently.

"My name is Mrs. Newell. I am calling about your letter in answer to my advertisement in the *Boston Transcript*. I will be passing through Wellsville at three o'clock this afternoon. Can you arrange to see me?"

"Yes! Of course I can. Where . . . ?"

"I see that you live on Weston Drive. Can you tell me how to get there?"

For a moment I panicked. I didn't want my parents to know anything yet. Then I remembered it was Wednesday, the day my mother spent down at the Women's Exchange. I gave the woman on the phone the directions.

At three o'clock that afternoon a shiny black sedan pulled up in front of my house, and a plump woman got out and started up the walk. I took a last look at myself in the mirror in the hallway. I had put on a sleeveless green linen dress, my very best. Paige had gone with me when I'd gone shopping last fall with the money I'd earned in day camp. My hair for once had come out right after I'd washed and quickly dried it in the sun after the morning phone call. I wore a small pearl necklace and the tiny gold loop earrings that made my thin face seem rounder. I looked down at the green

13

sandals that matched my dress exactly, and I was pleased.

The doorbell rang and I went to answer it.

"Miss Prescott?"

The woman in the doorway was imposing in appearance. She was about forty years old, wearing a navy blue suit and a small flowered hat, under which stiffly waved reddish hair lay close to her head. She had piercing brown eyes and a sprinkling of freckles across her cheeks and the bridge of her nose, the kind of complexion you see on young, good-natured, redheaded girls. But she did not seem good-natured at all. I stood there a moment, overpowered by this commanding figure.

"Well, aren't you going to ask me in?" she asked.

"Oh, of course. I'm sorry!" I was half stammering.

I led the way into the living room. Mrs. Newell, following me, seemed to be sniffing out every last detail with her aristocratic nose, and making an unflattering appraisal of the room. She sat down in the red armchair, after brushing away some imaginary specks of dust on the seat. Then she spoke:

"Tell me about yourself. But please be brief. I have very little time to spend on this affair."

What a strange way to interview someone, I thought.

I told her about my school, my family, my local baby-sitting jobs, even about Ridgefield Day Camp and how they had no use for me this summer.

At that point she interrupted. "Why didn't they let someone else go and keep *you*?" How like my father she sounded just then!

I was so anxious for the job that I went on determinedly, ignoring her comment. Evidently she was not too displeased with me, for when I stopped, trying to think of something more I could tell her, she said,

"That is enough. You're not exactly what we had in mind, but you will have to do." She forced a smile. "I don't mean that quite the way it sounded. I'm sure you'll be adequate."

She then went on to explain my job. I was to be a companion to an old lady also named Mrs. Newell — this woman's aunt by marriage. There was a large house in Cranston, with some servants. My duties would not be too difficult. Mostly, I would help prepare trays for the old lady and spend time reading to her and making sure her days were as pleasant as possible. There seemed to be some hint of mystery about her illness. But I didn't feel comfortable enough to ask any questions.

The salary was a modest one, but included, of course, all my meals. They would pay my traveling expenses as well.

"Well, Miss Prescott? Does that satisfy you?" Her tone urged an instant answer.

I was suddenly overwhelmed. A wave of cold fear literally raised goose bumps on my body. Of course I was satisfied. But no one in my family — what I really meant was my father — even knew about this. Suppose I accepted and *then* my father refused to let me go?

The thought was appalling. I looked anxiously out the window at the quiet street, at the silent trees, unmoving in the dead summer air, and I knew what I had to do.

"Oh, I'm very pleased, Mrs. Newell!"

She gave a grunt of satisfaction. "Then that's settled. We shall want you to start on Monday."

Monday! So soon.

15

"Fine. That's fine with me," I said faintly.

She gave me a sheet of paper with written instructions on it. I was to take a bus at thus and thus hour, arriving at Cranston at thus and thus time. Actually, I hardly listened. I was caught up in the excitement of this momentous adventure. I remember thinking how strange it was that she did not ask for any references, or even to speak to my parents. Later, much later, I would understand — only too well. But in my enthusiasm I noticed nothing. My desperation to leave Wellsville overcame all fear, even my fear of confronting my father.

Today, still, I shudder when I remember my father's anger.

"You must be out of your mind. What makes you think you can take care of a sick old lady? I *forbid* you to go. And that's final!"

Normally, I would have wept, run to my room to escape his insults, his total lack of faith in me. But I felt that to lose now was to lose forever. I stood my ground, with my mother trying to help me.

It was almost midnight when my father said — to her, not me — "All right, Martha. She can go. But she'll never last out the summer! We'll be lucky if some disaster doesn't come of this!"

I tried to thank my mother, but she motioned me to go. She didn't want my father to get stirred up again.

I had to hold myself back to keep from flying up the stairs.

In my room I was too excited to sleep. All I could think was, "I've done it! I'm going! I'm going away from here at last!"

CHAPTER TWO

I STOOD in the bus station with my suitcase beside me, an umbrella and my purse dangling from one arm. In the other hand I held a box lunch: tucked under that arm were some magazines and a book Miss Anderson had lent me. She'd handed me the book with a whimsical bit of advice.

"If things get too rough, Melissa, read a couple of pages of this murder mystery. No matter what you're going through in real life, you'll be glad you're you and not the heroine of this book."

She was so pleased about my job. Quite a contrast to my own family when I had said goodbye to them that morning. My father's face was unyielding as I kissed him. My brothers, predictably, said:

"You'll be terrific!" This from Jody, hugging me.

"Just remember, Sis," Bob's voice, very solemn,

17

"if you fall on your face, we'll be here to pick up the pieces."

"Have you got everything?" my mother said anxiously, as she stood in line with me now, awaiting the bus. Her look of concern touched me deeply. I threw my arms around her.

"Thanks, Mom, for everything. I'll never forget how you helped me." Tears started in my eyes. "I swear you won't be sorry you let me go. I won't disgrace you or Daddy, or . . ."

"I'm sure you won't, Melissa. But we're your family. Even if — if things don't work out, you always have us to come back to." She smiled encouragingly.

Of course she meant well, but I felt that familiar pang of fear. No one really believed in me. Least of all myself.

There was a sudden rush of people around us, and then I was boarding a huge streamlined gray and silver bus.

I had barely settled in my seat when a stranger sat down in the aisle seat beside me. I stole a glance at him and his eyes caught mine.

"I assume this seat isn't taken," he said.

He was handsome, in a movie star way. His eyes were a deep green, his hair a tawny blond, his skin very tanned, in sharp contrast to his white teeth as he smiled.

"It is now," I said, teasing.

The corners of his eyes crinkled with amusement. "So that's the way it's going to be. I knew when I came on the bus that this was the best seat in the house."

My heart gave a little skip. Was he serious? Even if he wasn't, it made me happy to know that he had deliberately chosen to sit next to me. In

18

all the years I'd lived in Wellsville I had never met anyone like him.

"My name is Don Wilford, I'm twenty-two years old, and I'm going back to Undine University, second year medical school." He looked directly at me. "It's your turn. Don't tell me. You're twenty years old, your father is a bank president, you're a struggling young actress who's going to Hollywood by way of New England to seek her fortune in the movies. Right?"

"Wrong," I said. I felt a sense of freedom with him. It was easy to keep on this way. "I'm a spy. I'm on my way to Casablanca to meet a stranger named Sam."

"If he's a stranger, how will you know him when you see him?"

I burst into laughter. "Don't you ever give up?"

"Never. Not until I know all about you. Don't forget we're committed to each other for the next six hours, till we both get off at Cranston."

I was surprised. "How do you know where I'm going?"

"A fine spy you'd make," he said jestingly, looking at my ticket tucked into the steel border of the seat in front. "Now that I've cracked your disguise, *talk*!"

I told him about myself in a general way. He kept asking questions until he knew something about my family and our way of life. Once he interrupted.

"You know, Melissa, I know about your mother and your two brothers, but you haven't said anything about your father. How come?"

My cheeks reddened, though I tried not to show how his question had upset me. And again there was that funny little feeling in the pit of my

19

stomach. Suddenly I was confused. He sensed my discomfort.

"Hey, sorry if I said the wrong thing, Melissa. I didn't mean to upset you."

"You didn't say the wrong thing. My father is a very nice man. Really he is. I don't know where you got the idea I'm upset." It was all getting beyond me and I felt very uncomfortable. My father was right. I *didn't* know how to deal with people. Sooner or later, I always managed to mess up any relationship.

"Say, this isn't a fair trade," Don said quickly. "I haven't told you about *my* family. Here goes — my father is the town doctor in Bedford, Maryland, and I have orders to follow in his footsteps. Actually, I never could. He's only a country doctor — but the best kind. Pediatrician, internist, heart specialist, bone man — you name it, he does it."

I sighed with relief. We were back on the same easy footing as before.

Soon the realization came to me — he *likes* me! He's absolutely terrific — and he likes *me*.

Don's effervescent personality didn't leave me much time for such interior thinking. In a moment he was raising the lid of his attache case.

"It's only ten thirty, but my stomach says it's lunchtime. Have a ham sandwich?"

He pushed back the lid to reveal a very special picnic lunch. There were ham sandwiches and chicken sandwiches with the crusts trimmed off, two or three kinds of cheese wrapped in clear cellophane, contrasting with the vivid red and yellow and orange of fresh fruit — peaches, apricots, dark cherries. There were crisp brown cookies and even a small bag of chocolates. I couldn't conceal my astonishment. Don smiled.

"I know. I'm a glutton. A gourmet glutton."

I thought of the box lunch Mother and I had put together that morning. It showed about as much imagination as the life we lived in Wellsville. I was ashamed to open my bag of peanut butter and jam sandwiches, packaged devil's food cupcakes, and an orange drink in a paper carton. Don seemed unaware of my embarrassment.

"Hey! Peanut butter and jelly! My favorite. Try some of this Danish cheese with these biscuits and pass me one of those peanut butter jobs."

It was like that the rest of the trip. The wonder of it was the way we got along together. We laughed a lot and I know now it was because he brought out the best in me. I'd never had any sense of humor with a man. But Don and I were having every bit as good a time as Paige and I used to have.

The hours sped by. There wasn't time for me to brood about what lay ahead in Cranston. Don, with his irresistible curiosity, had managed to elicit some information from me.

"You mean you're going to be taking care of someone you've never even seen? In a house you've never visited? Weren't your parents upset about it?"

Weren't they ever! Mother had insisted on speaking to Muriel Newell. Evidently their telephone conversation had satisfied my mother. "They seem like very fine people," she had told my father that night. But what were they really like? I would know very soon.

Suddenly, the bus driver called out, "Cranston! All out for Cranston!" I could hardly believe we were there.

The rain was coming down in torrents. Don said,

21

"I've got to get a taxi, Melissa. It's getting rough outside. Wait here and I'll see if I can find one."

He left me in the small, dank station. Anxiety began to take over. Just a few miles away lay . . . what? For all the battle I had put up back home, I was scared of what I had gotten myself into. At that moment I'd have given anything to turn back the clock and be safe at home in my room.

Minutes later Don came in, his hair dripping, his trench coat sodden.

"Come on, Melissa! I was lucky to find a cabbie who was willing to make the trip to Wildemere."

He took my arm and we ran through the rain as the driver took our bags. In the warm, moist-smelling taxi, Don turned toward me and looked earnestly into my eyes.

"I don't want to upset you, Melissa, but . . ." his voice hesitated. Then he went on more steadily. "Three drivers refused to go out to Wildemere. When I asked them why, two of them flatly would not explain. The third is our driver. I talked him into making the trip, but he said the strangest thing."

"What was that?"

"He said, 'If I didn't need the money, I'd turn you down like a sack of hot potatoes.' When I asked him why, he said something about . . ." Don's voice broke off.

"Please, Don. Tell me what he said!"

"Let's not forget, Melissa, that this is pretty backward country. Folks here are superstitious. I'll bet they make up stories to scare themselves." He looked at my unsmiling face and said, "All right." He motioned toward the driver as we rode through the stormy night. "He says Wildemere is a swampland . . . riddled with quicksand mires. A really creepy place, judging by what he says. He claims a couple of people have even gone down in the swamp, under some rather peculiar circumstances."

He took my hand and said worriedly, "I couldn't understand him too well. He's a mumbler. But he talked about Wildemere as a place of 'strange goings-on.' When he mentioned 'the old woman,' I tried to find out what it was all about. He said if I asked one more question he wouldn't take us out there." Don sounded unhappy. "How do we know you're not getting into something you can't handle, Melissa?"

My heart dropped again. It was still not too late to turn around and go home. But at that moment the driver barked through the opening separating us from the front:

"We're almost there. Better be ready. I'm not spendin' any time hangin' around *that* place!"

That place we could now see through the rain-spattered windshield. It loomed like a huge, sharply angled monster against the dark purpled hills behind it. As we came closer, the angles became weird turrets, chimneys, parapets, relics of the Victorian era in which the house had been built. The winding road leading to the main house was blocked by a pair of tall black iron gates standing like bunched spears in the night, warning off any who might try to make their way into the darkened mansion. And mansion it was — for after the driver opened the gates and drove cautiously on the wet-slick road toward the house, we got our first full glimpse of Wildemere. It was awesome.

Huge overgrown trees shrouded the house. Thick-trunked, gnarled, they sheltered those nocturnal horrors I couldn't stand — *bats*. I shuddered as I heard their thin screams against the roar of wind and rain. Upstairs, on the top floor of the house behind a mullioned window, a dim, yellow light showed. The lower part was entirely blacked out, as if no one were living inside. The front door was a massive, intricately carved affair ornamented with grotesques and gargoyles out of some deceased Victorian woodworker's imagination.

As the driver went round the back of the car to get my bags, Don hastily scribbled something on a small slip of paper which he handed to me. It was a phone number and an address.

"You can reach me here. Remember that, Melissa. I may be in the lab or in class when you call, but you can leave word at this number. It's my dorm."

Before we could say any more, the driver had opened the door and was rushing us up the front steps. Suddenly a tremendous crack of thunder shook the ground, followed by a bright blue flame of lightning that illumined the front door in all its horrific splendor. I clutched Don and murmured, "Oh, Don! I'm afraid of this house!"

Then the door swung open.

Silhouetted against a pale light from within stood a tall, stolid figure, which I at first took to be a man. The figure motioned me to enter and, still grasping Don's hand, I stepped inside. I could now see a heavyset woman of perhaps thirty-five or forty. My first impression was a clear one. She did not want me there. The cold look on her grim face told me that. Her straight black hair was drawn tightly back from her forehead, raising her dark, heavy eyebrows in a disapproving manner. Her thin lips barely moved as she spoke:

24

"You must be Miss Prescott. You're late. I expected you in the afternoon."

"I — I'm sorry," I stammered. "The storm must have held up the bus. I had no idea. . . ."

"No need to explain," she said curtly. "I'm Mrs. Volke, the housekeeper. Who's this?" She looked sharply at Don, who broke into a smile and stepped forward with his hand outstretched toward hers.

"My name is Donald Wilford," he said in a friendly manner I was sure he didn't feel. "I'm a friend of Melissa's."

The woman ignored his hand; her lips tightened as she turned toward me.

"Are those your bags?" She indicated with disapproval my cheap blue suitcase and overnight bag dripping on the polished oaken floor.

"Yes," I said apologetically, "I'm sorry they're getting the floor wet."

"Well, pick them up and I'll show you to your room." Her voice was a command.

I started to follow her, but Don took my arm. "They're too heavy for you, Melissa. Here, let me help."

Mrs. Volke turned round from where she stood on the stairs. "That won't be necessary," she said sharply.

"Really, it's no trouble," Don said, taking the heavy bags from me and starting upstairs.

Mrs. Volke looked at Don for a long moment, then turned and quickly mounted the stairs.

She led us to a gloomy room on the second floor in the rear of the house. I could hardly see the furnishings as there was only one small lamp lit on a table beside a huge Victorian four-poster bed. Don had just put my bags down in front of

25

a cold gray stone fireplace, when we heard shouting from below. We couldn't make out his words but it was apparent the driver was about to leave, with or without Don.

Don said good-bye and started to leave, then stopped in the doorway and called back, "Don't forget, Melissa, I'm just a few minutes away if you want me." He looked coolly at Mrs. Volke. "I'll be seeing you again, I'm sure. Good night."

He ran down the stairs, the front door slammed, and moments later the cab pulled away with a roar.

With Don by my side, I had felt some security. Until this moment, the full impact of this woman, this house, my uncertain future, hadn't really hit me. I felt terribly alone.

The housekeeper's sharp voice cut the silence. My face must have revealed my thoughts, for she said:

"Well, you're on your own. You're a lot younger than I expected. What good you'll be doing Mrs. Newell, I'm sure I don't know. But it's *their* headache."

There was no mistaking her hostility. Whoever "they" were, she bore them no love. And she was angry that I was there to look after the old lady.

I don't know where it came from, but I felt a sudden strength. I had come to do a job, and this woman was not going to keep me from it.

"If you will take me to Mrs. Newell — Mrs. *Margaret* Newell — I would appreciate it, Mrs. Volke." I forced myself to smile. "She must be expecting me."

Mrs. Volke shook her head in annoyance. "If you came when we expected you, you could have met her. Now she is asleep in her room. She's an old lady, and she's very sick."

Did I imagine it, or was that a satisfied gleam in her eye as she made this startling pronouncement? The younger Mrs. Newell had told me that the old lady was in a delicate state, which I assumed was natural in an elderly woman. But — *very* sick? What was I doing here? I wasn't a nurse, just a companion — an inexperienced one at that. The housekeeper sensed my discomfort and was enjoying it. She smiled a bitter little smile and leaned close:

"Didn't they tell you? . . . Well, you won't be here long. The old woman won't last through the summer."

I drew back, repelled, and she seemed to sense my distaste. Instantly she became the cold, unfriendly housekeeper again.

"Your dinner will be on the table in the dining room at eight o'clock." She glanced at a heavy gold watch that swung from a chain about her throat. "That gives you half an hour to unpack your things and fix yourself up." She cast a critical look at my disarranged brown hair, my wilted jumper and blouse. "And remember — we don't tolerate lateness at Wildemere." With which she swept through the door, leaving me alone.

I closed the door behind her and retreated into the room. The one small lamp was not enough to see by. I looked about for another light and found a switch against the wall. I snapped it on and a big cumbersome chandelier lit up overhead. Instead of lending light and warmth to the room, it cast a peculiar greenish glow, centering on a worn Oriental carpet whose flowered design had been erased decades ago by the feet of inhabitants long dead. The walls were hung with a heavy scarlet fabric figured with gold, but the gold was faded and the fabric had deepened to a dreary shade of maroon that lent a somber air to the whole room. The huge four-poster bed occupied one wall. The only other furniture was a dresser of deep mahogany, two straight-back chairs, and a small console with an oval mirror above it that was meant to be used as a vanity table. Last, but overwhelming even the four-poster, was a tremendous clothes wardrobe which stood in the corner like a gigantic wooden coffin upended on its haunches.

It was the most unpleasant room I had ever seen. Surely no guest or member of the family had ever occupied it. Whatever it had been originally intended for, I was sure it was now part of the servants' quarters. "Now you know who you are," the ugly room seemed to be saying to me. And in that moment I knew that my fantasies in the few days before I came up to Wildemere, imagining myself acting as companion and, in time, perhaps, friend, were totally absurd. I was one of the hired help. That was clear, or they never would have put me in such a damp, shabby chamber.

I sighed heavily and glanced at the fireplace. On the mantle, a chipped old baroque clock ticked away noisily. A quarter to eight! What was I thinking of? I'd wasted fifteen precious minutes and hadn't even started unpacking.

I threw open the door of the wardrobe, and a sickly, moldy smell met my nostrils. I didn't want to hang my clothes inside it, but I had no choice. When all my things were put away, I stepped into the dark hall and, opening the door next to mine, found a bathroom. On close in-

28

spection it was as bad if not worse than my bedroom. But there was no time to linger there. I took a moment to rinse my face and comb my hair, and then I headed down the dark staircase to the floor below.

As I reached the front hallway which Don and I had entered only a half hour before, I saw three separate doors leading off from it. I didn't know which one to take. Then the one on the left of the hallway opened and Mrs. Volke stood before me. What a terrible way she had of appearing from out of nowhere!

"Don't stand there," she said crossly. "I haven't got all night."

I followed her into an enormous dining room. Like the other rooms I'd seen, it was so badly lit I could not make out what it was really like. There was a long dark refectory table on which a dinner setting was laid out. Mrs. Volke silently brought in a plate with food on it, and as silently left. There was some kind of roast meat, and some vegetables and mashed potatoes. On a smaller dish, there was a cherry tart with a smooth creamy base to it. Either the food was very delicious or I was very hungry; I disposed of every mouthful greedily.

No one came in as I ate. Off to the rear, in what I presumed were the kitchen quarters, I could hear an occasional distant sound. I felt a terrible sense of loneliness. I pushed back my chair and folded my napkin as Mrs. Volke came back. The grandfather clock in the corner sounded the half hour — eight thirty.

"You may go to your room now," she said. I felt like a school girl taking orders from a stern teacher. "I suggest you get a good night's sleep. Your day starts at seven thirty downstairs in the kitchen."

At my inquiring glance, she went on, "My husband, Emile, will knock on your door at seven o'clock. Good evening." Without another word, she started to clear the dishes. I was dismissed.

Troubled, I mounted the stairs. In my dark, uninviting room I began to undress slowly. I looked at my reflection in the cracked mirror above the "vanity" table, and was surprised at what I saw. I had never thought of myself as being attractive. I was much too angular, too nondescript for that. But what I saw now was a face wreathed in disappointment. Was this the girl that Don Wilford had smiled at so warmly only that afternoon?

The old doubts came rushing back at me in a flood. Who did I think I was? Just plain Melissa Prescott . . . who'd gotten herself into a situation beyond her depth. Again.

Involuntarily a tear started from my eye. I brushed it angrily away. I couldn't let myself think like this. It didn't matter that nothing was the way I'd thought it would be. I must not think of anything but getting through the summer. I couldn't fail; if I did I would have to go back to the certain mockery of my father, with his everlasting "I told you so."

Still, when I got into the big hard-mattressed bed with the ancient hanging canopy above it, I shivered beneath the icy sheets. A heavy weight seemed to be pressing on my chest.

I lay in darkness for what seemed an eternity before I dropped off to an unhappy sleep.

CHAPTER THREE

A LEADEN gray rain was pelting against the window-pane. The three sharp raps on the door sounded, in my sleep-heavy mind, like pistol shots. I sat up quickly in bed in the morning half-light, my heart beating frantically.

"Who's there? What do you want?" I was only half awake.

A heavy Teutonic voice rumbled through the door. "Up! Time to get up! Seven o'clock!"

As I heard his footsteps going away, full realization came. Wildemere! It must be the housekeeper's husband, Emile Volke.

I threw off the bedclothes and, shivering in the cold, washed, dressed, and managed to look respectable by the time I descended the stairs and found my way to the kitchen.

It was a big, dark room, with a huge black iron stove, the old-fashioned kind — part gas, part coal stove. Mrs. Volke was poking the embers in the coal oven, and grunted an answer to my "Good morning," motioning me to a round oak table on which breakfast was waiting. Orange juice, a plate of hot oatmeal, a toaster with a plate of sliced bread beside it, a jar of strawberry jam. There was a silver dish with slices of thick fried ham, and a pot of steaming coffee.

I sat down before the food and ate in silence. If this unpleasant woman wanted no conversation, it was all right with me. Then her husband came into the kitchen, and she said,

"Emile, this is the girl."

He said nothing, but brought a mug of coffee to the table and sat down opposite me, staring at me intently. He was a bull-necked man, with a glossy head on which not a single hair grew. But by some strange biological quirk, he had wild red eyebrows above his pale blue eyes. His size was enormous, and I was repelled by his huge hands, thick-fingered, holding the coffee mug in a tight grip.

He ate in silence, but once his wife said something to him in a language which I could not understand. He replied in the same language, and they both glanced at me. What were they saying? I wondered. I uneasily finished the meal, and picked up my dishes to carry them to the sink, but Mrs. Volke intercepted me.

"No," she said harshly. "That is not for you to do. In this kitchen *I* am the boss. I and only I handle all the dishes. I and only I cook the food. That goes for the old woman's meals too." She glared at me. "Understand?"

"Yes, of course," I said.

"You may be the old lady's *companion*, but *I* am responsible for her. Don't ever forget that."

She was so nasty I was tempted to answer back, but her husband was watching with sharp interest, and I held my tongue.

"You may go now," she said.

"When can I see Mrs. Newell?"

"After she has had her breakfast and rested a little."

"And when will that be?"

"In a little while," she said impatiently. "Go to your room. I will call you. Don't ask so many questions."

She turned back to the stove. I bit my lip, stung by her words. As I left the room, Emile looked after me with an odd expression on his face.

At about ten o'clock, without knocking, Mrs. Volke threw open my door and said, "Come with me. I will take you to her."

I followed her down a red-carpeted corridor to a wing of the house that was very unlike the part I lived in. We walked through a delicate Gothic archway to a charming room that seemed to serve a dual purpose. It was furnished like a beautiful Victorian parlor, but was obviously a bedroom as well.

Along one wall, in a high brass and inlaid ivory bed covered with a beautiful gold and blue satin quilt, reclined a white-haired figure — old Mrs. Newell. There was another old woman seated beside Mrs. Newell's bed, but there was no time to wonder who she was, for Mrs. Volke pushed me forward.

"Here she is," said Mrs. Volke. She turned on her heel and left.

"So you're the companion my niece has chosen for me," Mrs. Newell said.

Up close, even though the signs of age and illness were clear upon her face, she was yet quite lovely. Under a rather untidy mass of white curls her clear blue eyes, almost pansy-violet, shone brightly against a pastel pink-and-peach complexion. Her features were classic. It was clear that once she must have been a beauty. As she addressed herself to me, her voice was that of an aging Southern belle but with a commanding note behind it:

"Come closer so I can have a look at you."

Obediently I stepped nearer to the bed. She gave me a cool appriasing glance.

"You're very young," she said accusingly.

"I'm eighteen, I'll be going to college in the fall."

"Is this your first job? Well, my dear, speak up. Tell me what makes you think you can take care of me."

This was the start of a rapid-fire inquisition: *Where did you go to school? Are you an only child? Do you consider yourself well-educated? How old is your mother? What does your father do for a living?*

I managed to stammer out a few answers, all the while thinking of how I disliked this woman. She was spoiled, arrogant, unkind. The other woman was entirely different. She seemed almost as old as Mrs. Newell, but was dressed in a neat tweed suit that fit her slim straight figure well. She had smooth gray hair and a quick birdlike manner that belied her years. Her clear gray eyes looked at me with sympathy as Mrs. Newell threw question after question at me, until finally she broke in.

34

"Madge, for heaven's sake, can't you see the child's frightened? What is this anyway, an interview or a trial by fire?"

"Hush," Mrs. Newell reprimanded. "I'm the one who's a prisoner in this bed, Jennie, not you. I'm the one who has to put up with the idiotic plans my family makes for me — such as an eighteen-year-old nursemaid."

"Madge, try not to be rude. It's unworthy of you," the other woman said quietly.

"Very well. I'll try."

"And you might introduce me, don't you think?"

Mrs. Newell waved a fragile white hand airily toward her. "This, young lady, is Jennifer Hillary. We've been friends for more than forty years. Have you ever heard of her?" she demanded.

Jennifer Hillary. Where had I heard the name before? I tried to think, but it was no use, not with Mrs. Newell waiting for my reply.

"Well," she said, caustically, "since you seem to have not the faintest idea, Miss Hillary was, until a few years ago, a well-known writer of novels. Novels of suspense, of mystery, novels of . . . murder." Her pale lips curled in a half smile as I looked at Miss Hillary's gentle face. "Yes, my dear," she went on, "never judge a book by its binding, or an author by her books. Miss Hillary wouldn't hurt the proverbial fly. She's as soft as milk toast."

"Madge, please!" Miss Hillary protested. "Can't you simply *interview* this young woman?"

"There's no point in it, Jennie. She won't do." She turned to me, her face softening. "I'm sorry, my dear. I need someone older, more knowledgable, more — stimulating."

Miss Hillary said quietly, "Even if you're not feeling too well today, Madge, don't take it out

35

on this young lady." She patted her friend's shoulder. "Give her a chance. Please."

"Why should I?" Madge Newell said petulantly. "My life is so boring as it is, Jennie. Boring! Maybe it's because I'm too old. . . ." Her voice trailed off.

"Age has nothing to do with it," said Miss Hillary.

"Oh yes, it has," Mrs. Newell persisted. "Old people are either dull or ridiculous. Like the old man in the poem, Jennie. Remember? 'You are old, Father William, the young man said . . .'" she broke off. "That's funny. I've forgotten! How does the next line go?"

Miss Hillary looked puzzled. "Hmm . . . just a moment." Her eyebrows drew together in thought, her lips puckered. "Now let me think. . . ." she said. "'You are old, Father William . . .'" The two old women sat lost in thought, trying to remember.

I knew the rhyme they were looking for. In the Wellsville Public Library, Miss Anderson and I used to play a game called Quotations, reciting poems to each other, and the poem about the old man was a favorite of ours. I was debating whether to interrupt when Miss Hillary asked me,

"Do you know the poem we're thinking of, Melissa?"

Mrs. Newell said acidly, "Don't be ridiculous, Jennie."

Her sarcastic tone made the blood surge to my face. I said in a voice I hardly recognized as my own:

"But I do know it, Mrs. Newell." Her eyes widened as I recited,

" 'You are old, Father William,' the young
man said,
'And your hair has become very white;
And yet you incessantly stand on your
head —
Do you think at your age it is right?' "

I finished the poem and said coldly, "It was
written by Charles Lutwidge Dodgson, also known
as Lewis Carroll. He's also the man who wrote
Alice in Wonderland."

"Well, Madge," Miss Hillary drawled with
amusement. "What do you say now?"

Mrs. Newell raised her eyebrows. "Well!" She
turned to me. "My dear, I seem to have misjudged you."

"I'm sorry if you don't like me, Mrs. Newell,"
I said. "I was happy when they said you needed
someone to read to you. . . ." I stopped, unable
to go on with the lump I felt in my throat.

Mrs. Newell reached over and took my hand.
"I'm sorry for having been so rude, my dear. Can
you forgive an old foolish woman?"

She squeezed my hand, and a sudden wave of
tenderness for this sick old woman swept over me.
Her huge blue eyes held mine and I was about to
reply, when suddenly her grasp tightened and her
face went deathly white. Her eyes seemed to plead
with me and she became rigid on the bed.

"Madge!" Miss Hillary cried out. She ran to a
small night table beside the bed.

She hastily opened the table drawer, revealing
several vials of pills, packets of powder, and
other medicinal items. "Digitalis! That's what
the doctor said!" She was extremely upset as she

37

fumbled through the confusion of bottles with shaking hands. "Where is it? Can't find the right one . . ."

In the bed, Mrs. Newell's body all at once slumped. Her hand released mine and dropped limply to the coverlet. Miss Hillary turned to me, distraught.

"Can you find it?" she pleaded. "I can't see a thing without my glasses."

I ran to the table and she stepped aside to let me search. Luckily the very first vial I picked up was the digitalis. Miss Hillary took it from me and said, "Good girl! Get me some water!"

I ran to the bathroom and returned with a glass half full of water. Miss Hillary had somehow managed to force the pill between Mrs. Newell's lips. She took the glass from me and tried to hold it to the old woman's mouth. But her hand was shaking so badly some water spilled over the stricken woman, who began to moan. Miss Hillary thrust the glass at me.

"You do it," she said.

I had watched Paige administer medicine to her mother many times, so I knew what to do. I lifted Mrs. Newell gently from the pillow and put the glass to her lips, pressing it against the lower lip, making her mouth open.

"Mrs. Newell," I said. "Please — drink some water."

The old lady opened her eyes dazedly, and I said, "Please drink it. It will make you feel better."

She looked at me, then obediently drank. I lowered her to the pillow, where she lay back exhausted. The color began to return slowly to her cheeks.

Miss Hillary retreated to the bay window and I followed her. Her forehead was wet with perspiration.

"I don't know what I'd have done without you, Melissa. You were very quick." She shook her head disbelievingly. "I felt so helpless. I'm normally quite cool-headed. But seeing Madge in that condition . . ." She touched a handkerchief to her eyes.

"She's had heart attacks before," she went on, "but I've never seen one, until today. Poor Madge!" She shuddered, then sat silent, staring out at the green sweep of lawn. Then she rose and said, "We must call Dr. Perry to come over."

She returned to the bedside where Mrs. Newell was now resting easily, her face a normal color, her eyes alert. Miss Hillary leaned over the bed, and patted Mrs. Newell on the cheek softly, smoothing a tendril of hair from the invalid's forehead.

"Madge, my dear. How do you feel? Are you all right?"

"I'm quite all right, Jennie," Mrs. Newell said softly. "I've had these spells before. Don't make such a fuss." Her pansy-blue eyes met mine. "Come here, girl," she whispered.

I knelt beside her bed.

"Did I frighten you?" she said. "Don't be scared. I am not about to die — not yet."

"Of course not," I said. "Is there something I can do, Mrs. Newell?"

"You can stay, Melissa," she said softly. "You are very competent . . . very kind. I shall not forget that. Will you stay?"

"Yes. And thank you."

"I am glad you came to Wildemere . . . very

glad. . . ." She sighed. "Now I want . . . to sleep." She closed her eyes.

Miss Hillary looked at me and smiled.

"You'll be good for Madge."

There was a rustling at the doorway and then, "What is going on here?" an accusing voice said.

It was Mrs. Volke. She saw the bottle of medicine in my hand, and glanced at Mrs. Newell, lying there with her eyes closed. The housekeeper's body tensed and a comprehending look flashed through her eyes.

"An attack?" she said.

"Yes," said Miss Hillary.

"What is that?" the housekeeper snapped at me, indicating the bottle I held. "Did *you* give it to her? Let me have it!"

She snatched it from my hand. "Who told you to give her this medicine?" she demanded. She stood menacingly before me, her face hard and angry.

"*I* told Miss Prescott to do it, Mrs. Volke," said Miss Hillary. "Was I wrong?"

"This is not the proper medicine," the housekeeper said sharply.

"But I thought . . ." Miss Hillary began.

"Yes?" The housekeeper's face was a cold mask. "You thought . . . what?"

"I heard the doctor say 'digitalis' if she had an attack," she said.

"He said 'nitroglycerin,'" Mrs. Volke said with authority, holding the bottle only inches away from Miss Hillary's face. "Digitalis is wrong when she's that sick. She could have passed out for good. Why didn't you call me?"

Her manner was rude and insulting. Miss Hillary said, "There was no time, Mrs. Volke. I'm sorry, terribly sorry for the mistake. But evidently it did her no harm." She added, "Don't you think Dr. Perry should have a look at her?"

"Dr. Perry! What does he know?" There was contempt in Mrs. Volke's voice as the three of us walked slowly down the corridor. "Maybe if we changed the doctor, Mrs. Newell would get better. Since Dr. Perry got rid of the heart specialist, she is worse. Much worse."

"This discussion is getting us no place, Mrs. Volke. I think you should call Dr. Perry at once." Miss Hillary's lips tightened. "Perhaps it is time Mrs. Newell had a nurse."

The housekeeper's face whitened. "Have you forgotten, Miss Hillary? I am a nurse."

"I mean a qualified — a registered nurse." Her tone altered. "You have so much to do, running this entire house with no staff."

"I have Emile. We do not complain. So far we have been able to keep up with everything."

"And you've done a fine job too, both of you," Miss Hillary said in a mollifying tone. "It's just that I'm dreadfully worried about Madge." She put a hand to her forehead and said softly, "I feel a bit tired. May I come into your room a moment, Melissa?"

The housekeeper said with her customary grunt, "I will call the doctor. Now I must take care of my work."

Miss Hillary took one look at my room and said, "I wonder why they didn't give you one of the guest rooms at the other end, closer to Madge? Who told you to sleep here?"

"Mrs. Volke," I said.

"Hmm . . . that doesn't surprise me," Miss

Hillary stepped to the closed door and listened warily. After a moment, she came back and sat beside me on the bed.

"Someone may be listening," she whispered, "but I must talk to you. It's terribly important."

"What is it?" I asked.

"I cannot tell you everything now," she said, "but it would be unwise for you to remain in ignorance. There is something you should know, Melissa!"

I must have showed my surprise for she nodded and said:

"Mrs. Newell is in danger — great danger."

Her next words sent a chill through me. *Someone is trying to kill her!*

CHAPTER FOUR

I SAT stone-still in my chair, too shocked to speak.

"This is not a wild guess, Melissa. I know." Miss Hillary said emphatically, "I am sure someone wants Madge dead. Possibly someone in this house."

Involuntarily I glanced at the door. Miss Hillary shook her head affirmatively. "Yes, it could be Mrs. Volke. Or her husband." Her clear gray eyes darkened. "On the other hand, they may be entirely innocent. It would be dreadful to accuse an innocent person. I must go slowly, make sure of the facts. . . ." She broke off. "All I know is that someone at Wildemere is attempting murder."

What kind of house had I come to? I felt a cold chill at the back of my neck.

Miss Hillary said, with feeling, "I've scared you, poor girl. But I think you have to know what's going on. Madge is much sicker than her illness warrants. There have been several episodes where she has had attacks that Dr. David Gould, the heart specialist, felt were unnecessary."

"Why isn't he her doctor anymore?" I asked, remembering the housekeeper's words.

"Because he wanted to put Madge into a hospital for certain tests. Madge flatly refused. And Dr. Perry, the family physician, backed her up." She sighed. "Madge has always been strong-minded. But now, her life is at stake!"

There were tears unshed in her eyes. Although the old women were totally different, Miss Hillary obviously loved her friend deeply.

"Why would anyone want to kill Mrs. Newell?" I asked.

"Madge is a very wealthy woman. Don't let the neglected appearance of Wildemere deceive you. This property alone is worth a fortune. It has to go to somebody when she dies."

There was the sound of a board creaking out in the hall.

Miss Hillary got up. "I have to go now, Melissa," she whispered. "But I must warn you — trust *no one* in this house, relative or friend. Until we find the guilty one, I implore you, keep as close watch on Mrs. Newell as you can. Will you do that?"

"Yes," I said, in a voice as quiet as her own. "I'll try to do my best, Miss Hillary."

Some of her tenseness seemed to leave her. She said, "Observe the people who come to visit her. Keep tabs on her food and the medicine she takes. . . ."

"How can I do that? Mrs. Volke doesn't like me . . ."

"I know what she is," Miss Hillary interjected.

"She and her husband have been here many years — ever since they came from Germany. No one knows any more about them now than the day they came. They are close-mouthed people, competent, yet . . . strange." She paused.

"In your own way, Melissa, you can help. My dear girl, I'm asking you to play detective. We must cooperate in this. Let me know anything you see that you feel isn't normal."

She opened her purse and took out a yellowed printed card. "I live only half a mile from here. You can reach me at this number any time of the day or night."

I glanced at the card. It said:

> Jennifer Hillary
> The Cottage, Wildemere
> Cranston, Mass.
> Phone: 246-0330

"Why, you live here!" I said.

"Yes, my dear. Madge and her husband Henry were always like a sister and brother to me. When the sales of my books began to drop off quite some years ago, they insisted I move into the cottage."

She glanced at an engraved silver watch that hung from a delicate chain around her neck. "Goodness, I must be going! I had no idea it was so late."

At the front door she said, "Call me at any time, Melissa. I can be here in minutes. . . ." She broke off. The heavy velvet drapery separating the hallway from the rear of the house moved imperceptibly.

"Good-bye, Mrs. Volke," Miss Hillary said loudly. There was a pause and then, not Mrs.

Volke, but Emile Volke stepped from behind the heavy drapes.

"You called?" he said gruffly.

Miss Hillary shook her head. "I was just leaving, Emile. I will return after the doctor comes, to see how Mrs. Newell is."

As the door shut behind her, Emile threw a baleful look in my direction. Too absorbed with my thoughts to bother about him, I went upstairs to my room, weighing the events of the day.

I had never in my life been in touch with even the threat of violence. In spite of myself, I was frightened.

I did not trust the Volkes at all. And while I knew Muriel Newell, who had hired me, I had yet to meet any of the other people who lived at Wildemere. Who were they?

What kind of person would want to kill a helpless old lady?

"You're fine, Madge," Dr. Perry said. "I wish my heartbeat were as steady as yours is right at this moment."

"You'd say the moon was made of custard pie if you thought it would cheer me up," said Mrs. Newell. "You're a fraud, Gordon." Her voice was tart, but I could see she was very fond of the doctor.

Dr. Perry was tall, gray-haired, perfectly tailored, a model figure of a handsome man in his late sixties.

I had been sent up to Mrs. Newell's room with a tray of cookies and hot cocoa at four o'clock, just as the doctor arrived. While he was talking to the old lady after his examination, Mr. and Mrs. Bradford Newell had come in.

46

"Aunt Madge!" Muriel Newell had said, shocked to see Dr. Perry with her aunt. Calmly the doctor had quieted her fears.

"She's had a minor flutter, Muriel, that's all. I assure you she'll be just fine."

Muriel Newell looked quite the same as the day she had interviewed me in Wellsville, only less friendly. She briefly introduced me to her husband, Bradford Newell. He was short, slim, and rather dapper, and it was obvious that his wife was the dominant one of the pair. I wondered what hold this large, matronly woman had over her smaller but much more attractive husband.

"I would never lie to you, Madge," Dr. Perry said as he snapped his medical bag shut. "I've never been able to fool you for one moment, not since we were kids."

"Not that you haven't tried, Gordon," said Madge Newell, smiling. I envied the ease with which she teased the doctor, who obviously was charmed by her. I had never been comfortable or lighthearted with a man in my whole life — except for Don Wilford.

As I thought of Don, I felt a pang of loneliness. If he were really concerned about me, why hadn't he phoned to find out if I was all right after my strange reception at Wildemere the night before?

When the doctor was leaving he said to me, "Madge Newell is fortunate to have someone with a cool head about her." He added, "Oh yes, I heard all about it — from Miss Hillary. I've got an urgent call to make, but tomorrow I will give you detailed instructions about her medicine and so forth." He patted my arm in a fatherly way. "Nice to see a young face here. Should do Madge a world of good."

Muriel Newell perked up her ears when he said that. I got the impression she was not too pleased.

As we left the sickroom, Muriel Newell said to me, "I had meant to be here when you arrived yesterday, but Bradford and I had to be away . . ." she hesitated, ". . . on business. Wildemere requires a great deal of time in its management." She continued, "I'm sure you'll find your situation here quite pleasant. However, a word of advice." She came closer. "Do try to keep to yourself as much as possible. Mrs. Volke dislikes interference, and my aunt requires you just for some light reading and some errands, *only* at times when I and other members of the family are not available to her."

Unsmiling, she looked at me a moment and abruptly left.

It was apparent that to Muriel Newell and her husband I was little more than a domestic. At dinner that night, while I was allowed to sit at the table with them, both Mr. and Mrs. Newell either spoke directly to each other, ignoring me, or maintained a cool silence. Mrs. Volke seemed resentful as she served me, but evidently whoever acted as nurse or companion in this house was accustomed to eating dinner with the family.

After the meal I was happy to escape to my room, cold and gloomy though it was. It had rained all day and as night fell, a raging storm began once more. I got into bed and tried to read a magazine I had brought with me, but the lamp beside my bed shed little light and my mind was not on reading.

I felt desperately homesick. I yearned to be

back in my comfortable warm home with Bob and Jody and Mother. Could I last out the summer in this huge mausoleum of a house? If I couldn't, if I were forced to go home, it would mean facing Dad with another failure. Either way, the future looked grim.

I put out the light and tried to sleep, but in the dark I could hear every creak of the old house as it swayed in a wind that moaned against the windows like a ghost seeking shelter. I wished Paige were here with me. We might have been scared, but we'd have laughed together.

I tossed sleeplessly in bed for an hour, perhaps more. Downstairs something was making a constant noise; it sounded like a wooden shutter banging in the wind. I didn't want to stay in that dank room anyway. I snapped on the light and felt for my slippers beneath the bed. Putting on my thin cotton robe, I tiptoed through the hall past the door of the sleeping Newells. I had taken a book of matches with me and, lighting match by match, made my way downstairs to the library. During the day I had found the huge old room; it was lined with bookshelves running ceiling to floor and wall to wall, except for a marble fireplace on one wall and a pair of glass-paned doors on the other, leading out to a terrace.

I was surprised to see that the wind had blown the French doors open, and the rain was pouring in. I ran across the room and closed the doors, locking the catch. But I was now wet with rain and shivering in my thin robe. I was about to go upstairs when I noticed that a fire had been laid in the grate. The thought of my cold room upstairs undoubtedly made me do what I did next.

Quickly I crossed to the fireplace, struck a

match and held it to the paper nestling beneath thin twigs and heavy logs. Within seconds a hearty orange blaze was illuminating the room. I was so cold I didn't care if they scolded me the next day for lighting the fire. There was a deep-cushioned armchair by the fireplace and I settled into it, relaxing in the warm embrace of the fire's glow. My nerves quieted and I could feel peace descending, head to toe, through my body. I had not realized how much strain I had undergone in the past twenty-four hours. I soon fell into a deep sleep in the safety of the big chair.

How long I slept I don't know, but what made me waken was a vague sense of danger . . . of something happening outside. I rubbed my eyes and tried to see what lay beyond the storm-beaten panes of the French doors. At first there was only uniform blackness, then something stirred in the dark . . . something large and black, that even as I watched moved closer and closer.

Paralyzed with fear, I saw the French doors burst open, letting in a sheet of icy rain. A huge black-clad, black-hooded figure entered and slammed the doors shut. I cowered in my seat, hands clenching the chair arms, watching helplessly as the intruder advanced directly toward me. I opened my mouth to scream but a hard cold hand was pressed against my lips and I felt myself drawn sharply upward from the chair.

"Don't make a sound!" a deep voice said.

Limp with fear, I watched as the stranger threw back the hood of the black mackintosh he wore. In the flickering firelight I could now make out his features. Brown-black eyes glittered like a falcon's in a lean dark face.

"I'm sorry if I frightened you." The voice came

from deep in his throat. He took his hand away from my mouth and loosened his grip on my shoulder. "I don't blame you for wanting to scream, but I couldn't have you waking the household at this hour of the night."

I was still too shaken to speak normally. I said unevenly, "Who are you? What are you doing here?"

"I was about to ask the same question myself. And, I might add, with more justice. Who are *you* and what are you doing here?"

He had taken off his dripping raincoat and hood and was standing before the fireplace now. He was enormously tall, broad-shouldered, but lean-figured. His features were strong, aquiline, under a crown of wild black hair. His piercing eyes commanded me to answer.

"My name is Melissa Prescott. And I don't think I should tell you anymore . . . not until I know who you are. I have a right to be here. Have you?"

"I'm Bruce Murdock. Wildemere is my home." He cocked an eyebrow quizzically. "Does that meet with your approval?"

"But I haven't seen you . . . I mean . . ." I stammered.

"Naturally. I live in my own digs above the stable." He used a slightly superior, amused tone, reminding me of my brother Bob when he was trying to put me down. "You still haven't answered my question, and I'm waiting."

By now there was no point in playing out the charade. "I'm the new companion for Mrs. Newell. I just came last night."

"May I ask what you were doing downstairs at this hour of the night?" His eyes indicated the wristwatch on his arm that he extended toward me. I was appalled to see that it was three o'clock!

"I didn't realize it was so late. I couldn't sleep. I heard the doors banging and . . ."

". . . came down, lit a fire, and fell asleep by it." His eyes showed amusement. "It was the smoke from the chimney that drew my attention. One of the horses was having a bit of a problem and I was sitting up with him."

He came closer to me and his physical presence, exuding an aura of the outdoors, made me very aware of him.

"You're very young."

"Honestly, if one more person in this house says that, I really will scream, Mr. . . . ?"

"Murdock. And you may call me Bruce, even though I'm old enough to be your father."

"I doubt that," I retorted. "My father is fifty-six."

"Then I'm *half* as old enough to be your father." His features, so menacing before, now seemed handsome, lit by that engaging smile. I wondered that I could have been frightened of him for even a moment. I laughed with relief.

"That's a nice laugh you have," he said. "Tinkly."

Though he was speaking to me lightly, conversationally, he seemed distracted. He left me for a moment and walked toward the darkened kitchen quarters. There he stood and listened a moment. Hearing nothing but the creak and slam of the ancient floorboards and doors and windows of the old house under the battering of the storm, he seemed satisfied. When he strode back to me he said, I thought almost too casually, "Were you here today when Mrs. Newell had her attack?"

52

"Yes. I was right in her room."

"And the Volkes — where were they while it was happening?"

I didn't know this man; I didn't know if I should give any information to him, no matter who he said he was. Seeing my hesitation, he took me by the shoulders. His touch made me tremble, and his black-brown eyes searched mine, as if he hoped to find in my eyes an answer to some question. I felt my face redden and hoped that in the glow of the fire he would not notice.

He took his hands from my shoulders and turned back to the fire. For a moment he was silent, then he said angrily, "The fools!"

His face darkened with something I could not fathom. Was it rage, frustration, or — fear? I was bewildered. Had I done something, said something, to bring it about?

He said harshly, "There's something I have to say to you — and you'd better listen. Listen carefully." With an impatient hand he brushed his hair back off his forehead. "I'm not going to mince words. You don't belong at Wildemere. They've made a stupid mistake. But what's done can't be helped."

He came closer. "I can't imagine why any parents would let a kid like you take a job here. But I'll give you a word of warning. You'll be a lot happier — and healthier — if you keep to yourself. Do your job and don't get involved with the Newell family. If you remember that, you may be able to stay out of trouble."

His angry face scared me. He started for the French doors, then turned back.

"One more thing. There is swampland at Wildemere. Not only bogs but quicksand. Stay

53

close to the main house until you learn your way around." He said impatiently, "Why are you looking at me like that? Did you hear what I said?"

Too upset to speak, I nodded my head.

He grunted and then went on in that urgent, angry way, "Lock up after me. This time, do it right."

He walked out into the stormy night and was gone.

I fastened the bolt on the door and went back to the fire, my head spinning. What a violent man Bruce Murdock was! I couldn't understand his behavior at all. Was he related in some way to the Newell family? Even though his name was Murdock, it did not rule out his being a nephew, a cousin — or even an adopted child.

Child? Bruce Murdock was a man — more of a man, stronger, more threatening, and more exciting to me than any man I had ever dreamed of in my whole life.

That night, in bed, I thought of my brief encounter with Bruce Murdock. If I had offended him, bringing on that violent change of mood, I could not imagine what I had done. I only knew that the memory of him, his brooding eyes, his fingers touching my shoulders, aroused strangely disturbing feelings within me I had never known before.

CHAPTER FIVE

THE FOLLOWING day the storm stopped. The sun shone brightly on the fresh rain-washed grounds of Wildemere; the old house could not maintain its gloomy mien against the charm of the day. The honeysuckle and lilac bushes, freed of their dead blossoms by the storm, gave forth an aroma that was delicious. Forgotten were the fears I had been living with since setting foot within the eerie mansion.

Forgotten, that is, until teatime. Then a small group assembled in the old library: Muriel Newell and her husband Bradford, Dr. Perry, Miss Hillary, and a Mr. Pickett, who was some sort of real estate agent in Cranston.

"I tell you, Mrs. Newell," Mr. Pickett was saying as Mrs. Volke brought in a tea tray laden with an antique silver service, "the buyer I have in mind won't try to cut you down in price. He's a major land developer. All I ask is a chance to bring him out here to size up the property."

"I understand," Muriel Newell said impatiently, "but my — our — position is rather difficult. Aunt Madge — Mrs. Newell — is planning to move to Florida, permanently. The problem is she refuses to leave Wildemere until the fall. And by then . . ." she dropped her eyes with seemly concern, "dear Auntie may not . . ." her voice broke ever so slightly, "may not live to make the move."

Mr. Pickett clucked in sympathy, but there was no genuine sorrow in Mrs. Newell's voice. I was busy trying to set out the tea things, and my fear of making a mistake made me nervous.

Mrs. Newell said in a voice of reprimand, "We're waiting for our tea, Melissa," then turning back to Mr. Pickett, "I wonder how much . . . this is such a difficult question," she paused delicately. "Oh, Bradford, you speak to Mr. Pickett."

Bradford Pickett's weak chin faltered. "What did you wish me to ask him, my dear?"

"You know very well, Bradford. Go on, go on."

"What my wife, I mean Mrs. Newell, wants to know is if this big developer buys the land, how much would there be left over after taxes for the estate?"

"Estate?" Mr. Pickett seemed a bit bewildered.

"*Bradford!*" The name exploded from Muriel Newell's lips. She threw a look of disgust at her husband, who shrank into the wings of his Queen Anne chair. What would have followed then I don't know, for at that moment Bruce Murdock came in.

If I had thought him handsome by firelight the night before, he was dazzling in the light of day.

56

Even Muriel Newell responded to the vigor and attractiveness of this man.

"Bruce!" she said. "Come sit by me, dear!"

Dr. Perry greeted Bruce warmly and indicated the sherry decanter on the sideboard.

"No, thanks," Bruce Murdock said. "What I could use is a strong cup of tea and some of those shortbread biscuits. I was up during the night." He shot a glance in my direction and my heart leaped. "Bolivar stumbled on a rock in field seven yesterday and his hoof's been giving him trouble."

"We'll have to put him out to pasture one of these days," said Dr. Perry. "How old is he now, Bruce?"

"Fifteen years, I think. The poor old guy is falling apart. Like everything else at Wildemere."

"Bruce!" Muriel Newell said playfully. "You shouldn't talk like that, especially with Mr. Pickett here."

Bruce Murdock looked from under raised black eyebrows at Mr. Pickett.

"I'm back with an offer, Mr. Murdock. I hope this time you'll help me persuade your aunt to sell." He stopped as Bruce's face changed. "I know — Wildemere's been in the family for sixty years and you hate to see a stranger take over."

"Not sixty — more like a hundred," Bruce said sharply. "With very little effort, we could have Wildemere declared a historic landmark, which would make a lot more sense than having rows of matchbox houses or a shopping center erected here."

"We cannot hold back the march of time, Mr. Murdock. And since your aunt is about to move to Florida . . ."

57

Bruce cut in angrily, "That's a matter for the family to discuss. I'm against selling Wildemere."

Miss Hillary said before Mr. Pickett could go on, "You know, Madge might like a few of these muffins." Turning to Dr. Perry, she asked, "Doctor? Do you think . . ?"

Dr. Perry nodded. "No harm in it, Jennie — you know her sweet tooth. But no more than two. No jelly or jam with it, either."

As Miss Hillary went into the pantry, Bruce said to me in an undertone, "Aunt Madge is lucky to have Jennie around. She's her one true friend."

"You call her *Aunt* Madge," I said. "Is she really your aunt?"

"My father was Aunt Madge's nephew. I was five years old when my parents were killed in an . . . accident." There was pain in his voice. "Madge and her husband Henry raised me as their son. They never had any children."

"It was very kind of them," I said.

"Oh, yes. They raised Stephanie too. We grew up together." He looked at me. "Are you sure you're interested?"

"Oh, yes! I want to know. But who is Stephanie?"

He grinned. "Now it really gets complicated. You see, Stephanie is the grandniece of Henry Newell. She was an orphan too. The Newells raised us both."

I was not to know any more at that moment, for Bruce, seeing Miss Hillary start upstairs with the tray, said:

"Let me take that, Jennie. It's too heavy for you."

"Really, Bruce, you needn't bother."

58

"Melissa's had it a little rough here." His brown eyes met mine, then glanced away. "Sit down and talk to her."

"Oh, I'd love to," Miss Hillary said happily, relinquishing the tray to Bruce.

She settled herself beside me on the sofa and within seconds we were chatting. But my mind was on Bruce. He seemed for some reason to dislike Muriel and Bradford Newell, while they in turn probably resented his place in the family. The two of them were anxious to have Wildemere sold — and quickly. Then when the old lady died — which could not be far off — the resulting fortune, or a large part of it, would be theirs.

Miss Hillary might have been reading my mind, for as I forced my thoughts back to her, she was saying . . .

". . . because Bruce is the only one who doesn't seem interested in the fact that he is one of Madge's heirs. Still, who knows?" She stopped. "What am I saying? It could never in the world be Bruce. He's incapable of such a hideous act. I've known him since he came here as a youngster."

I waited for her to go on.

"Madge and Henry loved him as much — more — than a son. And so do I. He's a wonderful young man." She dropped her voice as Bruce re-entered the room. "He'd have made a marvelous villain in one of my murder mysteries. Temperamental, fascinating to women, a flamboyant personality. But moody — quite unlike Stephanie. Yet she understands Bruce so well."

There was a funny little pang around my heart at Miss Hillary's remark. Stephanie . . . Bruce had mentioned her too.

59

Miss Hillary continued, "Stephanie will be arriving next weekend. I haven't seen her in months. She's very beautiful, you know."

This time I identified the unhappy twinge. It was the same way I reacted back home when Dad compared me unfavorably with my brother Bob. Now Miss Hillary seemed to be saying *Stephanie is beautiful, while you are not*. Even worse was the jealous pain I felt at another girl's involvement with Bruce Murdock.

What is this? I asked myself. You never even saw Bruce Murdock before last night. You're eighteen and he's a lot older. There's a girl named Stephanie who's beautiful and understands him, whatever that means.

Then it happened. From upstairs there came a low moan. At first I thought it was an animal howling.

"What's that?" Muriel Newell said excitedly.

"It's coming from Madge's room!" Bradford said.

"It can't be!" Bruce said, coming into the room. "She was perfect when I left her a moment ago!"

The two Newells interlocked glances, then Muriel Newell said, "Come on, Bradford," and they left the room.

Dr. Perry picked up his medical bag, and started for the door. "Not another attack — not after yesterday. . . ."

I followed Miss Hillary up the stairs. When we reached the top Mrs. Volke appeared out of nowhere.

"What's this?" she asked. "Where is everybody going?"

She had something in her hand and as she spoke I saw her furtively drop it into her apron pocket.

I could not be sure in the dim light, but it looked like some small pills. What was she doing there? Was it possible that she, who was *upstairs*, had not heard the moaning we'd all heard so clearly down in the library? I could not believe it. She had to be putting on an act.

From the doorway of Mrs. Newell's room, Miss Hillary and I could see the old lady writhing on the bed.

"Where's the pain, Madge?" Dr. Perry was asking. "Where do you hurt?"

The old lady was fighting for breath. Her hands clutched not her chest, but her stomach.

"Is this where it hurts?" Dr. Perry touched the old lady's abdomen gently, and she nodded. He looked at her perplexed, but wasted no time.

"Quick!" he said to Bruce. "Get the ipecac! *Hurry!*"

I had seen the ipecac only the day before among the many bottles in the bathroom cabinet. I hastily stopped Bruce and said, "I know where it is!"

He stepped aside and I entered the bathroom, where I found the bottle and quickly brought it back to Dr. Perry. He took it wordlessly from me. Old Mrs. Newell's eyes were now closing, and he literally had to pour the emetic down her throat. Then he held a basin to the bedside as she spat up a strange greenish fluid. When she was finished she lay back, gasping, weak. The doctor prepared a syringe full of nitroglycerin and injected it into her arm.

"She's all right now. She should rest."

She was already dropping off to sleep. He said softly, "A nasty business. Very nasty."

As he spoke I noticed a fine white mist of powder in the blue Wedgewood saucer on the tray, next to the little sugar bowl that was kept up-stairs in Mrs. Newell's room with her tea things. At first I thought the powder was sugar, but it was not coarse enough in texture.

The doctor said, "I am taking the remains of this tea and the muffin with me. Although it seems hardly likely anything could be wrong with the muffins, since most of us ate the same batch."

I was about to tell him of the white powder in the saucer, but something held me back. Miss Hillary had said, "Trust no one." *Suppose Dr. Perry is the one?* I thought. *Suppose that powder is something peculiar?* All he had to do was say there was nothing wrong with it; we'd never know.

"Melissa, will you empty the contents of this cup into a small bottle, please? Then wrap up what's left of the muffin and bring them to me in the library."

"Yes, Doctor." I hurried out, delighted at the chance he'd given me. In the pantry I avoided Mrs. Volke's snooping eyes by turning my back on her while I poured the tea into a small bottle I found there, wrapped the muffin in tinfoil, and put both into a small paper bag. I furtively brushed the white powder from the saucer into a paper napkin and folded it up. Then I ran up the back stairs and, stopping in my room, put the napkin with the powder in it under some blouses in my bureau drawer. I hurried down to the library where Dr. Perry took the paper bag from me.

"Very good. I'll have these analyzed," he said.

"Why are you doing this, Doctor?" Bruce asked. "Why analyze that stuff?"

"For my own edification. I want to make sure it's what it seems to be, that it isn't . . ." Dr. Perry stopped there.

"Isn't what?" Bruce asked.

"Are you trying to imply that she was poisoned?" Bradford Newell said.

"I don't believe I'll answer that right now," Dr. Perry said.

"We've got a right to know!" Bradford Newell puffed out his cheeks like an angry rooster.

"Be quiet, Bradford," Muriel Newell said. "If Dr. Perry does not wish to tell us now, let's leave it that way."

Dr. Perry said, "Now listen to me, all of you. I'm going to set down a set of new rules. I want one person and only one to be answerable to me for what Madge takes into her system. This young lady," indicating me, "will be given instructions on how to administer Madge's medication."

Muriel Newell bristled. "Why her? I'm Aunt Madge's niece."

"I'm aware of that. With all due apologies to everyone present, I want to do things my way. This young lady has no connection with the family. Also, she kept a pretty cool head when an emergency arose."

Bruce looked at me quizzically, and I felt a blush spread over my face.

Turning to me, Dr. Perry said, "You seem familiar with sickrooms, Melissa."

"My best friend's mother was an invalid. I helped out sometimes."

Now everyone's eyes were on me. From Muriel Newell and her husband there was unmistakable hostility. Mrs. Volke sniffed contemptuously at the new turn of events.

"A wise choice, Gordon," said Miss Hillary, contentedly.

"Any objections, Bruce?" the doctor asked.

To my surprise, Bruce said, "No. She's just a kid, but — it's all right with me. Now if you'll excuse me, I've got to get back to work."

Bruce's leaving broke up the group. Dr. Perry led me back upstairs, where he explained in detail how Mrs. Newell's medicine worked. He took a bottle from his medicine bag.

"This is digitalis. She's to get .25 milligrams a day — two tablets of .125 each — one in the morning and one at night. Got that straight?"

I nodded.

He then told me about her other medication: a tranquilizer for her nerves, some vitamins and iron pills, a barbituate for when she couldn't sleep.

"Above all," he cautioned me, "*never* give her the nitroglycerin unless she's having an attack. The digitalis on Monday was a mistake."

I looked up from the pad on which I was carefully writing down the various kinds and amounts of medicines. "Shouldn't I keep the digitalis and the nitroglycerin in separate places?" I asked.

He smiled. "A very good idea. That way we won't have a recurrence of Jennie's mistake. She's normally very clearheaded. But she's terribly devoted to Madge, which is why she panicked. And," he added ruefully, "she's not getting any younger. None of us is. Which is why I'm glad they chose a youngster this time."

He added, "One more thing, Melissa. Don't let Mrs. Newell know that we suspect anything wrong with her tea this afternoon. She thinks it's just a stomach upset. Above all, she is not to worry. Worry alone can do her great harm."

"I won't say a word to her," I promised.

When the doctor left, I decided to check out my list against the items in the medicine chest.

As Dr. Perry had explained, there were the vitamins, tranquilizers, sleeping pills, nitroglycerin, digitalis. . . .

And suddenly I noticed something peculiar.

A vial of white pills with a label that said, "Dr. David Gould." The pills were identical in size, color, and shape with the digitalis.

Had Dr. Perry known about this other vial? What was in it? Why hadn't he mentioned it? Was he trying to confuse me even while he turned all responsibility for Mrs. Newell's medication over to me?

And what if the one marked "Dr. Gould" did *not* contain digitalis? Suppose I gave one of those pills to the old lady by mistake, would it make her sicker than she was?

I sat down on the window seat and looked out at the green lawn mottled with shade from the ancient cedars, trying to figure it out.

What about the powder I'd found? Why hadn't Dr. Perry noticed it? Or had he seen it and deliberately said nothing?

If it was a poison, who had dropped it into her tea?

Was it Dr. Perry himself? He'd been up to see Mrs. Newell a few moments before.

Was it Bruce, who had insisted on bringing the old lady's tray upstairs? Or Miss Hillary, who had prepared the tray? Or Mrs. Volke, who had hidden something in her pocket? Even Mr. Pickett, and the two younger Newells — all of them had had equal opportunity during their visit upstairs to Mrs. Newell's room before they'd gone down to have tea in the library. Any of them could have done it, by just dropping the white powder into the small sugar bowl.

I went to the tea tray and looked for the sugar bowl, to examine its contents. It wasn't there. I searched the room — but it was gone. Someone had taken it away.

At least I had proof that Miss Hillary was not just a kooky old lady. Someone was certainly trying to murder old Mrs. Newell.

I took a pill out of the vial marked "Dr. David Gould," wrapped it in a piece of tissue and brought it to my room, where I put it under my blouses, together with the napkin containing the white powder.

If I were going to be a help to Miss Hillary I needed to find out if either the pills or powder were poison. But how? Suddenly I thought of Don Wilford. He was the one who could help me. As a medical student he would have access to a laboratory.

If only he would phone! Why hadn't he called me?

CHAPTER SIX

THAT WEEKEND, the dark cloud of death began to descend over Wildemere.

I had gotten settled into the routine of the mansion, and even written a letter home, telling my folks all the good things about my job and leaving out the problems. To read my letter, no one would suspect the disaster that was brewing.

Friday turned out to be one of Mrs. Newell's cranky days. I'd start reading from one book, and she'd make me switch to another.

"Enough Shakespeare for today. I'm not in the mood. How about Robert Browning?" Minutes later, "Browning bores me. I'll bet he bored Elizabeth Barrett Browning sometimes too. Let's try Ogden Nash. He's always amusing." And five minutes later, "What's wrong with me? Or is it you, Melissa. Your voice is putting me to sleep!"

I said, "Maybe you don't want me to read to you today. Do you want to sleep?"

"No, I don't," she said, irritated. "Why do people always say old people and babies should get more sleep? Probably to be rid of us. Do you wish you were rid of me, Melissa? Do I bore you?"

"Not at all, Mrs. Newell," I said truthfully. She could be difficult, stubborn, out of sorts, often demanding, but never boring.

"I bore myself, my dear." She sighed wistfully.

Then I had an idea. "Would you like to play Quotations? It's a game Miss Anderson, our town librarian, taught me."

Her eyes brightened. "Quotations? How does it go?"

"One of us picks a quotation out of a book. The other tries to finish it, to guess who wrote it, or where it came from."

"It sounds like fun. Let's try it."

We started playing. I took a book of humorous verse from the shelf and chose a short poem. I quoted:

> "I've never seen a purple cow,
> I never hope to see one;"

Instantly she broke in:

> "But I can tell you, anyhow,
> I'd rather see than be one.

"That's Gelett Burgess! He wrote it!" she said triumphantly. "Am I ahead?"

"You are," I said. "Now you've got five points and I have zero. But I still get my turn."

"Poor girl," she said cheerfully, not meaning it. "I'm going to beat you in this game. I'm so glad you thought of it."

Happy that I'd been able to help her out of her bad mood, I smiled back at her. She looked at me

68

keenly for a moment, then said, "You know, you're quite pretty, Melissa. But you don't make enough of your looks."

I flushed self-consciously, but she continued in her willful, charming way, "Don't be embarrassed. It's true. I wish I were up and about. I'd take you down to New York City and really turn them loose on you — new hairdo, new clothes, new makeup — the whole works." She looked at me again and nodded, "Yes, the same sort of thing I did with Stephanie years ago. Made all the difference in the girl. She's quite stunning, you know."

"Is it true that she's coming here?" I asked.

"Day after tomorrow, I believe." Her voice became confiding. "You know, I've been longing to see Stephanie. She and Bruce have always adored each other. Of course, she was far too young for him. But now she's twenty-two and he's going to be thirty and the age difference doesn't matter anymore. Don't you agree?"

I nodded and felt miserable. The truth was that I was terribly attracted to Bruce Murdock. Judging by what the old lady was inferring, he and this girl Stephanie were emotionally involved with each other . . . and I didn't like it.

". . . as far as marriage is concerned, I don't want to push things," she was saying now. "But nothing would make me happier— and they both know it."

It was ridiculous for me to feel the way I did. Bruce Murdock represented something far out of my reach . . . a world not meant for me, Melissa Prescott, Plain Jane from Wellsville. But it hurt all the same.

"Oh, look!" Mrs. Newell pointed to a golden

globe outside the window. "Ivan!" she called.

The golden ball uncurled itself into a beautiful ginger cat. He yawned lazily and, as Mrs. Newell continued calling his name, padded into the room, stopped a moment, then leaped onto the bed. He purred loudly and rubbed his back against the old woman's thin white arm.

"This is Ivan. Terribly independent, as you can see. Is this the first time you've seen him, Melissa?" I nodded. She went on, "I thought so. Ivan hates storms. He probably took himself down to the cellar near the furnace the night you came."

"I've never seen such a gorgeous cat," I said, and the old lady beamed.

The rest of that afternoon was easy. I gave Mrs. Newell her four o'clock dose of digitalis, and after playing a game of dominoes, left her dozing off with Ivan curled up near her feet. It was a peaceful scene . . . a peace that was soon to be brutally shattered.

We had just finished dinner that night — Muriel and Bradford Newell and I — when the doorbell rang. My heart leaped as I saw who was standing in the corridor. It was Don!

In his light tan raincoat, belted tightly and with the collar turned up against the night air, his blond hair tousled, clean and shiny, his handsome face wearing a broad grin, he was a beautiful sight.

"Forgive me for dropping in without notice," he said, "but I had to pick up some chemicals at the lab in Cortlandt and I was just a mile away."

Emile stood near us like a watchdog posted to keep interlopers out. Ignoring him, I said to Don, "I'm so glad you're here! Please come in!"

Then I realized there was no place to go. I could not take him up to my room and where else in the house did I actually belong? But Don seemed to grasp the situation.

"I can stay only a few minutes, Melissa, and it's a great night. Can't you come outside for a while?"

I said to Emile, "Please tell Mr. and Mrs. Newell I'll be gone for . . ."

". . . fifteen minutes," Don said.

Emile grumbled something, but Don and I walked out between the two huge columns, down the white stone steps toward the garden, pale in the moonlight.

"Melissa, I've wanted to be in touch with you, but it's been a real rat race at school. And when it comes to trying to find an available phone, forget it. How are you?"

"I'm fine, Don. I'm so pleased you're here."

"I really shouldn't have stopped," Don said, taking my hand in his and looking at me closely, "but I've been worried about you. Do you like your job? How are they treating you? Everything okay?"

"Yes — and no. There's something I've got to talk to you about."

Quickly I told him what had been happening at Wildemere.

When I got to the part about old Mrs. Newell's strange digestive attack earlier that week, Don was extremely interested.

"You say she was retching?" he said. "Did her lips seem bluish? And tell me again what the doctor said about the tea."

It was his questions that made me remember the powder.

When I told him what I had done, I felt a little foolish, thinking I was making a big deal out of nothing. But Don was excited.

"You mean you scooped up some of the powder and saved it? Good girl!" He squeezed my hand.

We had been walking slowly around the house and now were heading toward the back, where I'd never been. The general rundown condition of Wildemere was even worse here. Some woods bordered the land to the far left; evidently there was swampland not too far off. The smell of decaying vegetation mingled with the scent of salt air. An owl hooted hollowly nearby, and I was startled. Don turned to me.

"Listen, Melissa, you seem to have walked into some peculiar setup here. I don't like it at all. I want to help you."

"Oh, Don, thanks!" I said, feeling relieved. "Ever since Miss Hillary told me her suspicions, I've been desperate to talk to someone."

"What's she like, this Miss Hillary? Can you trust her?"

"You've got to meet her, Don. She's a terrific old lady . . . very bright. Used to be a well-known writer. She and Mrs. Newell have been friends for ages."

"Well, if she knows what she's talking about, you could be putting yourself in danger. Whoever wants the old lady dead would want you out of the way as well."

That did it. Don's words crystallized the growing fear that had been gnawing at me.

"I know, and it scares me, Don. But what can I do?"

He stopped beneath an old beech tree that hung over us like a monstrous black cloak.

"You can leave here," he said earnestly. "Get out while you're still all in one piece."

"I couldn't do that."

"Why not?"

"Because . . . I *care* about that old lady." Trying to explain things to him helped me to understand my own feelings. "Don, no matter what happens, I couldn't possibly go away from Wildemere now . . . and leave that poor old woman to the mercy of those people. The trouble is, Dr. Perry insists she mustn't worry. He says it would only make her heart condition worse. Otherwise, I could warn her about the danger she's in. He's probably right, but it's another reason why I feel I must stay."

"Okay, Melissa. I understand, though I still think you'd be a lot better off if you cleared out now." He drew me closer. "But if you won't . . . I'll try to help you. Just promise me you'll be careful, won't you?"

"I promise."

"Fine," he said. "I'll never forgive you if you let yourself get bumped off."

I laughed at his joke happily; I could relax with him now that I'd told him my problems.

In the moonlight, Don glanced at his wristwatch. "Say, I'd better be getting back and I'll take that powder along with me. Think you can sneak it out to me?"

"Sure. It's upstairs in my bureau drawer. It'll just take a minute to get it."

I started away, but Don seized my arm. "Melissa, wait! Don't go yet."

What he had in mind I don't know, for in that instant we heard a sound nearby and something

73

moved in the shadows. Frightened, I grabbed Don's arm.

"Who's there?" Don asked.

Silence. Then from the heavy foliage, Bruce Murdock stepped out toward us.

"You!" His tone showed great displeasure.

"Bruce! Oh, you scared me," I said.

As I introduced them, I was wondering what Bruce was up to. How long had he been here? How much had he heard? Don was friendly, warm, smiling. Bruce was quite the opposite, barely acknowledging Don. Turning to me, he said, "I thought I told you not to roam the grounds. Especially at night. Not even with one of your boyfriends." He was rude, patronizing. He obviously considered Don just a kid. I said quickly, "He's — a friend. He goes to medical school at . . ."

I would have gone on, but Don's eyes stopped me; they seemed to be telling me, *Don't say anymore.*

Bruce's face darkened. "Never mind! I haven't time to stand here arguing. I've got to get back to the stable. Bolivar is acting up again." He said curtly to Don, "Nice having met you," and without waiting for an answer walked off into the night.

"Well! He's not exactly a ray of sunshine, is he?" Don said as we started back toward the house. "I'm glad you picked up the cue, Melissa. I didn't think he had to know all about me."

"I know. I guess I talk too much," I said unhappily.

"No, you don't. But from here on out, you'd better be very careful. As Miss Hillary said, trust no one." He added mischievously, "Not even me."

74

"Don, you're a nut!" Part of me was horrified at the words that had slipped out. I'd been raised to be different with boys than with girls. You didn't just make jokes or relax in the company of men. There was a difference between the sexes that called for another kind of behavior with them. Somehow I felt it was linked with my father and the way I feared him. But I couldn't understand it. Don didn't notice my confusion.

"I'll wait here, Melissa," he said at the front door. "Be careful. Don't do it if anyone is around. Don't take any chances."

Fortunately I was able to slip up to my room, get the paper napkin with the powder in it, and the pill, without meeting anyone. When I got to Don's car, he took the packet and kissed me lightly on the forehead. "Good night, Melissa. I've really got to dash now. I'll be in touch with you when I find out what's what with our mystery powder — and that pill."

With another warning to be careful, he got into his car and drove off.

I started walking back to the house, when something drew my attention to the upper floor. There was a faint glimmer of moonlight in one of the darkened rooms upstairs, and I saw someone watching me from behind the curtain in the bay window.

It was the second room from the corner, and I could see the figure silhouetted by the moonlight behind it. It was hard to tell if it were a man or a woman.

Whoever it was — he was in my room.

I ran into the house, my heart pounding furiously. I felt I had to catch the intruder. I raced up the stairs and along the corridor to my room.

It was empty, of course, when I got there. However, hearing a noise at the other end of the hall, I peeked down it to see a dim figure disappearing around the corner leading to the back stairs.

It was just a glimpse that I got, but the figure was unmistakable to me even in the darkness.

Emile Volke!

CHAPTER SEVEN

THE NEXT DAY Mrs. Volke was almost friendly as I prepared Mrs. Newell's breakfast tray.

I wondered why.

Had they figured out that I'd caught Emile as he'd sneaked downstairs the night before? If the Volkes were the ones trying to do away with Mrs. Newell, maybe they had now decided it would be wiser to stop antagonizing me.

But why would they want Mrs. Newell dead? Would they benefit by the old woman's death? If so, what could it be? Five, perhaps ten thousand dollars at most? Miss Hillary had said the Volkes were paid a good salary; they seemed quite content with their jobs.

Or suppose Muriel and Bradford Newell — who *would* profit by their aunt's death — suppose they were willing to pay the Volkes to do away with their aunt?

What if it weren't the Newells? Dr. Perry, the old woman's lifelong friend and physician, might well have been left a large sum under her will. But he was a doctor with a lucrative practice and no skeletons in the closet, according to Miss Hillary. So why he? The same applied to Miss Hillary. As an old friend, even if she were to inherit a large sum of money what would she need it for? She was almost seventy, living in a cottage she apparently loved, and her needs were simple. No, profit motive for Dr. Perry and Miss Hillary were definitely out.

Bruce? Did he really like living the way he did? Suppose all these years he'd resented being an outsider, an adopted child. Some adopted children never got over the loss of their parents. And Bruce was a man of complexity, of unfathomable moods.

In spite of the danger, I felt I belonged at Wildemere. Since I had been given the responsibility of caring for old Mrs. Newell, I had known a new strength. I felt needed. The life I led here was another world from the one I'd lived back home.

If only I had known how the mystery of Wildemere was deepening, how the game of death was about to draw me in as one of its players.

That noontime I was in my room freshening up for lunch when I heard sounds of activity downstairs. Usually the house was still as a tomb; today it was humming. A green utility truck was parked out in front but the thick cedar trees outside my window obscured my view and I couldn't make out who the visitors were. When I answered Mrs. Newell's summons I found her much brighter than she had been the entire week I'd been there. The reason for it was soon clear.

"I'm so excited, Melissa! Today's the day the

78

men start getting the house ready for the big event."

I must have showed my surprise, for she said, "Don't tell me they haven't told you about it? My party?"

"A party?"

"Really, it's too bad of Muriel. Still, I think I know why she — or any of them, for that matter — hasn't mentioned it to you." She smiled wryly. "I'm fooling them all, my dear. They all expect me to shuffle off this mortal coil, as Shakespeare said, especially since those last two attacks." She leaned close to me from her pillow. "Do *you* think someone is trying to harm me, Melissa? Please, I want the truth."

Remembering Dr. Perry's admonition, I said cautiously, "How could anyone harm you? Even if they tried, it wouldn't do any good. You're being watched much too closely. Since Dr. Perry showed me how, I give you every bit of medication myself, and I keep it all locked in the cabinet. I even know what food you eat."

"Melissa, you're the one sensible move my niece Muriel has made in a long, long time." She sighed happily. "Now what were we speaking about? Oh, yes, my birthday party. Just two weeks from today. I'll be eighty, you know. It's going to be a really big affair. I gave orders to give the old house a good going-over. Even though I'm definitely going to sell it, I want one last big splash at Wildemere before I leave it."

As the clock struck noon, Miss Hillary came in.

"Jennie! Come in, come in! Can you stay for lunch?" Mrs. Newell asked.

"Well, I hadn't really intended to. . . ." Miss Hillary began.

Mrs. Newell, with a grand sweep of her hand,

said, "Good! Then you'll stay. We must talk about the party."

Miss Hillary gave a little shrug and smiled helplessly. "You see, Melissa? I'm putty in her hands."

"Make that lunch for two, please, Melissa," Madge Newell said.

Downstairs three men were draping the furniture in the living room with drop cloths, the kind house painters use. In the kitchen, Mrs. Volke ventured no explanation while I made two roast beef sandwiches and a salad. I asked no questions of her, not wanting to be snubbed for showing any curiosity.

When I went back upstairs, the two old ladies were talking excitedly.

"It will be just like Madge's engagement party fifty years ago," Miss Hillary explained.

"Fifty-two years ago," Mrs. Newell corrected her. "I was eighteen, Jennie. Henry was twenty-three." She giggled, reminiscing. "I really thought of him as an older man. Remember, Jennie? You were sixteen and yet I always thought *you* were the one who should be getting engaged. You always had so much more sense than I did."

"It wasn't your maturity Henry was interested in," Miss Hillary said drily, "and that applies to all those young men who cluttered the veranda of your father's house. My 'maturity' is probably the reason I stayed beauless and unmarried all my life."

"Why, Jennie Hillary! That simply isn't so. You could have had plenty of beaux. Whenever Henry and I had a fight, he'd say, 'If I had any brains I'd have married a sensible girl like Jennie instead of a scatterbrain like you, Madge.'"

She looked at me with a faintly wicked smile.

"I wasn't the easiest girl in the world to live with. Spoiled rotten by my daddy. Never could have gotten away with my tantrums and schemes with any of the young men today."

I was watching Miss Hillary while Mrs. Newell spoke, and wondered: Did she regret never having married? Whose life would mine be like — Mrs. Newell's, or Miss Hillary's? Would I end up unmarried too? Yet both women, each in her own way, seemed to have enjoyed their lives.

I learned from their talk that all the family and many old neighbors and friends in Cranston would be at the party. It was to be a gala, not only celebrating Madge Newell's seventieth birthday, but, since she would be moving to Florida, it would also be a farewell to the friends she'd known for half a century. It would be a re-creation of her engagement party in every possible detail. The menu would be the same; the same music would be played; the guests would do the same old dances, the Charleston, the tango, the two-step, the waltz. Mrs. Newell would wear a white dress similar to the one she had worn that night.

Mrs. Newell said cryptically, at one point, "Who knows? Perhaps I'll be able to make a surprise announcement on July first, just as one was made at my party."

"What do you mean, Madge?" asked Miss Hillary.

"Wait and see," Mrs. Newell teased.

I wondered if I would be invited to the party. Or was I considered just one of the help? If I were invited, I had a problem. I had nothing to wear — I knew that the dress I'd bought back in Wellsville for the senior prom would be ridiculously out of place. From what I could gather,

81

there would be at least seventy guests, all of them dressed to the hilt for the big event . . . the final one . . . at Wildemere.

The house was in a kind of ordered chaos that day.

While I was fixing tea and dessert in the kitchen for the old ladies, Bruce came in. My heart leaped when I saw him, but I managed to conceal it. He seemed preoccupied — quite different from the way he'd been last night when he'd found Don and me together. Today he was acting as if I weren't there.

"Would you like some soup, Bruce?" Mrs. Volke asked. "Emile fixed a big pot of mushroom, beef, and barley soup. It's very good."

"How about Goldilocks? Doesn't she get any?"

Mrs. Volke said, "If she wants some, she can have it. She knows how to help herself."

I felt my face redden with annoyance, but I picked up the tray and walked out of the room. As I left I heard Bruce say, "Touchy, isn't she?"

Mrs. Volke answered something I could not make out.

When I got upstairs, Mrs. Newell said, "I hate those wheat biscuits, Melissa. Can't I have some of the ones with cheese?"

I nodded and came back down to the kitchen, where Bruce said, "Come and have some soup with me."

"I'll have some later," I said.

"Have it now," he persisted. "Keep me company."

"I can't. I have to take this up to Mrs. Newell."

"Then take it up and come back down." His eyes were regarding me with that half-amused quirk that made me feel like a foolish teenager. "Please," he said in a deep voice, impossible for me to refuse.

"All right. I'll be right down." When I came back I ladled out a bowl of soup and sat down beside him. He looked at me with that piercing gaze.

"I was just thinking . . . you've been here, what is it — two weeks? — and I haven't learned one single fact about you." He sounded as if he might be joking, but I couldn't be sure.

"That's right. I haven't learned one single fact about you either." The moment I said it I realized I sounded fresh. I hadn't meant to be.

"That's hard to believe," he retorted. "Aunt Madge and Jennie are a couple of pretty talkative gals. I'll bet you've heard many an earful in that room."

"No, I haven't. They do very little gossiping. And I've never heard them speak about you at all."

"Well, what would you like to know? If I tell you, will you tell me?" His voice was bantering; I felt that he was being condescending.

"I'm really not that interested," I said, and was instantly horrified to hear the words. What was wrong with me? What was there about this man that brought out the worst in me? I expected him to be angry, but he only laughed.

"Have I offended you? I didn't mean to." He put out his hand and placed it over mine. I knew it meant nothing to him, but the touch of his hard brown hand on mine once again sent that strange, exciting feeling through me.

I was dreadfully embarrassed. I hated this side of myself that betrayed me when I most needed to be able to think coolly. I did want to know about Bruce. I wanted to know all about him. But not in a joke, not as if he were doing me a favor.

He took his hand from mine. "Forgive me, Melissa. I know I have a tendency to treat you as if you were a kid sister — but I don't think of you that way. I really don't." He looked thoughtful. "I know what it's like to be young and alone in this place. It's the way I felt for a long long time — until one day, I felt I belonged."

He went on to tell me about his life at Wildemere and why he loved it so.

"College was not for me. I can't stand to be boxed in. I started studying to be an architect like my father, but I ended up in agricultural school." He grinned at me. "I'm just a farmer, Melissa. A plain, ordinary farmer. I'm only happy when I'm out-of-doors. If I had to do a desk job in a big city skyscraper, I'd flip out. Completely."

He broke off. "I'm talking too much about myself. Are you sure you're interested?"

More than anything in the world I wanted him to continue speaking to me like that, intimately, his eyes making contact with mine. I wanted to know all about him — every last detail.

I was so absorbed, I was only toying with my soup, and he went on. "My dad was an architect. The war was just over . . . he'd just come back from overseas. He was a kind of — war hero. Very daring and all that." His face softened. "He lost a leg in combat. Went on a mission that killed all six of his men and left him maimed for life."

He paused, and I thought that perhaps he was sorry he'd started talking about it.

"If you don't want to tell me . . ."

He straightened up. "But I do. I feel that it's important for you to know a lot about everyone . . .

84

everything . . . at Wildemere. I think it places you in an unfair — perhaps dangerous — position not to know. I was wrong to speak to you the way I did that first night in the library." He grinned at me. "I must have scared you."

"You did," I confessed.

"I was thoughtless, Melissa. I often am." He frowned and went on. "After the war Henry Newell was anxious to give up Wildemere and settle in Florida. He had my father draw up plans for the new home. My parents and I moved in here for a couple of months so Dad and Mr. Newell could work on the Florida project. It was to be even more lavish than Wildemere. Then it happened."

I could barely restrain my curiosity. "What?"

It was obviously difficult for him to talk, but he seemed determined to go on. He said in a low, sad voice, "There was an accident. My mother and father died here at Wildemere. In the marshland that borders the lake. They died together one night in a quicksand bog."

I gasped and put my hand to my mouth, shocked.

"That's why I was . . . worried when I saw you last night with that Don fellow. It's dangerous at Wildemere — particularly at night." He put his hand under my chin and slowly turned my face directly to him. "Promise me you will never, never wander out at night alone."

His eyes held mine; I felt half hypnotized by them. I said, "I promise, Bruce."

He looked at me for a long moment, then pushed back his chair. "All right then. That's settled. One less complication to worry about here."

So now I was just a "complication." I could hardly believe he could have changed so quickly.

In that instant the warmth and feeling of only a moment before was gone. In its place was the cool indifferent man he so often was. Apparently he already regretted having taken me into his confidence and wanted to put us back on the same basis as before. I felt pushed aside, rejected. I got up from the table.

"Excuse me, I have to go up to Mrs. Newell."

Saving what little dignity I could, I hurried out of the room and left him standing there. I went upstairs and shut the door to my room and started to cry. Bruce Murdock was much too much for me. I had been minding my own business when he had insisted I have lunch with him. Then, after making me feel important, a part of the life at Wildemere, he had tuned me out, with the air of a man who has just disposed of an unpleasant task.

I couldn't understand him. By the time my tears disappeared, I had made up my mind that I would stay away from him in the future. No matter what happened, I would stay away.

That was my determination, but I had no way of knowing that I could not live up to it.

And I had no way of knowing the terror that lay in wait for us that very night.

I was in a deep sleep. I had gotten into the habit of leaving my door open so I could hear any sounds from Mrs. Newell's room.

I awoke from a dream to hear a strange high voice, calling, calling. I sat up and rubbed my eyes. That funny, half-human voice . . . was it mine that I had heard? Had I cried out in my sleep?

Then I heard it again . . . an other-worldly

86

cry that seemed to be coming from the garden below.

AAIIEEOOO. The wailing sound sent shivers through me. I ran to the window and flung the shutters wide open.

Then I saw it. In the darkness, sitting on the stone wall separating the garden from the bushes, was a black cat. I sighed with relief. No doubt a friend of Ivan's come calling in the night. But then I heard the high, thin, ghostly sound again: *AAIIEEOO!* I saw the cat's jaws open, the cat was speaking . . . crying out a name!

Crying out:

Madge! Madge!

CHAPTER EIGHT

A CHILL ran up my spine as I watched, unbelieving. Suddenly the cat jumped down and disappeared into the darkness. But still there came that eerie spirit voice, keening, *Madge, Madge, Madge.* Ending on a note that trailed off into the misty night air.

It was terrifying. Then I realized that old Mrs. Newell's room was also in the front of the house. Surely, if she were awake, she must be hearing it!

I ran down the hall in my nightgown, hair flying behind me, heart racing, fearful of what I might find.

My worst fears were realized. In the moonlight streaming in from the window, the old lady was backed against the headboard of her bed in a paroxysm of fright.

"It's here! It's come to get me!" She was whimpering like a child.

I snapped on the bedside lamp and sat down

beside her. I was terribly scared, but I felt that I must not show it, that I had to quiet her down somehow. I took her in my arms, as if she were a small child; and I felt almost like her mother as I held her close and patted her.

"Don't worry," I said, forcing myself to sound calm. "I'm here, Mrs. Newell. I'm with you. Nothing's going to happen."

She was shaking with fear.

"Melissa! You heard it?"

"Yes, I did. But you mustn't be frightened."

"You don't know, you don't know! It's her! She's come back from the grave! It's Ellen, my old nurse, Ellen Coyne. She's come to get me!"

"No one's come to get you. No one can. Nothing like that is going to happen," I said.

"It's Ellen's ghost! I know it!"

Her eyes were dilated, and I was afraid of what might happen next. So I decided to take the risk.

I took her by the shoulders, and looked straight into her eyes.

"Mrs. Newell, you're too intelligent to believe in ghosts. I heard exactly what you did — and you're right. Someone *was* calling out there — but it was someone alive, not a spirit." She stopped whimpering and was paying attention at last. "Please, Mrs. Newell — listen carefully. Someone is trying to frighten you. But it's someone real — not a ghost."

She stared at me, her blue eyes measuring me. I nodded. "Someone is trying to make you ill, really ill. Whoever it is, we mustn't let him succeed."

Oddly, the information seemed to steady her. She said in a calmer voice, "No, we mustn't. That is, if you're right. But . . . how could anyone sound so much like Ellen?"

89

I thought a moment. "It would have to be some-one who knew you when Ellen worked for your family, when you were a child. . . ." I broke off lamely.

"Oh, Ellen stayed on with us long after I grew up. Why, she was working here in the household until she died," she said.

"When was that?"

"Let me see . . . eight? . . . no, nine years ago." She looked at me anxiously, her frail body still trembling. In a voice almost like a child's, she said, "Melissa, tell me the truth. You really don't think it was Ellen? Or that something is sending me a signal that I am going to die?"

"No, I don't. You know there are no ghosts or spirits."

"I've never believed in such things. But who would do such a thing to me?"

"That's what we're trying to find out."

"We?"

"Miss Hillary and I."

"Jennie?"

I nodded. She gave an enormous sigh. "Now I do feel better. If anyone can find out who's behind this, Jennie's the one to do it."

We spoke a few more minutes and then I got her the sedative which Dr. Perry had said she could have whenever she seemed disturbed. I heated a cup of cocoa, and as she drank it, she looked at me gratefully.

"I feel so much better, Melissa. I really do."

My eyes went to the purple damask chaise longue in the bay window. "I could sleep on that tonight," I said.

"Oh, Melissa! Would you?"

"Of course."

"Are you sure you'll be comfortable? It isn't really meant for sleeping on," she was protesting, but feebly.

"It'll be fine, honestly. I think we'll both sleep better too."

From a linen closet in the corridor I took some sheets, a pillow, and a lightweight silk coverlet. Within minutes I had made up a cozy sleeping place on the lounge. I kissed Mrs. Newell on the cheek and put out the light.

I settled down on the chaise longue, but my mind was racing. I kept remembering that weird black cat sitting on the fence, howling in the night. Had he jumped up there of his own accord, or had he been lured there? And what cat could be trained to jump on a wall and howl?

Then who could have been calling? The voice was high and thin. A man could have made that sound, if he were using a falsetto voice. Another thing: No lights had gone on in the house. Evidently I was the only one besides old Mrs. Newell who had heard. But the Volkes and Mr. and Mrs. Newell slept on the other side of the house — they need not have heard. Was it one of them who had made that strange sound? Whoever it was was trying to frighten the old lady to death.

The next day after breakfast, Muriel Newell came in with Mrs. Volke and made a big fuss when she found I had slept in her aunt's room. But the old lady told them in no uncertain terms.

"I want another bed brought in here — a studio couch. There's no reason why Melissa can't spend the nights in my room," she said.

"But why?" Muriel Newell persisted. "That's what I can't understand."

The old lady's eyes and mine met. By a tacit understanding, neither of us said anything about the voice calling in the night. That morning at breakfast neither the housekeeper nor Emile nor Mr. and Mrs. Newell had mentioned anything about it. Either they had not heard or were pretending not to.

"You're beginning to annoy me, Muriel," Mrs. Newell was saying, "I don't want to discuss it any further!"

And in that imperious way of hers she waved them out of the room.

While she was eating lunch, I went down to the library to read. The sun had shifted and the quiet, dark-paneled room was cool in the summer day. I sat in the big wing chair I liked so much; there was a small bowl of chocolates on the table beside me, and as I read I took one from time to time.

Suddenly I was conscious of whispering in the hall outside. By remaining very still, I was able to make out voices. It was Mrs. Volke and her husband. He seemed to be trying to keep her from doing something.

"It's all right, Emile! Leave it to me," I heard.

Then "You're taking a terrible chance! If the old woman . . ."

"Give me that!" one of them said; I couldn't tell who it was.

I got up and tiptoed across the deep Persian carpet to the doorway.

Mrs. Volke said to her husband, "You fool! You'll spoil everything if she finds out what you did."

Then, suddenly — "What's that?! Did you hear?"

"Hear what?"

92

"In the library."

"I'll take a look."

I sped back to the wing chair, but sat down hastily and accidentally knocked the candy bowl over with a clatter. Mrs. Volke came in at that instant and saw the chocolates strewn over the floor. Her face was purple.

"What are you doing here? Who said you could eat those? Look what you did!"

I looked at her coolly and began to pick up the spilled candies. "What I'm doing is taking my time off in the library. I have Mrs. Newell's permission to be here." At the nasty look she gave me, I added, "She particularly wanted me to try some of these chocolates. She said they were a gift from a friend in Zurich." I thought that if I got her angry, I might learn something.

She was furious, but there was nothing she could do. I was telling her the truth. Then I went on, hoping to rattle her, "Is there something wrong? I thought I heard you and Emile arguing."

That did it. She stepped forward and her voice was a whiplash of anger. "You'd better watch your step, young lady. I don't know how you got around the old woman, but I don't trust you!"

Emile appeared in the doorway. "She heard?" he said.

"Quiet, dumkopf!" she snapped.

"Just one big happy household, isn't it?" I said. I was being fresh, but I had learned it was not a bad way to deal with the Volkes. In their stolid, middle-European way they did not know how to cope with an American teenager. She gave me one last look, shoved her husband into the hall, and followed him out.

When I went up to the old lady's room, Muriel

Newell was there. "You can go out for a walk if you like, Melissa," she said. "Auntie and I will just have a nice chat. You won't be needed until five o'clock."

She spoke as if I were a servant. I thought, *She's trying to get back into her aunt's good graces by spending more time with her.*

I asked, "How would I get to Miss Hillary's house? She asked me to visit her."

"A splendid idea," said old Mrs. Newell. "Jennie loves company. Just take the path by the side of the house. It leads through the woods right to Jennie's door."

Leaving the house by the side door, I started down the path that began at the woods. The sun was bright and hot, so that when I reached the heavy growth of trees it was a pleasure to feel how cool it was in the shade. I walked along slowly, enjoying the beauty of the woods, paying little attention to where I was walking.

Suddenly there lay before me a clearing with a smooth grassy patch of land. In the center stood a small thatched cottage, gleaming white, with pretty green shutters and windows filled with flower boxes. It looked like a house in a fairy tale. A white ruffled curtain moved and there was Miss Hillary, calling through the open window, "Melissa! How lovely! Come round the front."

She threw open the door. "So you finally found your way here. I can't tell you how happy I am. Come in, my dear." She was genuinely pleased.

She led the way into her living room. "Now we can have a real tea party." She saw me looking around the room. "Make yourself comfortable. I'll be right back." She hurried off to the kitchen.

The room I sat in was charming. A graceful,

tufted blue chintz sofa and two small blue upholstered chairs to match were grouped in front
of a beautiful white brick fireplace. Delicate etch-
ings decorated the whitewashed walls. A low-beamed
ceiling added intimacy to the room. This house was
like Miss Hillary . . . inviting, gracious, charming.

In a few minutes, she returned, wheeling in a
tea table. In a shallow wicker basket, lined with
a white linen napkin, were freshly baked popovers,
giving off a mouth-watering aroma.

She watched anxiously as I took the first mouthful.

"It's fabulous," I said. "I've never tasted anything so delicious."

"I'm so glad. Have as many as you like, Melissa. When I was your age I had a wonderful
appetite." She sighed wistfully. "You're in the
best time of life, Melissa. Eighteen."

For some reason, the thought of home and my
dull life back in Wellsville came to my mind, and
I remembered the loneliness of that world.

"Maybe, but the way you live here, in this pretty
place, with all these lovely things around, and
friends you love up at the big house . . . this
must be a good time of life too."

"I have a lot to be thankful for, Melissa." She
sat down beside me on the sofa. "I've never had
much opportunity to be alone with you. And I'd
like to know all about you." She made a little
grimace. "We writers are a hopeless breed, in-
satiably curious."

So I told her all about myself, only half aware
that I had not felt this relaxed in all the time I'd
been at Wildemere.

"Having you up at Wildemere makes all the
difference, Melissa. I feel that whoever's threaten-

ing Madge is having a lot more trouble since you're there."

It was then that I told her about the cat in the night, and the strange voice calling for Madge.

She listened wide-eyed. At one point she broke in to ask, "It *was* Madge's name you heard? You said you saw a cat. Couldn't it have been just Ivan miaowing?"

"It wasn't Ivan. It was a strange black cat . . . and I heard the voice calling even after the cat disappeared. So did Mrs. Newell. It was no miaow. It was a woman's voice calling 'Madge,' clear as anything."

Her eyes flashed with anger. "Of course it's a trick, Melissa. It couldn't have been anything else." She sat frowning, lost in thought. "But who would do such a thing? Who would take such a risk?"

She didn't know about the argument the Volkes had been having that morning, so I told her.

"Maybe they planted that cat last night. Maybe that's what they were fighting about."

"Somehow, I don't think so. I find the Volkes' behavior most peculiar, Melissa. But while I can't explain why they're acting so strangely, I have lately begun to feel there's someone else whom we must watch closely."

"Someone else?"

She studied my face, then seemed to come to a decision.

"You must not tell anyone what I am about to reveal to you."

"You can trust me, Miss Hillary. I won't say a word to a soul."

"I won't be devious, Melissa. Last night as I lay in bed, I thought over what happened with

Madge's medicine that first day you started at Wildemere. You remember?"

"Yes, of course. The mixup in the bottles. We gave her digitalis instead of nitroglycerin."

"*I* gave her the wrong medicine, not you. I know Mrs. Volke thought I made an error. But I didn't, Melissa." Her clear gray eyes looked squarely at me. "I did exactly what Dr. Perry said. He said digitalis — and never mentioned anything about nitroglycerin. Or that it could do her real harm."

"You mean you think it was deliberate? That he didn't tell you because he wanted . . ." I finished lamely.

"I don't know what to think. Gordon Perry is a fine physician. It is most unlike him not to have mentioned what the wrong medicine could do to Madge." She shook her head incredulously. "I can't believe it. Yet it's not the only peculiar thing he's done." She passed a hand over her forehead and was suddenly sad. "Do you know what happened just a week before you came? He said he was going away for the weekend — Friday night to Sunday night — to Canada. But that weekend," she lowered her voice, "Saturday night I saw him in the woods back of the big house."

She went on, slowly, "He came to pay a house call to Madge on Monday, and told her what a lovely weekend he'd had in Canada. I can't believe it of Gordon. He's one of the finest men I've ever known. But why would he tell a lie like that?"

"Are you sure it was Dr. Perry? Maybe you saw someone who looked like him."

"It was Gordon Perry. He was just a few feet away. I couldn't have made a mistake. I wish I had."

Again she lapsed into a thoughtful silence. I sat quietly thinking my own thoughts, when suddenly she sat straight up in her chair.

"Wait a moment, Melissa. Things mayn't be all that black for poor Gordon. Didn't you say the voice from that cat you heard seemed to be that of a woman?"

"Yes. That's what it sounded like."

Her eyes lit up. "Listen, Melissa. I just remembered something else. Speaking in a high voice is one of Bradford Newell's minor talents. Years ago he played the lead woman's role in a play they gave at Chapman Military School. He was a big success."

She stopped, and bit her lip. "Melissa, you've given me a lot to think about. It's a mystery, all right, but it can be solved. The thing is, we must work quickly. Madge's would-be killer seems to be getting desperate."

She looked suddenly very tired. For the first time, every one of her years showed. I said, "If there's anything you want me to do. . . ."

She rose from the sofa. "What a terrible way to treat a new guest in my home. Forgive me, Melissa. I want to think about what you've told me. Meanwhile, let me show you the rest of the cottage. After that we'll have some chocolate layer cake. Come on, dear."

She led me through the living room to a small den, with an old-fashioned desk, a sewing machine, bookshelves, and a comfortable old rocker covered in cretonne. Next was the kitchen, also small, but neat and orderly, with a box of red geraniums in the sill. Her bedroom was cheerful, brightened by a yellow candlewick bedspread, cushions in yellow and green needlepoint, and a thick yellow hand-hooked rug on the polished floor. Next to her bedroom was a closed door.

"My workroom, Melissa. I'm tidy enough in the rest of the house, but I've got the writer's occupational disease when I work . . . the messier my workshop, the happier I am."

The next hour was a sheer delight. We talked and laughed a lot. Miss Hillary showed me some of the books she had written and told me how she got ideas for her stories. When I complimented her on the beautiful sofa cushions, she asked if I wanted to learn how to do needlepoint. I told her I did and she took me over to a big wicker basket beside the fireplace in which she kept needles, wool, canvasses, and painted designs all ready to be worked. I chose a design in the shape of a four-leaf clover, that was meant to be a case for a cushion, and we began working on it together.

When it was time to go, I said, "I've had a wonderful time, Miss Hillary. I've never enjoyed myself more."

Miss Hillary blushed. "Melissa, I didn't know there were girls like you around anymore. You're old-fashioned in a way and yet you're right up to the minute with your thinking. I have high hopes for your generation." She smiled. "Come on, dear, I'll walk you to the edge of the woods. It's all right in daylight, and it's the shortest way back, but I don't think you should ever come this way in the dark. Promise me you won't," she added anxiously.

"Why not?" I asked, remembering Bruce's earlier warnings.

"It isn't safe. You might lose your way, or . . . anything might happen."

"Then I won't come here at night."

I said good-bye and started back to Wildemere.

99

Dusk was not due to fall for another hour or so, but the sun had moved far over to the west and the woods were now in deep shade.

All the same, the forest was beautiful. In the peaceful glade, my thoughts began to wander — thoughts of home, of Don, of the sick old lady up at the house. And Bruce. As always my heart leaped as his face in fantasy came before me. I wished there were some way for me to talk as easily with him as I could with Don.

Then all at once a shadow caught my eye. Something was reflected on the trunk of a huge elm beside me, a shadow momentarily caught in a stray beam of sunshine that fell through the trees. Instinctively I turned around to see what could be causing it. There was a flash of black from behind a clump of bushes. Then it disappeared.

For a moment I thought it was my imagination, but then, between a small cluster of leaves I saw that deadly black flash again, and this time the bush moved. Something was after me!

A chill enveloped me. I went rigid with fright — then began to run down the path. I sped along to a point where it branched off. I was running as fast as I could. Left or right? I didn't know which to choose. Frantically, I took the left fork.

I heard my footsteps thudding, but the pounding of my heart was even louder in my ears as I ran furiously, half stumbling, half slipping on the fallen leaves. I looked back over my shoulder, hearing a sound in the bushes behind me, and saw a black-hooded figure slipping through the trees toward me.

The trees were thinning out now. Only bushes lined the way, and the ground beneath my feet was changing, becoming softer, spongy. It made it even harder to run, but I kept on, desperately, until I saw before me a rusted barrier of wire. It was a high fence, but directly ahead there was a break in it . . . an opening large enough for me to run through.

The ground beneath my feet now was swampland, but the footsteps behind me kept coming on, closer and closer. I felt a fearful stitch in my side as I tried to speed up but couldn't. Panic overcame me. Out of breath, filled with terror, I did not see the small clump of reeds that lay across my path. My foot caught in it and I fell face down on the damp marshy ground. The breath was knocked out of me completely. I couldn't get up. Still the footsteps came closer, and then stopped.

It was standing beside me.

I hid my face in my arms and clung to the ground. I felt the unknown horror bending over me and heard its breath. Helpless, knowing there was no way to escape, I began to cry — huge convulsive sobs I could not control.

Then something touched my trembling shoulders. A man's hand. From where I lay on the ground I involuntarily looked up and saw — Bruce!

My one thought was — *He's trapped me here in the woods. He's going to kill me*.

I screamed "No! No!" in a voice thick with terror.

"Stop that!" He knelt beside me. "What are you doing here anyway? Do you know what danger you're in?"

He lifted me from the ground, but I tried to shake free of him.

"You were chasing me," I said, half hysterical. "I saw you!"

Bruce stared at me as if I had taken leave of my senses. I took another look at him. He was dressed in his brown corduroys and tan shirt. "What did you do with your black hood?" I demanded.

"Whoa, there! You must have taken a pretty bad fall. What black hood?"

"I saw someone all in black, with a black hood, following me — in the bushes, through the woods. It was you! Then I heard your footsteps behind me."

"You sure did," he said. "Do you know what that is?"

His pointing finger indicated the small clearing ahead.

"*Do you know what this is?*" he repeated, angrily. "*It's quicksand!*"

He went on, "A few minutes in that, and you'd disappear forever! Just as my parents did."

I was too stunned to speak.

He cleared his throat. "I saw you running toward it and tried to stop you. Didn't you hear me call to you?"

"No," I said truthfully. "I heard nothing."

"Then you were too scared out of your wits to hear anything. If you hadn't fallen, it might have been too late," he said grimly. His eyes were dark and serious.

My lip quivered and my eyes filled with tears again. "Oh Bruce, if you're the one who's trying to kill Mrs. Newell . . ." the tears choked me and I couldn't go on.

"So that's what you think! And that's why you were frightened." His voice softened and he took my hands in his. "Listen, Melissa, if someone in black was here — and I'm not at all sure you didn't imagine it — it wasn't me. I don't want to kill my aunt. I want her to live. I love her."

I stood there, unable to speak.

"I'm sorry if I've been hard on you. Poor thing. Come here, you're trembling." He pulled me close to him, took out a handkerchief and wiped the tears from my eyes. Then, never taking his eyes from my face, he put a hand under my chin and tipped my head up to his. He held me tight and his warm lips touched mine. A flash of joy ran through me, a wild and wonderful joy such as I had never experienced in my whole life. My arms went around him in response to his kiss, and we stood that way for long moments. Then he took his arms away.

"I told you once you don't belong up here." His voice was harsh. "Well, you don't. I told you to stay close to home and you didn't. It will be a miracle if you last out the summer." His face clouded. "Come on, I'll take you back."

He strode off toward the house, while I followed behind almost in a daze, bewildered, and terribly hurt by that remark so like my father's — "You'll never last out the summer." I had to half run to keep up with his quick, angry steps.

When we reached the house, he said, "From here on, I want you to keep out of my way. I mean that. And you are to go no place outside this house alone. If you have to, get someone to go with you. Get that Don fellow or someone else. Understand?" He glared at me under fiercely drawn eyebrows.

"Yes."

He turned away abruptly and left.

The rest of that evening, as I brought Mrs.

Newell her dinner, then read to her and made her comfortable for the night, I had to force myself not to think about what had happened in the woods that afternoon. Alone at last in my room where I had gone to get my night things, I could not believe I was the same girl who had come to this house just two weeks before. All of a sudden I was alive. For something had happened between Bruce and me, something that might not have stirred him as deeply as it had me, but stirred him nevertheless.

Was this love? I must not believe that, my saner self reminded me. He is at least thirty years old and I am eighteen, a "country girl," and — according to my father — a second-rate one.

But all the thinking in the world did not help. I was in love with Bruce.

I slept in Mrs. Newell's room that night, but it was not a dreamless sleep. For even as my head whirled with thoughts of Bruce, I realized that tomorrow was Sunday.

Stephanie was due to arrive.

CHAPTER NINE

" 'HOW DO I love thee?' " said Mrs. Newell. "Your turn, Melissa."

" 'Let me count the ways.' Elizabeth Barrett Browning, *Sonnets from the Portuguese?*" I said.

"That's right," she said with a slight trace of annoyance. "Sometimes it isn't fun to play with you, you know so much."

My mind was only half on our game. The thought of Stephanie's imminent arrival made me dreadfully nervous. I did not have long to wait. A few minutes later a car screeched to a halt in front of the house.

"That's Stephanie!" Mrs. Newell said. "She's the only one who drives like that. Take a look, Melissa, won't you?"

I went to the window and saw a slender girl with long smooth blonde hair that the sunshine caught and rendered pure gold. A girl so striking she could have been posing for a TV commercial, stepping out of the old taxicab, taking up a multistriped, vividly colored suitcase. She looked up at the house, at the very window where I was, and caught me staring out like a country bumpkin. With a wave of her hand, she started up the walk.

"Melissa! Is it Stephanie? What are you standing there for?" Mrs. Newell demanded.

"Yes, it is. I'm sorry."

"Sorry for what? Don't always be apologizing," the old lady said, sounding slightly annoyed.

Sure, I thought. *I'm being put back into my place. The princess is arriving, and Mrs. Newell's got things back in perspective; she sees me for the ordinary creature I am.*

The door to the room was suddenly flung open and there stood Stephanie. Under that crown of blonde hair was a face molded into classic features, skin that was luminescent, dazzling green eyes, truly green, fringed by heavy black lashes. She flashed a smile, revealing white even teeth. It was a smile that lit her whole face, giving off a charisma so strong it was almost tangible. She was chic beyond words in a yellow pants suit.

I had never seen anyone so perfectly turned out. I stood like a fool and stared at her, thinking, *If I live to be one hundred I will never know how to put myself together like that.*

"Aunt Madge!" Her voice was the finishing touch to the perfect portrait of Stephanie. "So glad I'm here!" That slick prep school accent.

She smiled at me as she passed by to the bed. There she threw her arms around her aunt and hugged her warmly. Releasing her she said, "Let me look at you." She considered a moment. "Darling, you look fabulous."

106

"Stephanie, I look dreadful and you know it."

"You're gorgeous and you know it. You're Madge Newell, the belle of Wildemere."

She turned and said to me, "Forgive me! I'm so excited at seeing Auntie, I forgot. I'm Stephanie Newell."

Mrs. Newell said, "Oh, my dear, this is Melissa. Melissa Prescott."

"How do you do," I said stiffly, feeling like a Martian in the presence of these two elegant women.

"I've heard what a great job you're doing here, Melissa," Stephanie said quietly. "I'm grateful. We think a lot of Aunt Madge."

You're doing a good job, nice boy, good Fido, nice doggie. She was saying all the right things, but I felt I was being patronized. She was treating me the way the upper classes treated the help. And to Stephanie I was exactly that — someone her aunt employed.

"Have you finished decorating your apartment, Stephanie?" Mrs. Newell said. "If you need any money, just ask. It costs a lot to move about properly in society."

"No thanks, Aunt Madge." Stephanie dropped her eyes. Was she being evasive? I couldn't tell. "I don't need anything. Nothing at all."

Then Mrs. Newell began a long interchange with Stephanie, each bringing the other up to date. Once I tried to leave the room, but Mrs. Newell said, "No, stay. Just read or do something." I sat by the window and could only think of how jealous I was of Stephanie and of her knowing Bruce so well, and hated myself for it.

Occupied with my miserable thoughts, I scarcely heard Bruce come in. If I had any doubts about their relationship, they were quickly dispelled. They ran to each other, and embraced for what seemed to me an eternity. When Bruce let her go, Stephanie was breathless. Her eyes were glowing and she was radiantly beautiful. Bruce held her back at arm's length.

"There ought to be a law against any one female being allowed to look this great," he said and hugged her tight. "How I've missed you!"

"I want to hear all about the party," Stephanie said when she broke away from Bruce.

"Aren't you hungry, Steph?" Bruce asked.

"I am, but it can wait. Who's invited? Who's arranging everything? Tell me all," Stephanie said.

"Can I take her away from you, Aunt Madge?" Bruce said. "The poor girl's starving and I arranged for Mrs. Volke to make her favorite dish."

When they had gone, Mrs. Newell said, "I've waited so long for this. Those two belong together. Blood lines will tell, you know." She leaned close to me. "Don't tell a soul, Melissa, but that's the announcement I'm going to make the night of my party. I'm announcing the engagement of Stephanie and Bruce!"

That night as I lay in bed the old familiar pangs swept over me. *Dad was right about me. I am second-rate.* The thought of Stephanie and that perfection — from the tip of her blonde-capped head to the toes of her Gucci shoes — sent waves of jealousy through me. I must have been out of my mind to think Bruce could feel anything for a nothing girl like me. But that was just like me — imagining bright prospects where there were none. *"You're always letting your imagination run away with itself, Melissa,"* Dad always said.

He was right. I couldn't cope with the kind of situation I now found myself in. It was what I'd done all my life; try to take a giant step and then — take a terrific fall. Then Dad and the family would help me up, set me on my feet, set me straight. No wonder that sick feeling in the pit of my stomach had me in tears as I lay in the dark of Mrs. Newell's room, trying to hold myself together, trying not to waken her.

I would leave Wildemere and go home, where I belonged.

Sleep was impossible. That was why I heard the footsteps outside in the early hours of the morning. Who could be walking there at that time? I jumped out of bed. By the small night-light I saw that it was 2:15. Wondering who it could be, I ran to the window, but saw no one through the trees that masked the walk.

I stepped out into the corridor and a few moments later, two ghostly figures appeared out of the shadows. Bradford and Muriel Newell.

They were in their nightclothes, but Muriel Newell had a light coat slung over her arm.

"Who's that?" It was Bradford Newell's whiny voice. "Is that you, Melissa?"

"Of course it is! Be quiet, Bradford," said Muriel Newell in a commanding tone. Then, "Why are you up, Melissa? What are you doing out here?" In the semidarkness I saw her nudge her husband.

It was typical of Muriel Newell. It was my job to take care of her aunt and I was where I belonged. The Newells were in a position that needed explaining. But she wasn't the explaining type. She took the offensive.

"You should be with my aunt. What are you looking for?"

"I heard footsteps. I guess when you were out there. . . ." She cut me off at once.

"Out where? You're imagining things. Bradford and I were in the kitchen having a little snack."

"That's right, some of that leftover smoked turkey. Really delicious."

"Shut up, Bradford!" she said rudely. Then, to me, "We didn't hear a thing. Not a thing."

How could you? I thought. *The kitchen is in back and the footsteps were out front. That is, if you were in the kitchen.*

"You may go to bed now," she said, dismissing me. I didn't want to go. Something didn't add up. Yet I had no choice but to leave.

Back in the room I lay in bed, perplexed. Someone had said something that didn't make sense. What was it? I replayed the conversation over and over in my mind. Then I remembered. That late snack — they couldn't have had one. At least not with the smoked turkey. I clearly recalled Mrs. Volke's remark at about ten o'clock that evening. Emile had come in for a sandwich and I had distinctly heard her say, "No more turkey left, Emile. They ate it all up at lunch."

So the Newells were lying! What were they doing outside at two in the morning? Suddenly the memory of the cat crying in the night came to my mind. Either one of them could have arranged it, with Bradford or Muriel Newell impersonating the old nurse's voice.

I heard old Mrs. Newell sigh in her sleep and I went to her bedside. The room was moonlit, and I stood there looking at her in the silver light from the window. She looked so small, so helpless. Some-

110

one was threatening her life. It could be anyone at all; at this moment the Newells had again assumed the position of prime suspects. Miss Hillary was right. No doubt my sleeping in the old lady's room was making it difficult for whoever it was who meant to harm her. If she were not constantly and carefully and honestly guarded by someone, she could be dead before morning.

Only one road lay ahead for me. I had to forget about myself and my own problems. I had to concentrate every effort on keeping one defenseless old lady safe from the very real danger that threatened her.

I could not go home.

CHAPTER TEN

"SINCE WE'RE giving Aunt Madge a party, let's make it one to remember," said Stephanie.

"I'm definitely unenthusiastic," Bruce said. "But I'll cooperate. If only we could get Madge to see things differently."

"But we can't. You know that, Bruce. This is no time for us to upset her."

"What I do think, Steph, is that you ought to break your news to her. I don't approve of this duplicity."

I had come downstairs into the hallway and heard them talking in the dining room. Stephanie saw me and came out to the hall just as I was picking up the mail from the table. She had only just gotten to Wildemere and yet there were two letters there for her already. I was surprised to see that they were both addressed to "*Ms*. Stephanie Newell."

"Hi, Melissa." Stephanie saw the two envelopes I was holding. "For me?"

"Yes." I hesitated, then decided to ask. "I see they're made out to *Ms.*, instead of *Miss.* Is that something new?"

"Sort of."

"What does it mean? Does it stand for *Miss* or *Mrs.*?"

"Neither. And both." She laughed at my puzzled expression. "Well, if men only have to say *Mister* — which doesn't tell anyone whether they're single or married — women should have the same privilege."

It was a totally new concept for me.

"You know, I never thought about it. But I think it's only fair."

"So do I. It's just a matter of what we've gotten used to."

"How do you say it? *Missssss?*"

"It's pronounced exactly as if it were spelled *Mizz.*"

I tried it on my own name. "Ms. Prescott. You know, I like the sound of it," I said.

"I'm glad," Stephanie said, smiling.

"You'll be sad if you don't get into lunch, sister."

It was Bruce. "Come on in. You're both late." He said to Stephanie as we went into lunch, "What were you two talking about?"

She said, "Nothing you'd be interested in."

I couldn't help thinking how up to the moment Stephanie was . . . not only in her clothes and lifestyle but in her thinking.

Within moments we were all, including Miss Hillary, gathered round the luncheon table. Mrs. Volke had spruced up the dining room with masses of flame-colored gladiolas and a center spread of glorious tea roses. Ever since Stephanie had come,

113

the meals had been superb. Obviously Stephanie was a pet of Mrs. Volke's. Today's lunch began with French onion soup in brown crockery bowls; then came little guinea hens stuffed with wild rice and mushrooms, and to top it off, Mrs. Volke had baked some delicate pastry shells and filled them with juicy ripe strawberries and whipped cream that floated like a cloud above them. When the meal ended, Stephanie threw her arms about Mrs. Volke and kissed her. It was the first time I'd ever seen Mrs. Volke smile. A nasty thought struck me: If it were the Volkes who were trying to harm old Mrs. Newell, and if they were doing it for someone else, couldn't it be Stephanie? The next moment I hated myself for wanting it to be her. I recognized the ugly thought for what it was — pure jealousy.

"Come with me into the library," Muriel Newell said when the meal ended. "I'll show you what I've done so far."

We followed her into the library, which was still draped with the drop cloths the painters and workmen had left. On the huge circular coffee table were strewn various papers, some of which Muriel Newell held up.

"Here's the menu exactly as it was served at Madge's engagement party fifty-two years ago, in 1922. This," indicating some yellowed handwritten pages clipped together, "is a list of the floral decorations; this is for the linen, dishes, and so forth."

"Ooh, let me see," said Stephanie. She reached for the sheaf of papers eagerly. Bruce was amused by her enthusiasm and looked at her with an intimacy that made me turn my eyes away.

114

I'd been trying to put him out of my mind. I'd managed to put into perspective what had happened between us in the woods the day before Stephanie came. I knew I meant nothing to Bruce.

So I'd decided to encourage Don Wilford. He wasn't exciting like Bruce, but he was steady and what he offered might someday turn into more than friendship. Again the truth came home to me. I was constantly reaching for what was beyond me. Was I doomed to repeat this pattern for the rest of my life?

The next half hour was spent discussing party preparations. When we were almost finished, the doorbell rang. It was Don.

The moment he came into the room I saw his and Stephanie's faces light. And why not? I thought. Stephanie was positively stunning. I couldn't blame him. They were two beautiful people, and beautiful people were like members of a special club. It didn't matter how they met; they could spot each other wherever it was — Wellsville, New York, Italy, anywhere.

"Aren't you going to introduce me?" Don said to me, looking at Stephanie.

"Sure," I said, and quickly made the introductions.

Stephanie came forward and put out her hand to Don.

"I'm so glad to know you," she said, turning on all her charm.

His admiration for Stephanie was painfully clear. I felt he was making comparisons between us, comparisons not in my favor. I was unhappy and ill at ease until he sat down and we went on with the party plans.

Among the yellowed menus and dance programs, I saw a photograph of the original party back in 1922. It was a faded, browned picture of a group of beautifully gowned girls and perfectly tailored men, in the flapper-age mode. In the center were Henry Newell and his bride-to-be, Madge. Even with that ludicrous hairdo and outlandish clothes, the young Madge was gorgeous. Henry Newell — tall, laughing, and strikingly handsome in an old-fashioned movie star kind of way — was standing beside her. Next to them was a sweet-faced young girl ("There I am, Melissa," Miss Hillary whispered to me.) Next to her was another young man, almost as handsome as Henry Newell. ("Dr. Perry. He was just a medical student then," Miss Hillary said.) The rest were people I couldn't identify — relatives, friends. There was an enormous elegance in that photograph. It told of a world I never had known, never would know . . . the joyous world to which Stephanie and Bruce belonged. And, possibly, Don Wilford, I thought, remembering that gourmet lunch of his on the bus.

Yet something instinctively told me theirs was not a real world. This faded photograph of a party long dead; this house, Wildemere, with its faded elegance, elegance long dead; and the people in it alive but not really alive — I knew in my deepest self that Wildemere represented a way of life that wasn't relevant to the world today. In today's world, while there were still great differences in our society, it was our job to change it, to break down the barrier between those who had a lot and didn't care and those who cared a lot and didn't have.

I was shaken from my reverie by the officious voice of Muriel Newell.

116

"You realize there isn't a minute to lose. We've all got to start doing our assigned tasks . . . particularly getting to town to shop for the basics. Don't you agree, Stephanie?"

"Oh, I do, Muriel! The party's only two weeks away!"

"Exactly," Muriel Newell said smugly. "I think you should get into Boston today, Stephanie, and pick up the urgent items." She turned toward Bruce and said archly, "Bruce darling, you know Stephanie doesn't like driving in all that city traffic. You could drive her in, couldn't you?"

"I could, but I'm not going to," he said. "I've got the vet coming in to look at Bolivar, and a dozen chores that need attention. Can't spare the time."

"Giving me the brush-off?" said Stephanie, laughing up at Bruce. "Well, it isn't the first time. There must be some way I can get into Boston, outside of walking."

Did I imagine it or was that a clear invitation to Don? Whatever it was, Bruce said with annoyance, "Don't be cute, Stephanie. You're not the type. Muriel and Brad can drive you in."

"But we can't," Muriel Newell said. "We have some important business we must attend to in town."

Bruce flashed her a withering look. "I'll bet."

"Well, I have a car." It was Don. My heart sank.

"Come along, Melissa," he said. "We'll have fun."

Muriel Newell said, "I'm sorry, Mr. Wilford, that's impossible. The trip will take hours. Melissa cannot take the time away from my aunt."

117

She seemed to be enjoying the idea of *my* friend going off with Stephanie for the afternoon.

"Oh, no," said Don. "I thought we could all . . ."

"It's okay, Don," I said as casually as I could. "I do have to stay. But there must be something I can do right here to help with the party."

"Someone has to go up to the attic and rummage around," Stephanie said. "We might turn up some old things to make the party more authentic."

"I can sit with Madge," Miss Hillary volunteered, "while Melissa and Bruce poke through the attic."

Bruce frowned and then said, "Good idea, Jennie." He bent and kissed her thin cheek and she flushed with pleasure.

The clock in the corner struck the half hour — one thirty.

"We'll be down at two," Bruce promised Miss Hillary.

Stephanie took Don's arm in a proprietary way and said, "Thanks for lending him to me, Melissa."

"See you later," Don flung back at me over his shoulder as they went through the door. I thought, *No you won't, you haven't really seen me from the moment you laid eyes on Stephanie.* The worst of it was, I couldn't blame him.

So the house settled down, with Stephanie and Don gone, Muriel and Bradford Newell in their room preparing to leave, the Volkes cleaning up in the kitchen, Miss Hillary sitting with old Mrs. Newell, who was napping.

Though Bruce had warned me to stay away from him, here we were, alone. I couldn't understand how or why it was happening, and I didn't care. I wanted just to be with him.

We mounted the steep, narrow staircase that led to the unused attic at Wildemere and stood together before the heavy padlocked door. I could not fight down that wonderful wild happiness that was touch off by being near him.

"Why is the door padlocked?" I asked, mostly to break the silence.

"Aunt Madge had the lock put on when Uncle Henry died. Said she felt safer — attics scare her. Hmm . . ." he was examining it now, "this lock is rusted on its hinges. Get back a bit, Melissa. I'll try to batter it open."

I stepped back and he lunged against the door. The lock gave way instantly and he almost fell into the room. A delicious chill of fear ran up my spine as I looked beyond him into the dark forboding cavern.

"Come here, Melissa. But don't be scared. It looks a lot like Dracula's hideaway." In an instant I was by his side, terribly aware of his warmth and masculinity. My fear was forgotten, and all my good intentions melted away.

"I'll light a candle and try to see if there's another way of lighting up this dungeon," he said.

He struck a match and lit a candle; then, taking me by the arm, led me slowly into the attic. It was slow going in the dark as we made our way over misshapen forms of long-discarded furniture, piles of clothing, magazines, books, the thousand and one mementos people refuse to abandon, lest they lose a part of themselves.

"Ah ha! A lamp! Here," he thrust the candle at me, "hold this a minute while I try to find a socket."

119

While I held on to the flickering candle, Bruce scouted along the outer fringe of the room and found an outlet. In moments, he had the lamp on. It was made of bits of colored glass, green and red and purple and a ghastly yellow, and it gave off a weird glow that made the room even stranger. It was hideous.

Bruce and I broke into laughter. "What in the world Aunt Madge ever wanted with this monstrosity, I can't imagine," he said. He took the candle from me and his fingers touched mine for a brief instant. He quickly took his hand away, and said gruffly, "All right, let's do the job we came for. We'll start in that corner."

He was all dignity once again. *Why is he like this — friendly one minute, and the next, cold as ice? Does it have something to do with Stephanie?*

"Is there anything there?" he was asking.

We were at a turretlike niche where there was an old wooden coat tree on whose arms hung coats and dresses that had surely not been worn in many years.

"I'm not really sure what we're supposed to look for," I said.

"Neither am I. The point is I didn't want anyone up here whom we can't trust. Not with what's been happening in this house."

I should have been pleased by his frankness with me, but I wasn't. He had done it before, taken me into his confidence and then tuned me out.

He went on, tonelessly, "I guess we're supposed to choose a few things that might add to the alleged merriment of Madge's party. I don't know why we're giving this party. It's a silly whim — typical of the way the Newells indulge themselves. Costly and useless. Madge would be a darned sight

120

better off investing the money to send a couple of poor bright kids through college."

We plunged into the piles of junk for the next half hour; the emotional debris of people's lives: old portraits of grandparents, aunts, uncles, framed in antique gold baroque frames; a tarnished old chandelier; a Victor phonograph with a horn on top and a side handle to crank it with; a pile of jazz records from the '20's.

"That phonograph and records would be great to play the night of the party. If the machine works, I'll take it down." Bruce then indicated a pile of papers near me.

"Those magazines . . . what's the date on them?"

I picked one up and read aloud, "*Saturday Evening Post,* November 25, 1925."

"Great," Bruce said. "We'll take a stack of them downstairs and spread them around the library for the guests to browse through."

He put a record on and cranked the machine, and in a funny, hollow-sounding, tin-can voice, someone sang *I Lost My Heart in Avalon.* The music was corny, but romantic. Bruce's eyes caught mine and held them. Then he looked away and said brusquely, "Well, we'd better get on with it." He began to look through a huge carton near the window.

If that's the way he wants it, it's all right with me, I thought. I walked over to the wooden coat-tree to see what it held, and found a glorious long black velvet theater cape I just couldn't resist. Taking it over to a cracked full-length mirror against the wall, I held it up tight to my body. The old phonograph was playing that sentimental song from way before I was born, and I was pretending

121

it was 1920-something and was enjoying the effect of the lovely black cape and the corny old music when, reflected in the mirror, I saw Bruce emerge from the dark shadows behind me.

"What have you got there?" he asked.

I felt like a child caught dipping into the cookie jar by a stern and angry father. I stood there, unable to answer. He came closer, looking at my reflection as I faced the mirror. He stopped behind me and in the mirror I could see him frowning.

Then he said softly, "Melissa." He spun me about and pulled me to him, his lips meeting mine. He kissed me, and I felt wild with joy. There was no thought of Stephanie, of anyone, of anything in the outside world. I only knew pleasure and an excitement new to me and so wonderful.

Then he released me. Gently.

"What am I doing?" he said.

His face was distorted with an expression I couldn't understand. His dark eyes were distressed, and suddenly I couldn't bear anymore. I put my hands over my face so he wouldn't see me cry. I didn't want to break down before him — I didn't want to, but I couldn't help myself. I was too full of my feelings to hold back any longer.

He pulled my hands away from my face, and said, "Melissa — forgive me. Forgive me. I had no right to do that."

I shook my head, my hands still shielding my eyes. "I don't understand," I said.

"It's something I can't tell you. Something I can't talk about." His eyes clouded.

Then he said, in a more normal voice, "I promise you this will never happen again." He was carefully not looking at me. "Now you wait here,

Melissa. It's late and we've got to get back." There was a guarded tone in his voice now. "I'll take a look in that storage room at the other end and see if there's anything worth taking."

It was a jumble of words, said unconvincingly. He walked across the room to a partitioned cubicle in the dark corner, opened the Sheetrock door and stepped inside.

I stood there in the silent dark, waiting, sunk in misery. A minute passed, then two, then five.

It was eerie standing there alone, and I began to be scared. Why was he keeping me waiting like this? What was he doing?

Then, all at once, it happened. The light went out and the attic was shrouded in blackness.

I began to panic. "Bruce!" I called out in a voice high-hysterical.

No answer.

There was the sound of the floor creaking close to me. Helpless, I waited in the dark and heard that ominous creak again. I looked toward the doorway and then I saw it — silhouetted against the dim light — a horrifying black-hooded form swooping down upon me. A form just like the one that had pursued me through the woods only a few days before. I went limp with fear. My voice froze in my throat. I turned and tried to shield my head in my arms and then it came. I felt a mighty crack on my skull and saw a thousand lights explode in the darkness, and then I knew no more.

CHAPTER ELEVEN

"MELISSA! Can you hear me?"

A man's voice. A voice that I felt I should recognize, but didn't.

"I think she's coming to," said a woman.

I slowly opened my eyes but the ache behind them made me quickly close them again.

The woman's voice, anxious now, came to my ears again, "I hope she's all right. Her face is so white."

I opened my eyes again, and this time it was better. Slowly I looked around the room. My room. But how did I get there?

The voice at my bedside was gentle. "Melissa."

No mistaking the concern in that tone. I knew who it was.

"Miss Hillary," I said faintly.

"Yes, yes, Melissa." I saw unshed tears in her eyes. She leaned toward me. "Are you all right?"

"You're hurt," said the man's voice again. At the foot of the bed stood Emile Volke. Involuntarily I cried out.

"You! It was you!"

Emile's face remained impassive. Miss Hillary said quickly, "Please, Melissa. You mustn't say that. Whoever struck you, hurt me as well. Pushed me down some stairs." Miss Hillary had a look of real pain on her face. "Emile found me and helped me. He carried me down here."

My head was throbbing with a heavy dull pain and it was hard for me to concentrate on what she was saying.

"You had a close call, Melissa. So did I. Someone gave you a nasty blow."

The flood of memory came overwhelmingly back. Bruce and his tender look just before he took me in his arms in the dim light and kissed me. The light going out and my panic in the dark before I had turned to see that ominous batlike figure.

Miss Hillary was speaking again. "You seem to be all right. Bruce has gone to call the doctor. Don't talk now, Melissa."

Emile Volke came closer to Miss Hillary. "Your arm. It is bad? Maybe you are hurt worse than she is."

"No, Emile. I'm all right," she said, raising her arm slowly, then stopping with a wince of pain. "It's absurd. All my life I've been writing about dark intruders who bludgeon people over the head and knock helpless old ladies down the stairs." She smiled ruefully. "Now I'm the old lady who got knocked down the stairs. Serves me right."

Bruce was in the doorway; then he came in quietly, heading directly for me. For an instant

I relived those moments of terror alone in the dark attic, those moments when I called to him — and he did not answer.

He came to my bedside and stood over me.

"Melissa?"

Just my name, but it threw me into a panic. I turned my head away and lay trembling under the coverlet.

"What's this all about?" I heard him say to Miss Hillary.

"She's upset, Bruce. She doesn't understand yet what happened," Miss Hillary explained.

"And she thinks that I . . . you don't mean she thinks *I* had anything to do with it?"

"Be reasonable, Bruce. She's had a dreadful scare. She isn't thinking straight."

"Don't bother making excuses. And don't upset yourself, Jennie. Are you all right? Come here." A pause. "You must have taken a nasty fall. What were you doing on the stairs anyway?"

"I heard Melissa shout. I've never heard such a terrible cry. I rushed right up the stairs and the next thing I knew this . . . this dark thing came rushing down."

"And knocked you over," Bruce said angrily. "Is that it?" Miss Hillary nodded. Bruce said, "Did you manage to get a look at him, Jennie?"

"No, Bruce. It happened too quickly. I had just started up the stairs when that awful black thing," she shivered, "came hurtling down." She paused, thoughtfully. "It honestly didn't seem to be a human being. It was like an animal figure, with no face that I could see."

As she said the word, "animal," Emile gave a small start. He looked at Bruce and their eyes met. Then Bruce dropped his eyes and said: "Well, since

I seem to be upsetting our little prairie flower, I'll wait downstairs for Dr. Perry."

He did not look at me as he left, with Emile following.

"Don't feel bad, Melissa," said Miss Hillary. "Such a wonderful man, and yet he has these moods. He has a broad streak of unhappiness in him, and with good reason." She studied my face a moment.

"Melissa, I've had to revise my thinking about the Volkes being connected with the attempts on Madge's life. I truly don't see how Emile could have been involved in what happened today. I saw him go downstairs just before you screamed."

"Maybe not Emile. But why couldn't it be Mrs. Volke?"

"It could be," said Miss Hillary dubiously. "But it's hardly likely that a wife, living in the same house with her husband, could be trying to do away with someone without the husband knowing it. Even in the weakest of my novels, I would never have used that device."

"Do you have any other suspects?" I had a feeling there was someone else on her mind.

"As a matter of fact, I have. Someone who has both motive and opportunity." She mused a moment, then said reluctantly, "But I can't believe it. I can't believe he'd do such a thing, no matter how badly he might need Madge's money!"

My interest was aroused, and I tried to sit up in bed. All at once, the pain in my head was back, and I let out a small cry.

Miss Hillary said, "I'm sorry, Melissa. We shouldn't be talking. Just lie back until the doctor comes."

As if on cue, Dr. Perry entered the room with Bruce directly behind him.

"So soon?" said Miss Hillary. "That was fast, Gordon."

"We were lucky," Bruce said. "Dr. Perry was on call right near here and happened to phone in as I was speaking to his service."

"These little gadgets come in mighty handy." Dr. Perry indicated a small electronic walkie-talkie radiophone in his breast pocket. "This thing beeped at me and I came right over."

He put his bag down on the floor beside my bed.

"Well, young lady, now it's turnabout. Instead of looking after my patient, you're the patient." He spoke in a light tone, but he was looking at me searchingly. "Bruce said you've had an accident. Can you tell me about it?"

As briefly as I could, I told him. When I came to the part about being hit on the head, he interrupted me.

"Have you any idea what this . . . this bat figure could have been? I mean, could you see if it was a man or a woman?"

"No," I said. "I didn't see a face, or arms, or legs, just a big black — *thing*." Involuntarily I shuddered.

"All right, Melissa," Dr. Perry said soothingly. "I'll just look you over." He glanced at Miss Hillary and Bruce, who left the room.

Gingerly, with the softest hands imaginable, Dr. Perry felt my head until he came to a spot so sore I shrank with pain at his touch. He examined it carefully, then said, "That's a pretty mean bump you've got, Melissa! Fortunately, the club — or whatever was used on you — struck at the base of the cerebellum and glanced off. One inch closer to the thalamus, and you might have had a bad fracture." He added unhappily, "Whoever did this meant business. But we'll discuss that after I've finished."

I couldn't help feeling tense as he continued, taking my blood pressure, my pulse, and completing a fairly thorough examination. It was obvious that he was a fine physician; but he was Dr. Perry, a man whom I did not completely trust. Had he really been on a house call so near? It seemed quite coincidental. Somehow I did not believe his story.

When he finished, Dr. Perry called Miss Hillary and Bruce back into the room.

"She's been very lucky. The blow she took could easily have proven fatal."

Miss Hillary and Bruce looked upset. Dr. Perry said firmly, "She has a real concussion. She'll have to rest in bed for several days. What I'm most concerned about is the fact that if she was the intended victim, she's in real danger. And, as in the case of Madge, her attacker may very well be someone in this house."

A shiver ran through me as I realized that by remaining here — in bed in my room — I was exposing myself to another attack. And next time . . ?

Miss Hillary said, "You're right, Gordon. Someone must keep careful watch on Melissa." She turned to Bruce and said, "What do you think of giving Mrs. Volke the job?"

Bruce shook his head. "That's impossible. She'll have to look after Aunt Madge now that *she's* out of commission." His words made me feel like an inanimate object. "No, we'll have to take turns looking in on her. Between Muriel and Brad,

129

Stephanie, Emile, and me, I guess we can do the job."

The question was left unspoken: How did any of us know that among the ones who were supposed to be looking after me, there was not the very person from whom I should be protected?

Dr. Perry then turned his attention to Miss Hillary. He helped her remove her sweater, and since she was wearing a thin sleeveless blouse, was able to inspect her arm and shoulder. After a few minutes he said, "That was a nasty shove, Jennie. But I doubt it did any real harm, just a sprain. We'll wait till tomorrow. If any swelling or real pain develops, you can come to my office for X-rays."

Dr. Perry gave me a pill to ease the pain and help me sleep. I only half heard the discussion he, Miss Hillary, and Bruce had from then on.

"He came down the stairs like a cloud of fury," Miss Hillary said. "As I fell, I saw it — him — run down the corridor."

"He didn't go past me into the attic," said Bruce positively. "That I could swear to."

But you could be lying, I thought.

". . . If he ran down the stairs, Emile would have seen him as he responded to Melissa's shouts," said Dr. Perry reasonably, adding, "Emile says he saw no one."

And Emile could be lying, I thought. *And so could you, Dr. Perry.*

The pill Dr. Perry had given me took hold. A light, pleasant floating feeling tingled through my body to my very fingers and toes. The two men left, and as I watched Bruce go, Miss Hillary said, "Why, Melissa, you do care for Bruce, don't you?

130

I see the same soft look in your eyes whenever Bruce comes near."

"I don't know what you mean," I began, blushing.

"It's all right. I understand." Her voice was gentle. "But Bruce is the wrong one for you. It can only bring you unhappiness to love the unattainable, Melissa. I know."

In that moment, I knew. I said, "Were you in love with Mrs. Newell's husband?" I put a hand to my mouth as I realized what I'd said.

"Don't feel bad. You're right, Melissa." Her eyes looked at me earnestly. "I did really care for Henry. Very much. I have never felt that way about anyone else before or since. And that was fifty years ago." She shifted in her chair. "He was a prince of a man, Melissa. But Madge was the princess, and he loved her."

I said, in a rush, "How awful it must have been for you!"

"Oh, I suffered a lot in those days of my youth. That's why I'd hate to see you getting emotionally involved with Bruce, when there is no way that you can be with him. No way." She said quietly, "I have no right to talk about this. And I won't. Yet I cannot see you fall into the same futile love relationship I did when I was a girl. I should have left here and gone away and started a new life somewhere else."

"Why didn't you?" I asked.

"Because what I felt for Henry was stronger than my desire for happiness. My only joy was being with Madge and Henry, sharing their life and their marriage — by proxy." She looked at me with a fierceness that shook me. "Don't ruin your life, Melissa. Bruce is a fascinating man, but he is not for you. Go, before it's too late."

I had never seen her like this. Her voice was heavy with emotion. She said unhappily, "I'll miss you terribly if you go. But it will be best for you. Think about it, Melissa."

She plumped up my cushion and put a light blanket over me. "The doctor said you must keep warm. And rest. Close your eyes and sleep. I'll sit beside you and do my needlepoint."

To the rhythmic movement of her deft hands drawing the needle in and out of the floral fabric, I drifted off to sleep.

I opened my eyes to see Don. Don, with Stephanie beside him. He stood there tall and blond and solid. I put out my arms to him and he came down beside the bed and held on to me. I saw a slight frown on Stephanie's face.

"Are you all right?" Don asked. "You were trembling in your sleep. You must have been having a nightmare."

I felt snug and comfortable with his arms around me. While I instinctively hated playing the helpless female, I made no move away from him.

"I was," I said. "Oh, Don, where were you?"

"From what I've been able to gather, when you got zonked on the head Stephanie and I weren't very far away."

"No, we weren't," said Stephanie brightly. "As a matter of fact, Don and I weren't even together. His car ran into trouble. While he messed around with it, I got a lift to the gas station."

"Yes, the tow car came along and recharged the battery. Then Stephanie and I went into the city as scheduled." Don released me. Rising, he walked over to Stephanie. "Would you mind leaving me alone with Melissa? I'd appreciate it, Steph."

They had certainly gotten very friendly, I thought, considering they had only met a few hours before.

"Sure, Don," Stephanie said with a smile. Then she came to my bedside. "I'm glad you weren't hurt too badly, Melissa. See you later."

When we were alone, I told Don what had happened and what Dr. Perry had said.

"A mild concussion — but he wants you to take medication and stay in bed?" He snorted. "It's not as simple as you think, Melissa. I don't care what Gordon Perry says, it's not safe for you to stay here any longer. Someone's out to get you!"

"Why just me, Don? What about old Mrs. Newell? And that reminds me — what about that white powder I gave you to be analyzed? And the pill? It's been almost a week."

Don's expression changed. "I know. That's what I meant to tell you when I came here today, but what with the change in plans and everything . . ."

And Stephanie, I thought.

"What I would have told you, Melissa, is that powder is picrotoxin . . . a poison."

"How awful! Are you sure?" I asked.

"Sure, I'm sure. I stood by the laboratory technician while he ran all the tests on it. It's poison, Melissa," he said steadily. "Something like strychnine, at least it acts like it on the system. It's odorless and is used to treat people who have taken an overdose of barbituate. It causes cramps — you did say the old lady was doubled up with stomach pains, didn't you?"

"Yes. She was in real pain. Oh, Don, who could have done such a thing to her?"

"I don't know. Whoever it is, he's deadly serious. You don't fool around with poisons unless you are."

"I can't believe it's any of the people in this house."

"Well, I can," said Don. "Murderers don't always look like murderers. Some of the kindest people I've ever known look like perfect villains. You can't go by appearances, Melissa."

Then I remembered to ask, "What about that little white pill — the one I took out of the vial marked 'Dr. David Gould'? What about that?"

He hitched his chair closer to me. "That's something else, Melissa. Our would-be killer is not just messing around with poison. He's been fooling around with the old lady's medicine too. That little white pill is caffeine. Know what that does?" I shook my head. "It's used as a heart stimulant. No doctor would ever have prescribed that for a patient with a bad heart."

"Oh no! What would it do to Mrs. Newell if she got it by mistake?"

"Well, if she's supposed to get digitalis every day, and instead gets caffeine every now and then — her heart would deteriorate that much faster." His voice was grim. "I don't want to upset you, Melissa, though I know I have. But you must realize everything's changed now."

"I don't know what you mean."

"Listen, Melissa — I spoke to Miss Hillary when I came in and she agrees with me. You're just too young to cope with things as they are now."

"Well, I'm sure going to try," I said angrily. I resented his implication that I was a child. He certainly didn't treat Stephanie that way, yet she was only a few years older. "Don't try to talk me out of it, Don. As soon as I can, I'll be taking care of her again."

Before Don could answer, Stephanie entered the room. I felt like I was in some kind of public place. People just seemed to come and go as the inclination struck them. They must have been doing a lot of eavesdropping too, because Stephanie said, in that offhand way of hers, "Let the poor girl alone, Don. I know how she feels. I'd do the same thing if I were in her shoes."

"If this keeps on, she may not last to get into her shoes again," Don said sharply. "She's different from you, Steph."

"We're all sisters under the skin," Stephanie said. Then to me she added, "I'll go down and get your dinner tray, Melissa, and I'll sleep in Aunt Madge's room tonight. Actually I can cover for you until you're back on your feet again."

"That's very nice of you," I said.

"Not at all. She's my aunt, remember. And you're my friend." She smiled invitingly. "At least I hope we'll be friends."

"Thank you. I hope so." I made my voice as pleasant as possible, but I was confused. Even though it was Bruce that I thought of constantly, I didn't like the way Stephanie had gotten so close to Don so fast. He was *my* friend, and Stephanie probably had more men than she needed. Besides, she and Bruce were practically engaged.

After dinner, I took another of Dr. Perry's floating pills — that was the way I thought of them — and fell into a deep, deep sleep.

The shrieks came in wild succession. I sat straight up in bed and, ignoring the pain in my head, tried desperately to locate their source.

135

Old Mrs. Newell's room.

I hurtled out of bed and down the corridor exactly as I'd done only a week before. I had the dreadful feeling of *déjà vu*. At the doorway was Stephanie, backed against the door jamb, screaming. Old Mrs. Newell had just come awake. Her hair was awry and her eyes were heavy-lidded with sleep.

Stephanie began to moan, a weird animal sound.

"What's wrong with you? You're scaring your aunt half to death," I said angrily. "Are you out of your mind?"

She said nothing.

"What is it?" I demanded.

Slowly she raised her arm and pointed to the rumpled blanket.

Then I saw it, and understood Stephanie's horror.

Among the bedclothes, lying at the old lady's feet, was a furry orange blob. Her cat, Ivan.

He had been strangled to death.

CHAPTER TWELVE

OLD MRS. NEWELL'S face was a deathly white.
Stephanie and I each went to one side of her to
support her, when the Newells and the Volkes
appeared in the doorway. All four, as might be
expected at this late hour, were dressed in their
nightclothes. All four looked as if they had just
been roused from sleep.

Just then Bruce came upstairs, fully dressed in
his daytime clothes — brown corduroy trousers,
turtleneck sweater, sport shoes.

"Oh, good heavens!" Muriel Newell said when
she saw the dead cat.

"Shrecklich!" Mrs. Volke exclaimed in German,
turning her head away toward her husband, who
said nothing. Bradford Newell responded with a
shudder of his shoulders.

Bruce stopped dead, then came into the room.

"Stop standing around like fools! Will someone please help Aunt Madge out of bed while I dispose of the poor animal?"

We should have known then who had killed the old lady's pet. If I hadn't been so blinded by my own emotional involvement, the evidence was plain to see. The previous attempts to frighten the old lady — even the incident of the poison — could have been done by any one of them — the Volkes, the younger Newells, Bruce, yes, even Stephanie, could have done it. Even, I reminded myself, Miss Hillary. Or Dr. Perry.

But to take a helpless animal and with bare hands snuff out its life in such a senseless, brutal way was an act that could have been performed only by someone with a certain type of mentality. And there was only one person among them who had to be the guilty one.

By Friday, I had completely recovered from the attack in the attic, and was back on the job. The house was busier than ever; despite what had happened, old Madge Newell was determined to have her party. Bruce and I met only at the dinner table, where I avoided getting drawn into conversation with him. I still held the fearful conviction that if it weren't Emile, it was Bruce who had attacked me in the attic.

Whenever I had time off, I went to Miss Hillary's, where I could relax and be myself. Because of what had happened after my first visit, Miss Hillary refused to let me come or go using the path through the woods. After the episode of Ivan's death, she was even stricter.

"Bruce was right, Melissa. You mustn't go

138

alone into the woods. What happened to the cat was not only meant to frighten Madge — I believe it is a warning of what is about to happen next."

"You mean someone might try to do the same thing to Mrs. Newell?"

"Exactly. Or to anyone who gets in the attacker's way." She nodded her gray head vigorously. "Promise me you won't go into those woods again, Melissa. I'm sure if your parents knew about your situation here, they'd make you go home at once."

She was right. If my mother knew, she'd come right up and take me home. My father of course, would regard the whole situation as somehow my fault.

It's the kind of thing only you can get yourself into, Melissa, I could hear him saying, as I had heard him say so many times in the past.

I'd made sure my parents knew nothing. In my letters and phone calls back home, I managed always to dwell on the good things about Wildemere, "The grounds are so beautiful," "Mrs. Newell is just lovely to me," "Yes, mother, the food is marvelous. I'm putting on weight."

One day perhaps I would tell them all about everything, one day when I was back home for good; that is, if I ever got home again.

The day of the party drew closer. All the fine old silver was taken out, polished, and covered with plastic sheets on the long mahogany buffet. There was enough silver service for one hundred or more people.

"Uncle Henry and Aunt Madge were famous for their parties," Stephanie told me one day as we

139

stood side by side polishing the last few pieces of silver. "Aunt Madge could dash off a dinner party for twenty-five or thirty people faster and better than most women have a couple of friends over for lunch. Uncle Henry pretended he didn't approve, but actually he adored everything Madge did. He loved paying the enormous bills she ran up even while he grumbled about them."

"Do you remember him that well?" It seemed a good opportunity to find out about the almost mythical Henry Newell.

"I do, of course! He died when I was, let me think, twelve years old. I remember what a gorgeous man he was. Women fell dead when he paid them any attention. Even Aunt Jennie had a terrific crush on him once."

"You said once. What do you mean?"

"Oh, she got over it," said Stephanie.

"Really?"

"Sure. She's been trying to hook old Gordon Perry for ages." Stephanie laughed. "Isn't gossip delicious, Melissa? It feels so wicked."

When we had finished, Stephanie consulted her wristwatch. "I thought I'd run upstairs and take a look at the gown I'm wearing the night of the party, and decide what to wear with it. Have you got something special planned for the party, Melissa?"

"I'm not sure I'm invited."

"Not invited? Of course you are."

"No one's said anything to me about it and I don't know anyone who'll be there." I wished she hadn't brought the subject up.

"Don't be ridiculous. You know us — Bruce and

me and the family." She hesitated, then said, "And Don. I've invited him too."

It should have come as no surprise, but it did. Stephanie obviously had the Newell assurance; they dispersed their favors like royalty and assumed they could do no wrong.

"Is Don anything special to you, Melissa?" Stephanie asked. "You don't have to answer."

Her question took me by surprise, but I decided to be truthful.

"I don't really know. We met on the bus coming up here, and we've only seen each other a few times." I added by way of further explanation, "And usually under such peculiar circumstances."

"You can say that again. People running all over the place trying to bump other people off."

At the door to her room, Stephanie said, "Come on in. Now's as good a time as any to look over the dresses and pick one out."

As I hesitated, she took my arm. "Don't be silly, Melissa. I've got scads of them. No reason why you can't borrow one."

She was at the wardrobe, taking out a pale beige dress that stopped just short of the knees. She took one look at me, and returned the dress to the closet.

"Here's something you'd look great in."

She was holding up a long white dress that had all the simplicity of a Colonial gown — a big sash that would emphasize my small waist, and a flowing skirt that would add grace to any figure.

"How do you like it?" she asked.

"I love it. But I can't take it from you."

"I'm not asking you to take it, Melissa — just

borrow it for one night. What's wrong with that?"

"Nothing, I guess. I don't mean to sound ungrateful," I said lamely.

"Then it's settled," she said with finality. "Come on, try it on."

I slipped easily into the dress. Despite the difference in our figures — mine lean, lanky, more angular than her slim yet subtly rounded body — it fit me perfectly.

"I knew it! It's great on you!" Stephanie exclaimed. "It clings to you in all the right places — and it doesn't on me."

It was the most beautiful dress I'd ever had on. I felt I was looking at a stranger in the mirror — a very exciting stranger. I burst out impulsively:

"Oh, Stephanie, I adore it."

"I'm glad. I wanted you to like it." She smiled a funny little mysterious, Mona Lisa kind of smile and I got the uneasy feeling she was secretly congratulating herself, as if my taking the dress meant something very important to her.

She came closer. "I hope you don't mind, Melissa. But honestly, you could look smashing. Those fantastic eyes — and if you played up your features . . ."

I didn't know what to say. "Well, thanks. But I'm sure I could never be pretty."

"That's ridiculous! If you're not pretty, Melissa, it's because you don't *think* you are. The most important thing about being good looking is believing that you are."

I didn't know why, but I kept thinking:

Stephanie, I don't like you or trust you and you can't charm your way around me. I don't know what you've got in mind, but I know in my bones you're up to something. I'll wear your dress, because otherwise I couldn't go to the party. But, sister, I'll be on my guard against you every single minute!

Three more days. That's all that was left until the big night. Schedules were knocked askew as workmen and delivery boys came and went. Huge quantities of food and drink were sent in by the caterers in advance so that on Saturday they would have everything there for the huge buffet feast that was planned — the meal that would duplicate the menu from the 1922 party.

I saw very little of Bruce during those days. When I did, he was usually with Stephanie. I tried to steel myself every time I saw them together. When Bruce and I met, we barely spoke. Once, while I was washing some dishes, I felt I was being watched and turned around to see him standing in the doorway, watching me pensively. When he saw me looking at him, he left the room.

I retreated to Mrs. Newell's room and our word games. It was safe there. Luckily, she won the first game and it was a pleasant few hours. But by five o'clock she was tired and restless.

"Do you want a pill to help you relax?" I asked. "Dr. Perry said you may have one when you're excited. The party tomorrow has us all overstimulated."

"It's a happy excitement. But you're right, child. I'd better take one."

In the bathroom, I noticed that the vials in the medicine chest had been rearranged. I found the digitalis all right, but not where it was supposed to be. In its place there should have been a bottle of nitroglycerin, the medicine Dr. Perry said she must be given in the event of a heart attack.

When I had notified Dr. Perry about the caffeine pills, he had muttered angrily, examined all the old lady's pills, and thrown out everything that didn't belong there. But he had left the nitroglycerin and I had kept it carefully locked away.

I searched for the nitroglycerin everywhere, but it was gone.

CHAPTER THIRTEEN

SATURDAY, the night of the party, the house was ablaze with light from top to bottom. Outside, in a soft summer night made to order just for the Newells, flickering tapers glowed about the sweep of lawn leading up to the house. For once, the heavy overhanging elms, lit by candlelight and Japanese lanterns, were not the ominous sentinels they had seemed the night I'd arrived at Wildemere.

The party was to begin at eight o'clock. At six o'clock, Muriel Newell took over from me, explaining she would help her aunt to dress. She herself was already in her party dress, an unbecoming flower print that only emphasized her stocky figure. Around her throat, however, she wore a sparkling green necklace that seemed to me to be emeralds with diamond clusters and must have been worth a fortune.

"Don't let it fool you, my dear!" old Mrs. Newell whispered to me when Muriel left the room for a moment. "That necklace is a fake. A copy of one she once had that Bradford gambled away . . . some get-rich-quick scheme he invested in." She sighed. "He wouldn't mind a bit if this party tonight were my swan song. Don't shake your head, my dear. It's true. It's true of several of our other guests tonight. The Newell family is . . . improvident. They'd be much better off with me out of the way." We heard Muriel's footsteps returning down the hall. "But they're due for a big surprise," she whispered.

As I ran a bath for myself I thought of what Mrs. Newell had said. Dr. Perry had replaced the nitroglycerin when I'd phoned him about it. But someone had taken it . . . someone who might feel there was a chance the old lady would have an attack during the excitement of the party. Then, in the ensuing confusion, with no nitroglycerin available, she might die in what would appear a natural way.

But who could it be? I stepped out of the bath and began to dress, thinking of all the possible suspects. Bruce. His name came to mind first. All the old arguments persisted. He was old Mrs. Newell's favorite and surely remembered in her will. He loved Wildemere and its farmlands and was despondent whenever they discussed selling it. If he could do away with his aunt before she could sell it and go off to Florida, he would inherit while he could still hopefully possess Wildemere. For that matter, the same applied to both Muriel and Bradford. Down and out, relying on their aunt's bounty, surely they must be nervous at the thought of her changing her will, moving away, leaving them stranded. Stephanie? Not likely she wanted her aunt to die. If she did, I could think of no justification. But Stephanie was a girl of strong undercurrents. "Don't let her good looks deceive you," Miss Hillary had once said to me. "Stephanie has a steel-trap mind." I realized sadly that I knew no more about the identity of the would-be murderer now than I had when I first came.

I was all dressed and standing before the mirror when Stephanie entered the room. She was wearing a cloth of gold gown that outlined every curve of that perfect body. Her golden hair hung loose and gossamer soft to her shoulders. The tanned skin, brilliant green eyes, flashing white teeth . . . all blended into a flawless Grecian statue come to life.

I felt suddenly awkward, unattractive. There was that old sinking sensation in the pit of my stomach. That's who you are, Miss Inferior of 1974, I thought. Stephanie didn't seem to realize how I felt. She said, "You look lovely, Melissa. You really do."

"I love this dress, Stephanie — but it only makes me look plainer. If that's possible," I said miserably.

A determined gleam came into Stephanie's brilliant green eyes. "That's because you haven't done the finishing touches yet." She picked up my hairbrush. "Melissa, won't you please let me try a different hairdo and new makeup?"

"Go ahead." But I knew it was no use.

With sure, swift strokes, she began to rearrange my hair. When she finished, she brought me a pair of lovely chandelier earrings of seed pearls and gold. "Now I'm going to do your makeup. Hold still."

147

I watched a new me evolving, and was astounded. Yet it was my own self. Somehow Stephanie had managed to find the real me and heighten my looks, that was all. When she finished she stepped back and said, "Take a look in the mirror, Melissa. Go on. Get the whole impression all at once."

I stepped over to the long mirror and took a good long look at my reflection. I'd seen enough of the old Cinderella story in the movies to realize how corny the situation was. But still I could not believe my eyes. It was magic. All of a sudden I knew what Stephanie had meant by saying you had to feel beautiful in order to be beautiful.

I turned to her, my gratitude plainly written on my face.

"I know," she said with a smug smile. "Didn't I tell you you could be smashing?"

"It's wonderful! I don't know how you did it."

"After the party's over, I'll show you some tricks I picked up from a great makeup man in Hollywood." She glanced at the clock on the mantle. "Good grief! The party will be starting in a few minutes." Again that secret smile came to her eyes. "Tonight's going to be . . . a little special for me, Melissa."

"Yes?"

"You'll see." She patted me on the arm. "I've got to run along now."

She left the room. No matter how I hated to face the truth, no matter how she was flirting with Don — and she was — tonight Bruce and Stephanie would announce their engagement. I had expected it, but nothing could have prepared me for the terrible unhappiness I felt as I descended the stairs to await the arrival of the first guests.

CHAPTER FOURTEEN

I WAS LATE. I stood at the head of the staircase and saw several people clustered below, near the entrance to the library. I wished I could turn back, that they would keep talking and not notice me. There was Dr. Perry in a white dinner jacket; Miss Hillary in a lovely soft blue chiffon gown with an airy scarf draped round her shoulders; Brad and Muriel Newell, who were talking to Bruce, were on the either side of old Mrs. Newell, who was in a wheelchair.

The conversation stopped and they all looked up at me at the top of the stairs, and I felt my face flush. Bruce was striking in his white dinner jacket. His dark eyes flickered as he watched me descend. He neither smiled nor spoke, just stood, impassive.

"My dear girl, is it really you? You look positively beautiful. Come closer and let me see you!"

It was old Mrs. Newell. "You're exquisite, Melissa. I'll bet Stephanie had something to do with it. Come on, confess."

She was dimpling and smiling and being her most charming, but I was furious. The flash of anger I felt taught me how hurtful old Mrs. Newell could be. And if this was how I reacted to a simple remark, it was easy to imagine the genuine fury someone could be harboring after years of such treatment. Particularly if the loss of money, or status, were involved.

Bradford Newell had surely been the butt of more of old Mrs. Newell's withering scorn than anyone else in the family. He was always being put down by the old lady, *and* he was desperate for money — money which he hoped to inherit on her death.

Just then the guests began to arrive. Old Mrs. Newell's wheelchair was suddenly thronelike as she occupied it, wearing an elegant white gown and her diamonds, looking truly regal in the midst of friends and family gathered round her. Once again she was mistress of Wildemere . . . undisputed queen of the mansion.

By nine o'clock the house was overflowing with people. Outside a summer storm was brewing and the lanterns and torches began to flicker in the wind.

There was the sound of music, and Dr. Perry took me by the arm and led me into the huge living room which had been cleared to be a ballroom. A five-piece orchestra in colorful costume was playing Latin American music.

"Melissa, let's show them how to do the Argentine tango," he said gaily.

"But I don't know how!"

Ignoring my protest, he led me on to the dance floor, where several couples were already gliding smoothly around.

"Listen to the music, and let me guide you. With that graceful figure of yours, you must be a good dancer." He squeezed my hand and then assumed the first position of the tango.

Graceful? No one had ever said that about me before.

Hearing it from Dr. Perry, I suddenly felt less tense. Dr. Perry was not a young man, but he was a superb dancer. Anyone could follow him, and follow him I did. We circled the floor smoothly as the pressure of his hand on my back indicated a turn, a squeeze of his hand let me know when to dip, when to sway, how to move. My red gown rippled as we danced. All at once, miraculously, I *was* graceful.

"Melissa, you're a delight." Dr. Perry hugged me close. "It's a lucky man who'll be getting you one day. You do everything so very well."

Did you hear that, Dad? Did you hear what this man just said about me?

The thought was dizzying.

But then doubt crept in stealthily, and began to eat away. *Are you flattering me, Dr. Perry?* I wondered. *Do you meant it? Underneath your professional cheerful-doctor manner, what are you really like?*

"May I cut in?"

It was Don, unbearably handsome in a midnight blue tuxedo.

"Scoundrel!" Dr. Perry said, releasing me.

"Us sawbones don't get much time for dancing, honey. Just pretend I know what I'm doing." He danced me across the room, quipping and laughing.

151

Then we bumped into Stephanie and Bruce. It seemed to me Don must have planned it.

"Oops, sorry! Or something like that," Don said, looking at Stephanie. "You look sensational, Steph!"

Stephanie said hastily, "Oh, Don, Melissa and I know you say that to all the girls." Then she said to Bruce offhandedly, "I don't think Melissa should suffer through any more of this dance with Don, do you?"

Don said, "You asked for it!" He seized her and they danced off, leaving Bruce and me standing there. *Don, how could you?* I thought. *Bruce wants no part of me. Can't you see Stephanie's his girl?*

"I'm not too good at this," Bruce said, "but let's give it a whirl, Melissa."

He took me in his arms, and being this close was almost more than I could bear. I felt Bruce surely must know it. But his face, as he led me through the last few minutes of the dance, was a stony mask. The instant the music stopped he released me.

"Excuse me. I've got to take a look outside. If that storm gets heavier, it could be trouble."

My moment of glory had come and gone.

At midnight the band stopped. Madge Newell was wheeled into the ballroom where she motioned to the orchestra leader for a roll of the drums. I clearly remember the tableau at that moment. Madge Newell in the center, with Bruce on her left and Stephanie on her right. Next to Stephanie, Dr. Perry and Muriel Newell. Next to Bruce, Miss Hillary and Bradford Newell. Don, standing beside Emile and Gerda Volke, who had come to the doorway to watch. Mr. Pickett, only paces behind Madge Newell; I wondered why he was there, when his wife was across the room.

Mrs. Newell smiled and began to speak. "I first want to thank each and every one of you. Thank you, dear friends of mine and of my dear husband Henry, for being here. You've made this a memorable evening."

There were cries of "Hear, hear!" and a small explosion of applause. She smiled and held up her hand.

"As most of you know, I am planning to leave Wildemere and make my home — if God spares me to live that long — in a warmer climate, which a very famous physician," she glanced at Dr. Perry and everyone laughed, "believes might be more beneficial for my health."

Everyone sensed something important coming. There was tension in the air; you could hear the smallest sound clearly. My heart speeded up. Her next words would mean the end of all my dreams about Bruce, foolish though they were.

"Fifty-two years ago, in this very room, an announcement was made. Tonight I am about to make a similar one."

As the guests waited to hear more, Bruce Murdock held up his hand and stepped forward. Old Mrs. Newell started to protest, but Bruce silenced her.

"I'm afraid I must interrupt, Aunt Madge."

The waiters had been quietly passing glasses of champagne to the assembled guests. Now Bruce raised his glass high and said:

"I wish to propose a toast — a toast to Margaret Newell, my own dearest Aunt Madge — to

the incomparable, bewitching, and most beloved —
Madge! To her health and well-being! May she
live to be one hundred!"

Everyone in the room broke into thunderous
applause, and Madge Newell's eyes filled with
happy tears. She motioned to the guests to stop,
but the clapping went on and on. When it finally
died down, Bruce took over.

"I'm afraid I have unpleasant news. We have
just been informed by the State Police that, because
of the storm, there's a flash flood warning out."

There was shocked silence in the room. Outside
there came a giant clap of thunder, adding emphasis to Bruce's warning words.

Dr. Perry came forward. "The river is rising
rapidly, and the bridge at Millbrook will be
open to traffic for only a short time."

People began to talk in excited tones, but Dr.
Perry's voice overrode them. "While there is no
real danger, the police feel it would be wisest not
to delay our guests from returning across the
bridge as soon as possible."

Then Bruce came forward. "There will be people waiting to help you; if you will give them the
keys, your cars will be brought right up to the
door."

Within fifteen minutes, the only ones remaining
in the house were our tight little group. Old Mrs.
Newell said, "Well, really! Why wasn't I consulted
about all this? I am the hostess, you know."

Dr. Perry said, "Madge, behave yourself. This
is an emergency, although Bruce and I both tried
not to alarm anyone. There was no choice. They
had to leave."

She said, "What a nasty way for my party to
end!"

Stephanie said, "It was a gorgeous party, Aunt Madge. And it ended at the right time, while everyone was still enjoying themselves. That's what's called quitting while you're ahead."

"Don't be facetious." Madge Newell looked around. "I'll have a glass of champagne."

Dr. Perry began, "No, you won't. . . ." Then, seeing her disappointment, "All right — one last glass. You've had a big night and all the excitement you can handle."

Emile brought a glass of champagne to her.

"Sip it slowly," said Dr. Perry. "Then it's up to bed with you." He turned to Jennie Hillary. "I think you'd better stay over tonight, Jennie. If the storm gets much worse, you'll really be isolated in your cottage."

Stephanie moved over to the wheelchair, but Muriel Newell was there before her, bending down over the old lady to say something. At that precise moment there came a giant clap of thunder followed by a stab of blue-white lightning that flashed through the terrace windows, filling the room with monstrous heat. We stood helpless in that sudden blast of hot air, and I was scared, very scared.

Then the lights went out.

It was a blackness like none I'd ever seen. Goose pimples began to rise on my skin. Someone was breathing very heavily beside me.

Everyone started talking at once. Then there were sounds of furniture being bumped into, a chair overturning. Near me I heard the tinkle of breaking glass — undoubtedly old Mrs. Newell had dropped the champagne glass she had been holding.

155

In the dark, I heard Bruce clearly: "The storm's knocked out the electricity."

Then Madge Newell's voice, high, cool, imperious as always, "Won't someone do something? Let's have some light!"

Emile Volke's voice — harsh, guttural — was saying, "Madam, we will bring the candles in just a moment. Gerda, come with me to the pantry."

Bradford Newell and his wife Muriel voiced their separate complaints.

Dr. Perry said, "I'm right beside you, Madge. Don't be upset."

Don added his own reassuring, "Nothing to worry about, Mrs. Newell. Don't forget there are one and a half doctors in the room."

Someone laughed; then everyone did, and then we waited, in the dark of the room.

Suddenly there was a shriek and a thud. I tried to run to where I thought Mrs. Newell was. But in the blackness a hard muscular figure blocked my path. I could not see who it was, but I knew. It was Bruce.

He swiftly released me and I stood there, lost in the dark, stretching my hands out, trying to feel for some object, a wall, a piece of furniture, anything to help me get my bearings. But it was no use. I had no idea where I was or what was happening. There were strange sounds, a scuffling, something being dragged along the floor. A terrace window blew open near me and I felt the wash of rain on my face. I hastily slammed it shut, but I still did not know in which part of the room it was.

Then a candle flickered to life, and more candles, as someone entered the room. It had to be the Volkes. But the room was enormous and the half-dozen burning tapers gave very little light. Strange wavery shapes were thrown up on the walls and ceiling, a weird chiaroscuro of light and shadow, adding to the eerie ambience. I could see Mrs. Volke's face by the light of the candle she held. She said, "Emile has gone down to the basement to fix the lights."

Then, as if on cue, all at once the lights came on. I stood there blinking in the sudden brilliance. I looked around and found them all — Miss Hillary, Dr. Perry, Don, Muriel and Bradford Newell, Mr. Pickett near the doorway, Mrs. Volke — even Emile Volke had returned. Everyone there. Everything in place. Everyone accounted for. With one exception.

Madge Newell's wheelchair was empty.

CHAPTER FIFTEEN

SHE HAD disappeared.

Everyone spoke at once. Dr. Perry, standing right beside me, had a film of perspiration on his face, as if he had been under some strange exertion. He was wildly excited and I distinctly heard him say to Bruce, "It had to happen! You know it did!"

Stunned though I was, I searched each face, hoping to see a giveaway clue, something that would reveal who, among us, knew what had happened. But everyone seemed as shocked as I was.

Bruce said in a dangerously quiet voice, "All right. We'll start looking for her and we won't waste a second. Her life may depend on it."

Bradford said in his high whine, "I say, old man, don't be so melodramatic. She must be around someplace. . . ."

Between clenched teeth, Bruce said, "That's all

I want to hear out of you. Do you understand?"
Bradford nodded, instantly submissive.

"You and Muriel go upstairs and start looking."
Muriel Newell huffed indignantly, then shoved
her husband toward the door and followed him out.

"Emile, take the basement," Bruce instructed.

"But I was just down there," Emile protested.

"Do as I say." This was another Bruce speaking, in cold, clipped tones from a face that was a
frozen mask. I felt that underneath was a fury
struggling to be contained . . . a murderous fury.
In that moment, I could have sworn that he was
operating under some enormous guilt; that his
taking over was a cover-up.

We instantly started the search. Don volunteered
to look outside, ludicrous though the suggestion
seemed. He got a raincoat from the front closet
and disappeared into the stormy night.

Even as we searched, it seemed impossible that
the old woman could have disappeared from her
wheelchair, from that huge ballroom. We went from
room to room . . . the sun-room, the ballroom,
the sitting room, the library, down the many cor-
ridors and staircases leading up and down stairs;
and through the rear of the house, the pantry, the
kitchen, the laundry room. Then, fearfully, some
of us joined Emile and Gerda down in the deep,
dark, musty basement, with all its cupboards, the
furnace, the stored storm windows and doors, the
giant casing for the electric motor-driven water
pump that fed the house from the artesian well.
That dungeon-basement — its pervasive odor of
age, its dampness and an eroding, decaying chill,
all said that at its base Wildemere was rotting,
overcome at last by the years and the penetrating
swampland surrounding it.

Nothing.

I couldn't believe that something like this could have happened to the old lady I had gotten so attached to. Suppose — suppose she was gone for good? The thought was horrible. I looked at Miss Hillary's face, and it was a ghastly greenish-yellow color. On an impulse, I went to her side.

"We'll find her, Miss Hillary. You'll see."

She broke into tears and turned her head into my shoulder and sobbed.

Then Don reappeared through the front door, his borrowed raincoat dripping, his blond hair matted, drenched.

"She's not out there," he said. He took off his raincoat and stood before the newly lit fire to warm himself.

Bruce said, "It's unrealistic to think she could be anywhere except a few yards away from this chair."

He lowered his eyes as he spoke and I felt a chill. He knows something and he's not telling us, I thought.

Then he continued, "I don't believe anyone could have risked going out of this house with her and gotten away with it. What I think we should do now is retrace every place we've been." He turned toward Mr. Pickett and said, "That includes you."

Mr. Pickett muttered something and left the room. From what Bruce had said, "a few yards away" I got an idea. What was the nearest place of concealment? The guest closet in the front hall. It had already been searched, but I felt a compulsion to go there and look again.

My heart was racing as I pulled aside the deep rows of coats, jackets, raincoats, shawls, umbrellas, all the oddments one finds in a catchall closet, in even the best run homes. There was a huge cardboard carton way back in the furthest recess of the big closet. It smelled faintly of paint, and I realized it was full of drop cloths the painters must have forgotten.

I craned my neck to look behind it. Nothing. I started to back out, but I heard a sound . . . or did I imagine it? I waited. Then I heard it again — a faint sigh coming from behind that huge cardboard box. I stooped down and looked again and there, way back in a corner, under a hanging cloak, I saw a dark shadow, a crumpled form, and I let out a shriek.

They all came running. Bruce said excitedly, "What is it? Melissa, don't just stand there."

I could only point a wavering finger toward that dark shadow in the closet. Bruce stepped inside and, pushing me aside, bent down. I heard a gasp, and then he emerged, carrying the limp figure of Madge Newell, her eyes closed in a death-white face, the blood streaming from one side of her head.

Bruce carried old Mrs. Newell upstairs two steps at a time. The moment he set her down on the bed, Dr. Perry, with Don assisting him, went to work on her. He motioned us to leave, and we all trekked downstairs to the library to wait. We had no idea if she were still alive or not.

At one point, an emergency car from the local Red Cross drew up in front of the house and two men entered with several tanks of oxygen. We all knew what that meant. The old woman's heart was so bad that oxygen was needed in addition to the considerable medication Dr. Perry had available to him. At least she was not dead. How the car had gotten here in the storm was another mystery — the bridge must have been opened for the emergency mission.

We sat in the library while the Volkes made coffee and gave each of us a cup, anticipating a long wait.

At last — when the clock struck the half hour after three o'clock — Dr. Perry came downstairs slowly. His face was very grave.

"I've left Don Wilford upstairs. Needless to say, Madge cannot be left alone for a moment."

"How badly is she hurt?" Stephanie's voice was filled with tears.

"She's in a very bad way. Whoever did this ghastly thing to her, and for whatever purpose, it brought on a stroke. Madge is paralyzed."

You could feel the shock wave that passed through the group.

"Poor Auntie," Muriel Newell cried out. "Paralyzed!"

Bruce said, "What else can you tell us, doctor?" Don't hold anything back!"

"The paralysis may or may not pass. She's lost her power of speech completely. It doesn't look good for Madge . . . not good at all!"

I heard a moan beside me and Miss Hillary toppled over on the sofa in a faint.

The rest of that night Wildemere became an infirmary. We were kept busy fetching and carrying, both to Mrs. Newell's room and to mine, where Miss Hillary now lay.

"It's not too serious," Dr. Perry had said. "Jennie's no youngster, and she's had a bad shock. Seeing Madge in that awful condition simply proved more than she could take. But I've given her some medication, and as soon as the weather permits she'd be best off in her own home. Of course, I wouldn't want her completely alone all day."

His eyes asked a question of me. "I can help take care of her — if that's what you mean," I said.

"It's exactly what I mean, Melissa. With that matter out of the way, I can address myself to the care of Madge." He turned to the group again. "In view of what has happened, I feel it's time you knew that someone did indeed try to poison her last month." He ignored the instant, shocked reaction of the group. "I don't want to discuss it at this point. You must take my word for it, and we'll proceed from there."

He rose from his chair and said with authority in his voice, "I'll bring a trained day nurse in here tomorrow. I'll also make arrangements for a night nurse." He gazed solemnly at us, then his face seemed to sag, and he said in a breaking voice, "I blame myself for allowing Madge to be exposed to this. I will save her if it is humanly possible!"

In that moment, I knew in my heart that Dr. Perry was not, could not possibly have been the one who had sought to dispose of Mrs. Newell. No one could be acting out the emotion he was revealing.

The next morning I awakened on the sofa I had occupied in the same room as Stephanie. It was hard to believe the terrible storm of the previous night had ended. The sun was pouring in through the windows, and its warmth was balm to my aching body. I had evidently fallen asleep in a cramped position, exhausted. None of us had gone to bed until 4:00 A.M.

163

The sun was shining, but I was depressed, remembering what had happened the night before. I knew now that with all her faults I truly loved Madge Newell. I couldn't bear the thought that she might not recover. The idea of never talking with her again, never playing one of our silly word games, never seeing the gentle, graceful, queenly wave of her hand as she commanded all those in Wildemere to do her bidding, was unthinkable.

I got up and sneaked to the door of her room. I peeked in at her and was appalled to see her lying beneath a plastic dome that covered the bed, tubes from a machine connected to her arm. She was white-faced.

The nurse had already arrived. Her name was Barnes. Tall, solid, reassuring in a crisp white uniform with a starched R.N. cap set on top of her no-nonsense hairdo, she motioned me out when Stephanie came to the doorway. She shook her head and refused to let either of us into the room.

"No one is to visit her. Doctor's orders." She shifted her feet in their rubber-soled oxfords. "Where she *should* be is in the hospital, but Dr. Perry won't risk the ambulance trip."

I said, trying to be friendly, "My name is Melissa Prescott. If I can help in any way, I'd be glad to."

"All right," the nurse said coolly, "but I don't think so." Then an idea occurred to her. "Are you the one who's been giving her her medicines?" I nodded. "Dr. Perry told me about you."

Was that approval I heard in her voice? "Maybe you could relieve me during lunch and rest period. They can't expect me to go a twelve-hour shift without a break."

"I'd love to fill in, I really would," I said.

Actually, I made the offer without knowing whether or not my job was ended. What need was there for me with Mrs. Newell so ill? But if there was anything I could do to help Mrs. Newell get well, I wanted to do it.

"I appreciate that, I really do." Her face creased in a smile. She turned to Stephanie. "And you're the patient's niece, I suppose . . . Miss Newell?"

"That's right," Stephanie said. "I'd like to make the same offer, Nurse. Anything I can do."

"Thank you, but I doubt that I can take you up on it. This young lady is the only one who's to be allowed in the room. That's doctor's orders."

Stephanie bit her lip. "I realize that. And I have the greatest respect for Dr. Perry. Do you know him well?"

The nurse was friendly again. "Oh yes, I've worked on his cases for years. He's a wonderful man."

I knew what Stephanie was up to. She was trying to charm the nurse. Well, let her. I wandered to the doorway and tried to get a glimpse of old Mrs. Newell while the two were talking, but it was difficult to see anything from where I stood, and I didn't have permission to go in.

As I walked back to the two of them, I heard the nurse speaking.

"Well, yes. I did want to be a doctor. But back then, only men were supposed to go into medicine. That's why I trained to be a nurse."

So Stephanie's charm was working; she had the nurse unloading personal details.

"It's different today," Stephanie said.

"You think so?" the nurse said.

"Are you talking about that new Women's Movement?" the nurse continued curiously. "Some of the young nurses keep trying to get me to go to a meeting. I don't know what it's all about."

"I don't know too much, either," Stephanie said. "I only know that some of the things they stand for make a lot of sense to me." She patted the nurse's arm. "If you want, we could have a talk about it one day."

"I'd like that," the nurse answered, looking at Stephanie admiringly.

As we walked downstairs, I took a second look at Stephanie. The charm act was one thing. But she had surprised me nevertheless. I couldn't help thinking, *Look at her, rich, right out of the Social Register, beautiful, graduate of a top finishing school, and yet look how she had gotten along with the nurse.*

And those things she'd said. I was really confused. Was it right to feel like Stephanie? It would be a new way of thinking about life . . . new and exciting, yet frightening. Maybe the new freedom for women to think and act as equals to men would spare girls in the future from Miss Hillary's fate. She had loved one man. The big prize in a girl's life in her day was matrimony. When another girl married the man she loved, she had given up the idea of love altogether.

Why did women have to feel that way about men? About marriage? It was something I needed to think over. What it meant, though, was that perhaps having to give up Bruce (as if I had ever had him!) might not be as tragic as it seemed.

But it was impossible for me to believe that I would someday care for another man in that very special way I felt about Bruce.

After breakfast I rode home with Miss Hillary

in Dr. Perry's car. Dr. Perry helped me get her onto the sofa in her living room and then left.

This time I was the one who made tea, heated biscuits, and brought them in with jelly and butter. Dr. Perry had demanded that Jennie Hillary take it easy at home. "You're going to stay home and rest, Jennie. Melissa will be with you a good part of each day and do any small chores you need."

So there I was looking after two old ladies — one desperately ill, fighting for her life; the other just needing a little TLC — tender loving care. I was busy, but I liked it because I was doing something useful.

The days sped by, like they do when you're busy. On Friday, the doctor said that old Mrs. Newell's oxygen tank could be removed for brief intervals.

"She's improving," he said. "There's a definite sign of progress. Slight — but progress. With a stroke that's an encouraging sign."

Everyone at Wildemere took the news in varied ways. As far as I could see Stephanie and I were the ones who were most elated by Dr. Perry's report — and Muriel and Bradford seemed the least pleased. Since the old lady's stroke they both seemed to slink about the house, almost as if they were trying to make themselves unnoticeable.

That afternoon when I came into the library Bradford Newell was up on a small stepladder reading an opened book which he'd taken from the top shelf. Upon seeing me he slammed the book shut and, taking it with him, stepped down the ladder and almost ran out of the room. I thought that was odd — even for Bradford Newell. Yielding to impulse, I climbed the ladder and peered at the top shelf. He had taken the book from a space between two books; one was entitled *Poison, Its Effects and Antidotes*; the other was a ponderous tome entitled *Homicide*, with a subtitle, *Famous Cases of Death by Poison.*

Now I knew what the Newells meant when they spoke of Bradford as being none too bright. He might just as well have left a note telling what book he had carried away with him. For some reason, he was delving into the study of poisons. Why? Had he already made use of some? Did he plan now to administer a final fatal dose?

On Saturday morning, Mrs. Volke called me into the kitchen and handed me a wrapped package.

"It's a bit of fresh fish I've cooked, Melissa. There's some vegetables and a little salad too. If you take it over to Miss Hillary now, she can eat it for lunch."

"All right," I said, trying to conceal my surprise. It was the first time she'd ever called me by name since I'd been there. I wondered at her sudden meekness. She was almost friendly.

When I got to the cottage the shades were drawn against the morning sunlight; I thought Miss Hillary was asleep. I was disappointed because I was anxious to talk over Bradford Newell's interest in poison with her.

After knocking and getting no answer, I gently opened the door and tiptoed in.

I found her lying on the sofa, with the most peaceful look on her face. For a moment my heart stopped. She looked as if life itself had departed. Then I saw her bosom faintly rise and fall, she gave

168

a long sigh of exhaustion, and then opened her eyes and smiled at me.

"Melissa, excuse me. Sit down, my dear."

"Thanks."

"How is Madge feeling today?" she asked. "Is there any change?"

I shook my head. "Not really. She's out of the oxygen tent for brief periods, but her paralysis is the same."

Jennie Hillary winced. "Help me up, Melissa, if you will. I must talk to you. It's very important."

I gave her a hand and she sat up, a slender weak figure that willingly let me adjust her on the sofa . . . almost like a rag doll.

"Are you all right?" I asked.

"Don't worry about me, Melissa. This week has been difficult. But I come of hardy stock." She looked at me with grave gray eyes. "There's not much time left if we're to try to save Madge's life — if it still can be saved."

Her eyes glittered with anger.

"I know beyond all doubt who has been trying to kill Madge."

My heart leaped. "You do?"

"I've had plenty of time lying here to sort out the events of the past month. Every last detail. They all lead to one conclusion."

I couldn't hide my impatience. "Please, Miss Hillary! Tell me!"

"I will, but bear with me a while longer," she said anxiously. "The very fact that you *know* will put your life in danger. You must tell no one. No one!"

She shuddered. "I can't believe it, and yet it's the only answer. It is someone who has been in

169

or near every scene of attempted violence that occurred at Wildemere. Someone whom I have since learned has more motive than anyone else to want Madge out of the way. Think, Melissa. Do you know who I mean?"

My heart stopped. The idea was one so awful that I could not, would not, contemplate it.

Miss Hillary said gently, "I know, my dear, how you must feel. But there can be no way out except to acknowledge the truth and act on it. The would-be killer gave himself away the night of the party in that last attack on Madge. A person who knew the house well enough to move about effectively in the dark. A person with enough physical strength after he'd knocked her unconscious to carry Madge's body out of the ballroom into the hall, to move aside that heavy crate of drop cloths and place her in the darkest recess of the closet.

I could not speak, so horrible was the realization of what was coming next .

"Melissa, I do feel for you. But he is a man who relentlessly struck down an old woman who has given him nothing but kindness and love from when he was a little child. A child grown into a monster.

"I see that you know who it is . . . *Bruce Murdock!*"

CHAPTER SIXTEEN

OF COURSE, BRUCE.

What Miss Hillary had done was to give voice
at last to the ugly suspicions I'd had from the
beginning but refused to acknowledge, even to myself.

Bruce. I had felt him move in the darkness of
the ballroom only seconds before Mrs. Newell disappeared.

Bruce. That day I was being chased in the
woods, he had convinced me that someone else
had been following me. But he was the one who
had pursued me.

Bruce. Even in the attic when he'd come up
behind me . . . I remembered that strange gleam
in his eyes that had momentarily frightened me.
My skin crawled as I thought of what a narrow escape I had had.

How could he have done anything so vicious?

I could not bear to believe it, and yet the facts were there before me. Still, there were a few questions that remained unanswered, and I asked them now.

"How did he imitate Ellen, the old nurse's voice?" I asked.

"I've thought about that. It wasn't too difficult. Bruce has a small tape recorder. I have often called to Madge by name, even in speaking to her in everyday conversation. I have often said her name aloud, just that one syllable — *Madge*. All he had to do was stand outside her room, record her name once, and then rerecord it on tape. He could even introduce a hollow-voiced version. In the confusion of being awakened in the dead of night, as Madge was, she could easily think it was old Ellen's voice she was hearing."

"But the cat . . ?"

"For Bruce? The simplest thing in the world. He has a marvelous way with animals."

"Why? Why did he do it?" I found myself asking.

"For the plainest of motives. Madge recently told me — but I scarcely gave it any thought — that since Bruce would someday marry Stephanie, he would inherit the largest part of her estate, as nominal head of the family. In his eyes, Madge must die *before* Wildemere is sold so that he can own it."

Was there no way around the facts? With her fine, sane, logical mind, Miss Hillary had put all the information together and come to a conclusion all too inescapable. Even so, I still hesitated to accept the inevitable.

Miss Hillary, always tuned to the slightest reaction, saw.

"Let me show you something, Melissa. Sit there."

She crossed the room, pulled the drawer of the cupboard open, and removed a small black object from it. When she returned to my side, she held out her hand. It was a triangular piece of shiny black plastic, apparently ripped from a larger piece. A piece that was exactly like Bruce's raincoat.

She shook her head sorrowfully. "I found it in the bushes one day as I was gathering berries in the woods. It was clinging to the branch that had torn it off. I wish I had never found it!"

I burst out suddenly, unable to repress my feelings, "How could he treat Mrs. Newell that way? He *does* care about her. I've seen it. It doesn't seem possible he could bring himself to do the things he did." I was seizing any possibility. "Why, only a madman could. . . ."

"Melissa, there is a great deal you do not know." Beads of perspiration stood out on her pale forehead. "You've heard that Bruce's parents died in the marshland? Do you know what actually happened?"

"No," I said miserably. "Bruce told me it was an accident."

"It was hardly that." Her voice was scarcely more than a whisper. "His parents died in a suicide pact."

I was shocked. I felt an actual pain in my heart.

"There was a reason for his father's suicide, beyond mere depression." She leaned close to me. "Bruce's father was suffering from an illness that attacks the mind with no warning. It is known as Huntington's Chorea, and once it appears, there is a rapid disintegration — first mental, then physical. There is no known cure for it. It begins with

173

small symptoms . . . like little mistakes in adding up figures or in doing detail work, then very quickly the victim becomes confused, deranged, and dies.

"That is what happened to Bruce's father. Since he was an architect, small mistakes began to crop up in the blueprints and other calculations he was working on. He knew the disease was fatal, so he . . . took a faster way out."

I couldn't speak. Miss Hillary took my hand and held it. "You must know this, Melissa. Bruce's father's illness was not only an incurable one, but it can be inherited. It is passed on by the males in a family to their sons. That is the constant threat that hangs over Bruce's head — that one day he will become ill with the same disease. . . ."

Tears started in my eyes, and I saw that she was crying too. I was numb with sorrow. Now that I knew, I could not bear the thought of Bruce living out his life carrying a terrible burden like that.

The words spilled out: "Then that's the reason for his strange moods, his anger, his awful unhappiness."

Miss Hillary said, "But do you understand all the implications? I do not know if he is already suffering from the disease his father had — or even if he will ever actually be a victim of it. But certainly he is unstable and disturbed enough to have been trying to take Madge's life."

I was filled with a sense of shock, of loss, of disbelief.

"Are you worrying about what will happen next?" Miss Hillary said. I nodded, miserable. "That has kept me awake nights since Madge's stroke. How can we possibly betray Bruce? Yet he must be stopped."

"Do you think anyone else suspects him?"

"I don't know. I don't think so. I can't bring myself to tell them, either. I love Bruce too much. And because I do, I'm stymied." At my inquiring glance, she said, "Bruce has no one in the world except Madge and Stephanie. If we tell Dr. Perry or the Newells, they'll insist he be taken away. He will either be put in jail, or in an institution."

At her words, I broke into tears.

"You must be strong, Melissa. I'm an old woman, and I can't function alone. Yet something must be done. Don't forget Bruce's objective is to destroy Madge." She said sadly, "That is, if she manages to survive the stroke she's had. Even that may be unlikely. In any case, Bruce cannot be allowed one more opportunity to hurt her." She wiped her eyes. "I will need your help."

"Just tell me what to do," I said, meaning it.

"I have a plan, Melissa, but I haven't worked it out entirely. It would be a way of saving Madge and yet preserving Bruce's liberty, despite what he's done. It would take matters outside the hands of the authorities."

"It would? What is it?"

"I'll tell you when the moment is right. Until then, Melissa, keep very close watch on Madge's sickroom. Oh, yes, I know about the nurse. But she's only human. If she steps away for even a few minutes, it can give Bruce the chance he's been waiting for."

I felt a chill. "All right. I'll see to it that he doesn't come anywhere near her room."

"Good girl!" Miss Hillary said, and brightened enormously.

The next few hours were a nightmare for me.

That afternoon at about four o'clock, Bruce came onto the terrace and joined our group for tea. The hard knot in my stomach that I'd been living with since Miss Hillary's talk with me earlier, now tightened and a wave of nausea hit me.

Fortunately, Dr. Perry took over in his brisk way. "I've got a bulletin I think you'll enjoy. She's improving. There's a definite sign of progress."

We were all sitting under one of the huge cedar trees shading the terrace. Instead of hot tea, the housekeeper had wheeled out a cart of cold drinks — lemonade, iced tea and coffee, and a bowl of fruit punch. It was an innocent charming scene, like something out of an English movie.

Dr. Perry sat down beside me on the white wrought-iron sofa just as Mrs. Volke placed some trays of little sandwiches and cakes on the table before us.

Everybody began to speak at once. "She's really getting better?" "Wonderful!" "What did I tell you?" "What makes you think she's getting better?" "When can we see her?"

"We can't all invade Madge's sickroom at once," Dr. Perry said. "Remember, she's still almost completely paralyzed. But," he cocked his head on one side and said with a broad smile, "she is now completely conscious. I've taken her off intravenous feeding. What pleases me most is she's gotten back some mobility in her legs. Nothing much . . . she can wiggle a couple of toes. But that's a very good sign that she may regain her motor powers to a considerable degree."

I heard a small sigh beside me. It was Muriel Newell. Her husband, Bradford, said, "I told you, Muriel! She'll bury us all. She's basically as healthy as a horse." He paused. "What I mean is, I'm glad.

176

It's a good thing she's got such a healthy constitution, is what I meant. That's all I mean. . . ." he finished lamely.

"Bradford, keep quiet!" Muriel Newell said.

Stephanie spoke to Dr. Perry directly. "Has she gotten back her speech yet?"

Dr. Perry said impatiently, "Please try to understand. Madge is still a desperately ill woman. She has suffered a severe stroke; we've only just been able to take her off the oxygen. Now we'll try to build up her strength and hopefully keep her on a steadily progressing rate of recovery. But there's no guarantee that we can do it. She can't speak, she can't have visitors of any kind. There must be nothing to set her back. All I've said today is that, for the first time in a week, there is some indication that with great care and attention, she may recover."

Bruce, tall and square-shouldered across the table, spoke up. "Do you mean to say, Dr. Perry, that we're still not going to be allowed in to see her?"

"That's exactly what I mean," the doctor answered.

Bruce's eyes darkened and he said in a dangerously quiet voice, "What I can't understand is why Melissa has been allowed to be in the room when Mrs. Barnes and the night nurse are off."

"What do you mean by that remark?"

"I mean, she's just a child." The contemptuous way he said it was unmistakable. "Suppose Aunt Madge gets a setback — needs emergency help? What then?"

"I much prefer to have Melissa in that room than any other member of this group. Don't ever forget — Madge is only in her present condition

177

because someone . . . someone perhaps at this very table, tried to kill her." Bruce reddened angrily, and started to rise. "Sit down, Bruce. You know that Melissa is the only one besides the nurses who is above suspicion, who can be trusted to keep a watchful eye on my patient."

"The group at this table includes you, Doctor," Bruce said meaningfully.

"Don't be a fool," the doctor said as he rose from the table. "If I wanted to kill Madge, would I be trying so hard to save her? Would I have taken such a clumsy and violent method as her attacker did?" He turned to me. "Come with me, my dear. I'll instruct you in the new regime for Madge."

With a heavy heart I followed the doctor up the stairs. I had not relieved the nurse since early morning and at that time Mrs. Newell was asleep under the oxygen tent, looking more dead than alive. Now I was astonished to see her lying back against the pillows, her eyes open, her hair groomed, wearing a pretty pink bed jacket, very like the one she had on the first time I saw her. I ran across the room to her.

Dr. Perry came quickly to my side. "Wait! Don't excite her. Speak in a calm, slow voice. This first day of consciousness is a great strain — and most important."

Mrs. Newell's eyes focused on the doctor with what I could have sworn was a look of reprimand, but since she could not speak I couldn't be sure. When she again looked at me a tear welled in the corner of her eye and I wiped it away with a tissue from the box beside her bed. I said the first words that came to my lips.

"Oh, Mrs. Newell. I'm so glad you're better."

Maybe Dr. Perry didn't approve, but I couldn't help showing my emotion. Somehow in these weeks, my world had turned upside down. Mrs. Newell was family to me.

Nurse Lucas, the night nurse, who had retired to a corner of the room when Dr. Perry and I came in, now said, "You know, Mrs. Barnes and I swapped shifts today. I have a dinner date tonight. If you want to relieve me now, Melissa, I'll take a break for a few minutes. Then I won't be so tired by the time Mrs. Barnes comes to take over."

I welcomed the chance to stay with Mrs. Newell. The doctor left with the nurse, and I sat down in the chair beside the bed. For a long moment we regarded each other. Then she blinked her eyes. She seemed to be looking at me expectantly.

"I can't talk to you. I'm not supposed to tire you. Doctor's orders." And I smiled.

Again she blinked her eyes.

I shook my head. "Please, Mrs. Newell," I said, "let's be good and do what the doctor wants. That way you'll get better faster."

Again her eyes blinked. Now there was no mistaking it . . . a look of anguish.

"What is it? Are you in pain?" I asked.

No blink of the eyes, only that look of anguish.

"Then what is it? Do you want something?"

Blink!

"Something you want me to do?" I waited, breathless.

Blink!

So that was it! Her blink meant *yes*. If her eyes remained open, it meant *no*. She wanted something, this old game-player, and had devised a way of helping me discover what it was.

179

I started to ask another question, but at that moment Nurse Lucas returned.

"How's our patient?" she asked, in that phony cheerful tone old-fashioned nurses use.

"Fine."

She picked up the old lady's wrist and felt her pulse, checking it against her wristwatch.

"Well! What's this all about? Her pulse is racing. Is she upset about something?" Her tone was accusatory. "You'd better leave now, Melissa. I'll just give her a tranquilizer to quiet her nerves."

Mrs. Newell was blinking her eyes again.

"Listen, Miss Lucas, Mrs. Newell's trying to tell me something."

She cut me off with a quick: "Now, you listen, young lady. She's just come round after five days of being in a coma. She's to do nothing but lie there and recuperate. And I'm here to see that she does it."

I started to protest; she clucked like a hen and playfully pushed me to the door. But I knew I had not misread Mrs. Newell's thoughts. I managed to fling back over my shoulder loud enough so that she couldn't help hearing, "I'll be back! I'll be back and we'll play our game!"

Outside Miss Lucas said to me, "That was a naughty thing to do. We mustn't do anything to upset our patient." With another kittenish little pat she motioned me along. I wished she would stop acting like she was a schoolteacher and everyone else was ten years old. Mrs. Newell had something she wanted to tell me. The very next time I went on relief duty, I would open up the subject again.

At dinner that night there was a phone call for me. Stephanie and Bruce both looked up curiously

180

as I left the room to take the call. When I picked up the hallway phone, I heard Mother's anxious voice at the other end.

"Melissa, you've had us all worried. We haven't had a line from you in two weeks. Are you all right?"

"I am," I told her. "But Mrs. Newell had an accident. That's why I didn't write."

"An accident? What do you mean?"

Mother's voice abruptly broke off. My father came on the line.

"What accident, Melissa?" My mother must have been explaining to him because, after a pause, he said, "An accident to the old woman you're taking care of? Was it your fault? What did you do?"

"Nothing, Dad. I didn't do anything. It just happened."

"What do you mean? Nothing just happens." His voice was the same — harsh, demanding, the way I remembered it. I felt a rush of anger that I quickly repressed. This was no time to answer back.

Click. I heard it plainly — the sound of a receiver being picked up from a phone cradle. Someone was listening in on our conversation!

"I can't talk now, Dad. I have to go," I said. "Is everybody all right?"

"We're fine here. You're the one we worry about. When you get back you and I are going to have a serious talk."

"I have to go now, Dad. Good-bye."

I hung up and punched my fist into the back of the chair beside me. That phone call was a reminder of what awaited me back home. Wildemere's problems were deadly serious, but they were real. What went on between my family and me back in Wellsville was some kind of murky un-wholesome thing I couldn't deal with. What was a family supposed to be? Were the men supposed to put you down all the time, make you feel in-ferior? In the families back home, the men were the important ones — the women were nothing. What good could come of that?

Troubled, I returned to the table. Bruce gave me an odd look, but I had stopped trying to commun-icate with him and did my best to ignore him whenever I could.

We finished the meal in silence. Once, Bruce said to me, "How's your friend Don? We haven't seen him around here since the accident."

"I don't know," I said curtly and got up. "I don't think I'll have any dessert. Excuse me."

I went to my room and waited. A half hour later, Nurse Barnes knocked at my door and asked, "Can you come in and sit for ten or fifteen min-utes, Melissa?" My heart leaped. It was the op-portunity I'd been waiting for. I rushed out of the room, and went to Mrs. Newell. Stephanie was standing in the doorway. I said, "It's okay, Steph-anie. I'll sit with her."

Stephanie firmed up the polite smile on her face. "I'll stay with you, Melissa. I do so want to see Aunt Madge."

"But Dr. Perry said she still can't have visitors. I'm not a visitor."

She actually elbowed her way in beside me. "Neither am I. I'll just say hello to her and then pop over to the bay window and sit there quiet as a mouse. She won't even know I'm there."

There was a determined glitter in her eyes I didn't like. What was with her anyway? Was she sus-picious of me, afraid for me to be alone in the room? Or did she have another reason for wanting to be there? She had never acted this way before. But there was nothing I could do about it. I had to let her go over to the bed, where she said hello to her aunt, kissed her lightly on the forehead, then said to me, "I'll get a book from my room," and went out.

There was only a dim lamp lit beside the bed, but I saw Mrs. Newell's eyes looking at me eagerly. She couldn't smile, but she blinked her eyes . . . and I knew.

"Want to go on telling me what we started?" I asked.

Blink!

Her eyes shifted to one side.

"Are you looking at something special?"

Blink!

"At the bookshelf?"

Blink!

"Want me to search for a book?"

Blink!

"This book?" I indicated the book of Shakespeare we had played with the last time I was with her before the accident.

No blink. Her eyes were pleading with me. I tried to think of what book she meant. I picked up the book of stories about Sherlock Holmes.

No blink.

I couldn't imagine which book she meant. At one time or another, I'd read to her out of every book in that bookcase. I thought a moment, then pulled out the book of nonsense poems that always made her laugh. I showed her the book.

"Is this the one you mean?"

Blink, blink, blink!

I was obviously hot on the trail. But her eyes

183

were pleading with me again. I ran through the index, wondering which poem she meant, and then I took a chance. On page 56 there was the poem she'd asked me about the day I came for my first interview. I quoted it now:

" 'You are old, Father William.' "

Blink, blink!

Good! It was the right poem. But now, what about it? I tried the next phrase:

" 'You are old Father William, the young man said . . .' " and got no further, for at that precise moment Stephanie came back into the room and stood next to me. She looked curiously at me and the poetry book I held.

"Shhh," I said. "We're almost at the end of a little game, and — and she's having fun and yet it's not exciting her at all."

Stephanie looked at me hard for a moment. "I don't get it," she said, without a trace of her usual charm. Then she shrugged her shoulders. "Okay, I guess it's all right if you'll be finished in just a moment. But I don't see how someone can't have visitors but can be playing games."

She retreated to the window seat where I could feel her eyes burning a hole into my back. I bent over the bed again, and indicated Stephanie with my head. The old lady got the idea at once — and blinked. We had to be careful if Stephanie were not to discover what we were up to. But I couldn't have done it without Mrs. Newell's fine, bright mind. No matter that she lay there paralyzed and only just beginning to make her way back; no matter that she was seventy and I was eighteen; no matter that she was the last of a fine old aristocratic Southern family and I was a nobody.

We were the game players, and this was the most sensational game we'd ever played . . . a game of life and death.

I had to hurry, so I repeated the last line I'd spoken before Stephanie came in: " 'Young man'?"

No blink. So I was off on a wrong track.

I went back. " 'You are old, Father William'. . . ?"

Blink, blink!

"You?" I said.

No blink.

"Old?"

Blink, blink!

Old? What meaning did that have for her? My mind raced back over the possibilities, back to that first day again, back to . . . Mrs. Newell, myself, and . . . Miss Hillary. I said aloud, "Miss Hillary?"

Blink, blink!

"Is it about . . . your accident?"

Blink, blink!

"You think Miss Hillary knows who hurt you?"

Blink, blink, blink!

I wondered if I should tell her that not only did Miss Hillary know who had hurt her, but that it was Bruce. I hesitated, thinking of the terrible blow it would be to her to know it was Bruce. Unless she already knew it was he!

But I was not to be given a chance to continue, for a shadow loomed in the doorway — and there stood Bruce!

I flashed a look at Mrs. Newell, and her eyes went to Bruce and then back to mine knowingly, and then . . . furiously . . .

Blink, blink, blink, blink, blink!

185

So that was it! She knew it was Bruce! I bent closer to her and whispered, "Bruce?" and again she blinked.

"Oh, now! This won't do!" said a voice, and Bruce turned aside to let Nurse Barnes enter.

"Mr. Murdock! Now, really! You can't come in here!" Then she spied Stephanie at the window seat. She said to me, "Oh, Melissa, I'm disappointed in you. You know the doctor's orders!"

Stephanie got up and came over and said, "All I did was sit here, Miss Barnes." Then to me, "Let's go, Melissa."

She took my arm, although she could see I didn't want to leave the room as yet. Old Mrs. Newell's eyes were pleading with me. There was something terribly important she wanted me to know, but in her helpless condition there was nothing she could do. I wrenched my arm out of Stephanie's grasp and practically shoved the nurse aside.

I bent over the bed and said in a hoarse rapid whisper, "I know. I know what you want. And I'll do it."

Again came the knowing *Blink*!

"Here now, that'll do," the nurse said angrily.

I was aware of Bruce still in the room as I left, talking to the nurse. Obviously he wasn't going to give up seeing the old lady as easily as the nurse thought. I tried to slow up, so I could hear what was going on, but Stephanie had me firmly in her grasp.

Out in the corridor, she let go of my arm roughly. "I don't know what you were up to, Melissa, but I intend to find out." She was getting really angry. "Don't think you had me fooled; that was no game you were playing."

"I don't know what you mean," I said, trying to

sound offended. "Maybe it was wrong, but I was only trying to cheer her up." I looked at her with the most sincere, innocent gaze I could muster. It wasn't easy, but I held myself to it until she dropped her eyes first.

"Forgive me, Melissa," she said, subdued. "I guess we're all uptight. I'm sorry."

When we got downstairs, I excused myself and went into the library. There I sat before the fire and tried to think things out. I couldn't forget the look in Mrs. Newell's eyes when Bruce had walked in. She had registered an enormous reaction. Obviously she wanted me to go to Miss Hillary and discuss it with her. All right, I would go — but first there was something else I wanted to make sure of. Miss Hillary's piece of evidence — the torn black plastic fragment — was proof only if it were matched to the raincoat from which it had been torn.

I had to go to Bruce's quarters, get the raincoat, and bring it over to Miss Hillary. She would tell me what to do next.

I went quietly out of the same French doors that Bruce had stepped through the stormy night I'd first met him, that night when he'd been wearing the black raincoat that was to prove his undoing.

My heart was full of misery as I mounted the stairs to the upper loft of the barn where Bruce lived. I stood before a door that was half open. Through the aperture I could see a warm yellow light burning in a room beyond. There wasn't a moment to spare. Suppose Bruce decided to come right back to his apartment the moment he'd won — or lost — his argument with the nurse?

I stepped into the room, feeling like a criminal.

But what I saw made me forget those feelings for the moment, for this was the home of the man for whom I cared so much, and it lay before me, openly revealing itself and its inhabitant's character for the world to see. It was a charming room, furnished in heavy saddle-leather chairs and a settee. The walls were paneled in wood, but with a great stone fireplace dominating the main section. It was outdoorsy in feeling; no one could mistake this for a city person's quarters. It was in shipshape order; everything seemed to be easily accessible — books, hunting guns, some attractively arranged seascapes on the wall, a great bowl of marsh ferns growing in a huge old brass pot. The colors were brown and black and tan and a warm cinnamon, very like the shade of clothes Bruce habitually wore.

I could have stood there forever, drinking in the look and feel and scent of this place, and wondering how a seemingly wholesome man of taste and education, as this room revealed him to be, could have such a dark and evil side. But the sense of urgency was great — I had to do the job I'd come for, and get out fast.

I crossed to his bedroom, and made myself go to the closet door, open it, and start my search. There were two rows of clothes neatly hanging inside: suits, sport shirts and jackets, and — coats. I went through the closet thoroughly. There was a tweed overcoat, a tan trench coat, a dark blue formal coat, several three-quarter length jackets, a dark brown leather coat, even a kind of Eskimo parka with sheepskin lining and a hood.

But no black raincoat. None. And I'd seen Bruce in it myself that first stormy night I'd met him.

I realized the implications: He must have disposed of the raincoat when he discovered a piece had been torn off.

Certain it was not there, I walked quietly across the floor, snapped off the light, and entered the dimly lit living room. A huge shadowy figure was standing there, and I felt my heart drop as I realized that, unheard and unnoticed by me, Bruce had come in and was waiting for me.

CHAPTER SEVENTEEN

HE TOOK one long step toward me, barring my way. I tried to move away from him, but he put a hand on my arm.

"Not so fast! Not until you explain the meaning of this visit."

"I — wanted to talk to you. So I came over . . ." I began, knowing as I spoke what a stupid lie it was.

"Nonsense. I was upstairs with Aunt Madge and the nurse, and you knew that." His voice was low, but there was no mistaking his determination. "I want the truth, do you hear? What were you doing here in my house?"

It was impossible for me to think of an answer. In desperation I said, "I was looking for something."

His eyes glittered. "All right. Now tell me what it was." I stood there mutely. He took my shoulders in his hands and half shook me. "I'm waiting, Melissa."

I was taut with fear; I felt he could break me in two with those hands. His look was so fierce I thought he would stop at nothing. But still I could not tell him. If I did, it meant revealing everything. I must say nothing about the black raincoat. It would put Miss Hillary, alone in her house, in great danger. That was all I knew. But he was waiting for an answer, an answer I could not give him.

"What were you looking for? Tell me!"

"I won't tell you. You can't make me." My voice cracked, and I began to cry.

"Stop that. Tears won't help you now, Melissa. I want the truth." He shook me by the shoulders and began to back me up against the wall. His eyes were frightening. I bent my head, but he swung it up against the wall. I was panicked out of my mind. I could only think, He's going to kill me! Here. Now.

"Talk!" he said.

"I won't! I won't tell you anything — you murderer!" The words spilled out of me.

"So that's it," he said in a whisper.

"You can kill me, I don't care. But I won't let you hurt anyone else. I won't." I could not stop the wild sobbing.

He pushed me hard against the wall.

"Now you just listen to me. You've given me no choice, Melissa. I don't want to do this, but now I have to."

My eyes were racing wildly around the room. I looked desperately for some weapon I could try to reach, but it was a foolish thought. Even if there were something, I couldn't possibly break out of that iron grip. Nothing could save me.

And then from downstairs there came a wild

uproar. I felt the floor under my feet shake as the strange violent sounds reverberated through the barn. Bruce let loose his grasp of me and looked toward the staircase, from which I could now make some sense out of the sounds. It was Bolivar. He was pounding the barn floor and walls with his hooves, and bellowing at the top of his lungs. Surely something terrible was happening to rouse an animal to such a frenzy.

Without a word, Bruce raced down the stairs toward his horse. I looked about the room and ran to the window. It opened onto a low shed four or five feet below. I didn't wait one moment, just stepped out on the sill and jumped.

I landed on the roof of the shed and got down on my hands and knees and edged my way over, holding on by my fingers, then letting myself down to the ground below. I felt my knee scrape against the side of the shed as I went down, but it didn't matter. I had to get over to Miss Hillary's.

I ran in the darkness, along the wooded lane leading to Miss Hillary's cottage. I was still too full of what had happened in Bruce's place to be scared; moonlight lit the path, filtering through the trees and the thick bushes where once the dark intruder had trailed my steps. I determinedly ran on, trying to forget all about Bruce, thinking only of getting to Miss Hillary and working out with her a way of stopping Bruce in his now desperate and openly murderous intention to bring matters to the end he desired.

When I got to the cottage, a faint light was glowing in the window. I had to rap on the door several times before she heard me. She opened the door and her face lit up with a smile of welcome.

"Melissa! Come in — I'm delighted." She held

the door open and stood up on tiptoe to kiss my cheek. There was that lovely scent of lavender that was so like her; her gentleness and civility were so welcome after the harrowing time I'd just had that I went a little limp with relief. She noticed at once.

"What is it, my dear? What's wrong?" Her gray eyes were warm with concern.

I told her about my encounter with Bruce, and she was shocked.

"Oh, Melissa. You didn't. That was a big mistake, going to his quarters. Now he'll stop at nothing to get what he wants." Her forehead wrinkled with worry. "And Madge will find out that he's the one who's been trying to do away with her. Dear girl, do you realize how you've complicated matters?"

"I'm sorry, Miss Hillary. But I thought that if I brought Bruce's raincoat to you, you'd really have proof that he was the one who's been behind all the attempts on Mrs. Newell's life. I didn't mean him to catch me."

"It's true, Melissa — the raincoat should be enough to convict Bruce, but I didn't want to . . ." she broke off, as from the kitchen the whistling of the tea kettle began and grew louder and louder. "Wait a moment while I get the tea things, and we'll figure out what must be done now."

She left the room, and I sat there, bursting with nervous energy, unable to sit still. I got up and began to move about the room. Then my eyes lit on the needlepoint basket. That was it — I would take out the needlepoint pincushion cover I was working on. Maybe it would soothe my nerves. I raised the lid and began to poke around to find my sampler. I dug deeper and deeper, still not finding what I wanted. But there was something dark toward the bottom of the basket. Curious, I reached down and started to pull it up when I realized what it was.

A balled-up black plastic raincoat. A hooded black raincoat, with a triangular tear in it.

I was shocked. What was it doing here?

Miss Hillary hadn't told me that she had taken Bruce's raincoat. Why not? In order to destroy the one perfect piece of circumstantial evidence? That must be it. Bruce was *her* favorite as well as Mrs. Newell's. Between them they would do anything to save this man.

I heard Miss Hillary wheeling the tea cart from the kitchen. Hastily I slammed the basket shut and sat down on the sofa just as she entered.

"This is what I made today, so you'd have it tomorrow. Now you can enjoy it while it's just fresh-baked. Angel food with fudge icing."

I forced myself to act pleased. It wasn't easy, not with all the puzzling information I was trying to deal with. I started to babble nonsense, to cover up how upset I was.

"I'm so glad I could come here." I took a forkful of the cake. "Ummm . . . this cake is really delicious. You're too nice to me, honestly," I said insincerely.

As I ate, my mind was weighing all the meanings that plastic coat in her possession could have. Every tingly instinct warned me not to reveal that I knew it was there. If Miss Hillary were protecting Bruce, then she was no longer being open with me and I owed her nothing. If she were not, what was it doing in her house?

I was on pins and needles to get out of there. Since I didn't feel I could be honest with Miss

Hillary now that she was holding back information, I didn't want to get into any deep discussion with her until I'd had a chance to think things out alone.

But just then, she spoke: "We'll discuss the matter of Bruce later, Melissa. Right now, I'm anxious to know about Madge. How is she?"

I started to tell her about Mrs. Newell and her obvious desire for me to see Miss Hillary. But I couldn't. Caution sealed my lips. Miss Hillary was looking at me, waiting. That was when inspiration struck: A half truth very often serves the purpose when you're trying to keep information to yourself. Unquote. Miss Anderson.

"To tell the truth," I said, not telling it, "when Mrs. Newell and I were alone this evening, I got the feeling she was trying to tell me something."

"Do you mean she's conscious?"

I had forgotten that she did not know. "Yes," I said.

"She is? How wonderful!" Miss Hillary's voice broke; she put a handkerchief to her eyes, and I could see they were full of tears.

Better not get her hopes up too high, I thought. "She's still paralyzed, and can't talk. But I got the feeling when I was with her that she wanted to tell me something important."

Miss Hillary said thoughtfully, "What made you think that? If she can't talk, how could she communicate with you?"

So I told her about the blinking. But I didn't tell her that Mrs. Newell wanted me to see her.

Miss Hillary said, "Now we are getting somewhere, Melissa. You say she blinks her eyes. Very well, what we have to do is prepare a list of questions to which she can answer *yes* or *no*."

"That's a wonderful idea," I said, hoping I didn't sound too stupid. "Maybe tomorrow you can come over and visit and between us we can figure out what she wants."

"That's exactly what we'll do." She sounded much cheerier now. "What time will you be relieving Nurse Barnes?"

"I don't know, actually. But the one we can be sure of is Miss Lucas. She always takes a break around teatime."

"Then that's when I'll come over."

"Are you sure you'll be up to it? You still seem — not quite yourself," I said tactlessly.

"I'm old, Melissa. That's all that's wrong with me, and no one can cure that. But I'll see you at teatime tomorrow. You can count on me."

As I went to the front door, she said, "I don't like your going home in the dark, but I'll give you a flashlight. Wait." She got one from a drawer and handed it to me. "Be sure to stay on the main road. And don't stop for anyone."

"I won't." I gave her a quick hug. "Thanks for the cake."

I used the flashlight to see my way to the main road, and I started walking back. But I hadn't gone more than twenty steps before I realized I didn't want to go. I felt there was unfinished business back at the cottage. I couldn't just walk away.

I stopped, snapped off the flashlight, and tried to think. I began to focus on the night of the accident to old Mrs. Newell. I could remember what people had said and done after she'd disappeared. It was funny how clear my mind was in the quiet darkness. I could hear Bruce's voice again. And Mrs. Volke's. And Stephanie's. Everyone. In a blinding flash I heard Miss Hillary's voice earlier that very day when I had brought her lunch over. I particularly remembered what she had said about the night of the accident — and there was something that didn't make sense at all! Why hadn't I realized it earlier? I had to know.

I made my way back to the cottage. I reached the edge of the freshly mowed lawn, and trod softly on it to the side of the house.

At the kitchen window I crouched down, but I could still see Miss Hillary. She was stacking the tea things on the sideboard next to the sink. Obviously she was going to do the dishes. That would give me the opportunity I needed.

When I had first visited Miss Hillary, she had not allowed me to peek into her workshop. Now I felt that I had to know why.

I went to the back of the house, to a window that had to be the one in her workshop. I tried to see within, but it was hopeless. Inside the window a dark green shade barred even the faintest crack of light. I was taking a terrible chance, but I couldn't stop now. Cautiously I felt the sill around the many-paned window. And luck was with me. It was an oppressively hot night, and the window had been left slightly open — just an inch, but that was enough. Slowly I pushed it up enough to let me enter. The sill was about four feet off the ground and I could not leap up to it without making a terrible commotion. There was only one way to get in, and that was to shinny my way up to the sill.

I scratched my knee — the one I'd already hurt leaving Bruce's house — against the abrasive wooden shingles. Then I got my hands on the louvre windows and pushed gently against them. They

197

were strictly decorative, and had no latch between them; they swung back into the room easily. At last I swung my legs over the ledge and looked inside, and then I had to hold on to my senses to keep from exclaiming aloud.

Even if I live to be very old, I will never forget the scene that met my eyes.

CHAPTER EIGHTEEN

A GLOWING eternal light lit up the small room. It flamed in front of a mantelpiece over which hung a huge oil painting framed in an antique gold border. The painting was that of a young and handsome man in his late twenties, and had obviously been done forty or fifty years before — the style of the clothes told me that. Though he wore a neatly trimmed mustache, I could still associate his features with those of a man whose picture I had seen frequently at Wildemere.

Henry Newell.

The entire room was a shrine to his memory — a testimony to the ill-starred love Jennie Hillary had borne him. On every inch of wall space — on tables, shelves, in cabinets — were mounted relics of the past, not only pictures, but all sorts of mementos. Near a snapshot of a fish with Henry Newell standing proudly beside it were mounted the very rod and reel with which he had caught it. There was a class ring dated 1916 from Murchison High School, with the initials "H.N." engraved inside it, a diploma from Cornell University certifying that one Henry James Newell had received the degree of Bachelor of Arts. The other displayed items were enough to make a person sick with fright — ties, a sweater, a leather boyscout belt — probably worn by the boy Henry Newell at age eleven or twelve.

I stood frozen to the spot, stunned.

Where and how Jennie Hillary could have collected these unbelievably intimate items I could not imagine. But then I remembered Bruce's surprise when the attic door had given way so easily. Of course! Jennie Hillary, obsessed, must have been constantly looting the Newell mansion, scouring the attic, stealing these pathetic reminders of the man her best friend had taken away from her, a man dead more than twenty years.

And then the doorknob turned.

The door slowly opened, and Miss Hillary came in.

But this was not the Miss Hillary I had known. She looked the same, small trim figure, smooth gray hair, neatly dressed, only her eyes were two cold gray stones, expressionless, terrifying.

"Oh, Melissa, what a pity!" Her mouth was smiling a little, but those dead eyes held mine. "You couldn't accept things as they were, could you? You had to know." Her voice was as cold as her eyes. "Now you've made things too difficult. Too difficult for me to think of a way out for us."

That pronoun "us" frightened me as much as anything that was happening in this strangely lit cell.

"Why don't you say something, Melissa?" Her eyes came to life a bit, demanded attention. "Aren't you going to tell me what you think of my treasures? Did you truly think I was a woman who could live without love?"

I had to say something. "Why, no. No, I didn't, Miss Hillary. I mean, I didn't think. . . ."

"Oh yes, you did, my dear. You're the kind of girl who thinks a lot. But you keep it to yourself, just as I do."

She came closer to me, put a hand on my arm, and involuntarily I stepped back.

"Don't be afraid of me, Melissa. I would never harm you." At the disbelief she saw in my face she said, "Oh, I know — those others. I did harm the others. I admit that freely." Her thin gray eyebrows arched in a plea for understanding. "But I had to do it."

She is completely insane, I thought. *What am I going to do?*

Unconsciously I was searching the room for a way out, for a weapon if I needed one, for something. . . .

With a quick movement, Miss Hillary reached for what my eyes had lit on — a hunting gun mounted on the wall. She pulled it down and held it with the muzzle pointing at me.

"I can't let you go now, Melissa. Don't make me do anything to hurt you." She motioned with her head to a rocking chair that directly faced the mantel with the portrait of Henry Newell above.

"Sit down. We'll have a little visit."

What a mockery, those words. I sat down. With those eyes fixed on me and the shotgun now pointing directly at my head, I had no choice.

"That's my chair you're sitting in, Melissa. And

201

I'm glad you're here with me. It's fitting that you should be. You must know how very fond of you I am."

She sat in a small upholstered armchair a few feet off to the right of and slightly behind me. Her position put me at a terrible disadvantage. How could I make a move to get that gun? I was super-sensitized with fear. My nerves, like a radar beam, were telling me, *Don't move, don't get her angry, don't turn your head and look directly at her, don't say anything to upset her. She's a killer, watch out, watch out.*

"Look at him, Melissa. Look at my love. Isn't he handsome? Look at those eyes, that mouth, that beautiful forehead." Her voice hardened. "*She* took him from me. He loved me and she took him from me. She didn't love him, not like I did. She made him fetch and carry, she made him play up to her all the time, just like she treated all the others. She didn't care about him — not the way I did."

I put my hand to my cheek, and she instantly raised the gun closer.

"Don't move, Melissa." The voice crackled. It didn't sound like Miss Hillary. It was as if she were inhabited by two different people. One voice was the ice-cold, hard, dead sound of something inhuman. The other voice was soft and sad and sick and, yes, loving.

The soft voice again, "You know, Melissa, I am not a cruel woman. I want you to understand. You know I'm not cruel, don't you? Please answer me, Melissa."

"Yes, yes. I know you're . . . good." My heart throbbed in my throat, making my voice thick. Could she tell how frightened I was?

"You're quite right. Madge killed him. If Henry had married me, he'd be alive today. With her, it was all strain and fuss and selfishness. All she ever thought of was herself." The voice was cold-hard again, vicious. "That's how she killed him. But I'll pay her back." A strange moan twisted her lips.

What can I do to get away? She's a madwoman and I'm alone with her. And no one in the world knows I'm here.

The voice was soft again, soft and weary. "It's all over now. I know that. When Madge decided to sell Wildemere and take my last shred of happiness from me, what else could I do? I had to be rid of her. It isn't as if she deserves to live anyway. You see that, don't you?"

She wants an answer. Don't antagonize her.

"Yes, I see that."

"It isn't like it was with Bruce's parents. I truly didn't want to do what I did. They were good people. But if Bruce's father had finished the blueprints, Henry would have moved to Florida, and I would never have seen him again." A long, wracking sigh escaped her. "That was — unthinkable. So I had to act. And Bruce's mother had begun suspecting me. Woman's intuition, you know. I was so in love with Henry any woman would have guessed — any woman but Madge. Madge, with that enormous ego of hers." She passed a hand over her face, but not so slowly that I could make a move toward her. "Where was I? Oh yes, the Murdocks. Good, decent, but I had to dispose of them. So easy to do. My writer's mind, you know. Told *her* he was waiting for her down in the marshland. Got *him* down there first with a trumped-up story. There they stood in the moonlight, on the edge of the quicksand pit, each wondering what the other wanted. All it took was a quick push from behind." She leaned toward me, her eyes glittering with a kind of amazement. "Do you know, Melissa? They were both gone in less than two minutes? There was a suck and a gurgle, and the bog swallowed them up."

A wave of nausea hit me. *Poor, poor people.*

"The rest was easy. Mr. Murdock was an architect, you know. There were dozens of samples of his printing around. I can copy anyone's handwriting quite well . . . printing is a lot easier. Left a brilliant note — " She chuckled. "One of the finest things I ever wrote. No one doubted it for a moment. 'No reason to go on. With my terrible illness, the future is too bleak.' That sort of thing." The voice split again. "I made all that up about Mr. Murdock having that disease. I chose Huntington's Chorea because it can be inherited. That took care of that brat, Bruce. Spoiled little beast! Always coming between Henry and me."

I gasped, and she picked it up at once. "Shocked, my dear? Don't be. It was all for nothing — nothing. Henry, my darling Henry, became ill a few months later. Leukemia. Incurable. Of course he'd never have gotten it if it weren't for *her*. The strain of living with her. That's what did it."

Her voice was hoarse. She must be leading up to something. What? I waited, then she said in a low, warm, loving voice, "Melissa, you're the only one I can talk to. Darling girl."

That low caressing voice made me turn my head aside with revulsion. Instantly, the cold voice came.

"Don't do that. Don't turn away. Look at me. Do you hear?"

I turned back. The rigid face relaxed.

204

"The trouble is, I got so terribly fond of you, Melissa. That's what made it so hard for me to do the things that had to be done. Once you were there, it was so difficult to do anything about her food or her medicine. That's why I tried to frighten you that day in the woods when you left my house. I didn't want to hurt you; I just wanted you to leave Wildemere.

"I was almost glad when Bruce came along and spoiled my plan." She shifted in her chair, still holding the gun steady. "But you kept right on, my dear . . . interfering. So I had to try again. That day in the attic — I didn't mean to hurt you, just scare you off." A little laugh, then, "Besides, it gave me a chance to pretend I was hurt too, in case anyone was suspecting me. Oh yes, I'm clever. Years of writing murder books, you know." She paused, then I saw her expression change. "I saw him kiss you. You do love him, Melissa. Just as I loved Henry. But then she took him from you — she, the other one — Stephanie."

She got up from the chair and moved toward me, the gun leveled right at me. I started to shake with fear as the voice, the cold crazy voice came again, "Now I must ask you to make final arrangements. Stand up!"

I said, "Yes, Miss Hillary," and quickly got up on my feet.

Coldly, the voice dictated: "Go to the fireplace. Take out the logs. Take all the newspapers and books and pictures from that cabinet. Make a pile of them. A big pile. Place the logs on top of them. Then light the fire."

I stood still, horrified by her words.

"Do it. Now. Do you understand?"

So that was it. I would start a fire, and the

room would burn up, destroying all evidence of her obsession. Then what?

With the gun trained on me and that crazy voice directing me, I set to work building a pyre in the center of the small room, piling wood on paper, then adding more and more as she indicated . . . a small bookcase, a stool, an end table . . . wooden pieces that would make a roaring fire.

I stole a glimpse at her as I went about my grisly task. Her face was flushed, her whole stance and bearing that of a person in an almost catatonic state, rigid, mindless, obviously bent on violence, destruction.

She's going to burn me up in this room!

"Don't be afraid, Melissa. I see on your face that you know," she said in a suddenly kindly tone.

She'll lock me in and I'll burn down with the house and she'll say it was an accident. She'll say I came visiting when she wasn't home. Maybe they'll never find me at all.

Tears were beginning to fall from my eyes. I was crying silently, but she saw.

"Don't cry. Don't be afraid to die. I know, Melissa. I've suffered all these years. I know now it would have been better for me if I had died the day I lost Henry."

There was no way out. Even in her lunacy, she planned too well. She said softly, "That's enough, dear. Light the fire. Take a match from the mantel and light the fire."

I went to the mantel, and got a match from the box on top of it.

"Good girl. Now light it."

Almost as in a trance I struck the match and touched it to an edge of newspaper. Instantly it all leaped aflame . . . papers, books, wood taking hold incredibly fast. Within a few minutes the room would be a flaming furnace at the rate the fire was growing. With that gun on me, my death sentence was all too clear.

"Now sit down over there, and I'll sit here, and . . . let's talk, shall we?"

If the terror weren't so very real, what happened next was so ludicrous I could have laughed. For Miss Hillary sat down in her chair and proceeded to chat with me in the most reasonable voice, even as the fire blazed higher, even as the words she spoke defied belief.

"What a lovely fire. You're so efficient, Melissa. That's what drew me to you from the first. I never wanted to hurt you. I love you. You're *me*, at your age. Neither of us great beauties. But quality. That's what we have . . . quality. . . ."

Rambling on and on in that soft voice as the flames climbed higher and higher. The heat was unbearable. *I am going to die. I am going to die. Here, now, with this crazy woman.*

Can I leap at her and get that gun out of her hands? Impossible. We were too close. She would shoot me first, she couldn't miss, not at that distance, not even in her deranged state.

I thought of my family back home, Mother, Jody, Bob, Dad. What would they do? Mother would cry and so would Jody. Would my father?

"Perfect, it's perfect, Melissa. We'll go up together, my dear, in a puff of smoke. And no one will ever know."

The heat was intense. I raised my hands to my face to shield myself from the flames coming closer. I barely heard Miss Hillary cry out,

"Don't do that! Put your hands down, Melissa!"

Then came the sound of cracking wood. At first I thought it was the fire, and then I saw the splinters flying into the room as the door burst open. I saw Bruce and Stephanie and Don. Bruce leaped across a patch of flame toward me and that was the last thing I knew.

CHAPTER NINETEEN

THERE WERE stars and the sky was black and I
thought I was dreaming, but I wasn't. The night
was warm and there was a wave of heat sweeping
toward me and an orange glow coming from where
the heat was.

I was lying on the grass. I heard voices and
commotion; there were men in hip boots, wearing
helmets and carrying hoses and shouting to each
other. Don Wilford was helping a fireman carry
a hose that was spurting torrents of water.

I looked up and saw Stephanie bending over me.

"Melissa! Are you all right, honey? Melissa,
talk to me."

Muriel and Bradford Newell were standing
behind Stephanie and looking at me with sym-
pathetic eyes. To the left of Stephanie I saw
Emile Volke's back; I could not see beyond him.

I was tired, terribly tired, like a long-distance

209

runner who's finished a race of a thousand miles. And Stephanie was waiting for me to answer, kneeling beside me.

"I'm okay." Speaking was such an effort.

Stephanie smiled and took my hand. "Melissa, if anything happened to you . . . I can't tell you how awful it was thinking we were too late." Her voice — that perfect finishing school voice — had lost its cool, its polish. You're real, Stephanie. You care. You're real.

"We'd have been there sooner, but I'm not as bright as you, Melissa. It took me a heck of a time to figure out Aunt Madge's message."

Back it came, flooding memory with horror. Miss Hillary. Raving and hating and — a killer. It was warm there on the grass, but I shivered.

"Miss Stephanie! Don't you see you are upsetting her?" It was Mrs. Volke. It was the same harsh Germanic voice, but she cared. Why hadn't I known that before?

Then Emile Volke stepped aside and I was able to see across the lawn. Miss Hillary was walking on the grass. Miss Hillary with Bruce beside her; Miss Hillary looking wild-haired and disordered, just as I'd last seen her in that flaming shrine room of hers. Looking the same and yet not — she seemed shrunken, beaten.

I heard Bruce say to her, "Come along now, Jennie. We're going to take you to a place where they'll take care of you."

Dr. Perry slammed out of a station wagon and hurried over to them with a white-clad nurse beside him.

He took Miss Hillary by the arm. "Hello, Jennie," he said quietly. "Shall we go now?"

For a long moment she stood and looked at him

blankly. Then she smiled and said, "Yes, Henry. I'm ready. I've been waiting so long for you."

Dr. Perry and the nurse each took her by one arm, and they led her to the station wagon. I felt my heart would break.

Emile Volke came close to me and said, "I will carry the girl to the car."

He started to bend down, and then a voice said, "No, let me."

It was Bruce.

He picked me up in his arms and started walking to a car. Inside it, behind the wheel, was Don. He said, "Don't know what you think you've been doing, Melissa, but the minute I turn my back, you get into trouble." His voice was teasing, but his eyes were concerned.

Stephanie got into the back of the car with Bruce and me, and I saw her take his hand.

"It's terrible about Jennie, Bruce. But I think we're all squared away now, darling. Aren't we?"

Bruce sighed deeply and said, "Yes. I think so. I hope so."

He and Stephanie looked at each other meaningfully and I closed my eyes. They would be happy together; they were good people and they were close and warm, bound together by the common experience of many years. And when Bruce learned the whole truth about his parents, he'd be free of that burden he'd carried for so long.

Bruce looked over at me and said, "We're taking you back to Wildemere, Melissa. You'll be taken care of there. Think you can make it?"

"Yes, Bruce. I can make it." My voice came out a lot weaker than I would have thought. But I meant it. I could make it. I had learned I could stand up to anything. Even though it meant making it through a whole lifetime without this man whom I loved so deeply.

We were all gathered in the library. It was two weeks later and there we were — Dr. Perry, Muriel and Bradford Newell, Emile and Gerda Volke, Stephanie and Bruce, and Don Wilford. Old Mrs. Newell had been coming along in leaps and bounds, and the doctor had said she could be present at this meeting. She was in a wheelchair, with Nurse Barnes standing beside her, and she looked a lot like the woman she'd been when I had first come to Wildemere. Her cheeks had filled out, her color was good. She was rapidly regaining as much use of her limbs as she had had before the "accident" — and now the prognosis for her future state of health was good. She still did not have the power of speech, but Dr. Perry felt that it would return with proper physiotherapy, which had already been started.

"It's all here in this book," Bruce said. He was holding a small red diary-sized volume. "Can you imagine a mind so unbalanced? She was the one who wrote the note supposedly from my father. My parents had no intention of committing suicide and my father had no illness. That was all contrived by Jennie Hillary."

"It's incredible," Dr. Perry said. "I've read that diary from cover to cover and it's a complete documentation of poor Jennie's derangement."

"What an actress she was — to have fooled all of us for so many years!" said Muriel Newell.

"She didn't have to be an actress," said Don Wilford. "She had a dissociated personality. Two sides to her — one good, one evil. Neither half really tied up with the other. Whichever one she was being at the time, she believed in that part of her personality completely. Isn't that right, Dr. Perry?"

"It certainly is," Dr. Perry said, looking approvingly at Don. "You're going to make an excellent doctor some day, young man. Understanding the mental and emotional makeup of people goes a long way toward understanding their physical ailments."

"Wait a minute!" said Bradford Newell. "I'm not sure I follow all this. How could she have done some of those awful things? I mean like killing Aunt Madge's cat and . . ."

I was close enough to Madge Newell to see her wince. Muriel Newell picked up her aunt's reaction immediately and said her favorite three words, "Be quiet, Bradford!" She nodded toward the wheelchair. "We mustn't upset Aunt Madge. It's just as well to let certain matters drop."

"Not at all," said Dr. Perry. "Let me explain, Muriel, please. Your aunt has never been one to hide from the truth." He looked over at Madge Newell, who nodded her approval.

"Very well, then," he continued. "With her dual personality, Jennie on the one hand was able to be a tender loving friend and companion, as she most often was to Madge and to others of us present in this room. On the other hand, when her evil self was operating — the self that was out for revenge — she could perform acts of extreme violence, acts requiring strength she did not normally possess."

"You mean like . . . killing Ivan?" Stephanie asked, her eyes wide.

"Oh, yes! In the frame of mind she was in, it was not difficult for her to lure Ivan outside —probably with catnip left over from the night she lured the black stable cat out on the fence to frighten Madge. Once she had her hands on Ivan, she had the strength not only to throttle him . . ." He glanced at old Mrs. Newell. "I'm sorry, my dear Madge — but let's clear it all up, shall we?"

Again she nodded, though her eyes were bright with tears.

Dr. Perry went on, "Believing she was venting her wrath rightfully, Jennie had more than enough strength to kill Ivan, *and* to do something she could never have done in her other gentler personality — climb the trellis outside Madge's room so she could leave the poor animal on the bed."

"I can't believe it," said Stephanie. "Do you mean that's what gave her the strength to take Aunt Madge from the ballroom that night? Her obsession?"

"Certainly. She could never have done it otherwise. The entry in her diary reads . . ." Dr. Perry turned the pages, found the one he wanted and began to read, " 'Fate gave me my opportunity last Saturday at the party. When the storm began and the lights went out, I knew that it was the time to forever rid myself of my enemy! I struck her down, and I lifted her — she was like a feather in my arms — and I found my way in the dark to the nearest place, the closet. Oh, why did Melissa have to be at the party? Of course she was the one who found Madge! The girl has stood in my way before. If I did not have this strange feeling for her, she would be the next one to be removed. If she persists in playing detective, I will have to act."

Stephanie was the first to speak when Dr. Perry had finished.

214

"Melissa, did you know the danger you were in? When you went to her house that last night, did you know?"

"Not at first," I said. Everyone was watching me. I had told Dr. Perry the story of that last terrible night in the cottage, but obviously the others didn't know. They were waiting for me to go on.

"The first inkling I had was finding that raincoat of Bruce's." I didn't look at him, but I felt his eyes on me. "Even then, the fact that it was in her needlework basket didn't mean she was guilty. I couldn't be sure. What really made me know was when I left the house and thought back on her conversation earlier that day. She had said to me the guilty one had to be a person who could carry Mrs. Newell's body out of the ballroom, *move a heavy crate of drop cloths aside,* and place her in the back of the closet."

"I don't see what that had to do with anything," Muriel Newell said. "We all knew that's what happened."

"That's right," I said. "*We* knew — but Miss Hillary didn't. She passed out, remember? Before we had any discussion of anything. And no one spoke to her about it after that. She went home the next day and saw no one but me — and *I* never mentioned it. So how could she have known there was a crate in the closet, and that Mrs. Newell was behind it — unless she'd been in that closet herself?"

"That is very nice deductive thinking," Don said, smiling at me. "You've got the makings of a real Sherlock Holmes. You amaze me."

"Why?" Stephanie asked, those clear green eyes of hers looking directly at him. "Are only men

215

supposed to be clear thinkers? Or detectives?"

Don seemed bewildered. "I hadn't actually thought about it."

"Then do," said Stephanie. "Try thinking along those lines, Don. You may be surprised at what you'll come up with."

"Please!" Muriel Newell turned to Dr. Perry, cutting off the conversation. "Please finish, Gordon. Are you telling us that it was Jennie who was making Aunt Madge so sick all this time? Is that what it says in that diary?" The answer seemed very important to her.

"That's correct, Muriel. Jennie was the one who removed the nitroglycerin so it couldn't be used in an emergency. She's the one who replaced the digitalis with caffeine, to stimulate the heart. Which explains why Madge began to go downhill so quickly this past year, once the decision to leave Wildemere was made." Dr. Perry smiled at old Mrs. Newell, who was taking in every word. "But it's reversing now. She's getting back complete physical mobility. That's why I wanted her up in her chair and out of that sickbed."

Bradford Newell said, in his high thin voice, "But what about her speech? Why can't she talk?"

"She'll be talking away a mile a minute, as usual." Dr. Perry grinned at the old lady, who made a stern face at him, although his words pleased her. "Madge Newell will be a lot healthier when she comes out of this than she's been in many years. She's invincible."

This time I did not imagine it. Both the Newells looked crestfallen and were trying their best not to show it.

"What I can't figure out is where she managed

216

to get the poison she was dosing Aunt Madge with," Stephanie said. "Jennie never went into town."

"I think I can answer that," Dr. Perry said. "She got it right out of my medicine bag. When I had the tea analyzed and discovered there was picrotoxin in it, I should have known. Even so, I never would have suspected Jennie. It was too outrageous." He hesitated. "I even lied to get a chance one weekend to do some detecting. I said I'd been in Canada, when actually I was snooping around here, looking for evidence."

"We were all terribly concerned over dear Aunt Madge," Muriel Newell said, looking at her aunt with a big fake smile. "Why Bradford even did research on poisons in the library, to learn their effect on her. And we were constantly roaming around, thinking some outside person might have been involved. Isn't that right, Bradford?"

Bradford Newell's pale eyebrows drew together. "What? Oh, that was just *one night*, Muriel. Remember we went out and Melissa heard us?"

Muriel Newell said, "That'll do, Bradford!"

Bruce said, "No outsider could have poisoned Madge's tea that day. Jennie did it by loading Madge's sugar bowl with poison earlier that afternoon."

"Right," Dr. Perry said. "There was enough poison there to do her in. Jennie worked both ends against the middle. By mingling caffeine pills with Madge's digitalis she was overstimulating Madge's heart. There's no doubt the caffeine helped bring on the stroke." He shook his head. "With no one suspecting her, she played havoc with Madge's medication!"

"Emile and I thought maybe she was doing the monkey business," Mrs. Volke spoke up now in that tight-lipped way of hers. "When the nitro-glycerin disappeared, and we knew it was so important for Mrs. Newell, I took some from the bottle the next time you brought some, Doctor, and I kept it on me. That way, if Mrs. Newell had an attack, I would have the right medicine."

So that was what I'd caught her putting into her apron pocket that day! She'd been trying to protect the old lady, not harm her. I certainly had misjudged her. What she said next cleared up still another question.

"Emile and I watched everything that came into the house that could get to Mrs. Newell. One day Miss Hillary brought over some cookies she baked for Mrs. Newell. Well," her eyes flickered over to Emile, "he didn't want me to do it, but I didn't care. I threw them out in the trash. I didn't want to take any chances."

Which explained that strange, whispered interchange I'd heard in the library that day. And they'd sounded so mysterious and underhanded.

"All of us were trying to protect Madge — and Jennie Hillary kept outwitting us," Dr. Perry said.

Stephanie said, "I have my own confession to make. Knowing I was innocent, I suspected everybody else." She grinned at me. "Even you, Melissa." Then she turned to Emile, "And you, Emile."

"And us," said Emile, shamefacedly, "we — my wife and I — were watching you, young man." He pointed to Don. "We did not trust you. We thought, Melissa is a young girl. She does not understand the ways of men. Maybe he is — involved somehow. Gerda sent me to watch whenever you came to see her."

So I understood what Emile was doing in my

room that night — the night I'd run out to see Don! All the things that had been so very mysterious at the time were now all too obvious. The Volkes, who had seemed so hostile to me then, had only been trying in their rigid old-fashioned way, to do the right thing for Mrs. Newell and even for me. I suddenly felt very warm and close to everyone in that room, except Muriel and Bradford Newell, who were now making some idiotic comments.

Old Mrs. Newell was tapping on the table. She motioned to a pad and pencil nearby. I handed them to her and watched while she wrote a message. I read it, " 'I tried to warn you not to go to Miss Hillary's house alone. That's why I blinked at Bruce . . . so you'd take him with you. But you misunderstood.' "

I nodded at her. "I sure did. I was stupid."

She shook her head *No,* then picked the pad up again and wrote. When she finished, she indicated that Bruce was to take it. He picked it up and read, " 'Why didn't you and Stephanie want me to make the announcement that night at my party? You had a good reason, I hope.' "

It was funny. Even with her pencil the old lady managed to sound domineering. Bruce smiled and said, "Stephanie and I knew the plans you've had for us, Aunt Madge. You're not half as tricky as you think you are. And we appreciate it, but . . ." he hesitated.

"Let me tell her, Bruce," Stephanie said.

Madge Newell raised her eyebrows, obviously impatient.

"I'm going to give it to you right from the shoulder, Aunt Madge. You're a wonderful, bright, kind, and witty woman. But you haven't caught up

219

with the Generation Gap." Stephanie grinned imp-
ishly, then stopped and took a deep breath. "Know
what my job is, Aunt Madge? I work with Vista.
I teach in a slum area in Chicago. I live there too.
I love the work I'm doing." She hesitated. "I
want you to know all about it, Auntie. And I wish
we could talk about Wildemere someday. If you
didn't sell it, maybe we could make it into something wonderful for people. Poor people."

Mrs. Newell's expression did not change. Stephanie walked slowly over to her aunt, and sat
down beside the wheelchair. She looked at her aunt
squarely and spoke in a gentle voice.

"I know how indebted I am to you, Aunt Madge.
I can never repay you for what you've done for
me. But people have to do with their lives the
best they can. I don't like wasting my days going
to charity lunches and my nights running around
with the beautiful rich young men who don't know
what it means to earn their own bread . . . that
means their own living, you know." She grinned at
her aunt. "I like self-made men." She glanced
quickly at Don, who grinned back at her, then went
on. "But there's more. As I said, Bruce and I can
never repay you for all you've done for both of us.
We adore you. We'd do anything to make you
happy. But one doesn't 'arrange' marriages anymore, Aunt Madge," she said, in that quick, forth-
right way of hers. "If we were to have made a
toast the night of your party, it was going to be
a toast to the honesty of today . . . to the ability
to say what you feel and mean it!"

My heart began to quicken. What was she
saying? The bewilderment I felt was not reflected
in Madge Newell's face, however. She seemed to

220

understand what Stephanie was driving at; I did not.

"The thing is," Stephanie went on, "Bruce and I love each other. We really do, Aunt Madge. But we're not *in* love. That's why we can't get married, no matter how much we'd like to please you. No matter how much you'd like us to keep . . . all right, the money . . . in the family. Don't you see?"

My heart was thudding in my ears and I looked away from the two women, feeling I shouldn't be hearing this. I got up from my chair and took a step toward the doorway. Bruce moved toward me and put a hand on my arm.

"Don't go," he said.

"But, Bruce . . ." I began.

"Shh." He put a finger against my lips.

Old Mrs. Newell was shaking her head and reaching for the pad and pencil again. She picked them up and held them and stared across the room, lost in thought. There was dead silence as we watched her — Stephanie, Bruce, and I. Don had wandered off to the French doors that overlooked the garden, and his back was to us. The others sat and said not a word, just watched Mrs. Newell as she looked off in space, thinking.

Then she nodded. Her beautiful expressive blue eyes had filled with tears. She began to write.

When she had finished, Stephanie read the note softly, " 'I'm sorry. How tiresome it must have been for you both. How did you ever put up with me all this while?' "

Bruce put his arm around me and began to walk slowly to his aunt. We stood before her for a long moment while the blood thundered in my ears.

221

Madge Newell glanced up at us standing there; then, looking at Bruce, motioned her head in my direction. Beside me, Bruce said quietly, "Yes, Aunt Madge."

I was trembling now. The old lady took up the pencil and wrote: "First-rate girl."

Bruce turned me ever so slowly toward him and kissed me lightly on the forehead.

That night as Bruce and I wandered out under the trees in front of the house, he explained, "I couldn't let my feelings get the best of me, Melissa. I felt I was too old for you — and I had that awful burden in my background."

I stood mesmerized in the moonlight as he went on explaining, and it was still dreamlike when he took me in his arms. He didn't need to ask me anything. I was free at last to show the love I felt for him. The way I responded to his kiss told him all he had to know. When at last he released me, he said, "You'll be Mrs. Bruce Murdock. Or do you want to be called *Ms.*? Well, *Ms.* or *Mrs.*, you'll have to live here at Wildemere now that Aunt Madge has decided not to sell the place. Will that suit you?"

Suit me? Bruce was offering me Paradise and asking for my approval. But I had to keep my newfound freedom — and say what was on my mind.

"It suits me, Bruce. But I want to feel free to be me . . . Melissa. I admire Stephanie for what she's doing. Even if she and Don get together, she plans to go right on with her own work. Can't you and I . . . can't we both be doing with our lives what each one of us thinks is right, Bruce? If it doesn't interfere with or hurt the other one?"

"Hmm . . . so Stephanie's gotten you onto that wavelength, has she?" He grinned wryly. "The Woman's Movement. It's all pretty new to us men, Melissa. You must remember that. But a lot of it makes good sense. It needs . . . working out." He shrugged his shoulders. "If Aunt Madge can consider changing her way of thinking at her age, I guess we can manage. Did you know that Madge is considering staying on here at Wildemere?"

I shook my head. "No. You mean because the doctor says she doesn't have to go to Florida to live now?"

"The doctor?" Bruce laughed. "Stephanie! Stephanie is determined that part of Wildemere be built into a place where poor children can live. She has ideas for a building that would eliminate those quicksand bogs forever . . . a building for youngsters without parents, like Stephanie and I were when we first came to Wildemere."

"Oh, Bruce! That would be wonderful." I hesitated. "But suppose Mrs. Newell doesn't agree to it?"

"With Stephanie in there, pushing for it in her own sweet way? Aunt Madge doesn't stand a chance." He said thoughtfully, "Stephanie is probably right. A project like that might give Aunt Madge a new direction in life."

A thought struck me. I said, "Bruce, maybe I can work there, and help Stephanie."

He said nothing. I said again, "Bruce?"

His dark eyebrows drew together and his eyes glowed. "Why are we wasting this lovely night? Come here, Melissa."

On Saturday we are going home to Wellsville. I'm not afraid to have my father meet Bruce. Oh,

223

he'll make a fuss. He'll say Bruce is too old and not for me and I'm about to make a terrible mistake. It won't be easy. He'll put on a big scene. But Dad will no longer be speaking to the country girl who left his home two months ago. In this summer I changed . . . got reborn . . . came alive.

I believe in Bruce. I believe in love. Above all, I believe in myself. If I know who *I* am, if I know my own worth, even Dad can't break me down again. And it may not be as bad as I think. If the new world, and the new thinking, can come to an old woman like Mrs. Newell, in a faraway place like Wildemere — maybe, just maybe, it's beginning to make itself felt even in Wellsville. Maybe it's getting through to my brother Bob. Maybe between us we can get my father to see the light. Maybe not. But I'm going to try.